Steggie Belle

&

the Dream Warriors

ELIAS PELL

Steggie Belle & the Dream Warriors

Elias Pell

Cover Design & Page Illustrations by: Unfamiliar Spirits

Title Illustration by Elias Pell

First Edition 2020

ISBN: 978-1-9163446-9-3

www.eliaspell.com

Contents

"A dreamer is one who can only find his way by moonlight,
And his punishment is that he sees the dawn
Before the rest of the world."
-Oscar Wilde

"The child is father of the man."
-William Wordsworth

For Fiona, Alan, Ros, and all the others whom I can meet now only in my dreams.

Book 1

1

Author's Note: If...?

18th November

I have kept these secrets almost all my life. Never breathing a word of it to anyone outside our little group. Why? You might ask. Well, for now, let's just say that a great many adults have a knack for not accepting what they do not understand.

In the case of children, tall stories are dismissed as figments of fancy or make-believe. For adults, however, there are more serious consequences, all of which usually end in confinement, the turn of a key, a padded room.

It has been many years since I was a child. For that, I hope you will forgive me and not judge me too harshly. All this time, I have kept quiet: adapting and disguising myself in order to live unnoticed within a world of men and women. Avoiding at all costs the danger of discovery. Until now.

What is my name, you might ask? With what I must now confess, such a detail as my real name would not possibly matter. Whether I am a Tom, or a James, or a Max or a Michael, I will leave for you to decide. I will reveal only the name she once gave

1

me, so very long ago. The name which eventually, out of fear, I would abandon and disown. For it is the name which now, at the unlikely age of forty-five, I must re-assume for what could very well be the final time.

My name then is Mr Zoofall.

I have no way of telling where these pages may eventually end up, though privately, it is my hope that they will find their way into the hands of a powerful and wise child, one with the special gift of sensing the truth in the world around them. And if right now you are reading these words, then that shall be my humble proof that magic does indeed still exist, and that maybe, just maybe, all is not lost.

My advice to you, if you allow me, is simple. Stay alert and on your guard. Keep these pages safe and hidden, in the ways that only a child knows. Crawl by torchlight under the blankets of a bedroom fort, or climb up to a secluded tree branch, to read them. Tuck yourself away into that secret cubby hole or hiding place, which you, and only you would know. Be careful with whom you share these secrets of mine. Spread them among the special, for they are very real, and equally fragile. Whisper these truths, for it is of the utmost importance that they keep moving, that they be kept alive.

I am seated at my writing desk in the small square room in the attic. It is a dark and cold winter's afternoon, so cold in fact that I have several blankets wrapped tightly around my shoulders. There is only one window, and right now, outside, a fierce storm is raging. The rain is heavy, lashing against the glass in wind-driven waves, with the sound of a million needles. Every now and then, the room is lit by a flash of lightning, which I admit has startled me and made me jump, as it illuminates for an instant those murderous black clouds, carving their jagged paths through the night sky. The low rumble of thunder that follows is ominous and makes the hairs on my neck and forearms stand up on end.

I shouldn't worry so. I know that I am safe here, for now.

I have seven candles with me and will light them one by one. That is the time I have given myself to complete my story. There is only one way into the room, the trapdoor leading from the floor below… though I shall not be leaving here that way. I have sealed it firmly and have dragged the chest of drawers and other bits of furniture to cover the opening, just to be sure.

Other than that, the room is almost bare. A small single bed in one corner upon which, when I am done, I shall most probably never lie down on again. While to my right, the one thing up here with me, which I find reason to fear. I have covered it, of course, with a bedsheet so that it does not betray me, but that has not helped. For I know it is there. Biding its time, and waiting for me to finish.

Why cover a mirror with a bedsheet, would be a question you have every right to ask, and I promise I will explain all in due time. Time…. With every drop of melting wax, I am reminded that I now have less than seven candles worth of time to do so.

I must start at the very beginning, and allow these secrets to spill forth naturally, in a similar pattern to how I learned them.

For my destiny is set, my bed already made.

You see, what we found all those years ago is not often glimpsed, and even more rarely remembered. Yet we pushed onwards, deeper into that entangled darkness: exploring, discovering, and never looking back. Why?

The truth is quite simple: with her, we were fearless.

3

I shall take you back to when I was a child, a young boy: to the time when this all began. But lastly, before I do, I must try to deal with my original question: If...?

Such a small yet powerful word. It teeters on the very brink of the tongue, the edge of reason. It defies all boundaries; it wonders and enquires. It is truly a magical word, one of infinite possibilities. I believe that is partly why it is the word most loved by—and the best weapon of—a child.

You know, by its very nature, it terrifies adults. It forces open the doorway to self-doubt. It shines a light onto their lack of real understanding. It pokes holes in their laws, bursts their bubbles of well-established rules, and pops their carefully blown balloons of reasoning.

That is the path we must now take, where we must now journey, you and I.

If that is, you will follow?

2

Waking to the Dream

I was five years old when I first became aware of what was happening, although I hadn't the foggiest idea as to where it would lead. I was able to dream whatever I liked, and direct the dreams themselves as easily as if I were writing my own adventure books. The term "Lucid Dreaming" meant nothing to me at that age, and as far as I was concerned, I dreamed in just the same way as everybody else. It was to be several years later, and with great disappointment, that I would read the accepted definition.

My sadness came from the realisation that grown-ups, with their rigid systems of knowledge, could have got it all so badly wrong. I think it would be fair to say that I became a bit cynical at that point in my life. I tell myself now that I mustn't blame them. It's a condition, or rather a form of conditioning among adults, you see. An infuriating habit, to be sure, but one which deserves our pity, not our anger. They cannot help themselves, or as a great dreamer once said, 'they know not what they do'.

In their definition of "Lucid Dreaming", they focus on words like "awareness" and, perhaps least surprisingly, "control".

They really do obsess so about having, maintaining and most importantly keeping "control".

What we found, however, refused such terms of limitation and went far, far beyond.

And so, at that young age, my dreaming continued blissfully ignorant and undisturbed. My nightly adventures were rambunctious and free: storming castles, chasing treasure, and evading pirates on the high seas. Within those first years, I developed the ability to extend and stretch the dreams themselves. Almost as one would an elastic band until each dream became an endless saga. Bridging the boundaries of sleep itself, lasting more than months at a time within the real waking world. At that point, as I have already said, I assumed all of this to be totally normal.

The effects were not obvious at first. The shift came slowly, reality blurring between the waking and the sleeping world.

Imagine your favourite cartoon or television show being played inside your head—one in which you were not limited as a viewer, but were given a starring role. That was my life back then. Dreaming night after night and continuously steering the dream itself, with perfect ease, in whatever direction I wanted. As the weeks went by the setting would develop, sprouting new characters, growing deep and intricate stories, building a solid past behind an ever spinning present.

Over time I forged real and meaningful friendships with the characters I had created, although they felt every bit as real as the children I met in my waking hours. Every morning my alarm clock would signal a temporary curtain call. I would pause the dream, just as one does a television episode, and surrender my physical body back to the daylight. Every evening with the switch of the bedroom light, and my head upon the pillow, the exact same scene would re-appear, and the dream would resume.

I found some days were longer and harder than others. Although, whether getting into trouble with my parents or testing my courage against the meanest school bullies, no matter what might happen, deep down inside, I was always smiling. Patiently counting down the hours for the dreaming to begin again. Gradually the change was happening. I was falling out of love with the harsh, grey light of the real world, and drifting ever deeper into my dreams.

I had a vague sense that it wasn't quite the same for all the other kids at my school. I noticed how they lacked the sparkle in their eyes at *going-home* time, and sometimes even seemed upset about it. I remember mentioning my dreams once to them, and once was certainly enough. Their united looks of confusion and disbelief warned me to keep such things to myself, at least for the time being. Being a normal young boy, and having no brothers or sisters with whom to share my thoughts, I did not suspect anything abnormal or unique was going on.

Looking back at it now, perhaps all that had been missing was a sense of direction, of purpose, to tip the scales one way or the other. I was unaware that big changes were already on their way.

It was on the weekend after my tenth birthday that the accident happened.

As a birthday treat my parents had decided to take me on an outing to the Zoo. At that moment, I was already two months into my current dream, and a lot of regular characters and close friends were already in it. I had told them all about the upcoming trip, and boy had we made some mighty plans. Upon returning

7

from the Zoo, having seen all of the exotic animals up close, we would form a travelling circus. The largest of its kind, complete with all manner of beasts and monsters. Once ready, we would then set off to perform shows all over the globe.

The night before, my dream was full of chaotic excitement, as my friends and I hurriedly put the finishing touches to our circus. Painting bright and eye-catching banners on the sides of the caravans and constructing different sized cages in which we would showcase our magnificent collection of creatures. There were so many things still to be done, and I was so focused on the work at hand that at first, I barely noticed the strange boy. He had been hanging around on the outer edges of my dream for the last two weeks, sticking to the shadows and never getting involved in any way. Each time he had simply stood there, holding an ice cream in one hand, watching us.

I realised that he was coming closer, stepping forward into the core of my dream, and staring at me. I stopped what I was doing and turned to face him. He appeared to be a couple of years older than me, and as he drew nearer, still holding his ice cream, he reached out his other hand towards me. His lips were continuously moving, but no words were coming out. I studied his face long and hard, that boy, and even tried to approach him a couple of times. Although, on each attempt, it appeared that we were separated not only by sound but also by distance, as though some giant sound-proof bubble stood between us. The strangest thing about that boy was that I was unable to make him perform a single task. I could not bring him closer or force him to speak or even make him go away. That morning I awoke with a clear memory of his expression: his lips repetitively moving and a sense of urgency in his eyes.

The big day had finally come, and for once I found it hard to contain my excitement with regard to something about to happen in the real, waking world. The tickets were punched at the gate, and I moved like a whirlwind from exhibit to exhibit, from cage to cage, taking in everything I possibly could. The sounds, the smells, the way each of the animals moved and interacted, it was an amazing overload for my senses.

I pressed my nose up to the glass panels with glee, my breathing actually steaming those cold surfaces on several occasions. The tarantulas were particularly terrifying, with their many glistening black eyes and bristling hairy legs. Scary in an odd and sickly thrilling way. I spent a long time studying every detail of the Iguanas, fascinated by the idea of including horse-sized versions of those lizards as a star attraction in our circus.

"We could strap harnesses to their scale and spike-covered backs, and figure out a way to ride them somehow!" I said enthusiastically to myself.

"What was that?" my mother asked. I hadn't realised she was standing so close.

"Oh, nothing, nothing really," I said, returning my attention to that seemingly alien, reptilian world behind the glass. My mother ruffled my hair and smiled before neatly tidying it again and stepping away. I was too engrossed in my wild surroundings to notice at the time, but I believe my parents were genuinely happy at that moment. Standing back, they gave me some space, relieved for once to see their usually quiet and shy son, outwardly enjoying himself so much.

We moved on to the gorilla pen, and it was there that disaster struck.

It all happened in a flash, and yet interestingly the world

saw it in two very different and opposing ways. Perhaps it would be best to first describe what the entire adult world saw, what the CCTV captured, and what the newspapers would the next day report.

Much to the horror of the general public who witnessed the 'freak accident', a young boy was seen to stumble backwards, trip and fall through the barriers. Landing almost thirty feet below within the gorilla enclosure. As the alarm was raised with cries of panic and confusion, all eyes looked down aghast into the pen. Within seconds, one of the adult gorillas emerged from the undergrowth on the farther side of the enclosure, approaching the small and lifeless body. The zookeepers would later conclude that the following three chance factors were responsible for the unlikely outcome, and safe recovery of the child.

First, they declared, was the fortunate fact that the fall had left the child unconscious. That in itself they said was a blessing in disguise, as the cries and movement of a terrified boy would doubtless have provoked an aggressive and deadly reaction from the animals.

Second, that luckily the gorillas had only recently been fed. A fact which resulted in the animals being slightly more docile than perhaps at other times of the day, especially the males who were slow to respond at first.

Third, and by no means least, that the first gorilla to reach the boy was a female. More specifically, a female whose maternal instincts were sensitively heightened, having only a few weeks before lost an infant of her own.

It was their professional opinion that all three of the above contributed in what was to follow. Everyone watched, barely daring to breathe, as the giant animal stroked and finally settled down to guard the motionless child. Gently cradling and protecting him as the other males approached, baring their monstrous jaws, pounding the earth with their fists, and roaring an angry protest of fierce disapproval. The female maintained this heroic defence throughout those long, agonising minutes. Until the zookeepers were peacefully able to reach the injured young boy, in what would later be regarded as "a very lucky escape".

Despite the intensity of their focus, those hundreds of adult witnesses with their watchful eyes and logical minds somehow managed to misread everything. They were wrong on every count. Though it was so many years ago, even as I write these lines, I remember it all so crystal clear, as if it was only yesterday.

Here's what really happened that day.

First and foremost, I did not stumble or trip. I was backing away most deliberately, in a state of total fright. For, what I had seen was something which nobody else was aware of, or could have possibly understood. It was that very same boy from my dream, ice cream in hand, approaching through the crowd some fifty metres away. He was staring straight at me, though this time, unlike in the dream, his lips did not move. What truly sparked my reaction of fear, was suddenly hearing his voice inside my head from such an impossibly great distance. Like some nightmarish, unstoppable phantom, he approached. His eyes locked on mine, his closed lips tightly pursed in concentration, his voice invading my mind.

If only I had listened, if only I had trusted or believed.

My brain, however, was gripped by hysteria. By the time I truly heard his words, it was far too late. I was already falling.

"Don't go. I am a friend, don't move!" those insistent words of

11

his echoed as I fell. Though before I had even hit the ground, his voice had changed, more desperate and earnest. *"He's fallen in!"* the boy shouted, although those words didn't seem directed at me. Then the ground came rushing up to meet me, and I met it hard.

The pain came first. Before I could open my eyes, it washed over me like lava, burning me from the inside out. The shock kept me from moving, kept me from screaming, from even breathing. Just when I thought it couldn't get any worse, I remembered exactly where I was. My unbearable pain was utterly consumed by a pulsing, terrible fear.

In contrast to what the adult world believed, looking down at me, I was perfectly conscious. The boy's voice continued in my ear, sounding so very close now.

"You must trust me, and do exactly as I say. Stay totally still, there's no time to waste. We are here to help you, but you mustn't move a muscle! Just play dead."

Despite my undeniable terror, I obeyed, as even the slightest movement caused a violent surge of pain to shoot and throb through my injured arm. It was then that I heard another voice, barely audible at first, together with the slow and heavy thud of approaching footsteps. Slowly I opened one eye, just enough to squint at what was coming. I immediately wished I hadn't.

Less than ten feet away, lumbering purposefully towards me, was a gorilla of unbelievable size. Looking down at a distance from above, as I had been doing only minutes earlier, is one thing. But take it from me, lying helpless with your head on the ground at such close range is an entirely different experience.

When this gigantic primate came within almost an arm's reach of me, something extremely peculiar happened. The female gorilla paused. Doubtless, the zookeepers and animal experts would tell you this was down to some primal indecision or wariness, but I realised something very different. She was actually listening. Not to the boy I had seen, as his voice was still repeating his instructions calmly in my ear, but to something, or rather someone else.

I could hear it too, indistinctly in the background of my mind. It possessed an incredibly soothing, yet firm tone, and I realised right there and then without a shadow of a doubt that it was a female voice. A girl's voice. I had never heard anything quite like it. While I cannot lie and tell you that I understood a single word of what was being said, I knew with absolute certainty what this mystery "she" was doing. She was talking, or more precisely, communicating directly with the gorilla. The intense concentration I could see in that animal's eyes was incredible.

At last, the gorilla approached, positioning herself right beside me. I remained perfectly still as she reached out one enormous forearm, and laid it softly upon my broken limb. I expected more unbearable pain and had bit my lip in preparation, but there was none. Only a sensation of astounding warmth as those huge fingers caressed my injury.

Soon after that, she lifted me carefully, as though I was but a feather, and cradled me close to her. All fear had gone. I laid there listening to the heavy, rasping breaths vibrating through her chest, staring up into those large, dark and soulful eyes. There was a definite, immeasurable sadness to them, which somehow made me want to cry. Both voices were still talking, whispering their messages to the two of us. No other sounds seemed to matter; the shrill human screams from afar, and the guttural furious roars rising up from close by, they all faded away into distant insignificance. It was around that point I must admit, dizziness came over me: a black fog clouding my vision until consciousness was no longer mine.

I awoke that evening in the hospital. The bed surrounded by serious faces, expressions shifting gradually from worry to relief. The pain had returned. My body ached and was covered in bruises, my left arm was already in a cast. My mother was gently caressing my right hand, and although she was now smiling, there were signs of worry on her face, her eyes still sparkling and brimming with tears.

The doctors were speaking quietly to my father and glancing over at me every now and then. They seemed a bit surprised that I wasn't showing any signs of trauma or anxiety, but assured my parents that was a good sign.

"And how are you feeling, young man?" one of the doctors asked, bending towards me and shining a cool, futuristic-looking pen torch in my eyes.

"My head hurts a little," I managed to reply, my voice sounding strange. My mouth felt dry, and the doctor must have guessed it, for he was soon offering me water, which I sipped through a straw. He smiled down at me, before straightening and turning back to my parents.

"There's no sign of any concussion, which is fortunate. Other than the broken arm, it's really only superficial scrapes and bruises. Still, we do want to keep him in overnight, just to be on the safe side." the doctor said reassuringly. Both my parents were nodding along seriously and continued listening intently to his instructions.

I didn't mean too, but I somehow managed to make every

adult in the room laugh. Apparently, my response to the doctor's strict order—for bed-rest and plenty of sleep—was a little too enthusiastic.

In truth, I was exhausted, and couldn't wait to rejoin my dream and tell all my friends the unbelievable events which had befallen me. Little did I know then that my adventure was only just beginning.

My parents kissed me goodnight, and the doctors gave me something either for the pain, or to help me sleep. I eagerly obliged, swallowing the tablets like they were sweets. Soon my eyelids became heavy, and I drifted into a deep sleep, with what the outside world might have regarded as a peculiar grin upon my face.

I tried to re-enter my dream, but much to my surprise, something very subtle had changed. In the distance, I could make out all the usual faces of my friends, already hard at work, busy preparing the caravans for our upcoming circus. I re-added the token cast to my left arm, for dramatic effect in the story I was planning to retell and made my way towards them. Yet every step I tried to take was a struggle, as though I were walking knee-deep through treacle or glue. Instead, I found my feet being drawn, almost magnetically off towards my right, and it was then that I noticed the door.

It wasn't quite closed, and a vibrant, golden glow was shining out the cracks from within. I was confused as to why I hadn't noticed it before. I looked back longingly towards the circus and my crowd of awaiting friends. All our plans, everything I knew was right there. Turning away from it all, I continued moving towards that door.

I approached and pulled the handle, the door creaking

loudly as it opened. Beyond lay a spiral staircase made of stone, leading downwards, which was lit by blazing torches hanging from the walls. I made my way down, and at the very bottom found myself in a vast cavern with row upon row of ornate pillars leading off in all directions. Standing there amazed, at the foot of that staircase, I suddenly heard it.

It was the unmistakable sound of approaching footsteps. I felt nervous, like I was trespassing and shouldn't be there. I took two paces backwards up the stairs, all the while searching the gloomy darkness for any sign of movement. The sounds were getting closer, a strange plodding accompanied by heavy breathing, which struck me as vaguely familiar. My mind began to fancy shapes within the shadows.

There! There they were again. Something was definitely moving. My eyes grew wide. There was no denying it. Two figures were emerging from the dark. I froze momentarily as the two of them entered into the light.

On the left was that same boy, standing proud and tall, and smiling now. Instead of an ice cream, he was holding the hand of his companion: a creature less than half his height. I recognised those eyes instantly, although the overall size was very different. He let go of her hand and she scampered playfully towards me, almost dancing with excitement. I couldn't hold back my laughter, and dropped to my knees with my arms open wide as she arrived. It was that very same gorilla who had saved me at the Zoo. Although in the dream, our roles were wholly reversed. With her the—albeit very heavy—youngster that I now cradled in my arms.

Casually, and still grinning from ear to ear, the older boy approached.

"She insisted on coming with me, you know. Almost tore my arm off in her hurry to see you," he said with an exaggerated sigh. "I'm sorry about earlier at the Zoo. I really didn't mean to frighten you," he continued, "thought I could sneak up next to you before you saw me. Glad you managed to hear me when it counted though."

He took a seat on the floor opposite the two of us, tucking his knees up under his chin, and watched the baby gorilla who was still tugging at my shirt sleeve for attention. With a sudden start, the boy realised that he had forgotten to introduce himself, and did so before continuing.

"I'm Wolfe," he said. I shook his hand, and in that second I could've sworn I saw the tops of his ears grow slightly into points but convinced myself it must have been a trick of the light. Wolfe carried on obliviously in a very friendly manner.

"And that little monster there's Daphne, seeing as you two haven't been formally introduced. I wasn't really sure, well none of us were I suppose, how it would all play out, you see. We've tried reaching out to Skimmers so many times, out there in the waking world, but almost always nothing comes of it. No recollection at all, like we might as well be invisible."

"Skimmers?" I asked, not having heard that word before.

"Sorry, er, don't worry too much about all that, I can explain things properly later, that is if…" his words trailed off, unfinished. I waited.

"That is if…?" I repeated, slightly distracted by Daphne's attempts to get my attention. For although a tiny, warm bundle of fur, her grip was incredibly firm as she tugged at the loose folds of my jumper.

"Well," Wolfe finally continued, "it all sort of depends on

what decision you end up making. You see, not many often reach this point, which I guess would make us two of the weird ones," he said with a slight chuckle. "The choice you have to make at this stage is whether you want to keep going a little further, and join us, if you will."

He paused again as if to gauge my reaction.

"But, it's like she said to me, almost three years ago, when I was sitting exactly where you are now—though without that silly fluffball all over me!" I looked down at the little gorilla who was now sound asleep upon my lap, purring contentedly like a cat. We laughed again before he went on.

"She said it was important the decision be yours, and yours alone. No pressure, nobody forcing you to take this path." Wolfe looked away, back in the direction of the staircase. "We wouldn't think any less of you if you decided to go back to your friends and the travelling circus. She said there are no guarantees, but should you come with us, we will teach you, train you, and hopefully take you to places of discovery, the likes of which very few have even dreamed."

"You keep saying 'she'. Is that the girl I heard talking today at the zoo?"

My question appeared to surprise him somewhat. "You mean, you were able to hear her too?" I nodded affirmatively. "Talking to the animals?" I nodded once more. "How interesting!" he pondered this a moment. "Yes, she's the one I'm talking about. Most would call her our leader, though she'd have none of that sort of thing. It was her who made it possible for me to reach you, to talk telepathically out there in the waking world."

"But who is she? And where is she?" I asked, still confused.

"Who, Stegs? Hard to say really," Wolfe replied, looking

around the cavern uncertainly. "She sort of comes and goes, you see. She was sitting right there next to us, only a few moments ago," he pointed to an empty space beside us. My eyes followed the direction of his finger, astonished. My jaw dropping further as I noticed two fresh footprints, clearly visible in the dust. My look of amazement was met with another warm smile.

"That's how she is, you know. Always moving free, kind of like the wind. But perhaps you may be seeing her soon enough?" Wolfe said, winking and rising to his feet. Simultaneously and without a word, the baby gorilla jumped up too, wrapping herself around me in a farewell embrace.

"Tell you what," Wolfe said, retaking the gorilla's hand. "No need to decide right now. You rest up, and go have a wake on it. I'll be waiting down here tomorrow for you if you're interested?"

As I shook his hand and said goodbye, something clicked automatically inside of me.

"I'll be here, for sure!" I promised, to which Wolfe smiled before turning away.

"I had a feeling you might be," he answered with a wave of his hand. I watched in amazement as the two of them walked away. With every step, baby Daphne was growing, transforming back to her normal size. By the time they had almost blended back into the shadows, her colossal frame was towering over Wolfe's, as they continued on into the darkness.

I rose wide awake, the hospital room was bathed in the warm rays of the morning sun. My mother was still asleep in a chair beside my bed, and I hoped she was dreaming good dreams.

It was going to be the longest wait, the longest day I had ever endured.

Later that morning, as we were getting ready to leave the

hospital, my mother seemed cheerful. Fussing over me, in the way that worried mothers sometimes do, barely letting me do anything for myself. I was grateful for her tying my shoelaces though since, with only one working arm, even that would have been tricky. She was busy telling me the plan for the rest of the day while tucking in my shirt when the change came suddenly.

"And then we will get you straight back to bed, and I'll cook you your favourite—" she paused mid-sentence, her mouth wide open and a frown beginning to form. Something had caught her attention and seemed to annoy her.

"What is this?" she asked. "Who did this to you?"

On the outer side of the cast, which I hadn't noticed, was boldly written in blue ink the following message: "Get better soon, Zoofall!"

It was signed with two noticeably different styles of handwriting, "S. Belle", "Wolfe", and then followed by what looked very much like a baby gorilla's handprint.

I told her it must have been one of the nurses.

My mother was not amused, nor was my father when he saw it.

They took it in turns, scrubbing and rubbing away at it for hours.

...much to my private delight, it would not rub off.

3

Peeling Away the Onion

My training began immediately.

Over the months that followed, it became clear that Wolfe—and Wolfe alone—was to be my teacher and mentor, leading me layer by layer into their world. This introductory stage was long and sometimes difficult, but Wolfe took me under his wing, guiding me through it with unfaltering patience and kindness. He explained that, until I had mastered the necessary skills, the ancient training cavern with its seemingly endless rows of arches, would be our home. When he felt that I was truly ready, Wolfe promised that we would then venture out into the "dream world proper", as he liked to call it.

"First thing's first," Wolfe said, backing ten paces away from me, and then pointing his right arm, palm facing upwards, towards the stone floor. Fine white powder began pouring out of his seemingly empty hand, while he slowly walked anti-clockwise in a wide arc around that bare section of the chamber. The powder continued to rain down endlessly as he did so until a large circle was completed on the floor around us. The thick boundary glistened on the grey flagstones, encircling the two of us and reminding me of a wider version of a Sumo wrestler's ring.

"In order to survive within the dream world, there are several skills the individual must master, perhaps the most important among them being 'Defence'. It is only once dreamers have truly learnt how to defend themselves from any possible threat that they have nothing left to fear."

That was, as far as I remember, the earliest point in his tutoring that Wolfe brought up the subject of fear. It would not be the last time.

"Let's begin." he continued calmly and then, without any further warning, raised both hands from his side. Within them, he instantly fashioned two long and deadly looking swords which he held high at crossed angles, adjusting his feet and lowering himself into a seasoned fighter's pose. Less than five paces separated us and, although I wasn't sure of the rules or how serious the combat would be, I didn't hesitate. Concentrating hard, I clasped my empty hands together. I imagined the weapon within them, tightening the thought until it became solid, and created an enormous broadsword which gleamed under the warm torchlight.

Wolfe nodded and relaxed his posture, walking casually around the enclosure while keeping his distance, gesturing with one of his twin blades as he spoke.

"That's good but what we have now is a stand-off, a confrontation, you see? While such tactics might work in the waking world, here it is always the last resort."

"I'm not sure I understand."

"Well, if it comes down to a fight," Wolfe said, turning back to face me, "then the dreamer is forced to put all his faith in the weapon he has chosen. I mean, how confident are you really that your one sword can defeat me?"

I looked down at the blade I held and decided to go a little further. I modified it in the blink of an eye, increasing it by over a foot in length, and altering the handle guards to form two menacing, razor-sharp side blades. I smiled, swinging the new and improved sword from side to side. It made a dull, whooshing sound as it sliced through the air.

"Pretty confident!" I replied proudly.

"Really? And how about now?" Wolfe grinned.

Suddenly something was terribly wrong. The sharp end of the sword dropped instantly to the floor, its tip clanging against the stone surface, as though the weapon itself weighed over a tonne. I bent down, heaved and pulled with all my might, but failed to raise it even an inch off the floor. I looked up at Wolfe in confusion: his grin had only widened.

"You see," he went on. "Even if you could lift it off the floor, are you really sure you'd want to?"

I glanced down and gasped, automatically letting go of what was once the handle and taking a few steps back in sheer fright. My sword was no more. Instead, I was gripping onto the tail of an enormous king cobra, which then slithered around and rose up to face me. Its hooded neck was flattened and puffed out wide, its mouth yawning open to reveal long fangs and a forked tongue flicking out and hissing aggressively at me. At that moment, Wolfe clapped his hands sharply, and the serpent recoiled, sliding away across the circle before burrowing like a mole and disappearing beneath the flagstones.

I realised I was panting heavily, my heart still pounding, but Wolfe, in that soothing way of his, just strode over and placed a reassuring hand upon my trembling shoulder.

"You'll soon learn that, in this world, things aren't always as they seem!" He was still smiling, and gave my shoulder a gentle squeeze, then re-positioned himself on the other side of the enclosure with the cheerful announcement that I would come to hear so many times. "Let's go again!"

The weeks rolled by. Every night those defensive lessons continued, and gradually I found my ability and confidence growing. With Wolfe's unwavering encouragement and my acceptance of frustration and failure, we practised various methods and techniques, over and over again. In between these exhausting and very physical sessions, the two of us would sit and talk, leaning against the pillars of that underground cavern. It was during such breaks that Wolfe would teach me the finer details of the dream world and our position within it. As his pupil, I remained spellbound and in awe, listening to him for hours.

They had their own language, an unwritten tongue, a word of mouth language. So secretive in fact that even writing this down feels in a way like some small act of betrayal. They had terms and phrases for almost everything, a funny-sounding vocabulary which at first, I must say, I struggled to get my head around. To explain every word of theirs here would fill a hefty book, and require a tremendous amount of time; time which sadly I do not have. The first candle is already starting to burn low, so I must press on, be selective and stick as best I can to the basics.

They saw a very definite division between the waking and the dreaming world but believed both worlds to be equally real. They had categorised three different types of humans who one might from time to time encounter within the two interconnected worlds. For a reason I did not understand then, and still do not know, the theme behind these main classifications revolved around water.

"The largest group by far are the Indiacs," Wolfe explained to me very late one evening. "They are the most common type of dreamers, but within our group, we usually refer to them as Floaters."

"Floaters?" I repeated, in a clearly mystified tone. Wolfe nodded before continuing.

"Yes. The Floaters make up over ninety-five per cent of the whole of humanity. Chances are, almost everyone you have ever met within the waking world would fall into this category. They are the ones so firmly connected to the material world that they only visit the dream world to relax. They have made a habit of lying on their backs, floating on the surface so to speak, switching off their tired minds: to sleep but rarely to dream. In this state, they stare sluggishly up at the passing clouds, quite unaware that there is anything real, let alone an entire other world, existing right beneath them. It may come as little surprise to you that their numbers continue to steadily grow."

"Why is that?" I asked. Wolfe paused for a moment, biting his lower lip and shaking his head with a sigh.

"It's just the way the waking world has been designed by adults. When most children grow up, even the more gifted dreamers among them are lured away, trading the magic of dreams for maturity. I don't know why, but that's just the way it is." For a few moments, Wolfe seemed deeply sad, and I found myself wanting to say something, but couldn't find the right words to reach him.

"The second group are known as the Ostrasighted." Wolfe continued, quickly snapping himself out of those troubling thoughts and getting back to business. "We call them Skimmers because the way they dream could be described as very similar to the game of skimming stones." He proceeded to demonstrate by conjuring a perfectly smooth pebble within his palm and then launched it skillfully across the empty cavern. Every time it struck the floor, there came the hollow knock of stone on stone, and yet it submerged slightly before bouncing on, leaving small ripples fading outwards on the flagstones. Eventually, the pebble skittered off into the distant shadows, and silence returned.

"These rare individuals have the natural ability not only to bounce between various dreams but also to dip below the surface, catching quick glimpses of what lies beneath. Whenever we come across such dreamers, like yourself, we try to approach them." Wolfe let out a heavy breath again, staring at me with solemn eyes. "But normally nothing comes of it. They just aren't 'in tune' enough to be reached within their own dream, and are hardly ever able to be contacted directly in the waking world. Nearly all the Ostrasighted remain forever in that curious state of semi-awareness. Confused by, and often afraid of, the depths to which they can occasionally see.

"As you may already be aware," Wolfe continued. "Grown-ups are obsessed with labelling everything. Even things that they do not understand. Things which cannot be pigeonholed." I nodded fiercely in agreement. "Well, their befuddled term of 'Lucid Dreaming', would, in fact, fit rather awkwardly within the above two groups. Much to the annoyance of their order-loving grown-up minds, Lucid Dreamers would not fit neatly into either the Floaters or the Skimmers."

The confusion must have shown on my face, despite me nodding along, and Wolfe made an effort to explain it better.

"Instead, imagine these two types of dreamers as overlapping circles, and right there in that untidy segment where the two groups cross, would be where that adult definition would lie. Somewhere between the deeper restlessness of the Floaters, and the more baffled, nervous members of the Skimmers. Grown-ups would not like such messiness, that's for sure, but what are we to do?"

We both sighed wearily at that, knowing there was nothing to be done. Convincing adults to change their precious beliefs was a difficult task, even for other adults. For a child to do so, well, such a feat was probably impossible!

"And the third type?" I asked.

Wolfe had risen to his feet now, dusting the dirt off his jeans and then stretching as though limbering himself up for a marathon. There was an intense look of concentration in his eyes as he focused on the pillar rising up about fifteen feet across from us. He lurched forward, leaned back and then sprinted straight for it. He gathered furious momentum and, for a second, I thought he was going to kick off the pillar into a backflip. Instead, defying gravity, he continued running up that vertical surface. Only when he reached the curving overhead arch did he slow down, both arms outstretched for balance as though he was crossing a high-wire. He walked tentatively, one foot in front of the other until he made it to the highest central point. There he steadied himself and then shuffled around to face me. I found it hard to take him seriously at first, dangling upside down there like some vampire bat, but I couldn't help myself and had to applaud. Wolfe smiled, bowing courteously before answering me.

"The final group are known as the Omnivagas, but we prefer to call ourselves the Freedivers. There aren't a lot of us,"

Wolfe said. "For the last ten years, we have managed to keep well over one hundred and fifty members. When your training is completed, and you cross over to join us, the Freedivers will number one-seven-three in total. One hundred and seventy-three in the whole world, imagine!"

I pictured the billions of kids sleeping their lives away, and what a tiny percentage of that number, one hundred and fifty of them were. "So, that one-seven-three, the Freedivers, they're like us, and can also harness the power of the dream world, and move freely around it?"

Wolfe cocked his head reflectively. "Sort of, it's complicated you see. The dream world is so enormous, it goes by different names. For us, we mainly deal with the Rising Four."

He didn't elaborate, and I pressed him: "The Rising Four? What are those?"

"Um." Wolfe somersaulted down, landing neatly on the flagstone floor, then paced back and forth a bit before leaning up against one of the dusty stone pillars. "Well, there's the Astral Inferno, the Astral Tower, the Astral Sea, the Astral Cloud. It depends on the level and development of the dreamer, the Freediver, who is facing it."

He looked at me expectantly, and I frowned. "I don't get it. How can it have different names depending on our levels? That doesn't make sense."

Wolfe grinned at me. "You're still quite new to all this, and your mind is tempting you to view the dream world in a similar way to how you've been taught to look at the waking world, when in fact the two are so totally beyond compare. One is defined by its boundaries; made up of fixed laws and limits. While the other, in every imaginable way, is limitless."

Wolfe leaned closer to whisper to me as the shadows danced around that dimly lit cavern, and once again, for a split second, I thought I saw his ears grow upwards into a pointed shape.

"That might lead a clever person to consider this dream world as being something more like a galaxy, or universe." I nodded warily, and he smiled before shaking his head. "But still they'd be wrong. This …" he said, darting looks left and right, "this, Zoofall, is so very, very much more!"

Well, I don't mind admitting to you that in the beginning all of this seemed incredibly complicated and confusing, but Wolfe persisted. My training continued, seemingly without any end in sight. By the end of the fourth month, I admit, I was starting to get quite restless, and my patience was wearing thin. One evening, when I was particularly tired of training, I had almost had enough and decided to bring the matter up with him.

"Wolfe it's been four months now, and all we ever do is practise! I'm still not even sure exactly why all of this is so necessary. I mean, what is it that we need to defend ourselves from?"

He regarded me very seriously for a moment, as though weighing over in his mind whether or not I was truly ready. Finally, he nodded to himself and replied more cautiously than I had ever heard him speak before.

"I do understand, really I do. I was even more impatient and desperate to get out of here, back when I was in your shoes. Steggie has always insisted though, that 'Defence' must be mastered before a dreamer is to learn how to 'Move'." Wolfe smiled ever so slightly at my blank expression, before carrying on. "How else are the Freedivers meant to protect themselves from what exists on the other side? But, I suppose you're about ready for me to teach you—" Wolfe paused for dramatic effect, rapidly flicking both wrists in a building air-drum roll, until the whole cavern echoed and shook with that booming sound.

"—how to move, all by yourself!"

I managed to laugh nervously at the anticlimax, waiting for my fluttering heartbeat to return to normal. Although this new focus of my training seemed odd and only raised more questions in my mind. Back then, as far as I was aware, moving was a skill perhaps taken for granted, but one that I was fairly confident I had already mastered.

Moving, it turned out, in the dream world was a far greater, impressive and essential craft, than its waking world counterpart. A raw talent that required much practice, skill and a whole lot of nerves. In the waking world, movement is mostly tied to the limits of the physical body. In the dream world, however, it is solely bound by the grip of the mind, and the level of balance within the person's creativity. So specific to the individual dreamer that, Wolfe assured me, even after a Freediver's movement had taken place, a trace of it remained, and could be recognised or identified just like a personal signature. Concerning what was possible, in a nutshell: if one was able to imagine it, to hold fast, and manage not to fall from that swaying tightrope, then it could be done.

Wolfe continued, explaining that there were many ways of moving through the dream world, but for ease, we were to start with windows.

The impact of my first successful experience was one I shall never forget: revelationary and terrifying. And without Wolfe's support, one from which I would have run a mile. It was to be my first view of the Astral Inferno.

Seated in that cavern, he told me to picture a window,

complete with frame, curtains and sill. I concentrated and did as I was asked, and there before the two of us it appeared, with gnarled and weathered wood, rustic, simple and quaint. The view it offered was of a countryside setting, idyllic rolling hills, shimmering peacefully in a midsummer haze. I remember the tone of his voice, stressing the importance of his next instruction, all the while, his hand placed firmly, reassuringly on my shoulder.

"Now, we both know that 'outside' is not real. Yes? I need you now to stay focused on the window, keep it stable. For it, like you and I, is real! Clear your mind of everything else and calm your thoughts. No outside, only us and that window frame."

A minute later, once I was truly relaxed, Wolfe reached forward and casually began picking with his index finger at the top left corner of the dusty window pane, the way one would to remove a sticker.

"You're doing good, that's it, everything calm, open and clear, and now, just like taking off a plaster …" then, with one swift move, he tore away that false countryside image, as though it were made of paper or fabric, a simple poster or painting. What was revealed beneath blew my mind. Dread swallowed me whole, and even to this day, I find it difficult to put into words exactly what I saw.

It was utter chaos. On the other side of the glass, hundreds of dark shapes were moving, pressed up close, squashed and struggling. The noises were sickening, long nails and claws scratching at the windowpane. I saw the flash of many eyes and dripping fangs amid the oozing, writhing forms; a pit of slithering unrecognisable shapes. It was what, at that age, I had always imagined could be lurking and waiting behind my bedroom cupboard door.

I was terrified, and my reaction was instinctive. My mind pulled the curtains closed at once, but that was not enough. Gripped by a racing fear, I hastily added thick, heavy iron bars across the window. I barricaded it with wooden boards, and a wall of bricks, before finally dropping an enormous portcullis down between us and that dreadful portal. It all took only a matter of seconds to throw everything my imagination could muster at it.

Wolfe had been watching me the whole time, an intense gleam in his eyes which I later learnt was genuine fascination. Once my breathing had returned to normal, he waved one arm over everything my mind had built, and it vanished in an instant so that only the shadowed cavern remained.

"Scary, isn't it," he said with a smile, "mind you, the first time that I saw it, I couldn't even think of doing what you just did. I only panicked, and froze completely!" He then muttered, half to himself, "She will be interested to hear about this, I'm sure."

"What … what were they?" I stammered, still in shock.

"All in good time, don't you worry. Good job though, seriously," Wolfe replied, patting me on the back. "Windows are a good way to begin. In essence, they are simply gateways, or portals, through which when properly trained and prepared, we can travel through the dream world. As to the 'they', well that requires a longer explanation but for now, simply put, they are a fraction of the beings, or entities, with whom we share the dream world."

"They didn't seem particularly friendly!" My remark caused Wolfe to chuckle.

"Some are, some aren't. You can find all kinds on the other side. Like sharks with the scent of blood, many of these creatures sense innocence and inexperience and will rush to crowd such a beginner's window or opening, as you have just seen. Swarming desperately, like moths to a flame. The more you learn, the warier most of them will become, and the more distance they will keep. Otherwise, it can be very dangerous out there, and easy to get lost, or worse!" He smiled at my pale and worried expression. "Perhaps now you understand better why she insists that every one of our group must first be trained in defence."

I shuddered at the thought of what I had witnessed out there in the beyond, and from that moment on, took all of my lessons far more seriously.

4

A Field Trip of Sorts

The next couple of months were an intensive mixture of theoretical and practical techniques, together with what Wolfe liked to refer to as "Real World Wisdom". Piece by piece, he taught me ways to survive, to move and most importantly, to escape. He also shared with me a vast amount of secret knowledge. What I found most fascinating was the way, throughout all our lengthy conversations, I began to see how these two parallel worlds—the waking and the dreaming—were so incredibly interconnected.

History, as understood within the waking world, is linear, like an endless conveyor belt, marked with precision by events chronologically through time. The history teacher focuses mainly on dates and places, and on solid evidence that is visible and able to be documented. As a result, so many hidden things go unwitnessed: destined to fall by the wayside, passing unnoticed beneath their radar.

Perhaps it will shock you, as indeed it did me, just how many ideas, discoveries and inventions originated and were brought to earthly life, knowingly or not, directly from out of the dream world. Over the countless centuries and lifetimes, going back to before the history books were even written, the greatest minds and most intelligent of mankind have scavenged, unearthed and retrieved mysteries from the world of dreams. An army of brave individuals, delving into the darkness, recovering secret information through the ages.

From ancient prophets, philosophers and scientists, to musicians, artists and writers, all up to the present day. Lone explorers ranging from randomly enlightened Floaters, and the flashlight fearlessness of curious Skimmers, all the way to the more refined wariness of Freedivers. They brought back to the waking world these discoveries from such an inexplicable place.

How, you might ask, were these heroes to be welcomed?

Exploding back upon the earthly stage, loaded with their pockets full of wisdom, a fortunate few were accepted and admired. Most, however, were ridiculed and rejected, only much later to be revered as "ahead of their time". While a great many were also persecuted and even punished! So is the way of the waking world, I am afraid. Yet very little of this will be found within the dusty volumes which line the library shelves. Back then, at such a young age, I did not know the names of these exceptional men and women, those daring figures, those spearhead dreamers.

I have studied them since. They are legion. Too many to list here in full. From Buddha to Joan of Arc, Plato and a man called Jung—remembered within our group as "the King of the Skimmers".

This may be foolhardy, but if you are ever feeling brave, ask your teacher or the nearest adult you can find, about a man by the name of Albert Einstein. Ask them how he came upon the idea of "the speed of light"? Or whether with another man whose name was Isaac Newton, it was the apple falling, which led him to the notion of gravity? I predict they will attempt to confuse you with complicated reasoning and calculations, rather than admit their ignorance. Very few would feel satisfied to say as an answer that such things came out of dreams from which these men had just awoken!

A final thought on the relationship between humanity and dreams was given by an artist named Salvador Dalí: "One day it will have to be officially admitted, that what we have christened reality, is an even greater illusion than the world of dreams."

I live in hope for such a day.

But Wolfe's revelations did not stop there. Perhaps he had planned the whole thing all along, or maybe he had just sensed that I was going a little stir crazy being stuck within the confines of that repetitive routine. Whatever his reason, when I exited the spiral staircase, re-entering the training cavern one particular evening, I found Wolfe waiting beside two fairly large backpacks.

"I thought it would be a good idea for the two of us to get a bit of fresh air. To go on a little adventure, if you're up for that?"

He didn't have to ask me twice. I was nodding vigorously before he even finished the question.

"Are you sure you feel ready?" he insisted.

"I've never felt more ready in my life!" I answered without hesitation, worrying that if we delayed leaving for even a moment, Wolfe might change his mind. I slung one of the rucksacks over my shoulder, never considering the real importance behind his question. Nor did I notice the deep concern, bordering almost on anxiety, that was clearly visible in his eyes. At last, I was getting out of the training cavern, and anywhere had to be better than there.

"Very well," Wolfe said, hoisting the other bag onto his back. "This way, follow me."

Any hopes I had, of seeing a freshly constructed window, or glowing portal in the distance, were quickly destroyed, as I realised quite dishearteningly that we were not, in fact, leaving the cavern. It turned out that the cavern just went on and on, seemingly towards infinity. This didn't seem to bother Wolfe though. As we walked, he went on to explain in great detail what was undoubtedly, to me, the most eye-opening elemental truth of all. A fact which, once exposed, would mean never seeing either world in quite the same way as before.

"What I'm about to tell you is perhaps the greatest secret in existence." he began, making sure that he had my undivided attention. "The stuff of myths and legends, every fabled creature ever described, was not a product of the overactive imagination of humans. No. These beings were—and still are—all too real. Every hushed tale ever told around the campfire, the kind that curdles the blood, which makes one's hair stand up on end and encourages listeners to huddle closer to the light of the flames: all of these entities exist within the dream world."

My eyes widened at the impossibility of what I was hearing. All of a sudden, the shadows that encircled us seemed to press a little closer. As though the things of which Wolfe spoke lay in waiting there for us, hidden by the gloom.

"The grown-ups of the waking world have long forgotten this. And yet, I can tell you that I have not only seen them with my own two eyes but have walked amongst them on the other side. Perhaps the easiest way to understand is to imagine all those stories of mythical creatures, from Unicorns to Trolls or Fairies as nothing more than faded paintings. Like rough sketches or poor quality photographs, gathered by the occasional glimpses or encounters in dreams through the recent ages." I nodded along as he spoke, paying great attention to his every word.

"They are images of what actually exists, made by a mind most often out of its depth, scrambling to make sense out of the extraordinary unknown. Of course," Wolfe said, making a point of warning me with a very solemn stare. "Like with many first impressions, such portraits are full of mistaken assumptions. Misunderstandings are most common when people try to judge the nature of an entire species as a whole.

"Some of these legendary beings did not even begin their existence within the dream world but, once upon a time, lived alongside us within the waking world. Take Fairies for instance," Wolfe explained. "They were around long before humans showed up. They were about as close to perfection as the waking world has ever seen. A species living in complete harmony with nature, who—over thousands of years—had learnt how to feed off the energy of the mountains, rivers and forests. Without their help and kindness, humankind would probably never have dared to venture out from the shelter of their caves.

"What happened to them?" I asked, and it was one of the first of my questions that Wolfe answered straight away.

"Their trusting nature was to be their weakness. They had taken pity on primitive humans, had tried to help them advance, and had even managed to form a treaty across the animal kingdom, that humanity should be left alone and excused from the laws of the jungle.

"The Fairies never saw it coming. They had no concept of the term betrayal. By the time those sacred forests had been set ablaze, and the carcasses of the woodland animals had been found slaughtered and half-eaten, it was already far too late. The Fairies themselves had already become infected by the—all too human—capacity to cause harm. They had developed a habit for mischievous trickery, and gradually as the cruelty of their actions grew, so too their most tragic fall from grace had begun.

"Their wings, those delicate angelic wings which they had evolved over thousands of years as a symbol of the balance achieved, were starting to wither and fade. Meanwhile, our species—having grown bold and strong and in the delight of arrogance—made a now long-forgotten, yet fatal mistake. We attempted to enslave the remaining population of weakened Fairies, and in so doing, transformed a once-loyal friend and ally into an eternal foe.

"Some of the fairies were captured and imprisoned, and echoes of their suffering are still seen today when one stumbles upon a child taking pleasure in plucking the wings off flies." Wolfe shook his head, wearily. "Shameful."

I felt a mixture of emotions at that moment. Both a deep sorrow, learning what had happened to the Fairies; but also a simultaneous surge of excitement, discovering these creatures were real. I wondered whether, at some point in the near future, I myself might be lucky enough to encounter them.

"The majority of them fled," Wolfe continued, "seeking refuge in the one place those clumsy human hands were hard-pressed to reach: the dream world."

There was a long pause, and his voice trailed off as though he had become completely lost in his own thoughts. I struggled to hear what Wolfe said next, his words barely even seeming to be his own.

"Invisible and eternal patterns. Things going full circle. All paths, no matter how seemingly independent, are interwoven and linked."

I paused, confused by those strange words and watched Wolfe closely, trying to figure out what he meant. He didn't notice me staring, just carried on obliviously, walking straight past me. As I turned to follow the direction he was headed, I froze, realising that our surroundings had changed. Having been so totally engrossed in Wolfe's story, I hadn't noticed, but the cavern had completely transformed. No longer were there cold, grey flagstones underfoot. The ground was soft, with scattered patches of grass and moss, and a rich smell of fresh soil was in the air. Thick vines and tangled creepers lined the sides of the path that we were on, the cavern's pillars almost completely hidden beneath the overgrown vegetation.

The further we went, the murkier the forest became, dark shadows shifting into deeper greens. Wolfe walked with purpose, both hands gripping the straps of his backpack until we reached a clearing where we both halted. In the middle of that open space, the earth sloped gently into a raised mound, and from it stood a magnificent and ancient oak tree. Centuries of growth had divided its enormous trunk, which branched out low in all directions. A vast web of roots had risen all around it, as though guarding the tree's centre which lay open, appearing hollow.

"Have we crossed over? Have we entered the dream world proper?" I asked timidly, in not much more than a whisper.

"Not quite," Wolfe replied, continuing on towards the darkened heart of the oak. "But this is about as close as one can get to it, without fully crossing over. We should hurry though, we're already running late!"

"Late? What are we late for?"

Wolfe turned back, grinning briefly. "Come on, Zoofall. There's someone I want you to meet."

I stepped into the wide central pit behind him, and it was only when Wolfe moved to one side that I saw it. Amid the parts of the sprawling trunk which rose up all around us, there was a hole.

"This is where it gets a little dirty," Wolfe said, before dropping down on all fours and crawling on ahead into the narrow tunnel. I followed nervously, feeling my way along that dark and musty warren. Time and distance were tough to judge. Sometimes it felt we were headed down, at other points the cramped tunnel seemed to curve upwards. I lost all sense of direction, just focusing on staying close to the sounds of Wolfe's feet shuffling on ahead of me. After what seemed like miles, warm golden light filtered in, silhouetting Wolfe's scrambling frame like a halo. We pressed on, a sense of excitement building within my chest.

When I emerged above ground, blinking in the firelight, at first, I didn't notice the other person sat cross-legged within the enclosure. The old oak tree was nowhere to be seen. Instead, a solid wall of shrubbery grew high on all sides. A matted mixture of wild ivy and fern, bracken and brushwood twisted upwards towards the starlit sky. The area inside, some thirty feet wide was flat and clear of debris, the soil smooth and dry. For some reason it reminded me of a massive, over-sized teepee, sheltered from the elements and with a wide opening in the roof from which the hazy smoke billowed away into the night.

In a ring around the roaring campfire, low tree stumps were evenly spaced, and it was upon one of these polished stools that the unknown figure was perched. Wolfe stood between us and, with a waving arm, gestured for me to step forward.

"Zoofall, I would like to introduce you to one of the Freedivers' most important members, Everly Kitt."

As I approached, the tall girl rose gracefully to her feet. I raised my right hand, uncertain of protocol, whether to wave or offer it forward for it to be formally shaken. Everly Kitt beamed warmly and batted my arm away, hugging me with great enthusiasm and force, as though we had known one another for years.

"It's so good to finally meet you," she whispered closely in my ear, before pulling away and turning towards Wolfe, her expression more serious. "As for you, forty-nine," I frowned quizzically at hearing her call Wolfe that. "It is my firm belief that you are quite incapable of turning up anywhere on time!" she tutted scoldingly before her playful smile returned. "Please tell me that you at least remembered to bring the marshmallows?"

Wolfe gasped, then grinned, producing three large bags from within his rucksack and holding them victoriously on high. I studied Everly Kitt carefully as their light-hearted banter continued. She was a few years older than me and had such an air of confidence and authority that it put me immediately at ease. I don't think I had ever met a girl quite like her before. She was strong and fierce, while also radiating a mesmerising warmth and charm which made her shine and almost glow. Seeing her standing there, with her hands firmly on her hips, made me think of those mighty Amazon female warriors or a young Queen Boudica. I found myself smiling, watching in genuine admiration as she circled the campfire, inspecting the crackling flames.

"Zoofall," she spoke sweetly. "Would you mind fetching

us some more firewood from the pile in the corner over there, before we get started?"

I obeyed without giving it a second thought, hurrying over to the stack of already chopped logs at the far side of the enclosure. I did not notice Wolfe flinch at the suggestion, lowering his gaze to the ground and biting his lip in the way he did when he was nervous. As I crouched down to start loading my arms with as many pieces as I could carry, an owl hooted somewhere off in the distance.

My senses suddenly seemed to shift into overdrive. Time slowed, and instinctively I knew that something was wrong. Without turning around, I saw flashes like urgent premonitions of what was going on behind me. Wolfe and Everly Kitt had separated and were creeping towards me, silently approaching from either side. My ears pricked at the unmistakable sound of a blade being swiftly unsheathed.

I spun around, whirling on the spot as Everly Kitt launched a long and jagged spear in my direction. Rolling to one side, I heard the shaft bury itself in the woodpile, and caught a glimpse of another identical javelin growing out of her same throwing-hand. Wolfe charged at me with a fearsome battle cry. I steadied my breathing, clenched both fists and remembered every lesson he had taught me. It had all led to this very moment. I did not hesitate, unleashing every ounce of my imagination at those would-be attackers.

A sturdy red brick wall shot up, over six feet high, just in front of Wolfe and I heard him slam violently into it, unable to stop in time. Everly Kitt had leapt into the air, wielding her spear high, overhead. I crouched, waving one across the ground and where she landed just a few feet from me, the earth rippled into a thick and viscous pool of mud. She sunk into it, almost up to her knees, and struggled to wade through, only sinking deeper into the squelching mire with every movement that she made.

Wolfe emerged from behind the wall, red-faced and rubbing at his nose. This time he fashioned a club, the bulbous head of which was covered in three-inch spikes, before running at me once more. In desperation, I threw a metallic boomerang at him, but he dodged it skillfully. It did not come back. Wolfe smiled deviously as he looked over his shoulder to see both points of the boomerang embedded deeply in that red brick wall. He was about to charge again when a sudden loud click made him look down to where a large iron shackle was now tightly fastened around his ankle. As he jumped wildly at me, the heavy chain I had created between the crook of the boomerang and the shackle became taut, stopping him in mid-flight. Wolfe came crashing to the ground, his head striking the soft, plump pillow that I just had time to create beneath him—he was a good friend after all.

Everly Kitt, who had been watching this from where she was, stuck waist-deep in the mud, couldn't help but laugh briefly upon seeing this. She then scanned the now empty enclosure, not seeing where I had pressed myself back against the foliage, blending in perfect camouflage into that wall of greenery. Her eyes darted blindly back and forth before, with a final cry, she threw her spear randomly in the general direction where I had been.

I managed not to move a muscle. The spear protruding from incredibly close to where I stood. I closed my eyes and concentrated hard, raising the entire woodpile off the floor, and swirling the pieces around Everly Kitt like a tornado. As the furious cloud spun around her, I was able with extreme effort to transform each wooden wedge into black and leathery bats, frantically slapping and flapping their wings as they circled.

"Alright! Alright!" she cried out in surrender. "We give up. Now, how about you give me a hand up out of here? It's starting to smell pretty bad!" I came out of hiding, pulling out the spear that had only just missed me and changing it into a rope, one end of which I flung towards her. Wolfe was getting gingerly to his feet, rubbing at his bruised knees and elbows.

"I'm sorry I couldn't tell you," he said apologetically to me. "But then, I guess it wouldn't really be much of a test if you knew it was coming."

"A test?" I repeated, then in a slightly wavering voice looking back and forth between them. "Did I pass?" To this question, they both simply smiled and nodded. No words were necessary as the three of us walked back, arm in arm, towards the campfire.

We sat there, discussing many subjects until late into the night. We laughed and joked, as marshmallows floated through the cool night air. We used our minds to move them in and out of the flames, until they were melted and toasted, cooked to a sweet, sticky, dripping perfection. I remember listening with fascination to all of Everly Kitt's stories, but above the rest, one stands out in my memory the most, when, amid the hiss and spit of the flames, that night she spoke of Witches.

Of how, putting to one side all the stereotypes and prominent misconceptions, Witches were, in fact, the chosen few, the "good apples" so to speak. Who, during those awful days of fighting, were selected to be taught. Initiated into the lesser known "Light and Dark Arts" by the last of the Fairy elders before they departed and crossed over. They were entrusted to pass on these occult practices and traditions. In the faint hope of restoring the beauty and balance to the waking world: the much loved and sorely missed original home of the Fairies.

"In the Witches' defence," Everly Kitt said. "They held out as long as they could. You don't have to look too far into the past to understand the decision that they finally made. At a time when the waking world had been whipped into a frenzy of suspicion and fear, they were hunted down so mercilessly, until there was only one option left open to them. To retreat into exile, as those before them had been forced to do. To leave the world which they had known behind, and cross over into the dream world."

The more I listened, the more I learnt that these "migrations" were not altogether unique. Whether forced by the need for survival, or to withdraw from long-running feuds, it became clear that several of these supposedly mythical creatures had at some point, and for a good reason, made the transition. Everly Kitt even hinted that on a handful of occasions entire human civilisations, the Mayans, for example, had decided to uproot and relocate to the dream world.

It was the sum of all of these stories that led me to ask what I thought was a harmless question. Though it appeared to disturb Everly Kitt, jolting her out of the jovial mood, in a way that I found quite startling.

"Has a war ever been fought between the two worlds?"

Her face turned noticeably pale, and her lips lost the angle of their usual smile. She didn't reply for what seemed an eternity. When the words finally came, her voice was trembling and clearly nervous.

"Some answers are better kept as secrets. That'd be a question best suited for Steggie, asked very carefully, and much further into the future." I began to worry that I'd ruined the evening, but then Everly Kitt's infectious smile returned. "But, don't you worry, you'll be seeing her very soon, Zoofall. He's definitely ready," she said, having turned to Wolfe. "Why don't you bring him on through for a late supper tomorrow evening? And, forty-nine," Everly Kitt said sharply, with an almost motherly smile, "do try not to be late this time!"

So it was that after almost six months, if I remember correctly, my training was finally over and I was able to leave the confines and safety of that cavernous chamber. With Wolfe and I, early the following evening, opening a well-calculated window out into the brimming unknown, where it was said that the mysterious Steggie Belle and the others were waiting.

Ah, Steggie Belle.

I still remember so clearly the one time during the early stages of my lessons when I thought I caught a glimpse of you. Wolfe and I had been busy planning ways for dealing with unexpected situations when it happened.

I had reached over to pick up a measuring-ruler which had been resting up against one of the nearby pillars, and in its reflection I saw you, standing right behind me, looking down over my shoulder at the work we were doing. Your dark hair wild and windswept, with one jet black curl falling rebelliously down over your face.

By the time I turned around, you were gone, vanished without a trace.

But I was sure that I had seen you.

I remember you were smiling.

I remember you were beautiful.

47

5

Foot on the Ladder

We flew like birds that night.
I remember stepping through that window into
darkness, with Wolfe by my side. I could tell he was
excited, but I had no idea where we were going or what was
going to happen. The floor was made of wood and sounded
hollow, and as my eyes gradually grew accustomed to the lack
of light, it appeared we were in a small room, perhaps, from
the vaguely outlined shapes, a bedroom. Wolfe had walked on
ahead, crossed the enclosed space and, without a word, walked
straight through the closed door in a flurry of gold sparks.

I blinked several times unbelievingly and, as those strange
lights faded back to darkness, realised that I was indeed alone.
It was then that I heard the noises. Indistinct at first, a distant
foreign humming, made up from all sorts of sounds. There
was an odd chattering—not human, though familiar and all-
encompassing—reminding me in some way of that trip to the
zoo. There was music too: a soft, steady ghostly rhythm drifting
down from somewhere up above. I stepped across those creaking
floorboards, pausing as I raised a hand to reach for the door

handle. Putting my hand back down by my side, I took a deep breath, closed my eyes and walked straight through that solid wooden door.

My jaw dropped open, and for a few seconds, I stood blinking in disbelief at what lay before me. To say it was a treehouse would have been a mammoth understatement, like calling the Eiffel Tower a footstool. It was like a giant adventure playground, a sprawling three-dimensional city set on many levels, woven through the majestic treetops, all interlinked with narrow walkways, plank bridges and rope ladders.

Fairy lights dangled from vines, lining every path and route, a fantastical web of shimmering trails glowing warm against the silken night. Although hidden from view, the animals were out there, almost welcoming my arrival with their wild, exotic calls and raucous cries rising up into the sky from their fathomless kingdom. The smells were lush and fragrant, fresh as the morning dew, and so powerful that they seemed somehow alive, wafting through my nostrils in a deep and pungent green.

I spotted Wolfe, standing halfway across a long and sloping rope bridge, leading through the branches towards some lofty central structure. He was smiling, beckoning me to follow and, looking past him, I could just make out a line of eager, beaming faces looking down over the railings from up above, awaiting us.

The rope bridge ended at a small platform which encircled an enormous tree trunk, with beautifully carved steps snaking their way around it to form a spiral staircase. Upwards we went, emerging finally at the corner end of a broad, open decking area. All the others crowded around us, the atmosphere celebratory, and I felt that the party had most definitely begun. From the sheer number of children present, I guessed that this must be everyone, a complete gathering of the Omnivagas. As the evening progressed, I was to learn another very important fact: that there was a definite hierarchy amongst them.

As I mingled and was introduced to the many new names and faces, it became clear that I had adopted a second identity of sorts. While several called me by that peculiar name she had given me, Zoofall, most simply referred to me as one-seven-three. It appeared customary amongst the Freedivers to address one another by these numerical names, which I learnt reflected their rank and position. Similarly, it was that night that I again heard Wolfe being called by his other name, number forty-nine.

Unknown to me then, I was only minutes away from a face to face meeting with the whole 'Inner Circle', the Elite within the group. I had managed at some point to break away from the ongoing revelry and look around a little. The place was breathtaking. Perhaps fifty metres wide and well over a hundred metres long, the wooden platform, bordered by waist-high ornate railings, was positioned high above the jungle canopy. It jutted out over the surrounding trees, offering magnificent views in all directions. Quite simply, it was paradise.

I had not, at that age, ever seen photos of the Amazon rainforest, but years later, I would find in those images the closest comparison to what I saw that night from the Treetop summit. There were no walls up there, only twisted wooden beams, rising up to support a slanting roof cover made from massive interlaced leaves. Enormous dragonflies appeared to have made their home up there: some resting idly upon the wooden railings while others swirled in impressive formations round and about our heads. Their bodies were beautifully coloured with sunset oranges and turquoise blues. That night I remember one landing passively in my open palm, allowing me to inspect its four delicate and black-laced wings closely.

In the centre of this decking area was positioned a long rectangular banquet table, already laid with fine silver cutlery and tall crystal glasses. Beyond the table, tucked away towards the farthest corner was the source of that magical music. A line of floating instruments, tightly formed in a semi-circle, moving back and forth without musicians, playing out their lively enchanted tunes.

At the opposite end from the spiral staircase where Wolfe and I had entered, I noticed yet another bizarre feature. There was a point where the railings ended, and from that gap what appeared to be a pier or jetty, some twenty metres in length, stretched off into the distance. It was the sort of thing one would expect to find by the seaside or lakeshore, not projecting out over those immense and darkened treetops. It looked so authentic that I half expected to see rowing boats tied up along its sides where the ancient wooden posts rose up at intervals from the uneven weathered planks.

As I stared in confusion at that empty gangway stretching out onto the night sky, the strangest thing happened.

Suddenly a faint shape appeared. Framed against the unbroken darkness, it was the shape of a person, ash-white and opaque, with the delicate consistency of mist or vapour. It was walking down that jetty towards us, gliding gently, becoming more visible with every step. Behind it, on either side, more shapes appeared. I stood transfixed, could not move nor cry out, could only watch wide-eyed as this phantom procession approached. At the edge of that main decking area, the ghostly group halted, and all the other Freedivers fell silent.

Stepping over the threshold, those fog-like figures transformed into flesh and blood, to a unanimous round of applause. The Elite group of the Freedivers had arrived and in the middle of them stood Steggie Belle.

All the other children rushed past me, swarming excitedly around these new arrivals, with a clamour of questions. I felt a familiar hand upon my shoulder. It was Wolfe, and he took that opportunity, until calm was restored, to fill me in a little on what was going on. All the while, as he spoke, through the bobbing, bustling chaos, I caught glimpses of Steggie standing motionless in the distance, looking intently in our direction.

"We're all ranked by our skill and ability, you see," Wolfe explained. "All except the Inner Circle. They're the ones who closely monitor our progress, and they decide who deserves to go up or down. As our newest member, I'm sorry to say that you have to start at the bottom rung, so to speak, but between you and me, I don't think you'll stay down there for long. You'll get used to it, just don't be surprised if others sometimes call you by your rank: number one-seven-three."

I nodded. "And you're rank number forty-nine?"

"That's right!" Wolfe replied with a hint of pride. "As you can see, the Inner Circle is made up of the strongest ten from within the Omnivagas. They are set apart, and no longer subject to individual ranking. While Steggie is our natural leader, in reality, she refuses to hold more weight or power than any of the other nine."

As I scanned the members of that Elite group, my eyes fell upon a friendly and familiar face.

"Everly Kitt's one of the Inner Circle?" I half asked, half exclaimed in surprise, wincing at my decision to bury her waist-deep in foul-smelling mud only the night before.

"She sure is," Wolfe replied, before lowering his voice and leaning closer. "The thing is Zoofall; rumours have been going around for ages, that the Inner Circle's thinking of expanding their numbers. Just last month Steggie announced it was true: they want to increase the group to twelve members. That would leave two possible spaces open, a chance for two among the Freedivers to become one of the Elite."

Wolfe's voice became distant, yet his eyes shone with focus and determination as he spoke his final words on the matter.

"It could be a year, or maybe five until those spaces open up. Nobody knows, that's the truth of it. But there's one thing which I'm sure of," he hesitated, glancing over at the Inner Circle in profound admiration, before turning back to me, grinning wildly. "When the time comes, I will be one of those two!"

The evening continued in a most extraordinary fashion. As we all spread out, ready to take our seats around that great table, I noticed that none of the Inner Circle stayed separate from the rest, but were dotted about quite randomly amongst the other Freedivers. It came as an even greater surprise to see Steggie pass quite humbly by the grand throne-like chair at the head of the table, which I had quite naturally assumed was meant for her.

She took her place amongst the others, and it was only then that she looked at me and smiled, motioning me with her open palm towards that vacant seat at the head of the table. I remember thinking that this must surely be a mistake, and yet every friendly face seated there turned my way, mimicking her gesture until every hand was pointing to that prestigious place. Overcoming my astonishment, I forced my feet to move, and as I did a burst of applause erupted, growing in momentum and volume with each passing second.

I was unable to hide my blushes, realising that I was, in fact, the guest of honour that night, that this whole gathering had been designed as a welcome party to celebrate my arrival. From the corner of my eye, I caught sight of Wolfe beaming proudly and cheering loudly from his seat. The warmth in my cheeks told me they had most likely turned a shade of scarlet, and though I couldn't stop smiling, was greatly relieved once I was seated and the noise eventually died down.

From out of the silence, each member of the Elite group rose without a word from their various places. They all shared a secretive grin, bowed their heads and closed their eyes. At that moment I could have sworn I heard their voices, although their lips were not moving, and whatever language it could have been was entirely unknown to me. All the other children around the table remained respectfully silent, the tropical night air filled with expectancy. It was then that the magic began.

It started almost like a fine drizzle, barely visible amid the glow of the fairy lights. The most delicate golden glitter was falling lightly down from above and rapidly growing stronger. Whatever was happening, it was certain from their strained expressions of concentration that the Inner Circle were the ones doing it.

Looking up I could barely make out the roof of leaves above us: everything was awash with the now torrential rain of gold. I reached out and allowed the tiny grains to run over my hand, watching in amazement as they fizzled on my palm and tumbled off over my wrist. It had the texture and actual warmth of the sand you would expect from the deep Sahara dunes. The banquet table was barely visible, and still, the sand kept coming, piling up like snowdrifts, cascading off the table corners, and falling all around us. It was an unimaginable scene, and I remember thinking as I sheltered my eyes, squinting through the raging sandstorm, that this must be what it was like to live inside an upturned hourglass.

Suddenly the glistening flurry vanished, and as my eyes readjusted to the gentler glow of those twinkling lights what remained seemed equally incredible, some sort of magical mirage. Not a grain of golden sand could be seen. The entire table was filled, stacked high with a sumptuous feast beyond even the most imaginative of dreams. Our bulging, greedy eyes were quickly overtaken by the overpowering seduction of smells. Necks were craned as I, along with many others leant forwards as if hypnotised, led by our noses. Fresh steam rose, flavours and aromas drifting through the air, causing fingers to twitch and our mouths to water. One hundred and seventy-three enthusiastic faces and rumbling stomachs, all ready to pounce.

There were too many choices, so much temptation that my eyes darted back and forth with indecision. I finally selected an enormous oven dish and reached towards it, holding out my plate. A large serving spoon rose up into the air as if possessed, and set straight to work, carving out a generous portion with great skill and care. My mouth filled with saliva as I watched the lasagna being lifted, with thick strings of melted cheese still attached as it was transported to my waiting plate. More heaped spoonfuls of the rich and creamy sauce were quickly added, and it was then, once I had finished being served, that I noticed something truly astounding.

I saw that a girl, seated two seats to my right was receiving food from the exact same serving dish as me. I thought it strange that she should be cradling a large bowl between her hands but then realised that instead of lasagna, she was getting ladle after ladle of some kind of noodle soup. I looked around in shock and in that moment saw the two boys to my left getting food from another large tray. The furthest boy had a towering pile of French fries on his plate and was vigorously shaking a bottle of ketchup. At the same time, the younger one sitting next to me appeared to be dining in reverse, tucking into a bowl of multi-flavoured ice cream, arranged in different coloured scoops. I marvelled at this magical scene, as it became clear in my mind that every one of us was eating to our own individual heart's desire.

That evening, up there above the highest treetops, we dined like gods.

The feast went on for hours, without a single bowl or plate ever becoming empty. I tried to learn as much as possible that night about the group and their then mysterious ways. I was introduced to so many people that I must confess it became a bit of a blur of names and number rankings. I recall noticing the range of ages around the table: I was fairly certain that I was somewhere towards the younger end of the scale, with the youngest of the group looking about eight, and the oldest members appearing fourteen or perhaps fifteen years old. Steggie herself was a hard one to place: while definitely not the eldest, I would have guessed at that time she was about twelve or thirteen.

The boy seated on my left was very young and extremely talkative, even despite the rapid mouthfuls of food he kept shovelling in. He was #152, and his name was Puddle, which I remember thinking was quite unfortunate, and I was about to ask the reason for it when the boy to Puddle's own left, Rick-O-Chet #60, jumped in to explain.

"I was Puddle's teacher at the time. Like Wolfe has been training you," he began, much to Puddle's dismay, the younger boy perhaps realising then that his own, more flattering version of events was not going to be told. "I knew he was going to be a handful from the first moment I met him. He had a funny way of approaching most of the things I tried to teach him."

Puddle groaned loudly with his mouth still full, but Rick-O-Chet carried on regardless.

"He seemed to really struggle when it came to picturing and maintaining the image of a window, you see. I'm sure you remember your first encounter with the Astral Inferno?"

I shuddered at the memory, the horror of all those dark creatures swarming up against the window I had made, and nodded emphatically.

"It scared me half to death!" I managed to say. Rick-O-Chet merely laughed in amused agreement.

"Well, as it turned out, my star pupil here had something else in mind for his first experience of the Astral Inferno. Isn't that right, Puddle?" Rick-O-Chet ruffled the younger boy's hair playfully, but Puddle didn't reply. Others were listening to the story now, and Puddle had lowered his face in embarrassment.

"I'd only turned my back on him for a moment, half a minute tops, but when I looked back, he'd only gone and opened his first portal all on his own! You can imagine my shock at seeing not only the wide puddle there on the floor, but my young friend here thrashing wildly about with his head and shoulders completely immersed within it!"

A roar of laughter went up from everyone who was listening, Puddle himself now forced to grin at his own foolishness.

"So there I was," Rick-O-Chet continued, "the one

responsible for his safety, desperately holding onto his kicking legs and trying to pull him back out of it, before the Inferno reached him. If it hadn't been for the, er, *unusual* choice of the opening itself, I reckon those beings on the other side would've gotten to him quicker, and probably given him some nasty scars to remember them by. So, after that mess, the name kind of stuck. You'd think that experience would've put him off, but nope ... puddles are still his favourite way of travelling, even to this day!"

"I am totally able to make windows now, though!" Puddle insisted in a red-faced attempt to defend his own honour. "I just choose not to, that's all."

"That's true," another young girl piped up, seated on the other side of Rick-O-Chet. Her name was Crumblina, her rank one-three-three. "Last week, Puddle made a window that was big enough for our entire group to escape through. No water involved at all."

"If that's true," interrupted another Freediver, who was positioned opposite her and introduced himself to me as Turtleback, rank forty-five, "then how come all my clothes were damp and dripping when we returned from *that* particular outing?"

More good-natured laughter followed, rolling back and forth along the banquet table.

To my right was a girl who was quite a lot older, and while polite and well-mannered, she seemed very preoccupied talking to those further down the table, using terms I had not then learnt, to discuss things I could not entirely understand. I remember her name was Miss Avant, and her telling me with evident pride that she was rank #19.

"Don't mind her," Puddle whispered quietly in my ear. "She

often ignores the newcomers and younger members. You see the girl sitting next to her? That's Bluebell; she's number eighty-seven. She's awesome, and one of my closest friends, but just look at the way Miss Avant's talking right over the top of her head as if she's not even sitting there."

Before the dinner had finished, I also heard fragments of another conversation going on a little further down the table. An older boy was sitting beside Wolfe and was questioning him quite earnestly. His name was Hammerhead, and he had not spoken to me to reveal his personal rank. I recognised him as one of the Inner Circle.

"I don't know," Wolfe was saying rather defensively. "You know how it is; we've been going through the basics, like we're supposed to!"

"But you must've noticed something? Felt something? You know as well as I do, 'they' just don't move or imagine in quite the same way the rest of us do."

Wolfe shook his head once more, "I've told you, I'm not sure. Everly Kitt was definitely impressed with him last night. He's fast alright, and he said he could hear her in the waking world, talking to the animals, but none of that means he is or isn't. Not for sure, anyway."

The older boy looked a little annoyed and ran a hand through his rust-brown hair. As he turned his back to me, I saw he had a long wispy lock of hair dangling down the back of his neck. It looked bizarre—like a hairdresser had accidentally missed it for more than a year, allowing it to grow. Puddle must have seen my raised eyebrow, for he followed my gaze, sighed and then lowered his voice to fill me in.

"That silly thing's called a Rat's Tail," he whispered, "but

don't let him catch you looking at it. He's very proud of it …
he thinks it's cool. It just makes me think of one of those rope
swings, you know, the kind you find in adventure playgrounds.
Makes me want to grab it, and swing from it." Puddle paused,
seeing me nodding along, and frowned very seriously. "But don't
ever do that! Hammerhead's got a real bad temper, and he would
go totally crazy."

"But why would someone want to grow something like
that?" I asked, still struggling to understand the appeal. Puddle
shrugged the question off.

"Who knows, he's French, and apparently that hairstyle's
really popular there."

I thought back to a weekend trip my parents had taken me
on the previous summer. We had visited Paris and, try as I may,
I couldn't recall seeing any other kids there with that haircut.
Mind you, those two days had been spent running madly around
visiting every impressive landmark and tourist site the city had to
offer. Hammerhead was continuing his conversation with Wolfe,
and I did my best to eavesdrop on what he was saying.

"They are pretty rare these days, and it's been a long time,
that's all. It'd be good to know one way or the other."

Wolfe seemed troubled by this. "And Steggie really thinks he
might be one?"

"She's absolutely sure of it," the older boy responded quickly.

"Well, she's not often wrong about these things, is she?"

Hammerhead glared back at Wolfe. "The last time she was!
And the Shifter ended up crossing too many times, and that was
nearly the end of us all." His voice had risen enough that the
rest of the table turned to look at him; he motioned for Wolfe to
lean in closer and dropped his voice. I shouldn't have been able

to hear him, but somehow his voice was as clear as if he were whispering in my ear. "If there's a chance he is one, I'll just have to keep a very close eye on him, that's all, and you'd be wise to do the same, forty-nine."

At that moment, the older boy turned towards me. I quickly looked away and pretended I was listening to another of Puddle's rambling stories. It was an uncomfortable few seconds, and I could feel Hammerhead's suspicious eyes burrowing straight through me.

Could they really have been talking about me? And who, or what were these "Shifters" he seemed so nervous about? Questions swarmed inside my head, but I would have to wait a long time to discover the answers.

A short while later Steggie Belle rose slowly to her feet, and all those gathered there fell into a hushed silence. As she opened her mouth to speak, the whole world was lit suddenly by a blinding flash of lightning. She turned in the direction it came from, as did I and everyone else. Several seconds passed before a monstrous rumble of thunder rolled its booming course across the sky. Beyond that wooden jetty and the miles of unbroken jungle, we saw the electrical storm unfold across the horizon. A series of jagged forked lightning bolts unleashed upon the world, those random trails exploding into the darkness, and suddenly, somehow, not seeming so very random. They lashed down from above like some demonic fisherman casting his hook or stabbing his spear into the shallow waters, angling … searching.

A chill was in the air. That distant storm was picking up pace and headed in our direction. Steggie calmly assessed the situation, turning her attention back to us with a broad smile.

"It's always a special moment when a newcomer arrives at

our door, and I wanted to thank you all for coming tonight to welcome another dreamer, another Freediver into our family. Zoofall, please stand up and take a bow."

I did as I was asked, blushing once more through a fresh round of applause. As the cheering continued, I realised that somehow her voice had crept stealthily inside my head.

"I know you can hear me, and it's alright. Welcome home, little brother, welcome home."

Our eyes were locked across that table. She was smiling as she repeated that private message over and over inside my mind until the clapping had stopped. She then winked knowingly at me, before continuing with her speech.

"And so, as tradition seems to go, the time has come for a story to be told." Before Steggie had even finished uttering those words an unexpected celebration had begun. Every child's hands had started pounding at the table-top, drumming an ever-quickening beat, until it reached a deafening crescendo. Steggie couldn't help but giggle and raised one hand in an instant command for silence.

"Zoofall, as our guest of honour the decision of what the story will be must fall to you."

One hundred and seventy-two children all turned in unison to face me, and many animated voices rose into a tangled clamour, all offering and pleading their personal suggestions.

"The time she escaped the Imp thieves in the poisoned swamp!" one shouted.

"When she discovered the underground Aztec temple!" another insisted.

I was inundated with topics from underwater prisons and enchanted labyrinths to ferocious hunts and haunted cities.

My mind was spinning, and I remember wondering how could I possibly choose. Each subject sounded better and more intriguing than the last. Meanwhile, I noticed that Steggie Belle had stepped away, focusing her attention back on the rapidly advancing storm. The texture and pressure of the air had changed, more humid, damp and heavy now, and a tropical wind was blowing the hanging lights to and fro. Sheets of rain could be seen thrashing the jungle canopy, and the lightning was getting closer.

She made a quick decision, and returned to the table at once, an urgent spring in her step.

"Now, now," she began soothingly, "don't confuse the poor boy! It must be his choice, and his alone." An ominous clap of thunder roared menacingly overhead. "Besides, we can't stay here. The top of the world is no place to be, on a night like this! Let's head to the cave, and continue there."

There followed several groans and murmurs of disappointment as, everywhere I looked, Freedivers were pushing back their chairs and creating all manner of windows and openings in preparation to travel. I saw to my left Puddle was living up to his name, a glistening, watery portal already formed upon the wooden floor beside his chair.

Steggie interrupted by coughing loudly, a mischievous grin spreading across her face.

"Who said anything about windows? After all that food I think a bit of exercise would do us good."

There was a brief silence, as the others realised what she meant. Then the crazed whoopings of delight began, as the fastest among the group were already on their feet and running from the banquet table. I can tell you quite honestly that, right

63

then, I had absolutely no clue what was going on.

"Just make sure everyone heads straight there, no stopping for too much fun along the way!" she called out with mock seriousness as the other children rushed enthusiastically past her.

I stood up and watched bewildered as the crowd raced headlong towards the jetty. It was a stampede of feet stomping and thumping their way down the length of that pier and, much to my alarm, none showed any sign of slowing down. I winced as I saw the frontrunners reach the edge, launching themselves off the final plank at full speed. Like fabled lemmings falling from a cliff, one by one, they hurtled down towards the lofty canopy below.

I noticed something else at that point. Near the very end of the jetty on either side, on top of the furthest two raised wooden posts, two statues were positioned, like stone gargoyles guarding the treehouse against the outside world. As each child passed that edge, they reached out to touch either the left or right statue before making their death-defying leap into the darkness. Very soon there weren't many of us left up there and, swallowing my fear, I started heading in the same direction.

As I took my first step out onto that rickety pier, my stomach dropped as I realised how very high up we were. Up ahead I saw the last of the youngest children disappear over the ledge, their high-pitched giddy screams fading as they went. I felt a hand upon my shoulder. It was Wolfe, and his final words were not very reassuring.

"You'll love it! Just like falling off a very big log. Only mind the trees, the lightning, and the ground!"

With that, he strode casually up to the edge, chose the right statue, which was clearly that of a cat, and touched it before turning back to face me.

I almost jumped right out of my skin. Something about him had changed. Standing there with his back to the abyss, he smiled and winked at me. His eyes ... they were no longer human! It was unmistakable. They flashed emerald green out of the night, the pupils long and almond-shaped and unquestionably feline. He leant back into a graceful backward dive, and was gone.

I took a deep breath, stepped up to that same ledge, and peered over—sheer, immeasurable darkness. The storm was raging all around, the wind gale-force and violent, but through it all, I thought I heard the faint sound of joyous laughter rising up from below. The statue to my right was indeed a cat, and looking to my left the other was an owl. I gave myself a moment to think. Then it struck me: night vision.

It was at that very moment I knew I was not entirely alone. It was Steggie Belle, and we were the last two remaining up there on that pinnacle.

"We really should be leaving here soon," she said, drawing level with me amid another terrifyingly close crash of thunder. "Besides, the cleaning crew has already turned up." She jerked her head to indicate behind us. "They're harmless enough, but sometimes they have been known to get confused, and blur the line between what is food, and what is not!"

Glancing backwards, I saw the main table was overrun with an army of strange-looking monkeys. They were scampering all over the remnants of our feast. Everywhere, food was being played with, eaten, and flung around with little regard for etiquette.

"We will go together," she continued, placing her hand in mine. She must have already touched the statue, for when she turned back to me, it was with mesmerisingly bright cat eyes. I reached for the owl. As my fingertips brushed against the stone, my sight changed as instantly as if a visor had been clamped down over my eyes. Looking down it was no longer pitch black, but a bizarre and shimmering spectrum, a superhuman clarity, with which I could see everything.

Far below was the rest of the group: specks of radiant light weaving their way like fireflies in and out among the multitude of ancient trees. We jumped as one. I heard her voice whispering again inside my head.

"We have so very much to discuss, you and I."

The feeling was indescribable, the words *weightless* and *free* failing to come close. The second that falling became flying was unforgettable, a moment of pure ecstasy.

Of course, the feeling of leaves slapping my arms and face as we crashed through the highest foliage helped to keep me focused. It was all very real, and one needed to keep one's wits about them. With Steggie's help, I soon found my balance and, following her lead, I attempted a series of somersaults and corkscrew spins, failing on the first couple of tries but slowly getting the hang of it. With my confidence growing, we began pulling off manoeuvres I had not thought possible, hurtling through the air, trying to outdo one another. We made our way through that endless rainforest at speed, diving, twisting, soaring. We glided and carved a breakneck course between the trees and branches.

The storm was hot on our tails, but for the most part, we kept ahead of it. At one point we were so distracted with our acrobatics that the storm overtook us, heavy curtains of sheet-rain falling all around, half blinding us as we ploughed our way through. The thunder, so loud that it seemed to split our skulls, and the nearby flashes of lightning threatening to incinerate us both and strike us from the sky. We sped on, keeping low and desperately trying to break free from that tropical downpour. Finally, we came upon a river; banked a hard right and flew west along it; staying barely inches above the rippling surface, using the mysterious pocket of an airstream.

How long we flew for was difficult to gauge. What felt like only seconds was more likely minutes or even hours, as in the distance the dark shape of a mountain range grew steadily bigger.

I was exhausted when the two of us landed gently on that open and precarious, rocky ledge; there we took a couple of minutes to catch our breath. The cave entrance was located less than halfway up that particular mountainside, carved into the overhanging rock-face above our heads, dome-like and tall like a giant's mouth frozen in full yawn. We stood there at the entrance, watching the furious storm which was still headed our way. Behind us I could just make out the excited voices of the other Freedivers, echoing faintly from the depths of the cave's long tunnel. I don't know why, but something about the storm seemed terribly wrong, and my words just tumbled out.

"Something else's out there, isn't it?"

Steggie looked at me very seriously but didn't say anything, only nodded gravely, and looked back towards the storm. Behind us, deep within the rock, where the cave curled away out of sight and narrowed into a tunnel, we could just see the warm reflection of flames, flickering in their eternal fight against the shadows.

"The others will be waiting for us," she said softly, still gazing out at the lightning-lit storm. "You must choose your own story, not theirs," she went on. "We can only find our own truths by asking our own questions. It's the only way to truly live your dream."

I hesitated a moment; then my question came to me.

Perhaps it had always been there.

"Tell me the story of how you found this group of Freedivers?"

She smiled and placed her hand once more in mine.

We turned our backs on that dark and threatening sky, and followed the sounds of laughter, echoing from deep within the cave.

6

Shelter from the Inferno

S teggie squatted down by the fire to warm her hands, while we huddled close together under heavy blankets, waiting for her story to begin. The dirt in which we sat was copper coloured in the light of the flames. The sloping walls rose up at angles all around us, with scattered alcoves and ridges worn into the rockface, that created raised places, like royal boxes in an opera house, where members of the Inner Circle were perched. The chamber was dry, and somewhere in its upper reaches one could hear the squeaking chatter of bats and the leathery flapping of their wings. They navigated the ceiling with their unseeing eyes, around and about the long and razor-sharp stalactites which hung pendulously pointed in our direction.

The wood crackled and spat in the fire-pit, as the flames licked their way hungrily over them. Steggie cleared her throat: as I was soon to discover, she had a style of storytelling which was so sincere, so fluid, that it captivated and united the audience as one. She had a natural flair for the dramatic; would be still and earnest one minute, then the next, explode like a dynamic spring, leaping, jumping, spinning and twirling, acting out the details as she went. I can only hope that my memory of her tale will do it justice:

"Everyone here can remember their first terrifying glimpse of the Inferno rushing up to meet them at the window. My experience, however, for reasons I couldn't understand at the time, was far more subtle.

"I was five years old when it happened. It was a day that I had been longing for, back in the waking world, more than even Christmas. I could barely eat my breakfast I was so excited and, let me tell you, brushing teeth becomes a tricky business when you can't stop jumping up and down and smiling at yourself in the mirror.

"It was to be my first ever time horse riding, and I knew without a doubt that it was going to be the greatest few hours of my life. I was quite surprised when I saw the horse, with its rust-brown back and upper body, while the underbelly, chest and face were a creamy white colour. I thought it looked exactly like a Hereford Cow! My father noticed it too and even made a joke about it, but it didn't matter to me. I thought he was the most elegant and majestic animal I had ever seen!

"I was so concentrated, so in awe, that I never noticed the trainer's hands disappear from alongside me, nor the encouraging voices of my parents fade away. I was having the time of my life. All of a sudden, the horse reared up, and I closed my eyes for just a second, holding onto the reins as tight as I could. Reopening them, I was stunned to find that he had cleanly vaulted over the fenced enclosure. The landing was a little rough, but I felt proud that through it all, I had somehow managed to hold on. I never once looked back as we broke across the neighbouring field and off down the narrow dirt track beyond. Both the sun and the breeze felt pleasant upon my skin. We were free, the pair of us, and onwards we went at a steady gallop."

I remember it was at this early point in Steggie's story when she was describing her horse jumping over the high fence, that I became distracted by the other children around me. Many of them had let out sharp gasps, followed by excited cries and cheers all at the exact same moment. I looked from side to side, studying the faces of those nearest to me with growing curiosity. It was their expressions that caught my attention.

Broad smiles were reflected in the flickering firelight. Many of their mouths hung open, gripped with such fascination that their tongues poked out over their lips. It was as though the Freedivers were a hypnotised audience, transfixed to the spot. It reminded me of how my father, after a long and tiring day at work, would sit staring at the television screen for hours, except for one very peculiar difference. Nearly all the other children's eyes were firmly closed.

I swivelled around further, checking as many faces as I possibly could. I discovered they were actually squinting. Squinting with their eyelids scrunched so tightly together that they may as well have been shut. There was one exception. From his raised and shadowed alcove, Hammerhead's eyes were piercing and glinting red as they reflected the flames. He was glaring straight at me.

I shifted back around, feeling slightly unnerved and decided to follow suit, closing my eyes. Suddenly the cave burst into a dazzling display of colours and light. The wall directly behind where Steggie stood was illuminated like an enormous cinema screen. It was clear that she was controlling it somehow, for the images projected were a perfectly timed visual display of the story she was telling. I tried squinting, to see what would happen, and found that doing so allowed me to view both the movie itself, while also watching Steggie's silhouette dance animatedly around her stage below. It took some effort and getting used to, but I continued squinting, listening and watching in amazement. I became totally and helplessly absorbed in Steggie's story. My hands clasped eagerly together, aware that my mouth too was gaping open like all the others.

"There was nothing to concern me or cause alarm," she continued. "Nothing to suggest that I had in fact already crossed over into the dream world. I never glimpsed the Astral Inferno in the way you all did, for some unknown reason it kept its distance, allowing me to pass straight through. I first suspected that something wasn't quite right when I became convinced that my lesson surely should have finished long ago. That feeling became a certainty as, from a leafy hilltop, the two of us watched the sun setting over in the west. If I had been all alone at that point, I might have been afraid, but my four-legged guide and new best friend seemed quite content, determinedly pushing on, as though he knew exactly where he was going.

"That evening, I named him Tiger, something which my father would certainly have disapproved of. He would have lowered his reading glasses, wiggling the corners of his moustache, as he often did when not impressed, and would have told me sternly, 'You can't go naming a horse that looks like a cow, Tiger. Whatever next, dear girl!' But this time he was nowhere to be found, and so I did, and Tiger he was named."

Laughter filled the cave, echoing through every crevice as the image of her unamused old father faded, and Steggie's tale resumed.

"We journeyed far together, days blending into one another,

never coming across any other person. I didn't realise it then but, as we ventured deeper and deeper into that wild and lonely world, we were getting more and more lost.

"On some occasions during those first few weeks, I was sure that I actually heard the voices of my parents, though they weren't calling out my name desperately as I had presumed they would have been. Quite the contrary. My father's tone appeared more serious than usual, demanding answers from someone, using words I struggled to understand. Meanwhile, my mother was patiently reading out loud, and I recognised they were my favourite stories which she used to read to me at bedtime. Try as I may, I could not find the origin of their voices, as though they were somehow living within the very wind itself.

"I decided those echoes must be coming from inside my head, the product of a homesick mind playing tricks on me, recreating memories to combat my loneliness.

"Eventually, Tiger and I reached a great and barren shoreline. The winds were strong, and the ocean stretched away as far as the eye could see, the crests of the waves a gurgling white and roaring spray. All around the air seemed laden with salt, which stung my nose, cracked the skin around my lips, and formed a thin crust around my eyelashes.

"We headed south, staying close to the seafront, Tiger leaving scuffed hoofprints behind us as he ploughed his way through the loose sand. It was as another evening approached, with the sun slowly sinking towards the golden, tiger-striped sea, that my horse and fellow travelling-companion stopped. Instinctively I felt that something was wrong. Turning his head back around towards me, Tiger snorted violently, as though letting me know that he sensed it too. I ran my fingers reassuringly through his mane to keep the two of us calm. It was then, with instant alarm, that I noticed we were sinking. I panicked as the thought flashed through my mind: quicksand!"

My eyes were glued to the screen, my heartbeat racing as I watched in horror. The shoreline was so bleak, so immense that it made Steggie and Tiger seem all the more forlorn as they struggled so desperately in the sand. The waves continued to pummel the beach, the wind rising to a screeching frenzy all around them.

"In fright, I leant forward," Steggie continued. "Throwing my arms around his huge neck. Looking down, I could see his hooves and ankles had already disappeared beneath the sand. I clung on hopelessly, shaking my arms in an effort to make him move."

The horse refused. His head turned towards Steggie once more, one massive, dark, oval eye looking straight through her with unspoken wisdom. She appeared to freeze at that moment, and in the cave, we heard his words, sounding so clearly, deep within her head.

"There's no need to be scared, Steggie. I've made it as far as I can for now. Your path goes on much further, and there are so many things you need to learn."

Steggie continued to sob as the two of them sank lower and lower.

"But I don't want you to go." she cried. "You cannot leave me here all alone."

Tiger whinnied soothingly as he spoke. "Now, now, you mustn't worry so. You will not be here alone, and I shall not be altogether gone, no more so than I was ever truly here. This is the time for you to be brave and to believe in yourself."

Her feet were resting then upon the soft sand, his upper body going under. She gripped him ever more tightly, feeling his warmth and hearing the steady thump of his calm heart.

"We shall meet again, Steggie Belle."

"You promise?"

"I promise," he replied, and with that I watched Steggie run her hands through his smooth coat, stroking the softness of his long mane, as the horse disintegrated and fell through her fingers like sand itself, leaving Steggie kneeling on her own, upon the beach. She remained there for some time, the relentless sound of the sea crashing nearby, before rising shakily to her feet. She carried on walking quickly, aware that the sun would soon be gone, as it melted like liquid lava beneath the waves.

As the final rays lit up the sky in magnificent hues of purple and pink, in the very distant corner of the screen, I spotted the cottage up ahead.

It was set on a raised bank just off the beach, overlooking the endless sea. From the edge of the dunes, clumps of dry saltbush began to grow, patches of lifeless green continuing on into an overgrown and tangled garden. A mess of tall shrubs, withered trees and strange shapes silhouetted in the twilight, all leading their way up to the stone property itself. There was an intense stillness about the place that unsettled me slightly as I saw Steggie make her way up from the beach. I could see a warm light glowing from one of the small square windows, which must have filled her with the hope of escaping those bitterly cold sea winds.

As I watched Steggie walk through the garden, I noticed several of those dark shapes were in fact statues, and even in the failing light, she paused to marvel at them. The level of detail was astounding, clearly sculpted by an artist at the top of their craft. Many of the statues were of human figures, while others appeared to be mythical. Some were in very strange positions indeed, fitting neatly into the surrounding landscape itself. All of them, however, seemed to have one fascinating feature in common. Each one that she inspected, was positioned and facing directly towards the stone cottage.

One was almost the size of a bear, but the face was more canine or wolf-like, and there was a definite portrayal of movement, its muscles taut and in mid-stride, as though lunging forward at high speed. Another was of a warrior of some sort, in an equally aggressive pose, heavily armoured and with a massive axe raised high behind his head, as though ready to swing.

Perhaps the most bizarre of them all, which she came upon much closer to the house, was clearly that of a pirate. The real swashbuckler sort, whose body language suggested great stealth, creeping his way forward. Without a doubt, this statue must have been purposefully constructed and then positioned with that particular garden in mind. He was pressed right up close, following the contours and angle of a nearby tree. The two were so perfectly aligned that the statue appeared to be gripping the very tree bark itself with his left hand, peering out from behind that cover with cunning intent, and a dagger still held firmly between his teeth.

"I was quite fascinated by it all," Steggie continued, "and wondered how the artist had managed to create such magical and lifelike sculptures. Perhaps, I thought excitedly, it was the artist who actually lived there. I climbed the few steps up onto the veranda and headed towards the door. I knocked twice upon it and waited. At first, there was no sound or response, then I thought I heard a brief shuffling from inside. I raised my arm to knock again, and just as I did, the door flew open.

"I was blinded by the light pouring out from inside, and I used my upheld hand to shelter my eyes, squinting at the blurry figure who now stood there."

On the cave wall, I saw Steggie, bedraggled and frightened in the doorway.

"Sorry to bother you," she said, "but I am lost and alone, and I saw your light. Could I come inside and stay for a while?" There was no answer, only silence and the sound of the distant waves. "Please?" she added, suddenly remembering her manners.

Her attempt at politeness, however, seemed to have quite the opposite effect, as though her request had caused great concern, or offence.

"Begone little Devil! Your skills hold no power over me, Evil One. Begone!" a voice roared at her, and in the confines of the cave, its echo rolled, disturbing the bats so that they launched themselves flapping and squeaking in fright. The indistinct figure leant forwards and down towards her, suddenly revealing its colossal height. Through the haze, I also became aware that this person was carefully, intently studying Steggie's eyes. Something seemed to change. "Who are you?" The voice was still rather gruff, but undeniably female.

Steggie explained who she was, and the situation she had found herself in, which seemed to put the figure slightly more at ease. She straightened herself in the doorway, though in the deep twilight, with the light shining from behind, her appearance was still a silhouetted mystery.

"It's not safe for one as young as you to be out there all alone. Especially not on a night like this. You'd best come inside."

Her tone seemed somewhat forced, and her words ended

hesitantly, as though she instantly regretted her decision, but she moved to one side, all the same, allowing Steggie to enter. As she did, Steggie glanced quickly up at her, and we observers were able to see the woman more clearly. She seemed to be wearing a veil over her face, the kind that a bride would wear to a wedding, made of intricate white lace. There was also a tangled thickness to her hair, dark and wild, and while silhouetted there in the entrance, it appeared to be caught perpetually by the gusty wind, buffeted, swaying, moving. Steggie stepped into a well-lit room, and my first impression was that it was incredibly cluttered and well-lived in, in a cosy kind of way. In the silence of the cottage, we heard the woman close and triple bolt the door behind her.

"My name is Euryale," the woman said, still with the same hesitance but in a more welcoming manner. Steggie's own voice drifted through the cave to tell us, "By then it was far too late. I didn't manage to step back in horror, or even scream. Everything went dizzyingly dark, and I fainted right there upon her sitting-room floor."

The images behind her faded to black, and I opened my eyes properly, unsure what was going to happen next. Steggie stood there motionless, and the shadows seemed to press down, weighing heavily upon her. There was a sadness to her gaze, which suggested loneliness and made me feel that she was keeping something secret from us. She appeared infinitely older than her age and somehow broken by it.

She noticed me looking at her and forced a smile. "When I awoke I found myself lying on the sofa, wrapped up under blankets, and straight away I saw Euryale sat quietly in an armchair on the other side of the room, watching me from behind her veil."

The large screen behind her brightened, the story resuming once more, and there was Euryale, saying, "I must apologise. I didn't mean to frighten or upset you. I don't get much in the way of company any more. It has been centuries since I have had a genuine, amicable visitor and, well, even the simple things can be so easy to forget. I am sorry, child, for giving you such a scare, and assure you that I have no desire to hurt you or do you harm." A heavy hood now covered her head and shoulders.

"I am sorry too," Steggie stammered now sitting bolt upright and clearly still nervous. "You were kind enough to give me shelter, and I didn't mean to offend you." she looked down at her hands, fiddling with them uncomfortably in her lap, and couldn't bring herself to look up again for quite a while. "Can I ask, did I really see what I think I saw? Were they really real?"

Euryale nodded slowly then, with a degree of apprehension, pulled back and removed the hood. Her hair was quite literally alive, what I had assumed was the wind, was actually a tangle of slithering serpents, mottled black and dark green, overlapping one another, and issuing aggressive hissing sounds.

"Are they dangerous?" Steggie finally spluttered in amazement.

"Deadly poisonous every one of them," came Euryale's reply, "best you keep your little fingers well clear of them for the time being. Give them a chance to weigh you up and get to know you, and then we shall see."

Steggie could not hide her astonishment and began questioning the veiled woman further. "I just don't understand. How did such a thing happen to you? And who exactly are you?"

"Ah," Euryale said, "the who's, the how's, and the why's. Those things can often take a very long time. Let me get some soup going before I begin." With those words, she rose and shuffled over to the fireplace, and swung a fair-sized cooking cauldron, which was hanging from an iron hook, until it was positioned directly over the flames.

"That night Euryale confided in me her remarkable tale," Steggie whispered to us, before turning around to face the screen herself. Within that isolated stone cottage, sheltered from the howling gales, the incredibly tall woman told us of her past. Her age was quite impossible to guess without seeing her face clearly. Her figure was athletic and lean, her voice young-sounding and soft yet, as she leant towards us, her spine appeared crooked and humped around the shoulders, suggestive of extreme age.

I was born the middle sister of three, on a beautiful island back in the waking world, several thousands of years ago. My younger sister was accused of a crime which she did not commit, and we two elder sisters, believing in her innocence, stood defiantly by her side. As a result, all three of us were punished, destined to suffer a lifelong curse. We were to be rejected, abandoned and eventually seen as an enemy of mankind. As we would soon discover, our problems had only just begun.

We were branded as monsters—and once seen as such—fear and hatred transformed our story into a legendary lie. Yes, our radiant locks of hair had been replaced by nests of venomous snakes, and our sight had been so cruelly and dangerously altered, but that was where the true understanding of mankind ended.

It was told that we possess immortality and, while it may have appeared that way to mortal men, it was not so. The three of us had merely been blessed with the secrets of longevity, which made a century of earthly time equivalent to only a few months for us; a fact that made our punishment all the more severe. It was also said that we sisters had terrible fangs, brass hands and monstrous claws for legs.

At that point in her story, Euryale got to her feet, raised her flowing gown a few inches, and did a little dance upon the spot, as though to prove a point, exposing her nimble and elegant feminine legs, before continuing.

We are indeed able to produce such defensive weapons if genuinely threatened, but thanks to the curse put upon us, in reality, there has rarely been such a need. Damned as we have been, with a single look that most often kills.

She made a point of that "most often", and continued to explain in more detail. She said that from her experience it is very normal for men to see exactly what they want to see, and that in such a way the sisters' curse itself was wholly misunderstood. Like with the transformation of their hair, so too their new sight was purposefully aimed to make them unapproachable. That was the essence of their punishment! So it was ruled that any man or woman with lies and deceit in their minds, or harbouring hatred in their hearts, with just one look into those three sisters' eyes, would instantly be turned to stone. Although I could not see it, I believe behind her veil Euryale wept at that point in her tale.

For us three, we would come to discover an ugly and awful truth which, with the passing of centuries, would make us wish that we could close our eyes for good. We learnt the hard way that nearly all beings have a tendency of hiding such thoughts and emotions beneath the surface, tempting the three of us to think that a connection was possible, tempting us to believe. Every attempt we made led only to more heartache and a gradual loss of faith. Time and time again, each home in which we tried to settle, soon became nothing more than a silent hall filled with cold, haunting statues.

At last, feeling we had no other option, we decided to withdraw from the world and return to the long since deserted island from which

we came. To live out our long lives in the misery of solitude. It became clear, however, that the world of men would not let us. For the years to come, we were hunted, pursued, and repeatedly attacked. The Fates refused us peace. Then one day, an unimaginable horror reached our shore.

Perhaps the greatest hero among men had accepted a challenge and came to join the fight. His target, and chosen victim, was the youngest of us three, whose name was Medusa, and through trickery and guile that ego of a man—that Perseus—found her.

A very different story has been told and accepted as to what happened there that day but we, the last two remaining Gorgon sisters, know the terrible truth.

As he approached, viewing her in the reflection of his shield, Medusa dared to dream one final, impossible dream. So desperate to believe a connection could still be found she looked into the reflection of his eyes which seemingly would not be turned to stone, and our baby sister went to him with open arms, and hope, and love. She was slain without mercy by his devilish hands, and the coward fled.

Three sisters had become two, and the world of men rejoiced. Legend has it that the Gorgons are the embodiment of rage and fury, so you consider and decide what's true? With our beloved sister murdered, it would have been well within our power to seek revenge, make the hunter the hunted, to open our eyes and create a worldwide quarry, destroying mankind forever.

Instead, we mourned, then together with my older sister, Stheno, we abandoned the waking world which had betrayed us, crossing over into the dream world.

Her story ended quite abruptly, and Steggie turned back towards us, continuing her narration. "After a minute or two, I found myself asking, 'Where is your older sister now, Euryale?'.

But the mouth behind the veil remained closed, and for the rest of that first night silence was the only answer to my question."

Steggie paused a moment, as behind her the cottage scene forwarded to daytime, the small windows becoming flooded with rays of brilliant sunlight. Suddenly an odd sound reverberated through the cave, causing every one of us to flinch. I recognised the sound instantly, and that sickened me, my frustration boiling over. It had no business being there, not now!

7

Crime and Comeuppance

The sound wouldn't stop. It had interrupted the flow of the story, and the movie on the screen had frozen. Only the noise continued, harsh and shrill, steadily rising in volume. It was my alarm clock, but I refused its call, clinging onto the dream for every last second that I could. I realised all the Omnivagas were now looking at me, and I felt the desperate need to apologise. That was when Steggie's voice softly snuck inside my head.

"Don't worry, Zoofall. We'll be right here waiting for you. You won't miss a thing."

"I'll be back as fast as I can," I promised telepathically, glancing quickly around the cave and feeling more reassured, before consciously blinking up out of the dream.

I slapped the alarm clock off, so violently that it actually toppled off the small bedside table. Heaving myself up and out of bed I fished around on the floor for the clock, saw the time and let out a wretched groan: it was a school day.

A merciless, steely grey light was seeping through the curtains, promising nothing but the dreary tedium of the waking world.

I drifted without interest, like a zombie, through my uninspiring daily routine. Putting on my uniform carelessly in the semi-dark, stuffing the dreaded school tie in my trouser pocket and stumbled downstairs, vaguely following the smell of burnt toast coming from the kitchen.

"Looks like someone got out of bed on the wrong side today!" my mother remarked, sensing my glum mood. Her unbreakable cheerfulness, which had a way of stimulating others to smile, failed to infect me that day. All I could think about was Steggie's unfinished story. I stared mindlessly at the cereal before me, spooning it in and barely chewing, while my mother tried in vain to smooth and flatten my bed hair with warm water. I could tell my silence worried her, a maternal instinct that something was wrong, but I simply didn't have the energy to pretend that morning. There was concerned sadness in her eyes, as she stood in the doorway, half-heartedly waving me off.

It had rained heavily, the night before. I rode my bike to school on autopilot, carefully steering around the puddles with a newfound sense of respect, instead of splashing straight through them. The morning classes fogged past me in a muted humdrum haze. I feigned interest through maths, made a mountain of pencil-shavings during geography, and daydreamed through art.

It was during the history class, which was right before our lunch break, that I decided enough was enough. I was inspired by my teacher reciting Hannibal's supposed response to his generals when they insisted to him that it was impossible to cross over the Alps with elephants.

'I will either find a way, or make one!'

The spark of determination was kindled inside me. I had to return to the dream world, to the Freedivers and Steggie Belle, sooner than the rigid, ticking wall clock would allow. I had to escape this prison-like maze of chalkboard tombs by whatever means necessary. The rest of the lesson was spent quietly plotting. The minute hand appeared to taunt me, shuddering but almost resisting to move around the clock face. It seemed an aeon, time stretching out like treacle before eventually, the high-pitched school bell rang.

I waited for the predictable rush and fury to diminish, as every child within the building spilled outside. Pacing the tarmacked playground amid the joyous whoops and bustling bodies, I continued to weigh my options. Faking an illness seemed like the safest bet. I knew which pitfalls to avoid: over-acting was a definite no-no. I had watched several of my classmates over the years ruin a perfectly good lie with exaggerated pains and symptoms. The school nurse was nobody's fool, she had been in the job for over thirty years, and had seen and heard it all. She had the sharpness of a bloodhound for sniffing out trickery, but if I kept it simple, I believed my odds were fair. A ten-minute sprinting session to create the cold and clammy sweats, then two minutes with my forehead pressed to the radiator, and perhaps finally if I was feeling brave enough, a glass of salty water to make my stomach really churn. I grimaced at the thought. Despite knowing that vomiting would certainly seal my performance's success, I still wasn't keen on the idea.

To that date in my school career, I had never got into any serious trouble, and perhaps for that reason, I hadn't considered any more drastic options. Standing there alone under an overcast and dismal sky, my plans were very soon about to change.

From the corner of my eye, I spotted a small commotion start to unfold on the other side of the playground. I paused and then, against my better judgement and with a heavy sigh, I altered my course and began casually walking in that direction. I had no idea what I was going to find, or what I was going to do about it when I got there, but my feet pushed on, as though magnetically drawn to the looming trouble.

It was then as I drew near that I heard the sobbing. It was so faint and indistinct that the coward inside of me tried to persuade me it had not been real, to turn around and just walk back the other way.

Not much was visible through the tightly massed group of figures, so I continued on around them, in the hopes of a better view. I had strayed far too close to that agitated group when suddenly Terry Mortlock straightened, rising a full head and shoulders above the rest.

Terry Mortlock wasn't just your standard bully. His cruelty and viciousness made even his closest allies uncomfortable. He was older than me and in his final year, before hopefully moving on to the senior school, assuming he wasn't expelled first. I even had the impression that the teachers were wary of him, counting down the months until that particular boy would no longer be their problem. It was a general and well-known rule among the entire school to stay well clear of Terry Mortlock.

A glimmer of an insane thought flashed through my mind, just one word: *fight*. I quickly chastised my rebellious brain: *You want to go home to bed, not end up stuck in a hospital bed, eating through a straw!*

At that moment, I believe I still could have run away, but some invisible current carried me straight on into that whirlpool of imminent danger.

"No need for that ten-minute run anymore," I muttered

under my breath, feeling a cold trickle of nervous sweat begin to roll down my temple. Pushing and squeezing my way through the scrum-like wall of older boys, I made my way towards the group's hidden centre. One of the younger boys was hunched over on his knees crying, as all around him those grotesque and leering faces laughed. I recognised him as being in the year below me, but couldn't remember his name. Bending down beside him, it took a moment to try and figure out what had happened.

Scattered fragments of what was once a bird's nest, and about half a dozen brightly coloured but broken eggs lay before him. A thick, mucus-like liquid was leaking from the cracked and shattered shells, horribly flecked with red.

"He killed them!" the younger boy was saying between heaving sobs. "Killed them for no reason at all." I noticed then that he was cradling the only undamaged yet fragile egg within cupped hands as he rocked there back and forth.

Suddenly our world grew darker, as behind us a giant had stepped forwards, eclipsing the clouded sun and casting the pair of us into shadow. *No need for that salty water*, I thought, as a wave of fear and nausea swept through me, making my stomach somersault and spin. With a strength I didn't know I had, I rose to my feet, planting myself between the cowering younger boy and the savagely delighted bully.

"It's the Zoo-freak!" Mortlock announced: a nickname he had invented after my accident, which I was not too fond of. He took a step closer, using his height to his advantage and staring down at me intimidatingly. "I didn't realise you were into other animals," he continued. "Thought you were just a gorilla-lover."

I said nothing, fairly certain that he had exhausted his very limited imagination.

"We've got a problem, see," Mortlock hissed, clamping one meaty hand upon my shoulder. I could feel the strength in his grip and couldn't back away. "Bird-brain here didn't have any lunch money to give me, and then he made a mess all over the floor. But seeing as the two of you are *such good friends*, I figure you can pay me the money that he owes. How does that sound?" It didn't sound much like a question, and his buck-toothed sadistic grin grew menacingly thin. "Then the two of you can just walk away... without us having to feed you both what's left of his little pets."

I nodded quickly, trying not to flinch at the disgusting image his threat had conjured in my mind, and thrust my left hand deep into my pocket, desperately searching for any money at all. Never had I wished so hard for the school bell to ring again, summoning us back to class.

Mortlock appeared satisfied with this reaction and loosened his grip on my shoulder. It was as I rooted around the depths of my pockets that a sudden calmness came over me. Fear vanished, and was instantly replaced by cold and steady logic. My train of thought became rapid and precise.

Use the element of surprise. Plenty of witnesses. Not just a scuffle though, or you'll end up staying later in detention. Make it count. If it's serious enough, they'll send you straight home.

My fingers found what they were looking for. As I withdrew the shiny one pound coin, I noticed a teacher had spotted the group of us acting suspiciously and was marching our way. *Even better*, I thought wickedly, a smile starting to form. Anger was growing inside me, spiralling into rage. I remembered Wolfe's words about what mankind had done to the fairies, I heard Everly Kitt's story about the witches. I remembered the feeling of flying. I remembered those poor, broken eggs.

Without further thought, I flicked the gold coin upwards, spinning it high into the air. Terry Mortlock's eyes followed its trail closely, his face turning skyward, perhaps in preparation to catch it. My right hand had automatically clenched into a fist. It came swinging up in slow motion, but at such high speed that I thought it was possessed. It missed Mortlock's chin—which was what I had been aiming for—by inches, but followed through, connecting forcefully with his nose. Silent shock swallowed the playground as a frightening quantity of blood sprayed out in all directions. Mortlock staggered backwards with tears in his eyes, reeling unsteadily and in a daze, before collapsing to the tarmac floor.

What happened next is mostly a blur. I remember being whisked away, the teacher leading me directly to the Headmaster's study. Then angry voices and appalled reactions from the grown-ups assembled in the room, followed by a brief phone call, after which I was informed that my mother was on her way to collect me. I vaguely remember grinning like a maniac through it all, even when the Headmaster explained the severity of my punishment, in a stern and disapproving tone.

"Two days suspension, effective immediately!" were the only words of his which stuck. I recall my mother's face when she finally arrived. It was flushed in a way I had never seen it before, an unforgettable fusion of anger, disappointment, shame and embarrassment, as she apologised on my behalf. Then came the long and silent car ride home, during which the adrenaline finally faded, and I began to realise how much trouble I was in.

"Your father has left work early and will back any minute now. Then the three of us will sit and talk," she said matter-of-factly once we were home, handing me an ice-pack for my bruised and swollen knuckles, without any of her usual care or affection.

The talk was long and serious. They made me feel tiny. They made the room spin. *Violence is never the answer*, was drummed into me repeatedly, in hundreds of different ways. I made no excuses, and hung my head low, like a convicted prisoner, as their long list of punishments was slowly recited. No television or computer games for a month. No cycling, or going out or seeing friends on the weekends. Homework and endless chores were to be my life from now on within the waking world. Then, there it was in all its glory.

"And straight to bed after dinner. No exceptions!" I sensed the faintest bit of hesitation in my father's voice as he delivered that final punishment, and after they sent me to my room, I listened to their hushed voices as they continued their discussion.

"...standing up to the school bully," my father said quietly. "In a way, I'm proud of him."

"Really!" my mother tutted, before adding gravely, "And I'm not so sure about sending him to bed early." True panic flooded my mind at hearing those dreadful words. "You know as well as I do how much he loves to sleep. It feels like we're rewarding him somehow."

"I know," my father agreed. "But there's nothing we can really do about that. We can hardly force him to stay up late against his will."

There followed a short period of stifled laughter, drifting up from downstairs. In the growing darkness of my bedroom, my smile was barely visible as I lay my weary head upon the pillow and snapped my eyes shut. Moments later, from beyond my eyelids that still were closed, came a warm orange glow which filtered through. It danced and flickered in a way I recognised only too well, my heart leaping for joy, knowing at once that I had returned. Opening my eyes slowly to the firelight, the first thing I saw was Steggie Belle smiling at me from the other side of the cave.

8

How She Found Us

"**D**oes it hurt?" Wolfe asked, examining my knuckles with great interest.

"Just a little bit sore, that's all," I said. We were squatting side by side, close to the campfire in the cave. The place had been half-empty when I first arrived, but gradually, one by one, the other members were returning.

"Where's everyone else?"

"Just waiting for them to come back." He saw my puzzled expression. "They have to reconnect with the dream, and that can sometimes take a bit of time."

I stared into the flames, not saying anything straight away, grappling with reason and trying to get my head around it. Then, as with the blink of a lightbulb, the obvious solution came to me.

"Time zones! If the Freedivers are spread out all around the world, then we're living in different time zones, right? When some of us are heading for bed, others might only just be getting up and going to school."

Wolfe had been nodding slowly as if in agreement but sighed as I finished speaking.

"See, that's your mistake. You're trying to figure this out with Floater logic and… and common sense! That's never going to work around here." He abruptly changed the subject: "So, you took him down with just one punch? That's impressive. You keep your cool like that in the dream world, and you'll be rising up through the ranks in no time!"

I found it easier to focus on my victory than to consider how the Omnivagas could possibly all be dreaming together at one time.

"It was a lucky punch really," I confessed. "Honestly, I'm not much of a fighter."

Wolfe tutted and shook his head, smiling. "I imagine that bully's face might disagree with you there!" Wolfe's grin faded, his voice becoming sombre. "But seriously, Zoofall, you're not worried that this kid's gonna be looking for revenge? If I were you, I'd try to grow eyes in the back of your head."

The thought hadn't even occurred to me, but from that moment on, it was all I could think about. My stomach started to twist and knot. The two days suspension would carry over into a long weekend, but then the following Monday I'd be right back there. In my mind, the school turned into a hellish battleground, full of dark corridors and blind spots where Mortlock could be lying in wait. I shuddered and swallowed down my rising fear.

"It's good to see that you're able to take care of yourself over in the waking world." the unexpected voice broke in from behind us, making me almost jump out of my skin. It was Steggie, and she continued speaking in that no-nonsense way of hers. "Bully, you say? An older boy I'm guessing?" I nodded shyly to both questions. There was clear contempt in her voice. "What's the coward's name?"

"Terry Mortlock," I said, feeling for a bizarre second that I was betraying a trust which the school bully definitely didn't deserve. Steggie Belle stared pensively off into the distance, committing the name to memory, before unleashing a broad, reassuring smile.

"Don't worry about him, Zoofall, he won't be bothering you again. I'll make quite sure of that!" Her promise was cemented with a courageous smile. Without another word she quickly turned on her heel, zig-zagging a path through the other members, and getting ready to begin the second part of her story. As she left, I turned back to Wolfe in distress.

"Mortlock's as mean as he is huge. There's no way Steggie could scare him off or beat him in a waking world fight! Besides, I'm not even sure we live in the same country."

It was Wolfe's turn to laugh, patting me on the back as he did so.

"Who said anything about the two of them meeting in the waking world? She'll get to him where he's weakest. Don't look so pale, Zoofall," he whispered, leaning closer. "Steggie eats bullies like him for breakfast!"

Moments later, a silence of eager expectancy settled within the cave and, with all the Freedivers present and accounted for, Steggie raised both arms up high. She twirled gracefully on the spot as the bright cinema screen re-emerged from the shadows above her head, her voice spirited and enchanting.

"Over the next few months that rambling old cottage became my home, with Euryale teaching me the necessary skills which would allow me to survive and stay safe."

We watched various scenes of the two of them training together, the complexity of the lessons soon became baffling and

far beyond my understanding. As a way of showing her thanks, Steggie worked on Euryale's garden, attempting to add a little beauty back into the overgrown chaos. On numerous occasions, we saw Steggie tentatively offering whatever insects and mice that she could find as a sort of peace offering to Euryale's hungry and viciously temperamental hair. Over time their hissing stopped, and those poisonous fangs were no longer bared threateningly in her direction.

"Euryale and I became close friends," Steggie continued, "although I often felt that she was holding things back from me as if she had built an invisible wall around her tortured heart. After those first three months it appeared my training was over, and perhaps if I hadn't acted so recklessly that day, our relationship would have come to an end right there.

"I found her late that afternoon out on the veranda, sitting in the rocking chair, as she so often used to do. She would spend hours each day just rocking back and forth, looking out from behind that veil at the endless waves as they crashed and rolled in towards the shore. That appeared to be her favourite pastime, although I sensed a great, unspoken sadness watching her there. I waited patiently for the right moment to interrupt her with my question."

We watched the scene unfold before us on the glowing screen, Steggie's voice sounding timid at first.

"Euryale, that first night when I knocked on your door you seemed to think I was someone else. Please, it's been bothering me ever since: who did you mistake me for?"

The creaking chair ground immediately to a halt, as though her words had surprised or frightened Euryale in some disturbing way. Even the snakes seemed a little on edge as the tall woman slowly turned to face her.

"Oh, Steggie dear, some questions I'm afraid are better left unasked," she replied with a shake of her head, "some answers are just too awful. Some knowledge comes at such a perilous price that it must only be shared with a very trusted few."

At first, Steggie seemed confused, and then her head dropped until her chin was almost touching her chest as if she regretted bringing it up.

"You don't trust me? Have I done something wrong?"

"No, no dear girl," Euryale said, taking her hand and pulling Steggie close so that she was standing level before her. "I do trust you. I trust you so very much more than most, but for the sake of protection, certain lines must be drawn. Some secrets must remain secrets."

I believed in that instant Euryale was smiling at her, I could almost hear it in her voice. Nothing, however, could have prepared any of us for what came next. Steggie's body lurched forward suddenly, her fingers rising in a flash with no time to weigh the risks. With the swiftest of movements, she snatched and lifted up the woman's veil. Euryale was a split second too slow to stop her, with even her terrified scream arriving too late.

"Steggie no!"

That cry tore through the cave, disrupting the bats' sleep again and causing the entire audience to jump backwards, gasping in startled fright. Euryale and Steggie appeared frozen for what seemed an eternity: as if they themselves had both been simultaneously turned to stone. Those eyes! I have never seen such eyes! They were fused and flecked with a thousand colours, swirling with indescribable depths as though galaxies were colliding inside them, dazzlingly brilliant and beautiful.

We were stunned into absolute silence. With not one of the Freedivers daring even to breathe as we looked up, witnessing that truly magical connection between Steggie and Euryale.

"Never in a thousand years," she finally gasped, tears falling down her angelic face. Then almost scoldingly, "why on earth would you… I could have…" but Euryale could not find the words, looking once more in amazement at the young girl, before cradling her close.

"It seemed the only way," Steggie told her, surrendering to the warmth of her embrace.

"Never change, Steggie," she whispered, not letting go. "Never change!" As the sun set that evening over the ocean, she held onto Steggie like a mother, like an older sister once more.

"I ended up living there with Euryale for almost a year," Steggie continued, "and it was she who introduced me to the deeper mysteries of the Astral Cloud, and beyond. The age-old rivalries and alliances that exist and are the very fabric within and between the two worlds. She revealed and taught me so many wondrous things.

"I remember, not long after that day, my utter surprise to discover that she had actual wings. Euryale had kept them modestly hidden under her cloak for that entire time, and I had assumed that the protruding lumps were merely a hunchbacked sort of growth resulting from her extreme age."

My eyes remained fixed on Euryale's strangely shaped shoulders, believing that—at any moment—the folds of her cloak would fall away as those magical wings unfurled. As Steggie's story continued, it was with some disappointment that I realised those wings would not be revealed just yet.

"She spoke at great lengths of the importance of harmony,

and how, as many of you listening here right now already know, there is a delicate balance that links our two worlds. A balance which must be maintained for both worlds to flourish successfully together. She explained how every action of ours, no matter how small, has a consequence. And how some various beings and groups were determined to upset and destabilise this natural balance for their own benefit and ends.

"Euryale insisted on taking me on journeys: showing me first hand some of the lesser-seen goings-on, far in the extreme outer reaches of the dream world."

My eyes returned in amazement to the glowing screen. The sceneries which were flashing by were wild and fantastical, like nothing I had ever seen before. I wished so very badly that we could have slowed them down somehow. We watched the two of them travelling at breathtaking speed, soaring high and unobserved like satellites, before plummeting down into the thick of it to walk amongst those curious tribes and clans. Euryale and Steggie seemed to be invisible to the local inhabitants, passing by them unnoticed.

"We moved through those turbulent realms like the most seasoned Shadow People." Steggie continued, as the screen showed them slipping in and out of secret meeting rooms where strategies were being discussed; watching entire armies in training, repeatedly practising for upcoming battles. "Euryale wanted me to see with my own two eyes, the constant dangers bubbling away beneath the surface of the dream world. She needed me to understand how, in every nook and cranny, trouble could be stumbled upon by the unwitting dreamer who wanders too far."

Every child within the cave marvelled at what we were

seeing. We realised that not all of their explorations had been limited to land-based civilisations. I found there was something spectacular about descending to encounter the scaly presences beneath the spectral blue waters. From the Starfish Soldiers wielding their sea-urchin spiked trident spears while endlessly patrolling the ocean floors. To the more sinister, self-appointed Crocodile Lords who, half-reptile, half-human, skulked through the shadowed roots of the mangrove swamps.

"One day Euryale announced a special trip, and we set off at the crack of dawn, soon coming across what appeared to be an entire army on the move. The creatures themselves didn't seem very physically threatening at all, even in their thousands marching row upon row."

I peered forwards where I sat, examining those strange beings which moved along the wall behind Steggie. I felt the giddying thrill of curiosity growing within me. Their bodies were thin and wiry, and even if they had stood up straight would not have measured over two foot tall. The way they moved was similar to a ferret or weasel, a sly squirming forward from side to side, bodies pressed close to the floor. More human than animal though, their skin was bald and wrinkled, and it was only in their crooked tiny faces that the malice showed. Beady-eyed with bony, pointed features, and rotten teeth visible behind wide and evil grins, stretching the corners of their mouths to the limit of their shrivelled skin.

"Some among you will surely recognise the horrible beings of which I speak, while a few of you will have had the misfortune of coming into direct contact with these infamous creatures. Well, of course back then I knew nothing of them, and so we followed in their wake at a safe distance."

"Who are they, and where are they going?" she finally managed to ask Euryale.

"These despicable things call themselves the Sophists but are more widely known by all as Temptors. This is a regular journey for them, day after day they make this exact same march. Although they may look like feeble little fiends, they possess a potentially diabolical ability. That brings me to the where: they are headed to the waking world."

"The waking world?" Steggie repeated, aghast and clearly not comfortable at the thought.

She followed Euryale along the bottom of a boulder-filled ravine which ended after several miles, opening out onto a vast, grassy meadow. At the far end of which a sheer cliff-face rose up to such dizzying heights that its top could not be seen, lost somewhere amongst the clouds.

"The Wall of Fuse-and-Flux," Euryale whispered as the two of them crouched low to witness what happened next.

The length of the wall appeared pitted with an infinite number of minuscule holes. There, much to my astonishment, I watched as the horde of Temptors spread out at the foot of the cliff and proceeded to contort and squeeze themselves into the individual holes they had chosen. It was an incredible sight to see and, despite great difficulty, one by one, the army disappeared through the rock face. Euryale was now shaking her head in dismay.

"I have little love left for humankind," she confessed, "but the day the Temptors found this place, the balance of both worlds was thrown in jeopardy."

Once the very last of those horrible creatures had wriggled their way right through, the pair made their approach. Up close it seemed even more impossible, the average hole was no wider than my thumb, and filled all the way through with strange, crackling electricity.

Euryale noticed the perplexed expression on Steggie's face and laughed upon seeing it. "They're slippery little devils to be sure, and the holes are even smaller on the other side! Don't look so worried. There's no need to start greasing yourself up just yet, I know a better way."

Along the base of the cliff ran a small gully, a narrow trickling stream, and I stared as Euryale bent low and dipped one hand into the clear water. My eyes widened. This was clearly not the regular sort of window which we used to travel around the dream world. It was the first Inter-World portal I had witnessed being made, a magnificent process of artistic beauty but not, as I was soon to learn, without its own fatal dangers.

Euryale looked suspiciously around the open field to make sure they were alone before beginning. Then her hand began to move, first in a swirling motion under the water, creating a mini whirlpool effect, before altering into a rapid upward pattern of swishing hand strokes, redirecting and manipulating the flow of the water. A liquid column grew, similar in a way to a lump of clay upon a spinning potter's wheel. Inch by inch it rose up against the cliffside. Both her hands massaging the water-jet faster and faster until her arms were almost a blur. Completely defying the idea of gravity, the base of this liquid column grew wider too, a gurgling, upwards rushing torrent of water.

Steggie gasped at Euryale's masterful creation.

"It's like… like an upside-down waterfall!"

A brief smile crossed Euryale's face. "I call it a Water-Rise Doorway," she said, taking a step back to regard her own handiwork, some three feet wide and seven feet tall. "These portals are extremely rare and special since they form a link—a bridge if you will—between the two worlds. This one leads to an exact location within the waking world."

At the top of the Water-Rise, I stared dumbfounded at the perfectly horizontal line of foaming spray, as though the water were hitting an invisible ceiling. Euryale was once again looking nervously all around them before she grabbed Steggie's hand and pulled her hastily towards the glistening doorway.

"We must be quick. We cannot stay long!" she said, stooping very low and nearly bending over double to fit her way through.

Her anxiety rubbed off on me and made me nervous, as I watched the two of them disappear. The screen view suddenly rushed towards that Water-Rise at high speed. A few of the Freedivers around me even yelled out, screaming as though they were on a rollercoaster, before we were sucked through straight behind them. In that last moment, far away in the distance, I thought I heard the faint echo of a bellowing roar.

We were now inside what appeared to be a darkened bedroom, and I was just able to make out the faint sound of snoring coming from nearby. Euryale was stood before us and had one of her hands placed gently over Steggie's mouth, in a clear instruction to remain quiet. The camera angle we were all staring at changed, rotating slowly and circling the entire room but remained focused on the two of them. As the movie swung around so that we could see Euryale and Steggie face on, a wave of shocked gasps rippled through the cave.

They were nothing more than two vaporous and misted forms, almost featureless shapes, hovering between the bed and the moonlit bedroom window. Behind them and to the right, the flowing Water-Rise had vanished, and where it should have been was only a long rectangular mirror, on the open inner side of a wardrobe door.

Everything was beyond confusing! To the point where it almost seemed reasonable that in the mirrored surface, neither one of them cast a reflection. The sudden thought of Vampires entered my mind, giving me chills and goosebumps along my forearms. Euryale quietly tugged her forward towards the bed a step or two. And that was when I saw it.

Next to the sleeping man, the dark, lean unmistakable shape of one of those Temptors. Its face was pressed right up close to the snoring man's ear, and there, in the dead of night, I heard its hushed and croaking voice. Though unable to pick up anything of what was being said, I instinctively knew that it could only be bad. The Temptor continued whispering, oblivious to the two of them being there, a sick trail of saliva dripping down from that wicked mouth, landing upon the poor man's pillow.

I was horrified and quite disgusted, but just at that moment, there came a rising rumbling sound from behind us, as though a train was approaching on some nearby railway line. Euryale clenched Steggie's hand tightly. The noise disturbed the sleeping man, and he rolled over onto his other side. It interrupted the Temptor too, whose red eyes flashed out of the darkness as he looked directly at us, before scrambling away to somehow squeeze his escape through a plug socket next to the bed.

Euryale dragged her back towards the mirror, hissing urgently under her breath.

"Stay close to me, Steggie!" before launching them both headlong back through.

They tumbled out of the Water-Rise, but from a sweeping

glance at the meadow it was obvious they were no longer alone. The entire cave appeared to shake, and through my hands, I could feel the ground vibrating as on all sides, a wave of terrifying monsters descended towards the two of them on the screen. A furious wall of brown fur, teeth and claws. It was the Wokhala, I later learned. The noise was deafening, like a fast-approaching stampede of giant grizzly bears.

Euryale was already on her feet. With lightning reflexes, she lifted her veil, and I watched as several of the closest attackers turned instantly to stone. But there were far too many of them. With her left hand, she reached up and pulled down the Water-Rise in one swift motion, like drawing down a blind. With her right, she fashioned a window which, having scooped up Steggie under her arm, she dove straight through.

As the picture on the screen gradually faded again so too did my agitation, unclenching white knuckles and finding my palms damp with sweat. But Steggie's story was far from over.

"Later that evening," she continued, "as we warmed ourselves by her fireplace, Euryale explained exactly what we had seen. How the Temptors had discovered ways by which they could cross over into the waking world. Having done so, they soon learnt humanity's weakness: The Floaters. It then became their life's work to target those vulnerable dreamers, whispering foul thoughts into their ears, and filling their heads with negative and hateful suggestions. By doing so, they found they were able to influence those men and women's waking actions, upsetting the balance and tipping the scales ever closer towards evil."

As I listened to this explanation, it made me think of all the cruelty and nastiness in the world. The memory of Terry Mortlock was still fresh in my mind, and I wondered if he too had been influenced by those creatures to act so horribly and to terrorise the other schoolchildren.

"When I asked her why all those monstrous creatures, the Wokhala, had tried so desperately to tear us apart as we had crossed back over, it wasn't much of a consolation to learn that we were in fact of very little interest to them."

"It was the Water-Rise Doorway to the waking world that they were after," Euryale said very seriously. "Through which they would have poured in their hundreds, given half a chance."

Steggie appeared to shudder at the thought.

"I needed you to see just how dangerous opening such Inter-World doorways could be." Euryale went on, hoping to clarify the matter. "It is extremely fortunate for the waking world that only the Temptors, with their limited capacity for doing harm, can squeeze themselves through those small cracks and fissures, you understand?"

Steggie nodded thoughtfully, mulling it over for a while until a frown began to form.

"But wouldn't the tiny Fairies surely be able to wiggle their way through those holes too?" she finally asked, to which Euryale laughed in genuine amusement.

"Indeed that's very true, young Steggie. But I have failed to meet a Fairy, in all my years, who could be convinced, bribed or even forced to cross back over, not while humans are still living and breathing on the other side. Not after what happened last time." Having said this Euryale paused, her face turned very solemn all of a sudden, which made even her snakes keep still. "I will teach you how to construct such openings and Water-Rise's on two conditions. You must swear to it on your life right now." Euryale waited to see Steggie's serious understanding and a sign of agreement before she continued. "That you would only ever open such a portal if you absolutely must: if you have no other choice. And secondly, that you must not teach this sacred art to anyone else. There are very few of us left who still know how to do such things, and other than a handful of Shifters, who possess that ability naturally, nobody else must know! That includes no teaching or training any of your friends, no matter how kind or loyal they might be. Do you understand?"

Steggie nodded gravely and swore an oath right there in the moment, bathed in the warming firelight, before a sudden thought occurred to her.

"But Euryale, I don't have any other friends. There's only you."

At this, she smiled lovingly at Steggie, with those mesmerising eyes of hers, before answering.

"You will, dear child. You will."

"I sensed our time living together in that little cottage was coming to an end. I remember watching Euryale on one particular day when she cut off a lock of her own living hair, tied a message around its neck, and sent it away, slithering through the sand like some sort of secret messenger. She would not discuss the subject further with me, and it was to be two weeks before a reply came."

Over Steggie's head, the cinema screen brightened, coming back to life once more as she spoke.

"The two of us had just finished supper and were listening to the sharp winds sweeping in off the sea, battering the old cottage with such force that they rattled the window panes. It was another night that I was thankful to be wrapped up warm inside."

There came a sudden, heavy knock at the door. It was a sound so unexpected that it made many of the other children—including myself—jump in fright.

"That in itself was a shock for me too," Steggie said, smiling down at our worried faces. "Since for all the long months I had been there, we had not received a single visitor."

We all watched with great curiosity as Euryale crossed the main room, before unbolting and opening the door. The unexpected guests began filing in, all dressed in the same crimson robes that reached the floor, their faces cloaked in the shadow of their broad, low hanging hoods. The greeting was silent and formal, made with respectful nods, and I noticed that Euryale never once lifted her veil in their presence, making me wonder whether those strangers could be trusted.

Once they were all inside, Euryale introduced the group to Steggie as The Coven of the North, and in unison, all thirteen pulled back their hoods. Now, I had never met a witch before, let alone a baker's dozen, but they did not resemble the drawings and depictions I had seen in picture books, not at all.

They had no broomsticks, no pointy hats, no hooked nose or protruding chin, no signs of boils or hairy warts, and no high-pitched cackle when they spoke. How best to describe them, I wonder? Serene perhaps? They seemed to fill the room with an aura of calm, even the smiles they directed towards Steggie seemed to affect her like a heavy sedative. Their skin was fair, their eyes were large and hypnotic, as though seeing or even saying more than could be perceived. Their overall complexion and delicate features gave them a graceful pixie-like appearance, and among them, there was an overriding sense of group togetherness that was difficult to ignore.

"It is done." One of them confirmed to Euryale who, although obscured behind the lace, seemed simultaneously both pleased and saddened by the news. Without delay, she walked to one of the bookshelves in the corner of the sitting room, and from its dusty upper reaches took down a long and ancient-looking scroll. Unrolling it fully on the wooden table, the witches gathered in a crescent around her, and Euryale beckoned Steggie to join them too.

Staring down at the faded parchment, my eyes flicked over it in excitement, though I was initially bewildered as to what it was. As the movie continued on the cave wall, Steggie explained to us that what we were seeing was one of the only known maps of the dream world, laid out in its entirety. From where I sat, it looked vast and incredibly complicated. An intricate labyrinth of crisscrossing lines, numbers and mysterious symbols. Although the map was printed on paper, it appeared to contain several dimensions, layers which sort of rose up or sunk further into its surface, the longer one looked at it.

"Show me where, please?" Euryale asked quite stiffly.

In response, one of the witches stepped forward and extended one arm over the map. As she did so, pointing with her index finger, the nail itself grew fantastically long, to the length of a ruler, perfectly straight and ending smoothly in a pin-like point. The witch's words came slow, her explanation crisp and stoic.

"We chose the two locations very carefully, as per your instructions, deep in the Ostery region, which in recent times have suffered very little direct threat. Both places are remote, positioned on the best ley lines, and are in an area in which

Omnivaga activity has been commonly reported. We have also spent the last week casting every spell of protection and harmony throughout both locations." Her elongated fingernail was now hovering just above the lower left-hand corner of the map. "Here, and here," she continued, lightly tapping two exact points quite near to one another. Both marks appeared to glow and almost pulsate in a fiery red colour upon the map, even after she drew her finger away. Euryale leant in very close, studying the parchment, as did her eager snakes, and she nodded in approval once she had finished her examination.

"Thank you for all you have done," she said, addressing the Coven as a whole, bowing as she did so.

The group returned the gesture and then turned in silence, passing by Steggie on their way towards the door. As the one who had been pointing at the map brushed by her, she looked for a moment deep into Steggie's eyes, and there in the cave we all heard the witch's voice communicating telepathically, deep inside her head.

"Until we meet again, Steggie Belle, blood-drenched under an ink blue moon."

I barely had time to wonder what on earth those strange words meant before, on the screen, the Coven neared the door and stopped. There, they raised their hoods in unison and promptly vanished, their empty robes falling without their wearers inside, like rose petals to the floor. Within another moment those deserted robes had disappeared too.

"But Euryale, they travelled without windows!" Steggie blurted out, in stunned confusion.

"Witches have many strange ways," Euryale replied, removing her veil and rolling up the scroll. Something still didn't quite make sense to Steggie about the Coven's departure and seemed to trouble her.

"But, if they can move freely like that, why did they bother knocking?" she asked.

Euryale grinned, returning from the bookshelf.

"Just because one can do something, it doesn't mean one always should. Besides, it would've scared us half to death if they had just risen up around us through the floor! How one decides to leave is one thing, but to enter, I find it always safer to knock first."

"Perhaps it had been the Coven's visit," Steggie said to us, "or all this talk of knocking which had prompted it, but Euryale sat me down that night, to answer one of my earlier questions."

"When you first arrived at my cottage," she began, "you asked me who it was that I had mistaken you for. The answer is a tricky one as, to this day, very little is actually known about them. When they were first sighted, they came to be known as The Lost Ones, and in the beginning, nobody realised exactly how dangerous they were. Most often they would take on the form of small children, travelling alone or in pairs. At first glance, there wasn't anything particularly strange about them, only the feeling way down in the pit of one's stomach that they were not at all what they seemed to be, and that something about them was very wrong."

"While the stories of various encounters with them grew, so too did a pattern in their behaviour emerge. They have a habit of approaching travellers on deserted paths or knocking unannounced at people's doors, claiming that they were lost and, if at someone's door, asking permission to enter. People who have encountered them would always claim there was an uncanny persuasiveness about them, as though they were attempting to control one's mind. It was soon after that, throughout the whole dream world that the disappearances began."

Once more, I found myself leaning forward, fixated on the screen and clenching both fists tightly, as I listened anxiously to Euryale's account.

"Many groups have tried, and still do, to track them or to figure out more about them, but as it stands, their activity seems almost random and unpredictable. Of course, there are many rumours, but at present that is all they are… just rumours. We refer to them now as Stalkers, and the only certainty we have is that they are beings of the utmost evil. There is only one feature that distinguishes them from normal children, and that is their eyes are entirely black, having no whites at all.

"Don't ever forget these words Steggie, and stay mindful of this warning," her voice was almost a whisper now, but very insistent. "If ever you should happen to come across such a child, you must not speak or engage with it. You must only run!"

There followed a long and harrowing silence in the cave, and seated there I felt a familiar shivering fear go up my spine, raising the hairs on the back of my neck. Steggie carried on speaking cheerfully to us, perhaps in an attempt to lighten the mood.

"The following morning, I found Euryale with a small bag already packed for me. She announced that this was to be the day of my departure. Among other things she gave me this."

At that point in her story, Steggie drew from her belt a strange whistle which seemed to be made of bone, with unusual almost hieroglyphic markings carved onto its surface. She held it up high so that all the Freedivers assembled in the cave would be able to see.

"She said that if I ever got into trouble or danger that I could not escape or handle, then I should use it to call her, and she would find me, wherever I might be.

"I spent most of that day finishing the path that I had dug from the beach, all the way up to that quaint stone cottage, winding its way through the now neat and relatively tidy garden, the pathway decorated along its borders with the loveliest seashells I could find.

"Once it was complete, I found Euryale in her usual spot out on the veranda, rocking back and forth, staring distantly out at the sea." We watched the two of them standing there side by side, with Steggie appearing to follow the woman's gaze.

"Euryale, what is it that's out there?" she asked gently. The answer was one I could never have guessed, and I looked up at the screen with a breaking heart as we saw tears rolling freely from those magnificent eyes.

"My sister, Stheno." Euryale finally replied, one hand wiping at her cheeks. "We tried, you see, when we arrived so many thousands of years ago, to live together as we had always done, here within the dream world. But, try as we may, it was impossible. For, the only thing we could see when we looked into each other's eyes was our little sister, and the memory of our loss was just too painful. So we parted ways, and now she lives in a cottage just like mine, on the other side of this enormous ocean. And I know, somehow I can feel her sitting there upon that shore, as I do now, watching the horizon and thinking of me."

She tried her best to comfort Euryale and held her tight that afternoon until the sun began to dip once more, and they both reluctantly accepted that it was time for Steggie to leave. They walked hand in hand down that pathway, past all those unfortunate statues. Away from the cottage which had become her cherished home. Down at the point where the garden joined the sandy beach, Euryale drew a doorway and, squeezing Steggie's hand, they walked straight through.

"Of the two enchanted safe places that the witches had built," Steggie continued, gesturing around them with her arms stretched wide, "she took me to this cave first. By way of another window, Euryale then brought me to the Treetop summit, and we stood together for a time, upon that highest platform, staring out over the forest below. It was the hardest goodbye I had ever made, but she promised me that we would keep in touch and that I could visit her any time I liked."

On the cave wall, the Freedivers watched as that final scene played out, with the two figures stood very close together at the end of the jetty.

"I don't want to be alone," she said, as Euryale stroked her hair soothingly.

"You have no need to worry, Steggie. You won't be."

"But what should I do now?"

Euryale smiled down at her and waved a hand around them. "Why Steggie, of course, you must go and light all the candles and fairy lights, and keep them burning. However else will they be able to find you, or know that you are here?"

"They?" Steggie repeated, confused. Euryale didn't answer, only winked and held her close. I stared as Steggie reached up onto her tiptoes, and kissed each of Euryale's snakes goodbye in turn. The tall woman then turned away, creating a window at the very edge of the jetty, before looking back at Steggie with those beautiful eyes of hers.

"Never change," she whispered again, raising one hand in

a final farewell as she climbed through the portal she had made.

"I did as she instructed," Steggie told us, as the cinema screen disappeared from the wall behind her. "And it took quite some time to get all the candles lit. Then I waited, looking out over the railings at the darkness of the night, wondering what the future would hold. A few minutes later, I thought I heard a distant sound. Then it came again. And again.

"I remember turning around, listening closely to the noises, as the first ones from among you started to arrive. Smiling to myself as I heard those adventurous footsteps climbing the spiral staircase towards me."

9

They Move in Pairs

The memory of that night and Steggie's story has stuck with me all these years. Looking back—with all that has happened since, and knowing all that I now know—I am left to wonder whether anything could have been done differently. If there was any way that the terrible and deadly crisis could have been averted. For over thirty years, this question has haunted me: a sick riddle offering endless self-doubt. I have learnt that such thoughts are nothing more than a forced medal, reluctantly worn by the lonely survivors. A tragic waste of time, an endless tunnel of despair, leading nowhere. "The clock ticks forever forwards, never back," as I recall Steggie once telling me.

And so the years passed, living among the Freedivers, and I found within myself the burning desire to rise up through the ranks, to one day earn a place within that prestigious Inner Circle.

Of course, from the outset, I was well aware that the odds were stacked against me, and that I had a very long way to go. I quickly learnt of the existence of a special room within the treehouse city where, positioned upon one wall and spanning its entire length, the ever-changing Leaderboard Chart was located.

At the end of every week, that table of names would be updated, and the excited havoc it sparked was a spectacle indeed! As soon as the changes had been made, chaos would ensue, and the boisterous race would begin. A tidal flood of Freedivers would rush for that room in hopeful expectation: hurtling down through the trees, tumbling across rope bridges, cutting corners at any cost and swinging like Tarzan on matted vines in a crazed effort to get there first. All the while, Steggie and the Inner Circle would be watching in amusement from the railings of that highest platform.

Though the rankings were hugely competitive, there was a close-knit, underlying sportsmanship to it all. With each joyous promotion, others inevitably would slip a place or more. So there existed within that furore a giddy fusion of celebration and commiseration, a warm camaraderie as—above all else—we were family.

It took some getting used to, as you can probably imagine, continually adapting to these changes in rank, but that almost became half the fun of it. Addressing friends and fellow members by their number would often lead to a good-natured correction. Calling out: "Hey 127, how are you doing?" would on many occasions raise a response such as, "Excuse me? It's 124 I'll have you know," or, "Oh, I wish! It's 128 for now, but I'll claw my way back, you'll see!".

So, you're probably asking yourself, just as I did, how exactly did the positions change? Or perhaps most importantly, how could one continue to move up? Well, as I was to learn, it all came down to missions.

As a practising Omnivaga, and member of the Freedivers, every dreamer was required to participate in regularly set tasks. These missions were usually assigned to specific groups, similarly ranked and from three to five of us in total, and overseen by a more senior ranked member. That team-leader would monitor each dreamer's performance throughout, from the preparation and planning stages to the mission itself. On completion of the task, he or she would then give a report to Steggie and the Inner Circle, regarding each individual's merit and demonstration of skill.

There were all kinds of missions, ranging from simple deliveries and pick-ups, meetings and relaying messages to retrievals and excavations, stake-outs and investigations. The individual's rank would reflect the greater level of their skills and proficiency. Thus, the higher the clustered average rank of the group, the more challenging and dangerous the missions became.

In the beginning, as a novice whose rank was #173, quite frankly my position couldn't really get any worse; each mission a shot at glory. All I had to do was to focus and climb. It was shortly after the end of the second month, that Wolfe sidled up next to me early one Sunday evening, while everyone waited for the next update to be announced, and whispered discreetly in my ear.

"Rumour has it you're pegged to jump to #170 tonight. It seems Toe-jammer was impressed with what you did this week!"

Even now I remember, at that very moment, catching Hammerhead staring coldly in my direction from the other side of that upper platform. A couple of hours later, it was *not* finding my name down at the very bottom of that list when the exhilaration set in: I was moving up in the dream world!

It turned out that I had a knack, not only for mastering new skills, but for adapting to deal with unforeseen dangers, for thinking quickly on my feet and, perhaps most importantly, outside the box. With experience, the speed of my reactions also grew. It was just after my eleventh birthday when something unexpected happened, and my actions were to propel me under the spotlight. An event which, once it had occurred, meant things for me would never be quite the same again.

I was ranked #149 at the time and, as fate would have it, was on a mission alongside Puddle who, positioned then at #148, happened in a roundabout sort of way to assist me in what was later to be much discussed and referred to as "an incredibly close shave".

All the preparations had been carefully laid out, and the mission itself hadn't been categorised as being particularly dangerous but, as with so many things in the dream world, appearances were often deceiving.

The four of us met in one of the lower cabins of the Treetop city. The mission was to be led and overseen by Rosethorn, a formidable and experienced Freediver, ranked #22. She paced back and forth across those wooden floorboards, waiting for the rest of the team to settle down. There was a slight tension in the air when she finally stopped, eyeing each one of us steadily in turn.

"We have our orders. Our mission is to complete a thorough search of an old abandoned mansion. A building which is located just within the edges of the Forests of Crepusculum. The mansion was built long ago as an outpost fort by the first Druids ever to have crossed over from the waking world. The mission is relatively straightforward," Rosethorn continued, leaning back against one of the timber walls and folding her arms. "It is widely known that the mansion once contained an impressive library, and while those books might not be directly useful to us, Steggie and the Elite have decided we should investigate the property anyway. It is up to us to search the ruins from top to bottom, and to bring back whatever remains, rather than let those books and relics fall into the wrong hands."

"Like a treasure hunt!" Puddle interrupted excitedly, rubbing his hands together. I found myself smiling at his enthusiasm, but it wasn't long before all good humour had vanished from that cabin. The fourth member of our group, a slightly older boy named MarbleTap, ranked #150, who had remained silent until then, suddenly spoke.

"This place we're headed to, it's not the same mansion where that legendary cult was based, all those centuries ago, is it?" For a moment Rosethorn appeared to be taken aback by the question, then nodded warily in agreement. MarbleTap raised his eyebrows and leant over, whispering to the two of us in a confidential tone: "Rumour has it the place is haunted—seriously haunted and cursed!"

Rosethorn quickly stepped forward, seeing the fear spread across our pale faces and decided to intervene. "There's no reason for us to focus on gossip and superstition. Besides," she added, glancing at Puddle who was the youngest of our group by a couple of years, "name me a place in the dream world that isn't 'haunted' in one way or another? Any location that's ever been visited leaves a trace of who and what has gone before. That's only natural and certainly nothing to get scared by."

I was not convinced, and Puddle, who sensed that his age was being used to protect him from the truth, was having none of it. "I'm not afraid of any silly stories, so please tell us about the building's past. I mean, we should know everything about the place, if we're supposed to search it properly, don't you think?" He fidgeted nervously and looked to the two of us for support. MarbleTap and I nodded gravely, and the three of us waited for Rosethorn to tell us what she knew.

"Suit yourselves," she said, returning to the far wall, folding her arms and resting one shoulder casually up against the solid wood. So it was, that on the night before we were set to embark on that mission, we listened as Rosethorn explained in detail the history of the mansion.

It had a dark past, there was no denying that. It had been occupied for a long time by those mysterious Druids. And for many centuries their minds had become polluted by their quest for power. They had dabbled heavily and recklessly in the Dark Arts, and at the height of its power the cult had become known for its annual meetings, where destructively-minded and abominable beings would gather there from all across the dream world.

On these occasions, peculiar lights and eerie chanting would often be heard at night, and disappearances were frequently reported. Local communities were convinced that this cult was performing both human and non-human sacrifices but, despite numerous searches, no traces of any bodies were ever found.

It was to be two quite random events that would eventually divide this evil group, and scatter them to the winds. The first was a mass migration of Mountain Trolls, attracted to the area by the perpetual twilight and protective cover from the harmful rays of sunlight those dense woods offered. The trolls' territorial nature and vast numbers made life for the cult—especially their daily foraging—extremely difficult. Then came the storm. Some still insist that it was not merely a freak accident, but that the group was, in fact, attempting to harness the power of the storm itself, to intensify the ritual they were performing. Whatever the cause, the mansion was struck repeatedly by lightning that night, with large sections of the building reduced to smoking rubble. Those members who did not perish in the fire that followed were forced to abandon that cursed place, and the site had remained deserted ever since.

As a final warning to us all, Rosethorn went on to tell us of one enduring legend associated with the building. It was said that any unfortunate traveller who happened upon that dreadful place and was caught there after dark, was bound to fall victim to the mansion's curse. For inside, once the sun had set, the most horrible of transformations would occur.

First, every outer door and window to the building would close and be sealed shut with an impenetrable layer of brick, and then the most ghastly and gruesome faces would appear as if by sorcery from within the walls. There would follow a slow and ominous drumbeat, steadily becoming louder and drawing closer, accompanied by the former cult's demented, murderous chanting. Finally, a solemn parade of hooded figures would materialise out of the very walls themselves; those demonic monks with their sacrificial blades already drawn and glistening, closing in silently on all sides. The last thing one would ever see.

We were quick to spot one glaring problem with that tale, namely that if nobody had survived, how did the legend get out? Nonetheless, I don't mind admitting we were all somewhat spooked. When Rosethorn assured us we would be setting off at dawn, and coming back well before sundown, our minds were put a little at ease.

The dawn finally arrived.

Our team took a window to the closest known safe point and proceeded to make the rest of the journey on foot. With windows, you see, one can only travel safely to a location one has previously visited, otherwise one risked "travelling blind", or "Plunging" as it was more popularly known, which was never recommended. As none of us had ever been to the mansion, that was the way it had to be.

Despite this, we managed to make good time, and by mid-morning, the four of us were shimmying our way through the tall, rusted iron gates which stood imperiously at the main entrance to the grounds.

Through many years of neglect, nature had triumphantly reclaimed the land: brambles, thistles and ivy crept over everything that had been prominent before. We viewed what was left of that mansion with apprehension. The sprawling estate, whose former glory was all but gone, now lay derelict and rotten with decay. The fire appeared to have consumed and gutted the majority of it, but here and there, parts remained almost intact.

It felt strange at first, rummaging through those skeletal remains, but we were explorers, archaeologists even that day, unearthing lost treasures from a time begone.

We located what must have once been the main library, but what we found there was fairly disappointing. Those dry and dusty volumes would have only fed the flames, and most were now nothing more than ash and soot, and from that forsaken place, we were able to salvage a mere handful of books that had escaped the blaze. Undeterred, we continued our search, room by room and floor by floor. The upper levels posed a greater risk, with the floorboards and stairs groaning precariously beneath our feet, threatening to collapse with every step we took.

After lunch, we split into pairs in the hope of covering more ground, with Puddle and I taking one end of the property, and Rosethorn with MarbleTap at the other. By late afternoon our inspection was almost complete, and I was so caught up in sifting through the charred rubble, and broken jars, in what I guessed was once a pantry or walk-in cupboard, that I almost missed the secret bird-call.

It was a signal we had practised and previously agreed should only be used in emergencies, as a way of summoning the team together. I could tell it was our leader, Rosethorn, who had made the call, and therefore knew it must be serious. I returned to the kitchen and reunited with Puddle, who had simultaneously just made a quite extraordinary discovery of his own.

He had been poking around inside an enormous tiled fireplace, which was far deeper than he had expected it to be. He was intrigued by the fact that it was the one place on that scorched property where evidence of any fire was nowhere to be seen. As he had leant further in, one of his legs had banged against a set of fire pokers positioned to one side of the hearth, and suddenly the back panel he was running his fingers along had begun to move. The hidden doorway slid open, revealing a secret passage through a plume of escaping dust. Peering through the dark shadows, he saw a narrow staircase descending below ground.

When I arrived by his side, he made me look too, barely able to control his excitement. The air inside felt cold and stagnant, and a chill ran down my spine as we stared down into that darkened cavity. Then the bird-call sounded again.

"We have to tell Rosethorn about this!" Puddle insisted.

"We will," I assured him, noticing how our voices carried, echoing down that long staircase. "But first we have to hurry, she's calling us. Something's happened!"

The two of us made our way quickly through the ruins, doing our best to stay low and out of sight. We found them in a bathroom on the uppermost floor, crouching for cover beneath a rotten window-sill. Rosethorn beckoned us to join them, so we crawled on our hands and knees over the broken tiles and scattered debris to reach them.

She was trying to keep calm, but MarbleTap was trembling and as white as a ghost. It was only when I got close and looked at Rosethorn that I noticed the fear in her eyes.

"I spotted it a few minutes ago, down by the gate where we came in. I don't think it saw me, and so far it hasn't shown any sign of moving. Take a look if you want, just for God's sake, be careful!"

Puddle and I lifted ourselves up slowly and snuck a look over the edge of that window-sill. My eyes scanned the overgrown lawn below. Over one hundred metres of eerily silent grounds, leading to that tall, rusted main gate. My reaction did little to ease the tension in that bathroom.

"I see two of them," I whispered, to which Rosethorn sprung up by my side to see for herself.

Standing motionless on the other side of those iron bars, were a pair of young children, close to our own age. As we watched through that windowless frame, we heard their voices call out over the unnerving stillness of the area; their tone was cold and lifeless, lacking any emotion.

"Can we come in?"

We sank back down to the floor, all looking at Rosethorn to

take the lead.

"Couldn't they just be Floaters or Skimmers?" Puddle whispered. "You know, kids who just got lost in their dream?"

"This far inside the dream world?" Rosethorn said, shaking her head, "not likely. Besides, didn't you see their eyes? They aren't real children!" she bit her lip, weighing her options quickly before turning back to us with a short, nervous exhale.

Rosethorn made her decision. "This mission's over. Our best option, as far as I see it, is we cast a window right here, right now, back to the Treetop city. Our search was almost done anyway. Besides, if those things are what they appear to be, the risk in hanging around any longer would be far too great!"

It was then that Puddle hurriedly explained what we had found, down in the kitchen. A brief and frantic discussion followed.

"There's still time!" Puddle pleaded. "We could hide down there."

"Too risky," Rosethorn said, "besides, what if they found us? What if we got trapped?"

"No way I'm going out there. We should run while we still can!" MarbleTap's voice was shaky and faltering as he shrank further away from the window-sill.

Feelings were mixed, but curiosity prevailed over our growing, stomach-churning fears. A new plan was hatched, and Rosethorn hastily repeated it one last time, insisting that under no circumstances any deviation from it should be made.

"We go now, take everything we have already gathered down to that secret passage. We seal the entrance as best we can, and do a quick sweep of whatever might be down there. Any sign of danger, we leave! If we're dealing with Stalkers, make no mistake:

nobody has any real idea exactly what they are capable of!"

That decision was to be our first mistake.

While the others were gathering up the bags containing the few items we had already found, Rosethorn told me to check the gate one more time. I fashioned a pair of binoculars, with the hope of getting a better look. What I saw through the lens made my blood run cold.

There were two pairs of them now, positioned in the same place, on the other side of that gate, as still as scarecrows. I could clearly see those large, empty, soulless voids, so black that one could not tell for certain if there were eyes inside or not, but that was nothing compared to the nightmarish horror I was about to witness.

Suddenly, both pairs vanished in an instant, evaporated into the air only to reappear a moment later, still motionless and in pairs, but about ten metres closer, inside the grounds of the property. In shock, I dropped to the floor and scrambled back over to the others.

"We better hurry!" I panted breathlessly.

We took a window, the quickest route we could, back to the fireplace. Once through we managed to find a lever which locked the sliding panel shut behind us. While the rest of the team began their descent through decades of low-hanging cobwebs, I took a couple of minutes to rig up a makeshift alarm system next to that secret entrance. A zigzagging series of near-invisible fishing wires, from the trapdoor itself to those first few stairs, all strung up with little brass bells which would sound at the slightest movement.

It never crossed our minds as we leapt down those stairs that now, below ground, we would be totally unaware that outside the sun was already setting.

By the time I rejoined the others, it was clear that we had stumbled upon that evil cult's inner sanctum. From a bird's eye view, that mansion was just the tip of the iceberg. The basement area was vast and labyrinthine, a rabbit warren of doorways, stairwells, and diverging tunnels, branching off in all directions.

Pressed for time, we stuck to the central passageway, which ended eventually in a wide flagstone set of steps, opening out into a dome-arched vault. Everything appeared untouched and undamaged, and we marvelled at the rows of brimming bookshelves along the far wall. Such was our excitement that we failed to observe certain things about that place which should have raised cause for concern.

There were no doors and obviously no windows, being as we were deep underground, only the stairs by which we had entered. Nor did we stop to notice the walls. How—by the flickering light of our candles—the layers of mould caked upon them created an optical illusion of many grisly portraits, a line of hideous faces staring blankly at us from all sides.

Instead, we set down our swag bags in the middle of the room, and Puddle, MarbleTap and I began running back and forth, grabbing as much as we could carry off those shelves and dumping them in a fast-growing pile back by our bags. As we were doing this, Rosethorn had made a window right there in the centre of the chamber. She then turned her attention to stuffing the sacks to bursting point with all those ancient volumes. It proved to be an efficient system, and within less than ten minutes, the shelves were almost picked clean.

At that point, I knelt down beside Rosethorn to help her as, one by one, we started throwing the bags through the open window. Meanwhile, Puddle collected the last few remaining books, before joining us, forming a puddle portal of his own right there on the floor, and dropping all that he was carrying in his arms straight through.

So caught up and busy in our tasks, we didn't notice MarbleTap slip away. Neither did the significance of the first sound to reach us register immediately: a slow, low and distant drumming. The second sound, however, stopped all four of us dead in our tracks.

It was the faint sound of several bells tinkling, echoing along the passage towards us. I turned and caught sight of MarbleTap, standing almost ten feet away at the foot of a grand altar that the three of us had somehow not even seen. His hands were outstretched, reaching for an impressive golden book that lay open upon it.

"My God! They're inside. Freedivers, we are out of here. Right now!" came Rosethorn's panicked cry from behind me.

In the minute that followed, my vision and reactions became greatly distorted, as though every tiny nanosecond was being stretched out to the very limits of time itself in a dizzying and terrifying slow motion.

Looking back over my shoulder, I saw Puddle and Rosethorn's final manic effort to throw everything we had gathered through the portal. Then I heard a hollow, sinister clicking sound amid the increasingly rapid drums, and realised that MarbleTap had just picked up the book from the altar.

Doing so had triggered something, and I saw an arrow launch forth from the other end of the room. It sailed past MarbleTap, missing him by a hair, and instantly I judged its direction. With lightning speed I flipped the puddle-portal up off the floor and flung it on its side so that it hovered like an oval beauty mirror, barely inches in front of Rosethorn's face. At the very same moment that it got there, two-thirds of the arrow's shaft whistled straight into it, with only the feather fletchings remaining visible on our side.

My other hand was already moving in full swing, gripping the handle of a lengthy bull-whip my mind had fashioned. With a sharp crack, the other end of it wrapped around a very startled MarbleTap's waist. Still clinging to the book, he found himself being dragged quickly back across the room towards us.

A split-second later came the hissing sound of a hundred more arrows being released from their boobytrap prisons, hurtling in our direction. Much to my own surprise, even as I thought it, my arm swooped in a crescent wave, constructing in that fluid gesture a hemispheric bubble of thick crystal clear ice, protecting and cocooning the team.

Then a succession of powerful splintering thuds as those deadly arrows struck, shattering, embedding into, or deflecting off of the ice globe. Meanwhile, my hand continued waving back and forth, adding layer upon layer of solid ice to strengthen the inner shell. My body turned in a whirling spin, my eyes taking in every inch of that cursed crypt.

I saw Rosethorn still half-paralysed in utter shock, Puddle wide-eyed, his mouth still slowly stretching into a reactionary scream, and MarbleTap still lying by my feet, disoriented and struggling to undo the whip that was coiled around him. The beat of the drums rang deafeningly through our ears, accompanied by a strange, deep and morbid chanting. Out of every corner of the room, large hooded phantasmal figures were stepping out of the walls, converging on us with their scythe-like blades held high. The last thing I saw filled my mind with dread. At the foot of those stairs, stock-still and motionless, the line of Stalkers, a terrible death stare from those black pit-like eye sockets all aimed in our direction.

With a strength I didn't know I had, I picked up MarbleTap and threw him clean through the window, whip and all. Out of the corner of my eye, I glimpsed Rosethorn return to her senses, grabbing hold of Puddle and dragging him with her towards the portal.

Then came the awful ear-piercing sound of all those crooked blades slicing; scraping and digging at the ice, like knives scratching at a dinner plate. As I too headed for the window, I remembered the gold-encrusted book, saw it still lying on the floor and reached back to grab it. As my fingers grasped for the cover, to my horror, I noticed the line of children's feet, pressed right up against the other side of the ice.

Looking up, I saw those harrowing eyes, so close I could almost feel the darkness and rage within them. It was then that I heard their voices all chiming seductively inside my head as one:

"Come with us."

There was a persuasive strength in those words, as though they were wrapping invisible tentacles around my own will. It made me hesitate for just a moment. But it was a moment too long!

In that hypnotic daze, I barely saw that pale sinewed arm reach forward, forcefully burning and melting its way through the block of ice towards me. It gripped my forearm tightly for an instant before I managed to struggle free, back towards the window with the book under my arm. In the intense pain of the moment, I couldn't tell if the grasp had been scorchingly hot, or ice-cold, but I knew, either way, I had been burnt. With the crunching sound of the ice barricade splitting and collapsing all around, I dove through into the darkness, obliterating the window behind me.

10

Shooting for the Stars

It was some moments before any of us even moved. We had landed in a crumpled heap on top of one another, the bags and piles of successfully recovered literature having broken our fall. It was when we realised for certain where we were, and that we had somehow managed to all make it there in one piece, that the real celebration began.

Puddle burst open the door, allowing the fresh evening breeze to filter in, and let out a shrill victory cry which resounded through the, until then, peaceful upper canopy. We had to enlist the help of half a dozen more Freedivers to haul all that we had salvaged up to that highest terrace in one trip.

I remember Rosethorn patting my shoulder and squeezing it appreciatively, as we climbed towards the Treetop summit, but more than that I remember what she said, whispered hushed and low in my ear.

"I've never seen anything quite like that before, Zoofall, I really haven't. I… the whole team is in your debt. Just let me do all the talking, okay. There's going to be a lot of questions, and this is definitely going to cause ripples!" Then, motioning towards the thick book under my arm, she went on, "Make sure you give that to Steggie yourself, that thing could be really important."

We handed over all our spoils to the Elite on the upper terrace, and the three of us waited and watched from a distance, as Rosethorn delivered her full report of our mission to Steggie and the Inner Circle.

Although we were too far away to hear the conversation, it became apparent that her account was causing quite a commotion. The whole way through I could feel an uncomfortable burning sensation on my right forearm but didn't dare look. It was later that same evening when—managing to sneak away—I hurriedly wrapped a thick white bandage around my injured arm, and tried my best to ignore the pain, hoping that in time it would heal.

The general reaction among the Elite seemed to be that of concern, with anxious faces casting inquisitive looks our way while they listened. Only Hammerhead appeared to be openly indignant and almost angered by the details of the mission report. A couple of times I was sure I caught Steggie Belle looking directly at me and saw that she was smiling confidently, which was more than enough for me.

Well, as I was to discover at the end of that week, our dangerous little escapade was to have some rather astonishing consequences. I became aware that a Freediver saving the life of a mission leader, let alone orchestrating the safe withdrawal of the entire team, was previously unheard of.

On that Sunday evening, a special meeting was held, during which Steggie gave a summary of what had happened to everyone assembled, before making a formal announcement.

"Obviously, we are all relieved that the team returned safely, but the outcome of this mission could have been very different. It is only by the miracle of chance that nobody was hurt... or worse." She cast a quick glance in my direction before continuing. "What happened out there should serve as a reminder to you all. Not only a grave warning of the dangers that can arise at any moment within the dream world but also of the increasing threat posed by these mysterious Stalkers."

Steggie paused, making sure that her words had time to properly sink in, and then turned her attention to the four members of our team, addressing each of us in turn.

"Rosethorn, your decisions may well have been slightly hasty and unwise, leading your team into a truly perilous situation. Yet we feel that your foresight in preparing an escape window in advance, combined with the instinct to aid your team members to safety, even under the pressure of such a frightening close-call, are actions which should not go unrewarded. You are hereby promoted to the rank of #21, although a little bit more caution next time would certainly be recommended."

In-between each announcement there came a celebratory round of applause.

"MarbleTap, for your participation and spotting a possible treasure that the others did not see, you have our gratitude, although I hope you may have learnt the lesson that 'All that glitters, is not necessarily gold'. We feel it would be well worth exercising more caution in the future for you too. Promotion to rank #147.

"And Puddle, well, a peculiar young dreamer you are proving yourself to be! It was your curiosity that led to the discovery of those hidden vaults. And it was you who created— albeit unwittingly—the tool which would later be used to save

135

the life of your team leader, and one of our dear members. We are promoting you to rank #141.

"Which brings me last, but not least, to you, Zoofall," she said, turning to me with that mischievous smile of hers. "Never before have we heard of such a controlled and sustained act of heroism; an excelling of multiple skills in the heat of an ambush, especially from one of our newer members! So it gives me great pleasure to award you a promotion of distinction, the size of which is remarkable, even to me, rank #77."

There were gasps all around, followed by a massive round of applause that Steggie herself initiated. In that surreal moment, I heard several comments flying by: "He's clean jumped 70 places, that's incredible!" and, "He'll be catching up to our rank soon!" and such like, while I could feel that familiar red glow of embarrassment spreading to my cheeks.

Through all the chaos I remember hearing her voice once more, whispering privately inside my head:

"Good job, Zoofall. Soon you and I must speak, about matters of the utmost and grave importance!"

So it was that, having barely turned eleven years old, I had been propelled at an astonishing speed into the top one hundred of the Freedivers, that magical clan of dreamers born from the waking world.

Oh, how I wish I could write down in these pages all the extraordinary chronicles of each and every adventure we undertook. There are ones still wedged firmly in my memory that have not lost their shine or sparkle, standing out like shooting stars from among the many. Missions that would make your toes curl and your hair stand right up on end.

Like the time we had to negotiate safe passage and protection from the ever so temperamental Mermaidens of the Deep South Seas. To help us locate the long lost shipwreck of the Mary Celeste, whose original form had actually crossed over and sunk, leaving only a copy of the empty vessel back in the waking world. We searched its waterlogged innards for the body of the young sailor responsible, who had drowned clutching a stolen artefact close to his chest, and a secret map tattooed upon his inner lip.

Or when we managed to make it across the fissured cracks of the exploding Sulphur Plains, to reach and rescue an old Taoist hermit, who in return would teach some among us the basic art of harnessing and projecting the power of the wind.

Midnight sneaking through the Cutthroat Isles; or attempting the impossible of balancing and walking over the Rainbow Bridge; or the tricky practice of using multiple windows to ensnare a desperate fugitive or bloodthirsty beast.

All these and more were ours: a boundless array of death-defying feats.

But I must not dally or delay. The third candle has all but melted. My time is running short, and there is so much more to tell.

By my twelfth birthday, I had risen somewhat more steadily to the rank of #52. By the age of thirteen, I had made it as far as #28. I noticed through those years that I was under the constant watchful gaze of the Inner Circle. Of course, it is true that they liked to keep track of all the Freedivers: of each individual's growth and progression. Although over time, I came to be convinced that it was quite different in my case. It was as if that earlier mission had piqued their interest and made them suspicious, as though in some way they were expecting something equally important yet to come.

Out of all of them, it was Hammerhead alone who seemed to really have it in for me, maintaining a brazen attitude of distrust and disapproval as far as I was concerned. For my part, where it was possible, I did my best to stay well clear of him and his judgemental, hostile stare.

I feel it necessary here to note, as more of an aside, something that happened around this time, back in the waking world. I will deliberately refrain from giving any exact locations, for reasons I am sure you will later understand.

Although still separated slightly in the dream world by differing ranks, Wolfe and I had become best friends. Since our first real meeting on that fateful day at the Zoo, we had discovered that we not only lived in the same country but that we lived in almost neighbouring cities, separated by only about eighty miles.

Well, I remember sometime shortly before my thirteenth birthday, Wolfe telling me that he and his mother were thinking of moving house. It didn't take us long before we had set about planning, devising and plotting a devious little waking world mission of our own! The first part was perhaps the most complicated but, with a lot of research and carefully timed and subtle coercion, together with a little bit of luck, we finally had his mother searching for available properties within my local area.

His mother ended up taking a lovely old property on the outskirts of the city, no more than a mile away from where I lived. Our mission did not end there. Although the last part was a lot more frustrating and time-consuming, the rest was really all plain sailing from that point on.

In less than six months we, as both skilled and cunning puppet masters, had succeeded in not only becoming waking world neighbours but in coordinating the "randomly accidental" meeting between our mothers, which in turn blossomed naturally into a close friendship. There was, of course, the occasional unforeseen hiccup, like when my accident at the Zoo came up in one of our mothers' many conversations. At that point, they realised—quite flabbergasted—that all four of us had been there, right at the exact same time, on the exact same day. Luckily for us, they simply put it down to that conundrum of adult logic, of "it being a very small world", before laughing it off with another glass of Sauvignon Blanc and promptly forgetting all about it.

We felt quite proud of our success and were amazed at what could be accomplished with two minds working together in perfect symmetry. So it came about that Wolfe and I were able to cycle around to one another's after school. We spent ample time together and even arranged sleepovers at each other's houses to cross into the dream world together, all under the blissfully unsuspecting noses of our mothers.

I remember by the time of my fourteenth birthday, the gap between our rankings had already closed considerably, with Wolfe at #15, and myself right on his tail at #17. It wasn't long after that when the two of us were to set out and embark on our first mission together, and it was definitely one which neither of us would ever forget.

Before I continue with that particular tale though, perhaps it would first be wise to let you in on a discussion that Steggie and I shared, back when I was eleven years old. It was probably only a month or so after that mission to the ruined mansion of that terrible cult when, one evening, she took me aside, and we were able to slip away unnoticed to sit upon the furthest edge of the jetty and talk.

It was a quiet night, with only the gentle rustling of a

tropical breeze blowing through the canopy far below us. We were perched side by side, with our legs dangling over the edge, as though dipping our toes into that black velvet lake. I waited, a little nervously, knowing that a difficult question would soon be coming.

"Did you feel, or sense anything in that abandoned mansion, before the Stalkers showed up?"

I shook my head almost automatically in answer to her question, but that clearly would not suffice.

"I need you to really think, Zoofall, think harder." Her tone was insistent, so I racked my brain, working back through the memories of that day before replying.

"Well, not really, but perhaps there was a part of me that felt that we hadn't yet found what we were looking for: like we were missing something?"

Steggie nodded slowly, contemplating my answer though giving nothing away.

"And why do you think that those Stalkers arrived at those gates, on that particular day?" She eyed me closely, as if reading every muscle in my entire body for some sort of reaction. I hadn't considered those events from that angle before, but suddenly a horrendous possibility flashed through my mind.

"You think perhaps they were looking for something too?"

Her face remained stoic and serious, then she nodded warily.

"Something, or someone."

I am sure she probably saw my shock at such a suggestion, for I was unable to hide it well, but she continued nonetheless as if she hadn't.

"I've considered the matter fully, Zoofall, and from the detailed report that Rosethorn gave, it seems to me that there are two most likely possibilities. One would be that they too were trying to get their hands on this," she said, pulling out that large book, bound with gold which we had recovered, from underneath her cloak. "The other being that they were trying to get their hands on one of you!"

My stomach felt very queasy, rolling over and over like a tombola. I remembered with terrifying clarity all those dark and hollow eyes staring down at me, and those cold, inhuman words: "Come with us". I had heard their command inside my head and hadn't told a soul about it since, not even Wolfe, but right then I could see in Steggie's eyes, that somehow she already knew.

"What does the book contain?" I asked, desperate to draw attention back to the first possibility.

"We are still working on translating it all, as it's mostly written in obscure and ancient tongues. So far, it's full of powerful incantations, and forbidden castings, the likes of which should never be breathed. It does, however, mention an artefact, long-hidden or buried by time gone by, of which we know next to nothing. The book refers to it as 'The Anchor of Perspicax', describing it only as an object of unimaginable power and potential."

At that moment, she paused, and looked out over that dark and silent sky, before changing the topic completely.

"As I'm sure you're aware, the Inner Circle is deeply concerned. The accounts of how you moved that day, down in that sacrificial tomb, have got them scared. It's got them worried that we could be cultivating another Shifter."

"But I saved Rosethorn and helped protect the team. You yourself promoted me for it!" I responded in protest.

Steggie's expression turned sullen and detached, as though

141

her thoughts were returning to a place in the past, a place she did not wish to go, which caused her much discomfort.

"That's how it began last time," she whispered, almost speaking to herself.

Confused by this, I found a question suddenly formulating in my own mind: do you really believe that I could be one of these Shifters? And I opened my mouth to ask it, but Steggie answered before I had the chance.

"I cannot say for certain. Nobody can. That's the problem with Shifters, you understand? They are so few, and what they have comes from the inside. How and if it awakens, and to what end it will lead, is beyond the realms of forecast and prediction."

I considered her words a moment.

"But is there no way that I can tell?"

Steggie remained pensive for a moment, before replying.

"Does it still hurt?"

I swallowed hard. I knew exactly of what she spoke. Yet once again, I hadn't told a single person about it, had taken to always wearing long sleeves or jumpers, in both the waking and dream worlds, to avoid detection. I had been so careful. So how on earth could she have known?

"Not so much anymore," I mumbled.

"Show me!" she said rather adamantly, and so, with some reluctance I rolled up my right sleeve. Steggie leant close to examine the marks, clearly fascinated. Upon my forearm were the strangely blackened scars where the Stalker had grabbed me, so distinct that you could even see each individual scrawny fingerprint. She tutted to herself.

"And it's always still there when you wake up?" I nodded in agreement.

"But what does that mean?" I implored.

"I am not exactly sure, for as far as I know nobody's ever come close enough to be touched by one of them, and lived to tell the tale, anyway. It could mean something, or maybe nothing, but I will try to find an answer for you. For now, I will say this: Shifters often possess, so it is believed, an uncanny ability to 'carry things over', between the two worlds."

"What sort of things?" I asked, to which she shook her head, rising slowly to her feet.

"That I cannot say. But if you are what the Elite fear you are, it's important that you know one thing. We need you," Steggie's smile had returned, "I need you."

With that, she turned and left to rejoin the others. I sat there a while longer, thinking over the conversation.

A heavy gust of wind rose up, carrying with it a speckled, exotic-looking leaf, which drifted down like a feather to land upon the wooden plank beside me. I picked it up, turning it over in my hands to examine the intricate veins and ridges along its surface, a living patchwork design of such delicate detail.

Then carefully I folded it up a hundred times upon itself, clenching my fist, with that little green package gripped firmly in my palm. I did my best to concentrate, harder than I had ever done before.

I woke to my alarm clock, and the persistent calls of my mother from downstairs, telling me I was already running late, and summoning me to breakfast.

I drew my hand out from under the pillow, opening it slowly, barely daring to breathe.

A flickering smile grew upon my face, as the leaf gradually began to unfold.

Book 2

11

Shifting Boundaries

Whata started with a simple leaf at the age of eleven, was to become a private hobby, or, perhaps more accurately, an obsession of mine. Over those next few years, under Steggie's watchful guidance, I gradually learnt to develop this Inter-World ability. I quickly came to understand that it was by no means a one-way street, that carrying things in the opposite direction was also possible. Throughout those years it was Steggie who insisted that this rare gift of mine must be kept secret—a necessity I did not fully grasp at the time.

I remember it was on a particular evening when I had borrowed one of my grandfather's most precious war medals from its cabinet in the waking world to show her, that Steggie fully explained the gravity of my predicament. She took me to one of the more remote treehouse rooms, making sure that we had not been followed, but even that level of caution apparently was not enough. After locking the door behind us, from there by way of a window, we travelled back to that protected cave and sat by the smoking embers of the campfire, with only the bats as our witnesses sleeping somewhere far above our heads.

"Surely it would be alright for me to tell Wolfe about these things?" I asked, flipping the silver medal from one hand to the other. "I trust him completely, and know that he wouldn't tell anyone."

Steggie considered that a moment, then shook her head in refusal.

"Better to keep it between the two of us for now. If it were up to me, Zoofall, these abilities of yours would tempt me to put you up for testing, as a possible new candidate for the Inner Circle." She sighed frustratedly, as if not sure of how best to continue. "But you see, this is a part of a much bigger problem. I believe that you are showing all the early signs of developing into an advanced Shifter. Something which again, in my opinion, the Freedivers as a whole are in such desperate need of.

"Our problem comes from past complications, from events which have allowed fear and prejudice to grow. The way it is now, the Inner Circle are divided. Sometimes, in their better moments, they can see the potential benefits, but they are weighed down by doubt, scared and reluctant to believe. We must, I feel, be patient and try to find ways of making them trust and understand you.

"That is why, until we can build their faith in you, every unusual power and skill you develop must remain a sworn secret between you and me, not told to any other living soul but guarded to the grave!"

We swore an oath right then, in the dwindling firelight and the blood-red shadows. Steggie's eyes sparkled with a sense of urgency and genuine fear as she leant closer. There was such an intensity to her stare that I realised she was about to confide in me her darkest, most terrible prediction. Her final words on the matter clearly reflecting the dangers we were soon to face.

"A war is brewing, Zoofall. I can sense it. I can feel it in the very air. Though the hows and whens are still unclear, I have seen the terrifying *If*: our fate if we are unprepared for what is coming. The truth can be someone's greatest ally or their harshest companion; it can set a person free or fill the heart with despair. Our truth? We are far from being ready!"

From that night on, I understood the need for *cloak and daggers*.

I took great care to downplay any action or advancing skills which might cause unwanted attention or scrutiny in the dream world. I held back, acting dumb and playing innocent when questioned or observed by the rest of the Inner Circle.

Despite my ongoing efforts at misleading them, Hammerhead remained sceptical, a persistent thorn in my side. It became clear that I was not the sole target of his suspicions either, his untrusting mind unable to accept why Steggie should be spending such an unusual amount of time in the company of myself, a non-Elite.

All the while back in the waking world, I was becoming a collector, an illegal smuggler of sorts. In the deepest recesses of my bedroom wardrobe, buried beneath piles of disused toys and outgrown clothes lay the large old trunk that I had retrieved one day from our dusty attic. Inside were safely hidden the plunder and mementoes of my adventures. From the broken canine of a Saber-tooth Squirrel and a Siamese twinned four-leaf clover, to a chocolate-drop an Aztec chieftain had given us as a reward, swearing it was worth its weight in gold. And the tiny war-horn, no bigger than a thimble, which—long ago—successfully called together the divided fairy tribes to fight as one.

Perhaps to the untrained eye, all these artefacts would have seemed like nothing more than random trinkets and curious junk, but to me they were priceless, each one reminding me of wild crusades from places unparalleled in the waking world.

It was when I was thirteen, around the time that Wolfe and I were busy becoming neighbours, that Steggie gave me another little nudge, encouraging me to break the mould and broaden my horizons.

"Have you ever wondered," she asked me with that knowing grin of hers, "whether the 'carrying-over' must only include objects?"

I considered her words. "Do you mean it could be done with an actual person?"

"Well, as I'm sure you can remember from my story with Euryale, the use of Inter-World portals in such a way can be incredibly dangerous… and should never be attempted unless properly supervised."

All of a sudden, I found myself caught up in a wave of excitement as what struck me as an ingenious thought sprung to mind.

"But you and I could go together! We could cross over to the waking world. You could show me your home and where you live. With enough practice, who knows, we could almost be waking world neighbours, just like Wolfe and I. Then we could…" my words trailed off. The beautiful smile I had seen spreading across Steggie's face as I babbled my plan had faltered and slowly begun to fade. A single tear had formed, spilt free, and rolled smoothly down her cheek, falling soundlessly to the floor and soaking into the soil.

I realised my words had somehow stung, but I was at a loss to explain how. I could see in Steggie's eyes a yearning to open the barrier and let me in. For a moment, her lips parted, as though her secret was fighting its way to the surface, but she checked herself and sealed them shut. After a while, she wiped her face and managed a brief giggle, regaining her composure.

"Who knows, perhaps one day such a magical journey could be ours? One day. But before we get ahead of ourselves, try to think more along these lines," she said warmly, opening a window that took us directly back to that far end of the wooden jetty. Once more she left me there, returning to mingle and disappear in among the other Freedivers, her parting words echoing inside my head.

"It needn't only be objects."

I instinctively knew what I must do. Peering out over that darkened jungle, I reached to my left and placed one hand upon the statue of the owl.

I awoke with a start in the very dead of night. My bedroom was pitch-black and seemed strangely foreign. I stumbled clumsily over to the window and drew back the curtains to reveal the moonless night. I knew the back garden lay out there down below, though everything was silent and dark. I closed my eyes, squeezing them tight to concentrate.

Reopening them came as a complete shock. It was all that I could have dared to hope for and more. Everything outside was revealed in such startling clarity that it took my breath away. I could clearly see not just the flower beds, hedges and surrounding trees, or the patio table and chairs, and the discarded football right there in the middle of the lawn, but all that hid within the blackness: those slinking nocturnal mysteries. The night had come alive, and I realised in enlightened awe that I was by no means alone.

A fox was tiptoeing his way across the garden, skulking

towards his oblivious prey, a couple of sparrows out far too late, pecking and rooting around in the long grass. I must have moved the slightest fraction, for he froze, aware of me watching from that upper window. His eyes flashed an angry white in my direction, with the brilliance of aluminium ribbon burning, as the birds became alerted and quickly took flight.

Along the top of the fence to my left, the neighbour's cat was confidently marching away, tail held high as she traversed that wooden tightrope. She too turned to face me for a moment, apparently indignant at my intrusion, a field mouse hanging limply from her jaws.

I would discover over time from my many nightly vigils that it was not only the animals staying busy and taking advantage of the dark. A few weeks later, I spotted two burglars circling and preparing to break into a nearby property through a ground floor back window. After a quick, anonymous phone call to the police, I waited and watched from on high, witnessing the rather comical yet exciting chase that ensued. Two parties of fully grown men clambering over fences, stumbling blindly about in the darkness and crashing into all manner of obstacles from paddling pools and trampolines, to low hanging branches and washing lines, before the fleeing robbers were finally caught and led away.

Over the next months, I attempted to cross back over to the waking world with all kinds of skills and abilities that I had acquired on the other side. I say "attempted" because I soon discovered it was much harder doing so than I had previously imagined. Unlike with mere objects, concentration alone was not enough, it turned out that what was needed was an altering of one's own state of mind, together with great patience and unflinching belief.

I choose at this point not to go into complete details as to the exact range of successes I accomplished, lest these pages should ever fall into the wrong hands. Here I shall try to keep firmly to what is necessary for me to tell my story. I will, however, share with you a mistake I made around that time, which I have previously not admitted to any soul. It is with much regret and embarrassment that I recall the occasion when, in a minor sort of way, I ignored Steggie's previous warnings. I hadn't planned to, I hope you believe me, but it was a rather unexpected opportunity which, quite literally, fell into my lap.

I was sitting in a secluded spot within the Treetop city, minding my own business and eating a banana when it happened. One of those pesky tree monkeys, in a failed attempt to steal my food, lost its grip on the vine from which it was dangling and fell right on top of me. A desperate scramble followed in which, while I managed to apprehend the would-be-thief, he for his part succeeded in getting hold of said banana. Well, as I held him tight, and he furiously munched upon my snack, my mind suddenly clicked.

In an instant, we were both back in my bedroom, where I quickly realised the consequences of my mistake. The monkey broke free from my grasp and wasted no time in ransacking my room. Books went flying, posters were torn, and many things were broken. It took me almost two minutes to catch the reckless rascal as he swung around his new playpen. I was fortunate enough to be able to drag him by one ankle back under the duvet, pushing him ungracefully through a quick window, hearing him land with a thump upon one of the rope bridges just as I saw my door handle turn.

With a flick of the light switch and a horrified gasp, my mother was standing in the doorway. As she speechlessly surveyed the bombsite that was now my bedroom, I popped my head out sleepily from beneath the covers. My defence was pretty flimsy, claiming that I must have been sleep-walking, but my mother sniffed out the lie and was having none of it. I was grounded for two weeks and forbidden to watch any television for a month. The strict bedtime curfew of 8pm until further notice was the only indication that, even with the severest of punishments, every cloud has a silver lining.

Writing that down, I find I do actually feel much better, relieved to have at last spilt the beans on that minor mischief. So I thank you for your patience in hearing my confession. Now back to my story… Where was I? Ah yes: skills.

So it was that some weeks later, a fortnight in fact before the start of my first mission alongside Wolfe, I announced my intention to Steggie of attempting what was doubtless to be the hardest "crossing-over" skill I had yet endeavoured to undertake. She chuckled at the idea, but I believe she found my enthusiasm and determination endearing. But before I was to begin, she had some very stern and wise words of advice.

"The dreaming skill you will be attempting to master is perhaps the most classic of its kind, a universal desire ingrained in the minds of all people since time began. It's certainly ambitious, but you must be careful and never forget these two things! Never get caught, for such a talent would never be accepted by adults within the waking world. The second, and by far the most important: always start from the ground up, for goodness sake, for only a great fool would ever try such a thing in any other way!"

Every evening for the following two weeks, I persisted in my efforts, and with growing frustration each time I failed. I would stand for over an hour: alone in my bedroom or down the narrow alley which ran hidden from view along one side of the house. If someone had been watching, I imagine it would've looked pretty ridiculous. A boy standing with his head down and eyes closed, perfectly motionless as if he were praying, and every few minutes suddenly launching into a little jump up on the spot—which appeared to cause considerable irritation—before starting the process all over again.

I remember it was early in the evening on the day that our mission was set to begin, that the breakthrough finally came. My parents had just gone out for dinner, leaving me all alone, and I figured I had a good couple of hours to focus before Wolfe would be arriving to stay the night. After about half an hour of what was fast becoming little more than the slowest and most pointlessly dull exercise routine ever imagined, I tried yet again to centre myself, push aside all the negativity, and believe.

I jumped up as I had done hundreds of times before, felt gravity kick in and drag my feet back down to the patioed surface of the side alley. It was, however, to be a subtle moment that would change my life forever.

With my eyes still firmly closed, I was half-convinced that I had already landed. My feet were probably just numb from the same repetitively tiresome action, which was why I hadn't felt the hard smack of brickwork underfoot. Still, I didn't dare to look, like a ticket holder after the lottery draw has been announced, almost content for those brief seconds to allow my mind to believe that it really could be true.

Slowly, I moved my right foot out to one side, expecting that familiar crunching sound as it scraped over the ground. There was nothing. Don't be ridiculous, I silently told myself, before tentatively applying more downward pressure to my toes. There seemed to be no resistance at all, until suddenly—when it felt like both my feet were fully stretched and pointing vertically, like a ballerina en pointe—they struck something solid.

My breathing was growing rapidly faster and cautiously, preparing myself for bitter disappointment, I raised one eye open.

The reality of what I had accomplished struck me hard. On the outside, I somehow managed to remain calm, though, on the inside, every wild thought was screaming, rejoicing. The fact that I was only a few inches off the ground was irrelevant, flooding my mind with an altogether brand new sense of vertigo, for I was flying!

I think it's safe to say that if my first addiction in the waking world was dreaming, I had just found my second.

The hardest thing was struggling to keep this unimaginable news to myself when Wolfe arrived a little while later. I knew I couldn't tell him but my mouth felt like a ticking time bomb, threatening to explode and let loose my secret at any given moment. I held my tongue and waited until I saw Steggie again. At first, I don't think even she quite believed me. She remained speechless for some time, before her look of frozen shock finally melted into wary enthusiasm.

When she pulled me urgently to one side, away from any prying ears, there was such a seriousness in her lowered voice that it scared me.

"I don't think you realise just how rare this is," Steggie said. "Truthfully, I didn't think it would even be possible, didn't believe you'd be able to do it. Nobody can find out about this,

Zoofall, nobody! I'm worried about what might happen to you if others knew."

"What would happen to me?" I repeated, starting to feel uncomfortable. "Why would anything happen to me, I don't understand."

"There are certain individuals, very powerful individuals who I fear would do anything..." On hearing heavy footsteps nearby, she paused and waited until she was certain they had passed. "... And I do mean anything to get hold of an Omnivaga who was showing such signs of advancement. I can't tell you anything more right now. You're just going to have to trust me."

I was confused, but I could see how serious Steggie was and so nodded along earnestly. She left me there without saying another word, scurrying away quickly into the shadows.

As for flying, it became an ongoing private battle between me and the temperamental air. It took almost a full month of regular practice before I worked up the nerve and confidence to go any more than a few feet off the ground. Training became an obsession. I sought solitude for my training, and whether locked in my bedroom or deeply isolated in the neighbouring woods, I practised at any chance I got.

I had no idea just then how, within less than a year, my ability would be put to the ultimate test, with the fate of not only my own life but many others too hanging in the balance. Luckily though, on that particular evening when my feet first left the ground, I allowed myself to be distracted by Wolfe, such was his excitement for our upcoming mission. We went to bed early, crossing into the dream world together, and headed for the preparation room, where we would meet the other members of our team and the identity of our mission leader would be revealed.

12

A Harmless Game of Colour the Loser

Our high spirits sank like a stone as the figure turned to address us: it was Hammerhead, and I could see instantly from the devious glint in his eye that he was relishing this position of power. His attitude was cold and professional as he outlined the details of our task, but it wasn't long before both Wolfe and I felt targeted by his critical glare and strict remarks.

"There will be no deviations! No clever tricks, or reckless risk-taking!" he bellowed at the four of us sitting there, though I knew full well who those words were aimed at. "This mission is of a most sensitive nature, and its outcome is of vital importance, so my rules will be followed to the letter, my orders obeyed! Is that understood?"

I think it would be fair to note here that Wolfe and I had, in our own unique ways, built for ourselves not a bad reputation as such, but one that could easily have been viewed as questionable.

I was quite notorious for thinking outside of the box and gravitating towards the unexpected. Wolfe, on the other hand, was known for bending the rules at times, and for a tendency of being something of a practical joker. I was one of the very few who knew for certain that he had been behind the harmless prank at the last dinner gathering. When, after the meal was over, all those greedy, treacherous tree monkeys had swarmed the table—as was their habit—but this time all dressed from head to paw in fancy and formal butler suits. I know this, as he had enlisted my help as an accomplice.

There was also the time that the two of us had almost successfully infiltrated one of Steggie and the Inner Circle's rare "governing meetings" where outsiders were strictly forbidden. It had been a truly genius plan, cooked up from his mischievously calculating mind, and had so very nearly worked. We had shrunk ourselves right down and disguised as garden snails had advanced undetected towards the private discussion. The only thing we hadn't allowed for was the exaggerated distance, and by the time we had slithered our slimy way to within earshot, the meeting had come to an end.

Well, under Hammerhead's rigid leadership, it was clear that the two of us were to be forced to play the straight and narrow. Our task was basically a surveillance mission. We would be acting as spies, setting out to investigate a largely unknown territory into which nobody was particularly keen to go.

"Over the last couple of months," Hammerhead explained, "it has come to the Elite's attention that one species has grown remarkably inactive, to the point of having completely disappeared. The last recorded sighting of even a single Temptor was more than two weeks ago. This supposed vanishing has, as you may imagine, caused us great concern. The abrupt end to their routine patterns and predictable behaviour has Steggie worried. These evil little creatures, as all of you know, cannot be trusted!

"Our mission is simple, but one which could involve great danger and possible confrontation. We must track down the horde, follow their well-trodden route, and discover what the Temptors are up to, or what has become of them. We only have tonight to prepare, and will set out at first light tomorrow. Should we locate them and come into direct contact, I do not need to remind you of their vast numbers. Suffice to say, stealth will be our best weapon, as any potential encounter would result in the five of us being severely outnumbered."

So it was that Wolfe #15, ScaleFist #16, myself #17, BugBowl #18, and Hammerhead practised well into the night a broad range of manoeuvers and movements, from camouflage techniques to misting, scent sensitivity to a variety of defensive shields. This training was relentless, and it was just as we were finishing an exercise known as "perfect blending" that Hammerhead did something quite out of character.

"That's good," he said, strolling around the cabin inspecting each of us in turn, "I'm actually quite impressed with how well you're all doing."

Compliments from Hammerhead were, from my experience, uncommon to say the least. Instinctively I felt something was wrong, and cast a dubious glance across the room to where I knew Wolfe was currently hiding. The wardrobe looked completely normal, its varnished wooden surfaces smooth and seamless. If I hadn't watched him only minutes earlier gradually dissolve into that piece of furniture, I wouldn't have had a clue he was there.

Suddenly, right in the middle of the wardrobe door, not far from where the handle and keyhole were, one of Wolfe's eyes blinked open. I stifled a laugh. He looked ridiculous, but then

I realised that I probably appeared equally foolish, with my own eye staring out at him from near the top of the ornately carved wooden bedpost, which I had chosen to blend myself into. As though sensing a degree of hesitation from his team, Hammerhead clapped his hands three times and softened his voice slightly.

"It's fine, really. You can all come out now."

He waited patiently as the four of us slowly emerged from various corners of the cabin.

"So, I was thinking," he continued, speaking to us in a strangely cheerful tone, "before we set off since you've all been working so hard, perhaps we would have time for a quick little game."

I looked at Wolfe again: something was definitely not right about this. Without further delay, Hammerhead made a window out of the training cabin and ushered the four of us through. We were standing in the centre of a large circular arena, which reminded me a lot of pictures I had seen of the Colosseum in Rome. I looked around at the large dark gates, thinking that perhaps at any moment gladiators or monsters might swarm out to surround us.

Hammerhead clicked his fingers, and within the arena, a dozen or so barricades appeared, none of which were more than waist-high. "I like to call this game *Colour the Loser.*" Hammerhead continued, chuckling to himself. "All you have to do is use everything we've practised to hide, but do make sure you hide well."

"Ah, cool," Bugbowl said, upon seeing Hammerhead turn to face us holding what looked like some sort of rifle. "I love paintballing. I've done it a few times, and I'm pretty good. Say, where are our guns?"

"Who said anything about you getting guns?" Hammerhead replied, his smile widening as a thick blindfold appeared over his eyes. The four of us hesitated, looking at one another in indecisive fright.

"How... how long have we got to hide?" Scalefist asked nervously.

"You had two minutes," Hammerhead replied, grinning blindly in our direction, "but the countdown's already begun."

We scattered immediately. I dove behind one of the makeshift barricades, my mind racing. Seconds later, Wolfe slid behind it too, saw me, and seemed to regret his decision.

"We probably shouldn't hide in the same place," he whispered breathlessly before turning to leave. Right by my feet, I noticed a dragonfly, perched on a small pebble, blissfully unaware of the carnage that was about to unfold. I grabbed Wolfe's arm.

"I've got an idea. Stay here, and the two of us turn to mist right now."

"Mist won't be enough, he'll see us straight away, two squatting clouds. We'll be sitting ducks!"

"Trust me!" I told him, not letting go of his arm. I shrunk the two of us down to roughly the size of an ant, and Wolfe looked around, getting used to this different perspective but still seeming unconvinced.

"Well, on the bright side, I guess it's gonna be harder for him to shoot us, smaller targets and all." My only response was to point at the golden dragonfly. The creature now loomed over us, almost the size of a school bus. As we raced towards it, with my mind, I was already looping sturdy reins over its head and thorax. The giant insect flinched at this disturbance and, in a panic, I realised it was about to take off. Reflexively I lengthened those straps which were now securely wrapped around its body, the two ends trailing in the dust ahead of us. We lunged forward, grabbing hold of them and hanging on for dear life as the dragonfly took flight. For those first few seconds, we were spinning and swinging uncontrollably, colliding back and forth into one another as we hurtled through the air. Finally, the two of us managed to link ourselves together with another rope and the world steadied as we were dragged along, dangling beneath the enormous buzzing creature.

"Any idea of how to steer this thing?" Wolfe shouted over the roar of the wings. I hadn't a clue, not having considered or planned for this. In my head, we would have been sitting comfortably atop the dragonfly's back at this point, gently pulling at the reins and guiding the great insect with ease. I tried climbing up the strap I was holding, and only made it up a foot or two but noticed that by doing so, the creature veered off towards the right. Then, when I slid back down to Wolfe's level, the dragonfly resumed its course. I climbed again and waited a second or two as we arced through the sky before sliding back down beside Wolfe, satisfied with our new trajectory.

"Um, Zoofall," Wolfe said nervously while staring in the direction we were flying, "we're headed straight towards him now."

"I know. That's the plan."

"I'm uh … I'm not sure you're quite understanding the aim of this game. You do know we're meant to be *hiding* from him right now?" Before I could answer, he looked off to our left, scanning the rest of the arena. "You see?" he continued, nodding his head demonstratively in that direction. "Now that's a good plan! That's what I'm talking about." I followed his gaze and watched as Scalefist squeezed the last part of his body underneath one of the rectangular barricades itself, before silently lowering the barrier back down to cover him. "You see," Wolfe persisted, pointing for a moment before remembering he needed both hands to hold on to his own strap. "He's dug himself a hole directly under the barricade, and now he is safe in his own little underground trench. *Totally ... hidden ... from view!*" He emphasised those last words slowly and sarcastically. "But no. That's not good enough for you. Instead, we're charging straight at Hammerhead, with barely any time left, like some kamikaze fighter pilots."

I ignored his protests and leant closer towards him. "What was the name of that strange haircut he has? You know, the long bit at the back, that hangs down his neck? Puddle told me once, but I can't remember the name of it." Wolfe looked back at me, utterly mystified, or perhaps thinking he was talking to a madman.

"It's called a Rat's Tail. And if you're so interested in it, make sure you get a good look at it when we fly by. Once Hammerhead eventually stops shooting us, I'd be happy to cut your hair and try to copy it."

"Oh, we'll get a good look at it alright," I assured him, "that's going to be our hiding place!"

I laughed as Wolfe gasped, shocked by the insanity of the idea. Then his lips began to curl at the corners of his mouth, his eyes sparkling at the outrageous daring of it all. "Are you sure he won't feel the two of us holding onto it?"

"With the size we are, he won't feel a thing."

Hammerhead was starting to count the seconds down from ten in a booming voice, as our dragonfly approached him. That was when the plan almost went very badly wrong. We had to fly in as close as we could get and then, at the last moment, I would jump across to Wolfe's strap in the hope that our combined weight would cause the creature to swerve a hard left, circling around the back of Hammerhead's neck. In our nervous excitement, we took the flying insect a little too close.

He must have heard the faint buzzing drawing near and, still with his blindfold on, reacted as though it could have been a killer bee. One of his giant arms came up to protect himself, and we almost crashed into his monstrous open palm. More by luck than anything else the dragonfly managed to avoid a direct collision and zigzagged a frantic path behind him. Our straps were swinging the two of us wildly from side to side, so violently in fact that there wasn't any need for us to jump. One second we were sailing disorientated through the air, the next both of us were tangled up in the exact place we had been aiming for: the matted strands of Hammerhead's Rat's Tail.

Our team leader was himself still whirling around on the spot, flapping his arms in all directions until it must have occurred to him to simply take off his blindfold. Doing so and, once satisfied that he wasn't about to get stung by anything nasty, he paused as though sniffing the air for a scent, before bellowing his announcement. "Time's up Freedivers, let the hunt begin!" Wolfe and I looked worriedly at each other and braced ourselves. Nothing happened, and, much to our delight, we began to be carried safely around the arena, by none other than the hunter himself.

Bugbowl was the first to be caught. He had bravely hidden in plain sight, camouflaging himself perfectly against one of those metal gates, and later insisted to us that he had no idea how

Hammerhead had spotted him. It was a little nerve-wracking, hanging from the hair on the back of his neck, both of us unable to see what was going on. There came a quick succession of several shots, interspersed with painful yelps and Bugbowl's submissive cries for mercy. Through the silence that followed, we kept as still as possible and clung to his hair like lice.

It took him quite a bit more time to find Scalefist. We heard him muttering something almost to himself about "digging holes without an exit" being "nothing more than preparing one's own grave." Then came the sound of a barricade being forcefully kicked over and Scalefist hastily saying something along the lines of "you got me, you got me. I surrender!"

A couple of hopeful seconds passed, where I imagined our team-mate rising slowly with his arms held high, then another rapid burst of paintballs being fired. It was clear Hammerhead had no intention of taking any prisoners.

He continued to stalk the rest of the arena, searching the enclosed space twice before we could tell that frustration was setting in. "Not possible!" he repeated bitterly to himself over and over again, as he struggled to find any trace of us. At one point, while he was turning over yet another barricade, I caught sight of the other two members of our team, standing off to one side. Their chests were heavily splattered with multicoloured paint, and they too were looking around the empty arena in bewilderment.

Perhaps a minute later Hammerhead stopped dead in his tracks. He didn't move a muscle, and I knew he was up to something. Very slowly, he began to turn on the spot, and I realised that he was manipulating the air in some way. Billowing white and silky clouds were rising up from the dusty ground, blanketing the whole arena. That fine fog lingered there a while and then gradually started to dissipate until it was nothing more than faint and wispy tendrils. I discovered that, without any awareness or decision on my part, I had been holding my breath. Glancing over at Wolfe, I saw his face begin to contort and understood just a little too late what was happening. He raised one hand in desperation to cover his nose and mouth, but there was nothing he could do to stop it.

The sneeze erupted from him with such violence that it made his whole body spasm, tugging hard at the strands of hair he was holding on to. I winced at the sound which was so loud to us and wondered whether Hammerhead's ears had picked up on it. Unfortunately for us, he had.

There came a disorientating spin: the world a sudden vortex. We hit the ground hard, tumbling across it as—from the corner of my eye—I saw a dark figure rolling away, putting some distance between us. As Hammerhead rose to his feet, I understood that he had shrunk himself down to the same size as us. He was glaring at the two of us, one hand reaching behind to gingerly massage the defiled Rat's Tail where we had hidden. There was zero humour in his face.

In hindsight, I should have accepted the game was over and that we had been caught. I should have simply closed my eyes like a condemned man facing the firing squad, but when I saw him raise his rifle, aiming at my best friend, instinct took over. All of Steggie's warnings about keeping my abilities hidden vanished from my mind. As I lunged forwards, planting myself between the two of them and directly in the line of fire, I created an old-fashioned leather slingshot which dangled loosely from my right hand. Steadying my breath, I saw time slow, stretching out as I heard the click of the trigger, and the drawn-out whistling puff as the paintball was fired. As I watched it hurtling towards me, my right arm was already in motion, coming up in a perfectly timed swing. In one fluid movement, I sidestepped, catching the paintball in mid-flight within the slingshot's cradle, spinning and dropping to one knee as I released the coloured pellet back the way it had come.

All this happened in the blink of an eye, my body a whirling blur. It was over in a flash, Hammerhead jolting back in momentary disbelief, his mind trying to catch up with the fact that he had just been shot with his own paintball. The fingers of his left hand gently dabbed at the brightly coloured gooey mess upon his shirt questioningly. In those few seconds, before he came to his senses, Wolfe was busy behind me, returning the favour. I saw the thin plume of smoke drift out of the hopper, the part of the gun where all the other paintballs were stored. Hammerhead did not. He stepped towards the two of us, this time with anger in his eyes, pressing the trigger repeatedly and probably with no intention of stopping until the weapon was empty. Nothing happened, not a single shot was fired. Confused, he quickly shook the gun and tried again. Still nothing. It was only when he pointed the weapon downwards to shake it again, that all three of us noticed the thin stream of paint trickling out the end of the barrel.

I felt Wolfe's hand upon my shoulder, and he wasted no time in returning the two of us back to our regular size. Both Scalefist and Bugbowl jumped as we reappeared and approached them. They saw the lack of paint upon our clothes and stared quizzically at us, but Wolfe quickly ran two fingers across his mouth, miming that it was firmly zipped shut. They did not ask:

the four of us waiting silently for our team leader to return.

Hammerhead took his time, making sure—we later understood—that no trace of the paint remained upon his clothes. When he did grow back, large as life, returning to the arena, I noticed he was no longer armed. He addressed us curtly as a group, barking orders.

"The four of you continue practising the techniques I have taught you. I have to go," Hammerhead paused, flashing a glare my way, "and speak to someone. When I come back, be ready. The mission will begin at once!"

"You've really gone and done it now!" Wolfe said to me with a smirk, once he had finished filling the others in on what had happened. "I reckon Hammerhead's gonna be watching us every step of the way. I don't think he appreciated you colouring him the loser." He lowered his voice as we continued with our training. "You know, someday you're going to have to show me how you did that."

Hours later, when our team leader returned, still scowling, I don't think any of us felt entirely ready for what we would find as we set out through a portal with the dawn.

13

Into the Lair (and the Betrayal of Mirrors)

What happened on that mission will, I hope, begin to explain my current predicament. For it is, in part, why I am here, writing these lines by candlelight, barricaded inside my own attic on such a stormy night, with a cloth-covered mirror. Perhaps only at the end of my story will everything make complete sense, but for now, I believe I must open the proverbial door just a crack, and confess the roots of my inner turmoil. It has been a phobia that has both gripped and dominated my life, all these long and lonely years.

The subject? Why I am afraid of mirrors.

For, before that day, such a concept would have seemed quite absurd and even ridiculous to me. In the waking world, mirrors are seen as a harmless household accessory, something to brighten up a room, offering us a perfect reflection of our physical selves and the world we know.

A dishonest object in our daily lives, sometimes a person's best friend, other days their worst critic. In a modern age of beauty and celebrated vanity, they have been given an enchanting power over everything physical, a virtual trap of sorts, stemming from dependence. And yet, none of these things would make a person fear them. Ironically, it would be many years later when I was to see the eye-opening truth portrayed from the unlikely place of a television screen, in some totally unrelated crime show.

In the scene, a suspect had been arrested and was being questioned. Suddenly the camera turned to the other detectives, in an adjacent room, watching what was happening … from the other side of the mirror!

A two-way mirror. Where on one side, the person sees only himself and his reflected surroundings. Why would that person ever conceive the possibility that others could be standing so close, yet simultaneously invisible to his known world, staring him down and watching intently from the other side?

But not even this lesser understood fact completely explains what would become my inescapable phobia. I was still coming to terms with what it meant to be a Shifter and all the dangers that entailed. The "pull of mirrors" was something which I had not yet experienced. Not until the end of that mission: standing in a meadow, under the shadow of that wall. With only three-and-a-half candles left now, I will do my best to be brief in recounting what transpired on that fateful day.

I quickly realised that we must have been in the ravine from Steggie's story, where she and Euryale had followed the Temptors to the "crossing wall". In the distance, shrouded in clouds, we could see the vague outline of that impressive cliff, the Wall of Fuse-and-Flux. That morning, however, we would be heading in the opposite direction.

We split into two groups, always remaining in sight of one another where possible, each team working their way cautiously forward along either side of the main track. Mine and Wolfe's celebration at being paired together was to be short-lived, as it turned out that Hammerhead was to be our chaperone, keeping a watchful eye upon the two of us. The trek itself was difficult and time-consuming; the tracks themselves were old and barely visible, fading entirely in certain areas where the ground was smooth, resulting in puzzling moments of second-guessing, backtracking and several delays.

The further we went, the more the absence of colour and vitality was noticeable from the surrounding landscape. It was early on the second day that the monotony was broken. A low warning hoot from ScaleFist and BugBowl rose up from where they were positioned among the grey rocks and shingled slope on the other side of the path.

We halted instantly, dropping low to the ground and, in a similar manner to the threatened chameleon, blended seamlessly into the background. There we waited like a seasoned squadron of bandits, on the lookout for whatever was headed our way. Although, as we were very shortly to find out, we were not the only ones to be taking such precautions.

I remember, only moments before my eyes were to register the cause of those shuffling sounds, I felt the scars on my right arm start to tingle, then itch, then a growing heat and a throbbing sensation of unbearable burning. I stayed still and bit my tongue.

From around the bend up ahead, a most curious parade came into view. At first, we almost missed them for, in our defence, there was very little to be actually seen. It was not a trooping of Temptors, of that we were sure. They walked upright on two legs, and we watched in silence as that ghostly procession advanced, moving in a seemingly endless column of pairs. They had no definite form. Gliding past us like a phantom army of Shadow

People, featureless, expressionless, yet terrifying nonetheless.

There was, we thought, a slight similarity to the misting technique we would often employ, cloaking ourselves in a light and airy haze to avoid detection. However, there were subtle differences in what we then witnessed. Those figures appeared more solid, a darker, more tangible shade of grey, as though their bodies had somehow bottled the raging density of a storm or thundercloud.

They were passing by less than twenty feet from where we lay, and I could not take my eyes off them, transfixed upon that floating tide of what adults in the waking world would most likely have described as ghosts.

Ah, ghosts.

I will confess that, as a young child, I was both enthralled and petrified by the mere concept of ghosts. It wasn't until I rose up through the ranks of the Freedivers that I finally glimpsed and understood the real truth behind that elusive phenomenon.

Perhaps by this stage in my tale, it will come as no small surprise for you to learn the full extent of the misunderstandings that have been accepted by the learned grown-up world?

The vast majority of adults will tell you, should you care to ask them, with proud certainty that *there are no such things as ghosts!* But as we all know, that is nothing but a desperate bluff. I implore you to look closer as they speak, and recognise the fear of the unknown lurking deep behind their eyes.

The origin of my terror though was quite ironically the product of the greatest misconception on the matter, which has spread like a virus throughout the waking world: the assertion that ghosts are dead. Or more precisely, that ghosts are the spirits or souls of the dead, reaching back to torment the living from beyond the grave. That, of course, is not quite right.

"What are they then?" I hear you ask, and here I give my answer, a long-forgotten truth which, as it did with me, may well strike some instinctual chord within you. A faint yet recognisable fact that every one of us was almost aware of. Like a butterfly flitting weightlessly above our heads, always just beyond our reach.

Among the Freedivers they are referred to as "Movers" or "Drifters", and that, in the simplest way imaginable, is precisely what "Ghosts" are. The reason for their apparition state or appearance is relatively simple too. For the most part, they are not self-aware, although of course, as with most things, there are certain exceptions. Whether simply a mist, vapour or orb, a vague shape or more distinctive form, and all the way down to the faintest feeling or presence, the first thing to acknowledge is that these entities are very much alive.

There is a lesser recognised school of thought among some grown-ups which, even limited by its relative viewpoint, still manages to grope closer to the mark. Namely, that ghosts are in fact energies, residual echoes left behind. Close, but not exactly. For, while these entities are indeed physical manifestations possessing energy, it would be better to regard them as travellers of a specific sort.

More often than not what humanity has chosen to label ghosts, are merely separated selves, detached and free from the physical restraints of the body: projected forth into an eternal realm. Think if you will, should it help, of a rudderless vessel adrift upon the ocean, or a lonely candle burning defiantly against the limitless night. Perhaps a fragment of a notion, a longing, a question or emotion, personified and energised, set loose to roam the boundaries of both time and space, searching against all the odds to find its place, its meaning, its home.

How do most of these Drifters, these supposed Ghosts, end up wandering through such a labyrinth style maze of infinite doorways leading anywhere, separated in most cases from their conscious host? Mainly through dreams, of course. Even the lowest and most slovenly of Floaters have been known to summon up such passion and desire, to project a yearning part of their other self out into the cosmos.

As you may now very well suspect from these secrets which I share, the more accomplished the individual dreamer, the greater the power and potential awareness their Drifter can evoke.

You may remember Steggie's earlier story of how she and Euryale followed a Temptor through an Inter-World portal, emerging into a darkened bedroom. Well, make no mistake, as they stood there as two misted forms, had that unfortunate man awoken from his slumber he would have sworn wholeheartedly to anyone who would listen that he had seen two ghosts standing at the end of his bed!

Such things are the rare exceptions of which I previously spoke. Unusual occasions in which the vapour, the Drifter, or Ghost, might be aware, have a purpose, or even be an apparition so advanced, that it exists united with its actual self.

Perhaps one day, the subject will become the next frontier for the human race to explore, accepting with humility and bowed heads their previous errors and oversights. Then a library of books will undoubtedly be written on the subject. But that my friend is not the reason I disclose these truths here upon this page, no. I do so, and offer you this secret now, to hopefully spare you the unnecessary fears which plagued my early years.

And so I shall leave you with one last thought and suggestion upon the matter of Ghosts.

Should you be sensitive enough to ever feel the presence of "a Ghost", and brave enough to withstand it, try to remember my words and remain calm. Though it may seem strange and silly, try sitting with it, welcoming it, or even talking with it. For, while the Drifter might be unaware, or unable to communicate; most that I myself have encountered are more than a little lost or lonely, and you would be amazed how far a little compassion can go.

Well, all that is well and good, but back in the dream world the five of us were under no illusions that the march we had just witnessed pass by were neither Temptors nor waking world ghosts or Drifters, but something far more sinister. We watched them trail off into the distance of the way we had just come, before discussing what we should do.

"I think we should double back and follow them. See where they're going." Wolfe said.

"You're kidding, right?" Scalefist responded quickly. "There's only five of us! I mean, what if they spotted us? Who knows what they really are?"

"But if we keep a safe distance, there's no reason why they should notice us," I replied calmly, showing my support for Wolfe's idea. All eyes turned to Hammerhead, who was rubbing his chin and looking back and forth in both directions.

"We're not going after whatever that was. We stick to the mission, and press on." I believe, was his final statement. There was no arguing with him, and so we were forced to continue tracking through the day, at a sharply quickened pace.

The environment grew increasingly hostile, with no greenery of any kind, only jagged, crooked peaks and a tangled sea of gnarled roots with sharp, spear-like thorns. As night fell over that barren, rotten land, ahead upon the dark horizon, we spotted the reddened glow of firelight.

It seemed an eternity before we reached its source, and exhausted we crouched low behind what appeared to be volcanic rock, eyeing the scene before us with a mixture of dread and suspicion, all of us hoping that the sun would soon be coming up again.

The trail we had been following had ended without warning in a great cluster of raised mounds resembling giant anthills. Or the kind of sloppy castles one can make on the beach, right down at the water's edge where the sand is extremely wet, dripping in dollops and stacked precariously upon one another. Out of the highest tiers of those craggy spires flowed liquid lava, red as blood, steaming and hissing its course towards stagnant glowing pools below. Right at the very base of every mound lay an uninviting opening. Dark and rounded tunnels barely a few feet wide, narrowing as they disappeared, descended at angles below ground and into the pitch black. The area was so utterly morbid by night, and yet we were doubtful whether it would appear any rosier by day.

"I don't like it. Not one little bit!" Hammerhead kept muttering under his breath, changing his position repeatedly with perhaps the aim of seeing something more. "There should be guards posted at every entrance! Not deserted like this. The whole place is far too quiet."

"Perhaps they're all inside?" BugBowl piped up. "You know, like one of our Treetop gatherings?"

Our leader shook his head, and ground his teeth nervously, clearly not convinced.

"So, we wait them out then?" ScaleFist suggested.

Wolfe and I glanced doubtfully at one another, somehow instinctively knowing that was not an option.

We all guessed what was inevitably coming, and gulped down our fears, as Hammerhead repeatedly stretched and flexed his fingers, finally curling them into tightly clenched fists. His aggressive stance appeared at first to be a simple display of bravado, but I believe he was governed at that moment by his own stubborn nature, unwilling to back down an inch and determined to complete our mission, no matter what the cost. He then turned back towards us and outlined his plan with a steady voice.

"We will proceed in single file, as that's all the entrances will allow. We will stay tight and close together, and use transparent shields to protect us, both from the front where I will be and at the back, which will be you, ScaleFist.

"Wolfe, you will be in the middle of our line, and should the need arise, you will set up two safe windows, through which we can back our way through."

On paper, it would have seemed a sound plan, but faced with it, in the middle of the night, nobody was jumping for joy. The Temptor's Lair awaited us, and one by one into that cramped and stifling darkness we went.

Crawling forward on hands and knees, we made our way deep into that earthy dungeon. I was right behind Hammerhead and could feel Wolfe's hand grasping at my trailing ankle. The smell was horrendous, becoming steadily more dank and disgusting the further we ventured. For all we knew there could have been hundreds, if not thousands of those shrivelled little weasels lying in wait for us—using the tunnels they knew so well to surround us, their venomous red eyes flashing as they plotted our demise from the shadows. But even with all our experience of the dream world, we could never have guessed the scene we would eventually find.

The tunnel was becoming increasingly tighter and narrower, to the point where I was starting to doubt how much further we would be able to go. Both my shoulders were pressed hard against the crumbling sides, and for the last stretch, I was wriggling along on my belly, using my elbows to lever my way forward inch by inch.

It was then that Hammerhead, and consequently the rest of our team, came to quite an abrupt stop. My first thought was that perhaps he had got stuck, which would have been highly amusing were it not for our appalling location. What we were unable to tell, as our leader's frame eclipsed whatever lay ahead, was that the tunnel had ended in an even smaller hole, through which he was just able to squeeze his head and take a guarded look around.

He didn't move or communicate anything back down the line for quite some time, and we found it was that claustrophobic not knowing that really tested our nerves.

"The coast seems clear," Hammerhead finally whispered back to me, "but this is going to take some doing, so just hang on!"

Twisting awkwardly I relayed his message to the rest of the group. Next came the muffled sound of faint scratching and clawing as he set to work widening the hole, pawing away at the loose soil around the edges, enough that we would be able to squeeze through. He shuffled forwards and dropped down out of view on the other side. As he did so, my face was bathed in a hellish red glow, streaming in from beyond. I, in turn, struggled onwards to the edge where he had been and gasped.

A series of low-ceilinged halls stretched away as far as the eye could see, the whole place lit by a fiery devilish light coming from a large number of fuming lava pools. While infinitely more spacious than the route we had already taken, even in the tallest parts it was still not quite high enough for any of us to stand up completely straight. We had to proceed hunched over and stooped, ducking to avoid the entangled tree roots that dangled from the rafters. Once we had all exited the tunnel, we squatted side by side in silence, mouths wide open, attempting to take in the enormity of what we had stumbled upon.

The mystery of the Temptor horde's recent lack of activity had been unveiled in a truly horrific way. What we were looking at right then was the eerie aftermath of what could only be described as a massacre. Despite our lack of fondness for the vile breed, we all agreed that no species deserved such a brutal fate as this. We all remained perfectly still for quite some time, reluctant to investigate the scattered devastation in closer detail.

"What in either world could have done this?" It was Wolfe who had spoken, his voice choked with dismay, and we could only look at one another in confusion. The only answer that came was the crackling echoes of the bubbling liquid lava that spat and hissed in the background gloom.

The rows of long, low tables showed no signs of food: some had been overturned, while upon others were sprawled the lifeless bodies of the fallen Temptors. The carnage was immense, our minds struggling to comprehend the extent of such savagery. Down there, death was everywhere.

"How many of them do you suppose were living down here?" BugBowl asked, hushed and low.

"Perhaps some of them managed to escape?" I suggested, almost hopefully.

It was Hammerhead who at last took a few steps forward. His head was hung low, his eyes scanning the blood smears and debris as he attempted to decipher the chaotic signs of struggle and desperation.

"This was an extermination. Whatever it was, it took the Temptors by surprise," Hammerhead muttered gravely, continuing to look around. "This place is a tomb. It couldn't have happened too long ago. Some of these marks still seem fresh. This is not what we expected to find, but we're here now, and we need to pull ourselves together. It's still our mission. So I suggest we search this place as fast as we can, try to find anything that could give us some clue as to the reason behind this.

"And remember, Freedivers, don't turn your backs on any of those holes," he waved one arm, drawing our attention to the many darkened tunnel entrances that lined the perimeter walls. "We still don't have any idea what we're dealing with, and just because they're gone doesn't guarantee they're not coming back."

It was a grisly job, one which makes me shudder now at the memory of it. Our examination of the bodies gradually revealed certain patterns, though in some ways these only managed to raise more perplexing questions than concrete answers. The wounds we discovered that those poor Temptors had fatally suffered were quite distinct, but not wholly the same, falling into two quite opposing categories.

It appeared that almost a third of their numbers had quite literally been torn to shreds, with deep scars where long, razor-sharp claws had slashed and sliced repeatedly at their torsos. In contrast, the majority of the victims we found showed no such signs of beastly rage or violence; instead, in various places upon their bodies, there was evidence of at least one puncture mark, inflamed and swollen as though from some injection or an insect sting.

"What on earth could have done this?" Scalefist asked, not to anyone in particular, as we leant over one of the bodies.

"Looks like they were attacked by two very different types of enemies," Wolfe mused, having sidled up beside us.

"The thing is," Scalefist continued, "we all know the harm they do to the Floaters, back in the waking world, but no creature—however vile—deserves to be slaughtered like this. It's just wrong!"

"Especially in the safety of their own … home," Wolfe agreed, looking around the revolting place before finishing that sentence.

We found several small ante-chambers leading off from those long halls, and I only poked my head inside one of them before instantly regretting my decision and warning the rest of the team not to follow. It was impossible to tell what exactly those rooms had originally been used for, but the last thing to have occurred within them had been of a truly fiendish nature. I won't go into the gruesome details, but it reminded me of the descriptions I had read of medieval torture chambers.

We were beginning to lose hope of finding any definite answers of what had led to these atrocities when ScaleFist accidentally noticed something. He was in the process of examining one of the ferociously mauled bodies when suddenly the Temptor spluttered weakly and tried to raise his arm.

Well, I don't believe I have ever seen a person, before or since, jump so high in absolute fright. He called us over while rubbing his head, which he had bumped on the low ceiling in his panic, and we huddled close around that lone survivor. There wasn't a great deal we could do for the poor wretched thing, as his wounds were quite severe, but the four of us knelt and linked our hands over his damaged body, focusing on a pure white healing light that cascaded down over him. As we did this, Hammerhead placed one hand softly upon the creature's forehead and then lowered himself, leaning his ear right up next to those pained, twitching lips as the Temptor, struggling through rattling gasps, told his final story. As each garbled sentence emerged, our leader repeated them word for word as follows, for the rest of our team to hear and try to decipher.

"They broke the deal, snapped it clean through. Had no intention of fulfilling what was promised. Lies and tricks, torn portal fixed. Tricks and lies, a damned disguise. We let them in, mistake, mistake!" A fit of sputtering and coughing ensued; the effort of talking was clearly taking a painful toll.

"They knew we had the secrets, ate 'em all up, and swallowed 'em whole. But they weren't just after our secrets, they wanted more, wanted it all. And we let them in. Then all the questions, in-terror-gations, off in 'em rooms. We didn't know, nobody could've known!" As I listened to his story, I couldn't help but feel a growing pity for the wiry little creature.

"Then the screaming, and they wouldn't go, couldn't make 'em leave. Torture thinks I, forcing our brothers to cough up all the secrets we had swallowed. But no, it was worse. They keep taking and stealing, after the deeper Sophist magic which be the very part of us. They are Chimera. Adding to 'emselves to reach purr-fection. Not what they seem, hiding behind 'em masks. Not Sophist friends at all. Stole our essence. Ripped out our Thistle-Wisps, our Kundabuffers as that uuu-man Gurdjieff once called 'em."

Wolfe and I cast a despairing glance at one another, both realising that despite our best efforts, the healing we were doing was not working. The wounds were too severe, the creature too far gone. As if sensing this finality, the Temptor pressed on, a mixture of blood and spittle bubbling over his thin lips.

" 'Twas only after the claws came out. We had no place to go, no place to run. Invaded. Spoiled. We took to 'em tunnels. But the nightmare came buzzin', swingin' tails out 'em holes. Surrounded all, armies of wing, armies of sting and claw. The hornet and the scorpion shook hands! So much blood... and it was us that let 'em in. 'Til us Sophists were all so very quiet."

There followed another fit of coughing, and the Temptor's breathing became shallow and laboured. We had struggled to make much sense of what was said, and Hammerhead began demanding answers before it was too late. The answers we got would haunt us from that day onwards.

"Who are the *'they'* you speak of, Temptor? Who did this to you?" our leader insisted. The Temptor's eyes rolled back a deep crimson red inside his tiny skull.

"You call us Temptor, but we be Sophists! We do not tempt, we enlighten and let 'em tempt 'emselves! 'Twas the Lost Ones, but 'em not be so lost no more! You call 'em Stalkers."

That place seemed all the more awful at that moment. The putrid air, the hellish glow; the point at which solitude succumbs to silence. Hammerhead pushed on with his interrogation:

"Where did they go? You must tell us!"

"Once 'em got what was ours, and had 'tacked us with 'em claws, 'em black eyes disappeared, turned to mist and shadow smoke!"

Wolfe and I exchanged a nervous glance, as we began to realise what that meant.

"But where were they headed? Where did they go?" Hammerhead shouted once more. The Temptor's eyes shone maliciously up at all of us.

"Only place left for 'em to go now! Back to the gateway of Fuse 'n' Flux ... back to our wall." As he uttered those last words, his thin and crooked lips curled into a devious grin.

We were all in shock, taking in the implications of what had been said. But we didn't have very long before we were forced into action when the five of us realised we were no longer alone. While we had been distracted by the Temptor's revelations, out of those gaping, dark holes had crawled an incalculable number of tiny translucent scorpions.

Our team formed a tight circle as, much to our horror, a distant humming sound approached, echoing through the tunnels, while all around us, those scorpions began to grow. From behind me, I heard Hammerhead barking orders, instructing BugBowl to construct a window back to the ravine, as the hall came alive with monsters. Wolfe rapidly lay down a thick barrier of fire which encircled and protected us, while I whipped up the stagnant air, pushing it towards the flames, stirring them into a frenzy which rose up to almost reach the ceiling.

Turning I saw ScaleFist extend both arms forward, and watched as his skin rippled over into hardened reptilian armour. Hammerhead was rubbing his own hands together at such a speed they began to smoke. Before, moments later, they crusted over almost to his elbows with a heavy granite-like substance. Bending low both of them thrust their hands into the nearby lava pools, drawing out dripping globular fireballs which, again and again, they hurled at our attackers on the other side of the flames. There were high-pitched shrieks as some of them struck, and through the light of the roaring fire, we could see hideous dark shapes moving and swaying all around.

It seemed to be holding them at bay, until suddenly a massive, curved scorpion tail came crashing through, striking the dirt only a couple of feet away from us with a powerful thud. More soon followed, swinging and slamming down blindly at us, as we dodged those poisonous barbs, waiting on BugBowl to finish the window. Just as the hall started to fill with the disorienting and threatening drone of a thousand angry wings, we heard BugBowl cry out for us to make our escape. Hammerhead and I were the last to leave and, in a rare show of camaraderie, he didn't hesitate to push me through first.

Even back above ground, with that death-ridden landscape far behind us, and the window firmly closed, we still did not feel safe. The five of us racing full speed along the ravine floor. Desperate cries were yelled between us, as our panicked minds attempted to keep up with what was happening.

"Where are we going?"

"To the wall, they must still be ahead of us!"

"Is anyone else worried that those insects will follow us?"

"Do you think we'll be able to catch up with the Stalkers?"

"Even if we manage to, what are we going to do when that happens?"

That question was the last to be shouted, as it struck us all, like the harsh slap of reality, that we didn't have a plan. Soon we saw the Wall of Fuse-and-Flux rising high above us, though there was still no sign of that shadow column.

We burst out into that wide, open meadow, just as the first rays of the morning sun came filtering through the trees. The place was deserted. It was precisely as I remembered it from Steggie's story, though there was one thing standing there that none of us had expected. Not far from the foot of the cliff-face, prominent and proudly facing us, was an antique-looking long rectangular mirror.

Now, I don't want to come across as hypocritical or of preaching double-standards, since only a few pages ago I urged you not to fear what adults have come to refer to as Ghosts, out there in the waking world. However, standing there in that meadow, I felt an inexplicable wave of terror sweep through me.

The five of us approached the mirror with caution, stopping some distance from it, at which point an argument soon broke out.

"The Stalkers must have already made it here," Hammerhead stated authoritatively, which provoked a steady stream of questions. Did they leave the mirror? Could they have somehow passed through it? Used it like the Water-Rise portal Steggie told us about? And if so, where had they gone? While the rest began bickering over their differing opinions, I started to feel an odd sensation, snowballing and coursing through my body, tugging and pulling persuasively at me, like a magnetic attraction, towards that mirror.

I resisted and tried to refocus on the heated conversation.

"It doesn't look anything like the Water-Rise Steggie described. So I say we investigate and find out where it leads," Wolfe said determinedly. Typical Wolfe, charging in with both feet first. I would have supported his suggestion, had I not been struggling in that very instant to maintain control over my own body and mind.

"We will do no such thing!" Hammerhead responded. "We need to report straight back to Steggie, and tell her what we have discovered! Besides..." If I hadn't been distracted by my own internal battle right then, I would have noticed him cast a suspicious look my way. "None of us can be certain we'd even be able to make such a journey. I'm opening a window to the Treetop summit right now."

It was the last thing I remembered hearing, his rough commands mellowing into a slurring drool. Then came the sudden sensation that my feet were no longer my own.

It seemed to catch them all totally unawares as, without the slightest warning, all my muscles rebelled, surrendering to that hypnotic pull.

I charged straight at the mirror. I heard their shocked cries rising up in unison as, against my very own will and judgement, I dove straight through.

14

The One Who Came Before

I must have been gone for several hours, although truthfully I would have just as easily believed if it had been only minutes, or that years had passed. I did not remember consciously making the window through which I returned, but as I was later to be told, I tumbled out of one at the far end of that rooftop jetty, collapsing in a heap upon those ancient wooden boards. I vaguely recall the hollow sound of many feet rushing towards me, worried voices, someone pronouncing that I was dead, though thankfully they were wrong. Then nothing.

When I finally came around, I was lying on my back on a low divan, which was littered with plush pillows. I heard snippets of an ongoing conversation being whispered in earnest before they realised I was awake.

"... We can't be sure where the portal took him, let alone what he saw."

"It won't make the slightest difference either way!" I recognised the negative hostility behind that voice: it was Hammerhead, and he was far from finished. "Even if he does recover, he won't remember a single thing, I guarantee you!"

Much to my immense frustration at that moment he was right, for when I gently probed my recent memory, I found only a blurred, sponge-like amnesia lurking there. "Besides," he continued, "I saw it all. He was totally out of control. Just got sucked right in, with no thought of anyone else—the team, the mission, nothing! Reckless and dangerous, just like I've been saying all along. Exactly the same way it started with Simeon Scythe."

A few seconds of silence followed, during which I racked my dizzy brain, concluding that I had definitely never heard that name mentioned before. Then came a familiar voice, and with some relief, I listened as Wolfe butted in, defiantly defending my honour.

"I was there too, and I'm telling you all he did exactly what needed to be done. What any of us in his place would have done, had we been able to. I know Zoofall better than anyone, and he's nothing like the stories I have heard of how Simeon was."

Hammerhead counter-attacked sharply, with venom in his voice. "Nobody asked for your opinion, fifteen! You're not even part of the Inner Circle. Not one of *us*. You're only here because Steggie wanted him to see a friendly face if he wakes up."

"Perhaps it's time to tell the two of them everything? The truth about Simeon Scythe, and what we have discovered about the Anchor of Perspicax?" I knew it was Everly Kitt who had spoken, recognising her kind and soothing, almost motherly tone, but her words only seemed to enrage Hammerhead all the more.

"Are you insane? Definitely not! Those are private matters: subjects which we shouldn't even be mentioning, not with two non-Elites present. I call for Zoofall, when he wakes, to be automatically demoted, and an investigation to be made for his temporary suspension from the Freedivers. What do you say, Steggie?"

An agonising silence rolled slowly by. Through squinting eyes, I was unable to see her and, perhaps most worryingly, at first Steggie offered no reply. Then finally, privately inside my head, she spoke:

"No more pretending. No more hiding, Zoofall. It's time."

I understood. I quietly raised myself up, unnoticed, onto my elbows, startling all of those present with my question: "So, who's Simeon Scythe?"

There was a divided reaction among the group, ranging from joyous relief, which Wolfe vocally led, all the way to bitter scepticism, the ringleader of that particular sentiment I'm sure by now you can guess.

"Give him some space," Everly Kitt said, kneeling down beside me to begin her examination, as though she were my own private doctor. Wolfe obeyed but remained close by, peering over her shoulder, while the rest of the Inner Circle eyed me inquisitively from a distance. "You gave us all a pretty good scare," she continued, smiling softly while checking the mobility in my arms and legs. "Do you remember anything about where you went?" she asked in a hushed voice so that nobody else could hear. I shook my head. "Never mind, you're unharmed and safe, and that's all that matters for now."

I noticed Hammerhead still whispering insistently to Steggie, and felt a pang of despair as she nodded reluctantly to whatever he was saying. She made her way over, resting one hand on Wolfe's shoulder in either reassurance or consolation, as she brushed past him. The group fell silent, aware that a verdict was coming. Before opening her mouth, Steggie prepared me telepathically for my token punishment.

"Don't take this personally, Zoofall, individual rankings are the least of our worries right now, I promise. This is just to keep Hammerhead happy." I nodded ever so slightly as she turned to address the group out loud as a whole.

"We will go straight to the cave, for an urgent Inner Circle meeting. For the time being," she added, glancing at Wolfe, "the two of you shall come with us, as your input might be useful. Although I'm afraid, as a precaution, I have no choice but to demote Zoofall to the rank of #63."

I heard Wolfe huff and mumble his disapproval which only seemed to strengthen Hammerhead's satisfied gloating. Everly Kitt said nothing, only patted my knee as she rose to her feet and offered her hand to help me up, as the twelve of us marched solemnly in single file, following through Steggie's window with our footsteps echoing as we entered the cave.

Once we were comfortably settled around the roaring campfire, all eyes turned to our leader as she began, with some sadness, to tell the story of Simeon Scythe.

He had been one of the first dreamers to find Steggie up in the Treetop summit, all those years ago, and from the very beginning had shown signs of becoming an advanced Omnivaga and pioneering member of the Freedivers. When the Inner Circle was initially formed, he had by his own merit quite naturally found his place among them. Simeon and Steggie had, over time, become close friends and she had quickly seen how his extraordinary speed of development set him apart from the rest and had noticed traits which led her to suspect that he could be a Shifter in the making.

Heeding Euryale's previous warnings, Steggie had waited and observed him patiently until she was absolutely sure and not the slightest shred of doubt remained. She confessed, with sullen regret, that it had given her great pleasure to finally help him learn and discover the deeper mysteries in regards to his talents and gifts, including the art of constructing and navigating the Inter-World portals.

Simeon Scythe took all her lessons in his stride; the vast accomplishments he made were always tempered by his honest and responsible approach. For a long time, Steggie didn't have the faintest inkling that anything was wrong. She had trusted Simeon completely. She had been totally unaware of his growing obsession and desire for crossing-over, driven by curiosity and his need for more advanced knowledge.

Simeon had devoted himself to this secretive quest until, as both his confidence and his unquenchable thirst for more grew, he became complacent and careless. He had believed himself to be above the guidelines and careful precautions laid out by Euryale and those before her to protect the delicate balance between the two worlds.

As his actions had spiralled out of control, so too his reckless web of deceit unravelled and became exposed. His crime? In his arrogance, he had started to leave those dangerous Inter-World portals open.

The first event to reach Steggie's attention had even found its way into the local news from a remote region in Norway, back in the waking world. A handful of mountain trolls had succeeded in forcing their way through the neglectfully abandoned portal, wreaking havoc upon the local landscape. Several cases were reported of people, local fishermen and hikers, going missing and their vehicles later found crushed and demolished.

While rumours and theories were plentiful, thankfully

sightings had been few. Any witnesses were quickly discredited due to the fantastical nature of what they claimed to have seen. By the time an organised search had begun, Steggie had led a recovery mission alongside Simeon Scythe, who she still did not suspect of being responsible for those Inter-World breaches. They had crossed over and managed with great difficulty to lure the colossal culprits back into the dream world where they belonged. With no hard evidence remaining, the waking world investigation was finally called off, the story becoming nothing more than superstitious folklore and soon forgotten by most of humankind.

Sadly, however, it was not to be an isolated incident, but only the beginning.

Over the following year, the Freedivers had been forced to undertake many similar cross-over clean-up missions, risking great peril in the process. From hunting down the stunted, rabid demon dragons of Volcanaton, referred to among people as Chupacabras, in Puerto Rico, to the wailing banshees let loose once more upon the brooding boglands of the desolate Irish moors; from the adventurous Manticores to the last of the Sirens, yearning to perform just one more song.

Never once during all that time did Simeon admit his guilt or even halt his irresponsible practices ... far from it. When the finger of suspicion began to turn towards one of their own as a possible culprit, Simeon Scythe appeared to have already anticipated this eventuality and had planned accordingly. In a bold attempt to escape blame, he had gone to great lengths to frame a fellow member of the Elite, Hammerhead—a scheme that had so very nearly worked. Only when an innocent Hammerhead had been on the very brink of expulsion had the real truth quite by chance come to light.

The thing that had affected Steggie the most, the memory she could never forget, was Simeon Scythe's reaction when his mask of lies had finally slipped.

There was no remorse or apology, no acceptance of wrongdoing or seeking of forgiveness—only his inner nature blossoming freely to the surface. His resentment was evident. He told them they were fools. Naive dreamers no better than the Floaters, and that whatever punishment they could throw at him would only serve as a release, elevating him one step further towards his destiny. He was banished from the Freedivers shortly before Wolfe's arrival and left cursing the Freediver name and swearing a promise of dire revenge.

After that, stories as to his fate had been sketchy. He went rogue, wandering the wilderness for many months until an enormous reward for his capture was put upon him by the Coven of the North, who had accused him of stealing several of their forbidden ritual texts. At last, he was surrounded and caught attempting to cross the desert of Vumbi Bones on foot, though he refused to say where he had been headed or what he was doing there. Rumour has it he was then thrown headlong into the Pit of Obliviscor, a harsh sentence indeed. Many say he still remains there, howling madly from its inky depths, while others claim that he somehow managed to escape the confines of that terrible prison, though nobody could really say for sure.

"That," Steggie said in closing, "is the story of Simeon Scythe, the last Shifter welcomed into the Freedivers ranks and your predecessor, Zoofall."

The flames continued to crackle, shadows flickering across the solemn faces of all those present. I saw Hammerhead differently then, as he sat cross-legged, stabbing at the dirt with a piece of driftwood, obviously uncomfortable at having to relive that painful memory. I found I could understand Hammerhead's distrust of me now.

Shortly afterwards, our conversation began to turn to the Golden Book and the artefact known as the Anchor of Perspicax. It was then that, once again, we were disturbed by the most ungodly and infuriating of sounds. I jumped up out of bed and without thinking threw the alarm clock across my room, feeling instant regret as its dark fragments exploded off the bedroom wall. By that age, I was quickly learning that my temper had consequences, and almost always got me into trouble. I cursed under my breath at the unfairness of it all, and as I hurriedly dressed in the semi-gloom, it appeared that the cruelty of the waking world was not quite done with me. Karma came back to bite me, as I trod on a sharp plastic piece of the clock, which then sent me hopping and howling painfully through the darkness, banging my elbow and stubbing my toe.

15

Nightmare in the Waking World

Against all expectations, that day actually passed quite quickly, the hours at school becoming a hazy slush of droning teachers' voices. I remember failing a science test quite spectacularly by failing to answer even a single question, but other than that, the rest of the day was an uneventful blur. My mind was elsewhere, miles and miles away, desperately trying to recall what had happened during those missing hours.

It was during my last lesson of the day that the nightmarish memory returned. It was an art class, which was by far my favourite, as it often allowed my daydreaming to flow quite uninterrupted. I was so distracted that I hadn't even noticed what I had done. We were meant to be drawing a rather uninspiring bowl of fruit, but instead, I had sketched that long rectangular mirror, standing upright as it had been within the meadow. I felt it pulling me, as though sucking me down into the page, and that was when the terrible flashbacks began. Those sudden recollections thundered through my brain without mercy, and my clammy hands gripped the workbench in horror as my amnesia dissolved.

Once I had crossed fully through that mirror in the meadow, leaving the team of Freedivers behind, I had examined my new surroundings in somewhat of a daze. There was still a crisp, fresh early morning feel in the air, though now it felt frosted over with a sharp and wintery chill. My warm breath was clearly visible and hung suspended before my face in clouded plumes. I appeared to be inside an old medieval castle, with thick stone walls designed to keep the bitter cold at bay and immense flagstone flooring, smoothed and sunken by centuries of feet treading their repetitive paths upon them.

The place was magical and otherworldly, leading me to the assumption that I must have still been within the dream world, and that the mirror must have teleported me to some far off, unknown region. That was until I spotted the people. As I exited the courtyard, passing under the portcullis and out over the open drawbridge, they were everywhere, dressed in such an uninspired and mundane way that I realised this had to be the waking world. Though not entirely, for there was something wrong.

Not one of them was moving: they were as lifeless as cardboard cut-outs, or the mannequins one finds displayed in shop windows. I walked around them, through their clustered groups, waved my hands across their unflinching eyes, and even tried to scare one of them to provoke some sort of reaction, but nothing. The whole thing was quite confusing. Most of the people there were carrying cameras, an item one does not often find within the dream world, due to its limited and somewhat redundant power, so I concluded that they must be tourists or visitors to that place. I tried desperately to make sense of it, and my reasoning led me to believe that this was indeed a location within the waking world, but that I had somehow stepped outside of time itself. Perhaps I had fallen only a fraction out of sync with the present moment? I could not say for sure, but what remained was an implausible scene. A world displaced and caught within the click of a ticking clock. Stuck in either a frozen future or a painted past.

I looked around as much as I could. The town seemed magnificent, like something straight out of a fairytale. A network of bohemian-style buildings and cobbled alleys, enchanting spires capped with silky remnants of recent snow, all laid along the banks of a mesmerising river that snaked its way through the town in the shape of a horseshoe.

I was alerted by a peculiar noise, and followed it with rising curiosity to a nearby low wall, with railings running along the top of it. It was my first sensation of *déjà vu*, that subtle bridge where both worlds meet within the mind, silent ecstatic fireworks begging the individual to take notice, to remember something crucial. I found myself looking down into the dry castle moat, and what I saw made me doubt once again whether all of this could actually be real.

A family of bears was moving quite lethargically around the ground below. For a second I thought perhaps time itself had re-awoken and energised itself, but the rest of the world still stood as stiff as scarecrows. Only me and those bears were moving. I watched them for quite a while, as they lazily sorted through a bushel of apples, content in their warm fur coats from the frosty elements. At one point, the biggest among them looked directly up at me and nodded slightly as though acknowledging my presence. On the wall opposite, written in some archaic and foreign language, was a plaque which I was unable to decipher. A particular word appeared most prominently, etched elaborately and deeply into the sign, and I made a concerted effort to commit it to memory: '*Krumlov*'.

Suddenly and without any warning, time seemed to shift drastically. It was then late twilight, and there were fewer people to be seen on the streets. The ones who remained outside were now wrapped up warm and as still as ice sculptures. Heavy snow had fallen, burying my feet entirely. The town was lit up splendidly, sleepily glowing with a static beauty. Down below, the bears presently emerged from their sheltered den and looked up in unison, though this time not at me, drawing my attention towards the clear evening sky above. I sensed that something of great importance was going on up there, and without hesitation, I took off from the ground, steadily climbing into the sky.

Even when I looked down, it was with an absence of fear. As I rose higher, rivers became fine cobwebs and towns became pinprick specks, major cities nothing more than shrinking, shining thimbles. Entire countries melted darkly into one another and then faded indistinctly until continents and oceans became interlocked jigsaw pieces making up the globe. I suppose I slowed to a halt somewhere in the uppermost stratosphere, close to the boundary where space begins. That was where I found them.

There must have been well over fifty in total, all hovering, spaced out like fiery red satellites. Though they had no describable form, I knew exactly who they were. As I drew level, but deliberately not too close, the scars on my right arm began to ache and burn. Up there in that giddy, thin atmosphere, I had come upon that elusive shadow procession, that squadron of Stalkers. Despite my stifled panic, they did not appear to be aware of me: they were busy watching, waiting for something. Like a murder of crows perched high up on a telephone wire, or a band of silhouetted surfers positioned beyond the break, they hovered there, and I among them.

They exuded a sense of menace, and I struggled against the growing feeling that at any given moment, they would turn on me like a pack of hungry wolves. Thankfully though, the wait came to an abrupt end in an entirely different manner. Miraculously, it came from above.

The darkness came alive with cascading light. A meteor shower blazed and tore a course straight towards us. No two were quite the same, either in size or brilliance: some sparkled gracefully, while others fizzled with a near blinding intensity as they approached. I watched spellbound as those shooting stars sped past us. Falling all around and in between our scattered swarm, hurtling down towards the Earth. The locations where they struck the ground continued to burn golden and red, vibrant embers from such catastrophic impacts.

I saw meteors strike Africa, the eastern side of the Americas and saw several of them rain down all over Europe and further to the East. I even saw a few crashing down on the United Kingdom: two stars landing almost on top of one another. From such a height, it was clear that several were burning far more brightly, which made me wonder what sort of damage they might have done. Raging wildfires? Or devastating blackened craters?

Once the last one had landed, I saw that suspended row of disembodied Stalkers all flinch as one. It reminded me in a nasty way of how a line of athletes at the Olympics would tense up at the "get set" signal in anticipation of the starter's gun. There was something evil and calculating about it, which I did not like at all. Though I could not make out features or faces, I got the strong impression of malice, as though devilish sneers would have been spreading across their lips.

Then in an instant, they descended, swooping like vultures through the night. I went after them, keeping up as best I could, but they were just too fast. The distance between us began to widen, and I was left lagging, trailing helplessly in their wake. It was useless trying to chase them, so instead, I focused on concentrating on their movements. Searching for a clue as to where they were going and to what purpose. I watched, still from a great height, as the Stalkers appeared to alter their course, regrouping and then splitting off into almost a dozen smaller packs before they reached the ground, drifting apart and scattering like dandelion petals upon the wind.

It was only from such an elevated position that I was able to notice a pattern to their movement, a mutual objective shared by each group. They were travelling at high speed in those smaller swarms, targeting the sites where the largest meteors had fallen. Though Geography was one of my weakest subjects at school, I recognised Italy from its distinctive boot shape and watched as one such team of Stalkers swept straight past one of the smaller crash sites, which glowed almost like a rhythmic pulse, as though it wasn't even there. They continued northwards, cutting a direct path towards a much larger and brighter fallen meteor. I saw the exact same thing happening in other areas around the world.

It was almost at that precise moment I noticed, deep in the dark heart of Eastern Europe, a silver twinkle flash up into the night sky. As though someone was attempting to communicate a crude message in Morse code, an S.O.S call perhaps, from the reflective surface of a mirror? A mirror! It was then that I felt the firm tug, as though some giant octopus or Portuguese man o' war had wrapped a slimy tentacle around my ankle, pulling me sharply down.

I was absolutely powerless against that pull. Dragged against my will by an unseen force through the emptiness of that night sky. When I got closer to the ground, I saw the reflection shine up once more, recognised that curling horseshoe river, those fairytale spires and that magical castle. It felt like being sucked into the spinning centre of a whirlpool, and I knew right then it was the same mirror that pulled me back. I succumbed to its power, and filled my mind with thoughts of Steggie and the Freedivers, the Treetop summit, as the ground came rushing up and everything went dark.

The final school bell rang right on cue, but as the rest of my classmates filed out with noisy celebrations, all I could do was sit there shaking. When I finally got home, I phoned Wolfe immediately and arranged to meet him at the midway point between our two houses before it got dark. There, sheltered by the shadowed woodland canopy, as the evening light dimmed, I breathlessly told him everything.

"I have no idea what it all means," Wolfe said, his face extremely pale and appearing worried in the failing light. "But I've got a terrible feeling about this! You've got to tell Steggie as soon as you can."

That last hour before bedtime was the hardest. I was a complete nervous wreck, walking endlessly around my room until the time came to say goodnight to my parents. Finally, I could cross over and tumbled out into the shadow-filled cave once more, where thankfully Wolfe and the Elite were already assembled. I told them everything that I remembered, being careful not to leave out even the most seemingly insignificant detail.

With my story finished, I sat back down by the fire,

feeling drained.

They remained quiet for some time, considering my account and trying to make sense of those cryptic visions. The tale seemed to have greatly troubled Steggie, and soon she was up on her feet, pacing back and forth in deep contemplation, with a concerned expression on her face. When, at last, she turned to address us, there was apprehension in her voice, and her shoulders were pushed low and sunken, as though she was carrying the weight of both worlds upon them.

"Thank you, Zoofall, for presenting to us the details of what you encountered on the other side. What you have witnessed requires a great deal of further thought, and I don't want to draw too many early conclusions from it just yet. But these things I will say to you all right now. We must find out what those Stalkers are up to. It sounds to me that they're most definitely planning something, using that strange place as some sort of practice ground. From what Zoofall said, it sounds like some sort of parallel world, almost frozen outside of time. We can only assume that the Thistle-wisps they stole from the Temptors is what's allowing them to cross over, but why only around fifty of them? Is that their total number, or just a limitation for the time being? And what about this meteor shower? How does that fit into their plans? Is it a real event that they have learnt is due to strike the waking world, and if so, what energy are they after from these earthbound stars? Or could the whole thing just be symbolic, as a way for them to disguise their true intentions? All these things, we must figure out, and fast, for I fear that time is most certainly against us!"

I remember those words so clearly. I have long since wondered whether there could have been any way that I, as the chance prophet or forecaster, could have figured out those riddles in my vision, even just a little quicker. Would it have made any difference? Could it have stopped the dominoes that were already falling?

"You don't think that perhaps it has something to do with the Anchor?" Liquid Beat, another member of the Elite, asked, and was answered by low murmurings of thoughtful consideration from those gathered around the campfire.

Steggie eyed Wolfe and I seriously, making it clear that everything about to be spoken must be kept absolutely secret. Once assured of this, she then proceeded to give her answer slowly.

"Of that, we cannot be certain. Let us consider what we do know. As most of you are already aware, once we had finished translating those passages from the Golden Book, we were quite disappointed that it did not offer more exact details and information regarding the Anchor of Perspicax. Sometimes it was referred to as the greatest weapon in existence. Sometimes as the lynchpin which balances the scales between both our worlds. On another occasion, it was described as the angelic tool by which all living entities could be set free.

"The book did, however, provide us with a particular clue, namely the last known groups entrusted with the task of keeping it safe. Over the previous two years, the Inner Circle and I have led several missions intending to find more definite answers and to track down the Anchor's possible location. This is what we have learnt.

"It was the various Covens of the dream world who were initially charged with this duty. And as we have discovered, they frequently met to reach an agreement as to what was to be done with the Anchor, and who would be best suited to protect it from misuse. Even discussing the matter amongst their own kind, those witches quickly realised they had a big problem. The problem was—and still is—a common conundrum even among grown-ups in the waking world, when matters of power and responsibility arise, so I am told.

"For while there has never been a shortage of people eager to wield such daunting power, the irony comes twofold. Not only in the fact that those who desire such things are most often the least capable, and most likely to be corrupted by it. But also in that, the best candidates are those who genuinely show no longing or interest for it, but do all they can to avoid bearing what they see as such a burden.

"The witches listened as many of their leaders laid out reasoned arguments why each of them would be worthy of taking on such a role. Even a notorious Necromancer decided there was nothing to be lost in having a go, putting on quite a humble show, pleading his case with feigned sincerity. This served to remind the wisest among them that even humility can be faked, and so it was that the Coven of the North decreed that no witch should be nominated for such a task. That, by necessity, they would have to look for the Anchor's guardian in more unlikely places. As a result, their final decision was one not bound by logic and perhaps understood least of all by the rather unusual individual they ended up choosing, and duly approached.

"Pan, the former Forest God of the waking world, firmly refused the witches' request. He had a firm dislike of complications, and to him, looking after the Anchor spelt nothing but an endless series of complications! Pan enjoyed the simplicity of Nature, breathing life into his musical pipes, never aspiring towards a pleasant tune, but took comfort from the unpredictable melody of the wilderness. What use had he for such an unplayable and awkward instrument? Despite his reluctance, the witches did not back down, and he finally gave way, if only for the reason of being left alone to his own devices.

"As far as we can gather, Pan fulfilled his obligation, and held onto it for as long as he could, more than could have been expected by most, keeping it safe for over two thousand years."

She told us how he even managed to find several bizarre uses for that cumbersome and priceless artefact. From a simple stool on which to perch; to a post around which to tether his herd while he dozed lazily through the long summer days. During wild parties he had organised he would apparently stand on top of it, using it as a platform upon which to trot out crazy, nimble and lively dances on his goatish hooves. Legend has it that on one such occasion there had been a human dreamer among the crowd who, upon returning to the waking world, was desperate to recreate what he had seen, and as a result, the very first origin of Tap dancing was born!"

We all found ourselves smiling at Steggie's wild historical anecdotes, but it seemed a little strange to me, considering the gravity of my vision and it's possible consequences. I suspected that these stories were attempts at lightening the mood and not allowing fear and panic to spread. These suspicions of mine were later confirmed, when even Everly Kitt got involved, steering the conversation off onto more amusing tangents. I decided to remain silent, watching closely as Steggie continued with her tale.

"When he decided to pass on the Anchor of Perspicax to another protector, Pan thought long and hard, by his somewhat unique standards, about whom he could trust to carry on that torch. So it was, we have recently discovered, that with great discretion he relinquished the Anchor to a tribe, famous for their devoted obsession of respecting and maintaining balance within the natural order."

"Oh no, not the Woodland Fairies," Wolfe groaned. "Tell me he didn't give it to them!" This caused a few of the Inner Circle to chuckle, for Wolfe's resentment towards that particular group was well known. It had to do with that peculiar transformation and annoyance, to which Wolfe had for a long time now been a victim. I had noticed at various instances, from the first time I had met him, that his ears would often elongate into points.

"When Wolfe first joined the Freedivers," Everly Kitt explained, "he was ... how shall we say it, a little bit too overconfident."

"Zoofall doesn't need to hear that story!" Wolfe interrupted, his cheeks starting to redden, but Everly Kitt carried on regardless.

"It had been on one of his first missions that Wolfe's team had decided to take a break on the gentle bank of a woodland stream. The others had warned him not to fall asleep, for they were deep inside Fairy territory, but Wolfe had insisted that no Fairy was capable of creeping up on him and taking him by surprise. What was it you said exactly? 'I can hear them a mile off, my senses are so sharp. Just like the ears of a fox!'"

Wolfe let out another groan, burying his head in his hands in utter embarrassment.

"Well let's just say they did manage to sneak up on him and decided on a mischievous curse which would forever remind him of that day, and how brazen boastfulness can often lead a dreamer into trouble."

Steggie giggled briefly at the memory, before returning to

Wolfe's original question. "No, no," she assured him, "Pan chose a far wiser and reliable ally: the Loup Garou."

The group remained in stunned silence, and at least one of the Elite, Miss Dimity, was visibly shaken by the mere mention of that tribe. Steggie, of course, noticed this too and continued with her explanation in a more soothing tone.

"There really isn't any reason to worry so. I too have heard the fairy tales, told inaccurately and designed to frighten children but believe me, the Loup Garou are not to be feared in such ways, not by the likes of us at least. They too are yet another tribe misunderstood by human beings because of their differences. A species which was forced to emigrate and reside for the most part within the dream world. The Loup Garou are in fact quite marvellous beings, a far cry from the tall earthly tales of Werewolves and Lycanthropy.

"Their ability to change into different animals is a deliberate and controlled choice, not something affected by the cycle of the moon. Unlike with other changeling groups, once transformed, the Loup Garou remain themselves entirely, keeping their intelligence and reasoning, while taking on the natural strengths and instincts of the creature they have chosen to become. They keep mostly to themselves and are rarely encountered knowingly, even here in the dream world. The Loup Garou are fiercely loyal to any cause they align themselves with, and they are the ones who have hidden and still guard the Anchor.

"It is to them I have reached out, requesting a meeting, and any week now I am hopeful for an answer."

The twelve of us continued talking well into the night, putting forward theories and discussing options, along with other areas to investigate. We all agreed that the Freedivers time and efforts

221

should be devoted to three things: finding out what the Stalkers were up to; preparing to defend ourselves in whatever way imaginable; and following the trail to the Anchor of Perspicax. We assumed—from the wintery feeling of my dreadful vision on the other side of the mirror—that it might be only a matter of months before the dark forces that were brewing would reach their boiling point.

We were wrong. It was to be less than three weeks later when the real nightmare began, back in the waking world.

It was a blustery Friday afternoon. Autumn had arrived early that year and stripped all the trees bare. The days were growing shorter, strong winds rustling up the dry, brown, deadened leaves into a swirling dance, a constant reminder that winter was coming.

I was looking forward to spending two nights at Wolfe's house, as his mother was going away for the weekend and leaving us under the questionable supervision of his older brother. He was seventeen years old, nearly always scowling and appearing either angry about something important or angry that everything was unimportant. He viewed us as a nuisance and seemed most content when we kept quietly to ourselves. So long as we stayed out of his way, that meant one glorious thing: unlimited dreaming time.

I was riding excitedly home from school when something in one of the corner shop windows caught my eye. My bike wheels squealed to a halt, and I froze in horror at the news board out front where the current headline caption was printed.

"Ghostly Black-Eyed Children Spotted near Cannock Chase!"

I dropped my bike, which clattered noisily to the pavement, and I ran inside. Spending almost all my pocket money, I bought a copy of each different newspaper they had in stock before hurrying home. There, locked in my bedroom as dusk began to fall, I flicked through all those pages in a growing state of panic, tearing out any relevant articles I could find. Below are some of the extracts, which I read hastily through trembling fingers:

'Two nights ago, numerous reports were made of strange children being seen throughout that area of local woodland. Independent witnesses stated that when these children were approached, their eyes appeared totally black, almost hollow. They were spotted wandering alone or in pairs, with their age ranging from eight to sixteen years old.'

'One woman swears that the young girl she saw, peered closely at her before actually speaking quite rudely, saying the following nonsensical words, "Not you, Indiac. We have no use for Floaters!" before vanishing into thin air.'

'A local resident told us how on that same evening, there came a knock at his front door. Upon answering it, he found two young children, both with the same dark eyes, who told him they were lost and asked if they could come inside. The man claims he felt "an inexplicable fear" in their presence, and refused to let them in, calling the police instead. But that when the officers arrived soon after, both children were nowhere to be seen.'

The last article referred to a team of supposed ghost hunters, who claimed they had caught visual, recorded evidence of the child they had spotted. The photo itself was quite dark and grainy, but their report of what they had heard on their recordings out there in the woods made my blood run cold:

'We got plenty of strange sounds and voices out there, creepy messages and short phrases that seemed almost to be taunting us, such as, "We're looking… We will find the right door… We're stalking … He knows where they live" and perhaps most threateningly, "He's coming!".'

I scrambled over to my bed and threw some clothes into my rucksack. As I gathered up those torn out pages, I noticed the name of the newspaper that one of the stories was from, *The Daily Star*, printed neatly in the top corner. I shuddered at the awful connection, and piece by terrible piece the puzzle came together.

I remember glancing out my bedroom window and seeing that it was almost dark outside. I leapt down the stairs, and breathlessly called out to my parents, saying that I was heading over to Wolfe's house. By the time my mother had called back, telling me to have fun and to call if there were any problems, I was already out the front door. I grabbed my bike and quickly wheeled it out of the driveway. I froze dead in my tracks, with one foot raised upon the pedal.

The route which I usually took was blocked by four children standing motionless at the end of the road. Looking over my shoulder in the other direction, I saw a similar row positioned in the distance that way too. My mind raced, as I felt that sickeningly familiar pain burning its way along my arm. I turned around, taking my bike quickly back into the alley at the side of the house, and locked the gate behind me. I kept looking around and up at the sky, whilst fastening the straps of my bag tightly over my shoulders. Only one thought, one question was pushing its way repeatedly into my head: was it really dark enough to try this?

I had often thought about one day visiting Wolfe's house in such a manner, but Steggie's previous warning had always brought me back to my senses. I had never imagined that such a decision would need to be made under such dreadful circumstances, but I was out of options, and the Freedivers were out of time. I broke into a run, heading towards the back garden, before taking to the sky.

Surprisingly, the journey wasn't actually that much faster than it normally took by bike, and definitely half as fun, but perhaps that was because I was so terrified of getting caught. Constantly checking behind me in a paranoid and panicked way, and keeping low to the tops of the treeline for cover. I decided on a detour through the desolate woods, the furthest border of which backed onto Wolfe's house. A cold wind stung my eyes, making them water and forcing me to pause several times to wipe at them with my sleeve. The landscape was eerily silent, with only the occasional rustling sound as my trailing feet brushed through those very highest branches.

At one point, while I was scanning the darkening sea of green in front of me to make sure I was still headed in the right direction, a family of sparrows burst wildly from the foliage below me. They scattered and soared, chirping madly at my approach, and their sudden, unexpected chaos threw me momentarily off course. I hurtled through a patch of those uppermost leaves, thin branches whipping and lashing at my clothes and bare skin before

I was able to regain my balance. Looking back I saw those birds now circling far overhead, keeping well clear and most probably wondering what type of bizarre distant cousin I was to them.

Up ahead, I caught glimpses of Wolfe's rooftop near the border of that wooded area and slowed down until I was hovering just above the final line of trees. His garden far below was dark and still, and I decided at that moment to risk it, making a break for it and flying over the vast expanse of open ground. My heart was almost beating out of my chest, and it struck me that flying in the waking world wasn't quite the same incredibly free sensation when you had to constantly worry about being spotted or seen.

I went straight for his bedroom window, rapping on the glass frantically. I can't be sure which one of us was most in shock, but I am guessing that his first rational thought was that I must have been standing on top of a ladder since his room was on the second floor. His face turned white when he opened the window for me to clamber in and he realised that wasn't so.

"But ... but ... but how is that even possible?" Wolfe stammered, looking at me in wide-eyed disbelief.

"There's no time for that right now, you have to trust me!" I shouted urgently, rummaging through my rucksack, and pulling out the bundle of loose pages. "Just read these, and do it quickly!" I ordered, thrusting them into his lap. While he worked through them, I closed the curtains—ignoring his occasional gasps and exclamations—as I stared out through a crack in the fabric. I was focusing on the darkened line of trees at the end of Wolfe's garden, where the woods began. I thought I saw something: a shadow move. The scars on my arm were once again starting to tingle.

"What on Earth does all this mean?" he asked when he

was done reading, his voice full of fear. "That the Stalkers have crossed over fully into the waking world? What are they searching for?"

There was definite movement now beyond those trees, dark shadows advancing towards the house. My scars were starting to hurt.

"You mean, *who* are they searching for!" I whispered, and Wolfe was quickly by my side, peering through the curtains.

"No way!" was all he managed to say, as we watched six little figures emerge at the far end of his garden.

"We need to get out of here now! We've got to warn Steggie and the others." I said, stuffing pages of the newspapers back into my bag and slinging it over my shoulder.

"Seriously?" Wolfe replied, both hands pressed to his temples as he paced around the room, clearly starting to panic. "How do you expect us to fall asleep at a time like this!"

"We won't have to," I replied, opening his wardrobe door and running one hand along the mirror on its inner side.

"No way…" Wolfe repeated in amazement. "Are you sure that can even be done?" he asked, as we both heard a loud banging sound coming from the downstairs back door.

"I guess we're about to find out," I replied nervously, focusing as my hands began moving rapidly back and forth over the reflective surface.

We stepped out together from one of the Treetop city's lower rooms, leaving Wolfe's bedroom back in the waking world deserted. In haste, we made our way across rope bridges and up ladders, calling out continuously, but the place appeared silent and empty. We headed directly for the Treetop summit.

Bursting onto that upper platform, we found Everly Kitt,

going through defensive manoeuvres with a group of low-ranked Freedivers. We ran to her, interrupting her lesson.

"Where's Steggie and the rest of the Elite? We have to talk to them!" I demanded, forgetting both her seniority and my place.

"Steggie's gone to meet Euryale, and the others are all off on missions. We're the only ones here right now," she answered, clearly unimpressed at our intrusion—though she must have noticed the expression on our faces, for her next question resonated with tension and worry. "Zoofall, Wolfe, what's all this about? What's going on?"

"We're under attack! It's the Stalkers!" Wolfe blurted out. Everyone heard that, and panic quickly spread through all the members gathered there. Everly Kitt reacted swiftly, arming herself with her shield and long flaming spear, turning expectantly in every direction, on her guard and searching for the threat.

"Where are they? I don't see or sense anything."

"Not here," I rushed to explain, "it's happening right now, back in the waking world! The meteor shower. I've figured out what they were doing, what they were preparing for. All those falling stars, they weren't stars at all!"

Everly Kitt's face turned pale.

"I don't think I understand."

"Those stars, they were us, the Freedivers. We're being hunted!" In those next moments nobody spoke, everyone wide-eyed and open-mouthed, shocked and bewildered. I continued with my effort to convince her. "Where do you live?" My question seemed to take Everly Kitt by surprise.

"Why would it be important where I live?"

"Just tell me!" I insisted. I could see she was genuinely

scared now.

"I'm f-from Italy." she stammered, and I cast my mind back.

"From the north?" I added, "near the coast? About here?" I said, using my own leg as a simplified map of her country, and pointing towards the top of my shin. I knew that I was right; even before she spoke, I could see the terror and confusion in her eyes.

"How, how did you know that?"

I paused a second to construct my answer.

"Those large meteors I saw land: I think the largest of them represented the most powerful among us, the Inner Circle. They're targeting the Elite."

I felt Wolfe's hand touch my shoulder, gripping it tightly as he whispered in my ear, pointing towards the floor: "Look!"

We followed his hand and looked down, with Everly Kitt the most startled of us all. Her shield and spear fell to the ground. Her feet were disappearing. She had just enough time to raise her head, a look of total desperation in her eyes.

"Zoofall, help me!"

In the next instant, her body twisted violently up and away from the floor, lifted horizontally, as an unseen force attempted to drag her away. I leapt forward, grasping her tightly under one of her arms, trying to pull her back.

"Wolfe, I need you!" I cried, and in a second, he was there too, wrapping himself around her other shoulder. In the background, we could hear the other Freedivers wails and screams, as the three of us were all dragged helplessly across the platform.

"It's gone past her knees now! It's taking her," Wolfe grunted, straining through clenched teeth.

Whatever was pulling her was incredibly strong, and I could

feel my feet sliding across the wooden boards as we braced ourselves against it with every ounce of strength. We struck the barrier, dug our heels in and kept low, making one last stand, refusing to let go and surrender Everly Kitt to the night that lay beyond the railings.

Her body had now completely disintegrated from the waist down, and I held on as tight as I could, our faces barely inches apart. I could feel her fear, and hear her repeating something hysterically under her breath.

"I'm only dreaming, I'm only dreaming, I'm only …"

Then suddenly our grip dissolved. Her head and shoulders turned to vapour, leaving us with nothing left to hold on to. Our hands swept through the empty air in the hope of finding something.

Wolfe sank to his knees, shaking his head and pounding the floorboards in frustration.

Sounds of sobbing filled the air on every side, and my head spun.

I felt a nauseating swell of emotion rising inside of me.

I wanted to react, to scream, tear my hair out, or cry.

Because I knew this was only the beginning.

16

An Assassin Among Us

In Memory of The Elite: Steggie Belle, Hammerhead, Karmakaze, Miss Dimity, Harvest Gem, In-no-Scents, Stax, Liquid Beat, Lumen Chou, and Everly Kitt.

I wish I could tell you that I was wrong. That Everly Kitt was the only victim and member of the Inner Circle that we lost ... but sadly that is not what happened, and would not be the truth. It wasn't very long before Steggie got wind of what was going on and returned, immediately summoning the remaining Elite to that upper platform. She quickly divided the terrified Freedivers into two: herself and I, and Wolfe upon his own insistence, together with the eight other members of the Inner Circle were to stay right there, to tackle the unfolding crisis. Her instructions to every other Omnivaga assembled there were very simple:

"Return at once to the realm of casual dreaming, mix yourselves in among the vast number of Floaters, blend in and hide. Do not show even the slightest sign of deeper awareness or any sort of Lucid Dreaming. You are all to do so until I call for you, and if you must spend any hours back in the waking world, stay cautious and keep to public and well-populated places. Do not get caught anywhere all on your own. Be watchful."

Most of the Freedivers left quickly, keen to escape the heavy and almost suffocating tension which was in the air. I noticed some of the older members nodding solemnly towards the remaining Inner Circle before ushering the younger ones away to safety. Puddle approached Wolfe and me with brimming, watery eyes and hugged each of us in turn, as if silently acknowledging that this might be the last time we see one another.

Once they had all departed, the eleven of us turned our minds to creating some sort of plan. We sat close together at the head of that long banquet table, with the newspaper clippings I had brought with me, strewn between us.

Karmakaze was the first to speak. "If the Stalkers are coming after us in the waking world while we sleep, wouldn't it be better for us to wake up right now?"

"And do what exactly?" Harvest Gem replied, clearly unconvinced by the idea.

"We could run, or hide … I don't know. We could wake our parents, or call the Police even? We could do something, right?"

There was a half-hearted murmur of support at the prospect of getting grown-ups involved until Miss Dimity cut in.

"There's no way anyone would believe us. They'd think we just had a bad dream and would put us straight back to bed. Besides, who knows how far the Stalkers would go? They might even hurt our families just to get to us."

As the discussion continued, Steggie rose to her feet and

moved slowly around the table. She paused, standing behind each of the Elite in turn, and with both hands raised above them began reciting a series of strange words, in a language I had never heard before. As she did so, a turquoise light shone down from her hands, and within that light, tiny crystal flecks started to fall, settling upon each member's head and shoulders like a fine layer of glistening sequins. The change was immediately noticeable: each of them seeming to grow somehow, sitting a little straighter, radiating a new confidence and appearance of calm.

"It's the most powerful spell of protection that I know," Steggie said when she was finished, taking her seat once more. At that moment I almost said something, but she flashed a silencing glance at me, and so I obeyed, remaining deeply troubled by what I had noticed: that Steggie had not performed the spell upon herself. "Although," she continued rather sheepishly, "I have no way of knowing if it will be enough to shield you all back in the waking world."

Unfortunately, it was not long before we found out.

It was Lumen Chou who suddenly rose up from the table screaming in fright: "Something's got me, it's got my ankle!"

It happened in almost the exact same horrific way as it had with Everly Kitt. We were dragged around that rooftop platform as we clung to him; a chaos of panicked cries and chairs being knocked over as his body thrashed about wildly, suspended in the air as he began to disappear. Despite the combined efforts of all ten of us, we were not strong enough to stop it, and there was nothing to be done.

We were still panting, exhausted on the floor with our minds reeling from the devastating loss when Liquid Beat's whole body suddenly jerked violently away, his fingers clawing and desperately scrambling at the floorboards. Again we tried but failed to save him, and within minutes he had been taken from us too—the rapidly shrinking Inner Circle already down to only seven. It was a manner of attack we had failed to foresee, our concentration having been so focused on preparing to fight the Stalkers within the dream world. Now the Elite were paying the terrible price.

The tension was unbearable, like a row of lambs being led to the slaughter. Even worse though, as nobody knew who would be next.

"Has anyone got any ideas," Miss Dimity asked hesitantly, "how the Stalkers know exactly where we live? I mean, those details are and always have been kept a secret, known only to us."

"What exactly are you suggesting?" Harvest Gem asked in a tone that wasn't quite a question. "Surely you don't mean that one of us gave out that information? Has turned traitor?"

There was no need for Miss Dimity to answer. We all knew that was precisely what she was implying. Silent and suspicious glances were exchanged, as it dawned on everyone present that the guilty party, the person responsible for the killings, could be at that precise moment sitting right there among us. Looks of growing distrust multiplied, with everyone automatically becoming a potential suspect. I noticed Steggie take a few steps back, separating herself from the rest of us as the group's discussion rose into a clamorous melee of wild accusations. I remained quiet, watching and hoping to catch a glimmer of a guilty conscience reveal itself, although something in the back of my mind was telling me this wasn't right and that none of us was to blame.

Wolfe suddenly jumped up with a start, knocking over

his chair. I believe he must have seen Hammerhead looking dubiously at him, or even me, for the way he spoke was shocking: pure anger without any restraint.

"Don't you dare even think about pinning this on either of us!" he yelled, with both fists clenched and his cheeks flushed. "Everybody knows you've had it in for Zoofall from the start, and besides, as you keep reminding us *we're not even Elite*, so we don't even have that information!"

It was the first time I had ever seen Hammerhead at a loss for words. Quickly regaining his composure, he snarled at Wolfe then pushed his chair back, and began pacing around that platform in frustration, not wishing to sit still, doing nothing, for even one moment longer.

"This is ridiculous! We're wasting precious time and getting nowhere. It doesn't matter how they know, the fact of the matter is they do! This is not the moment for us to turn on one another. We need to stand together, as we've always done!" At those words, there was a general murmur of agreement, before Hammerhead continued. "And I, for one, do not want to sit here, just waiting to be next. I'd rather be awake and fight, and see what's coming!"

Karmakaze suggested a vote, one from which Wolfe and I were excluded because our physical bodies were not lying vulnerable back in the waking world. However, that didn't make either of us feel any safer. Sadly the result of the vote was divided, and this only led to further squabbling, until with some reluctance Steggie intervened.

"This must be a decision that each of us makes on our own. Right now. To stay here, or go back to the waking world. I will not influence anyone's decision, but I, for my part, have decided to stay."

So it was that the diminishing Inner Circle was divided once again. Of the seven remaining, only three decided to wake up, and they were Hammerhead, In-no-Scents, and Miss Dimity. Each had their own reason for going, but it was Miss Dimity's that I will never forget.

"I have to go," she said, her voice quivering with fear. "Trust me, I'd rather stay, but I just have to. My little brother sometimes climbs into bed with me when he's scared. I need to make sure that he's safe, kiss him goodbye and lock him in his own bedroom if I have to. I've got no desire to see what's coming for me … I'm shaking just at the thought of it."

"Then come straight back to us," Karmakaze interrupted, putting one hand gently on her shoulder, "once you know your brother's safe."

Miss Dimity nodded doubtfully, her eyes bravely fixed on his. "I'll try, I promise. I'm just worried that once I'm awake, there's no chance I'll be able to get back to sleep."

Before the three of them left, each fashioned a candle, which they then placed under glass domes on the table where they had been sitting. When each of them touched their candle's wick, a coloured flame was ignited, flickering gently, protected from the wind and synchronised to their individual heartbeat back in the waking world. We embraced them and said our farewells, wishing that it wouldn't be forever and that we would be seeing them again soon. Miss Dimity and Karmakaze seemed unwilling to let go of one another, as though there were still words left unsaid between them. Hammerhead patted me on the shoulder rather awkwardly, and for a second I thought his animosity had passed—until he opened his mouth.

"Just don't go doing anything stupid," he grumbled under

his breath, before turning away.

After they had gone, an almost choking silence settled upon us, which nobody seemed able or willing to break. The only movement up there in the Treetop summit was the sudden arrival of that familiar cluster of dragonflies. They caught my attention as they hovered in a line, facing us, before gently settling themselves down upon one of the railings. It reminded me of my vision from the other side of that mirror: those Stalkers hanging above the world, preparing to pounce. With great effort, I pushed that unpleasant memory from my mind. Refocusing on our current situation, I suddenly had an idea but resisted voicing it, because I wasn't even sure it could be done. Before I had even properly thought it through, I heard Steggie's voice inside my head, encouraging me.

"Go ahead, Zoofall, it might just work."

I cleared my throat to speak.

"Perhaps I could try to align myself with each of you—get inside your heads, and force you in your sleep to open your eyes? That way, if I were able to see through your eyes, I could find out if the coast was clear?"

It took some persuading, but of the four remaining Elite, Stax finally agreed to be my guinea pig. We sat facing one another fearfully. He closed his eyes, and I placed both palms upon his temples. Our breathing slowed, becoming shallow and almost as one. Through the darkness of my mind, the shift was subtle at first, my nose noticing something and striving for some form of clarity.

Intensely foreign smells, pungent spices and exotic fragrances invaded my nostrils and signalled that I had arrived. I thought I heard animals, not there in the room where I lay, but nearby, weary grunts and snorting accompanied by the faint hollow clang of cowbells. Stax's eyelids were heavy, as were the coarse layers of blankets under which he lay. They felt like pure pelts or animal hides as they rubbed against my skin. Before I succeeded in prying open his sleepy eyes, I had the distinct impression that wherever Stax lived in the waking world, it was a truly remote and wild terrain. It was very dark where he slept, so much so that at first, looking through his eyes, I saw nothing. Then gradually, my sight grew accustomed, picking out strange objects from my immediate surroundings.

Many things were hanging from carved beams above, glinting and swaying like superstitious and rustic pendulums. The room, from the little I could make out, seemed spherical and somehow alive, and it was only when I saw the wall closest to me shimmer and flap that I realised I must have been inside a tent of sorts, perhaps a wigwam or yurt.

My fascinated examination was cut short when I noticed vague shapes moving within the darkness. My terror was worsened by the fact that although I could see, my body—or rather his body—was like a block of cement, and I was unable to move a muscle. The shadows were circling and moving closer. I no longer wanted to see this, wanted to back away and hide but was helpless and trapped. Four figures slid from the gloom, closing in on all sides. Dark eyes all looking down at me ... at him. Their pale, expressionless faces were only masks of innocence, masks which gradually slipped the closer they got. Their gaunt and hollow cheeks clearly inhuman; their veins, flowing deep beneath that surface masquerading as a child's skin, were actually pulsating black. With immense effort, I pulled myself free and disconnected, back to the Treetop summit of the dream world.

Our foreheads were almost touching, and at the exact same instant, both our eyes blinked open. The threat was right there, like a dreadful premonition, it sparked and passed unspoken between the two of us. We both sensed it. With my hands still touching the sides of his face, I barely had time to gasp "Oh my God!" before it started.

His eyes darted desperately towards Steggie, then back to me. He had the wild look of a startled and cornered animal.

"They cannot be sto—" came the beginning of his scream, cut short, as he too was wrenched up into the air. All of us, including Steggie, grabbed hold of whatever part of him we could. Karmakaze and Wolfe, side by side, were straining and clinging to Stax's writhing torso. As our eyes met briefly, Wolfe shook his head in despair. Through all the heaving and contorted chaos, I saw Steggie holding his shoulder, kissing his forehead before whispering something softly in his ear.

Our cries of anguish sliced through the otherwise tranquil night as, up there in the Treetop summit, Stax was viciously devoured, slipping right through our very fingers and evaporating into dust. Not a single creature stirred in the forest below, as if they too sensed our hopelessness and loss. Just a simmering darkness, as silent as the grave.

The awful stillness which directly followed each attack was becoming increasingly difficult to bear. I was shaking and drained from channelling his sight, but very soon, our attention was redirected to a change in one of the candles.

It was the green flame of In-no-Scents, which had suddenly grown tall and thin for a moment, before shrinking and spluttering the next. The five of us watched, barely daring to breathe, as the symbolic battle represented in that single fragile flame ensued. Whatever was actually happening back in the waking world, the struggle didn't last long. That green flame was soon extinguished and in its place only a wispy thread of smoke that quickly vanished in the air.

We were miserable: broken by the *not-knowing*, and wallowing in the helplessness of waiting. It was Harvest Gem who finally managed to pull through it, stumbling upon what sounded like a brilliant idea.

"Couldn't Zoofall cross over? Straight into our bedrooms, wake us up, and carry us safely back here? Just as he's already done with Wolfe?" I saw a sparkle of hope in nearly everybody's eyes on hearing those words, but Steggie shook her head doubtfully.

"It would be far too dangerous. Besides, in order for someone to create a precise Inter-World portal, they need to have already visited the location. It's a limitation, just like the way we use windows to travel through the dream world: we can only go somewhere that we already know."

Harvest Gem looked disappointed by her words, chewing on his lip for a few moments, before re-opening his mouth, determined to reach a solution. But he never got a chance to share his idea, the Stalkers having reached his defenceless sleeping body. Before he had even been fully taken, while the four of us were still hanging on to his contorting body with all our might, Wolfe cried out, noticing that the sky-blue flame of Miss Dimity had also started to flicker. Her flame was being buffeted violently around inside that glass cover, as though exposed to repeated gusts of wind, and waning perilously low.

By the time that the last physical shred of Harvest Gem had dissolved through our fingers, her beautiful blue flame had also gone. Only one candle then remained lit upon that table, Hammerhead's, burning a fierce, fiery red. The ten members of the Inner Circle had been quickly whittled down to three, with only Steggie Belle and Karmakaze remaining up on that platform with Wolfe and I.

Karmakaze was the next to be taken from us. There was something in the way that it happened, with an unparalleled dignity well beyond his years, refusing to be broken, that impressed me very deeply. He broke the uneasy silence that had settled up there with a brave smile. I believe he had, at last, come to terms with the loss of Miss Dimity, and it was that acceptance which empowered him and set him free. He gave Wolfe a warm hug before approaching me.

"I'm guessing there's not much chance of you having visited the small town of Mullumbimby in Australia? That's where I'm from." I shook my head apologetically. "Never mind," he said, almost cheerfully, giving my shoulder a reassuring squeeze. "Don't give up on her, you hear? She'll need you now more than ever," he whispered softly in my ear, before moving on towards her. "You've given us more than we ever thought possible, and for me, it's always been a pleasure!"

I could see Steggie's eyes brimming with tears, as he bravely shook her hand before bidding us farewell. We stood and watched as Karmakaze strolled off casually down the length of that jetty, as though he hadn't a care in either world. When he reached the end, he looked back at the three of us with a smile still radiating warmth. He touched the totem of the owl, and remained there a minute, taking in the jungle vista one final time, then slowly levitated upwards, both hands wedged firmly in his pockets.

He didn't get very far before his feet began to vanish, as that diabolical, invisible force began trying to drag him back down. He fought it heroically, never crying out, not once, and soon he too was gone, swallowed by the night.

Without a word and with lowered heads, we returned to the banquet table, our worried eyes falling upon that last red candle, still burning strong.

"We can't just sit here waiting for them to find him. There's got to be a way for us to help!" I stated, after some miserable minutes had passed. Steggie shook her head once more.

"We can't, Zoofall. I'm afraid he's on his own."

Suddenly a fluttering movement to my left caught my eye. I heard the faintest buzzing sound as the insect approached, looping a wide arc around my head, before hovering for several seconds directly in front of my face, surveying me with its darkly obsidian and alien eyes. The dots began to connect in quick succession: the dragonfly; the game of Colour the Loser; the Rat's Tail.

My mind began whirring into life, and my excitement could not be contained.

"Where's Hammerhead from?"

"He's French," Wolfe replied distantly. "But you already knew that."

"But where exactly?" I insisted, turning to Steggie for an answer.

I saw her answer—the word inside her head—before her lips had even the chance to move and enthusiastically blurted my response.

"But ... I've been to Paris! I went there a few years ago with my parents. I can take us there!"

Steggie's expression changed ever so slightly, but for the first time that evening, I believe I glimpsed hope in her eyes. "It's going to be extremely dangerous," she warned, but I would not be dissuaded.

"Do you know his address?" I asked, and she nodded warily, though when she recited it to me, I realised I did not know the place. "I could make a crossing to the Eiffel Tower, or the Louvre?" I admitted, a little shamefully, "They're the only two places I can picture clearly." Steggie pondered that for a moment before replying.

"The Louvre. That'll be fine, I can lead the way from there. But we have to hurry, he hasn't got much time."

I immediately set to work constructing the portal, while Steggie explained to Wolfe why he would not be coming with us. She needed him for a job of the utmost importance: to stay behind and, should the two of us not return, to reassemble the remaining Freedivers in the mid-way point of the training caverns and to explain all that had happened, to guide them and keep them safe. Wolfe did not relish this new role and grunted his lukewarm agreement while scuffing the wooden boards in clear frustration.

Just as the portal was nearly completed, a terrible noise resonated through the entire Treetop summit. It was a burst of deep and menacing laughter, carried on the warm night wind and weaving its way up from the trees below, booming and echoing disturbingly in our ears. I didn't recognise the voice, but one look at Steggie left me with little doubt that she did, her complexion turning ash-white as though all the blood had drained straight from it.

"Oh, no," she mumbled. "Zoofall, we have to hurry!"

Without further delay, the two of us, hand in hand, launched ourselves through the Inter-World portal, back into the waking world, our destination: Paris.

The night was cold, and a fine, light rain was falling in sheets. The streetlights and the sparkling neon signs were reflected through the glittering puddles as we left the glass pyramid of the Louvre, which rose up bursting through the pavement like a crystal diamond.

"Follow me, quickly now," Steggie called as we dashed headlong down the slickly cobbled streets.

I noticed something peculiar, although at that moment there were more pressing things to worry about and so I never mentioned the matter. It was Steggie's appearance, as we raced through those empty streets under the Parisian moonlight. For, unlike me, who had reverted quite naturally to a waking world flesh and blood boy, she was still a gathered mist and vaporous form. I wondered as we ran whether this was because she had crossed over to the waking world as her "dream self" whereas I was returning with my physical self. Or was it perhaps a tactical decision on her part, a camouflage of sorts, to draw less attention and go unnoticed? I concluded that had to be the reason why and thought it best to follow suit, disguising myself immediately into a similar ethereal form.

I was glad she knew the way, as we continued further into that tangled, disorientating maze which shimmered in the darkness like some oil-slicked suburbia. When we reached the address, we saw a light still on in one of the uppermost windows and headed straight for it. Nothing could have prepared me for what we would see as we burst through Hammerhead's bedroom door.

One look and we thought we were already too late. A large amount of the furniture was overturned, disordered and out of place. In addition, there were more signs of a violent struggle, from long claw marks that had shredded the bed covers and carpet, to two contrasting blood patterns, which trailed and sprayed their angles and paths across the walls. I say two types of blood, but in truth, at that moment, I was only guessing as to the second. Instantly we recognised the thick, dripping dark red blood as being human. The other liquid, however, smeared across the room, though roughly the same consistency, was more glossy and jet black in colour, reminding me of octopus ink.

We were so horrified by that brutal scene that at first we almost didn't spot Hammerhead lying face down upon the floor. It was when he suddenly moved, letting out a pained groan, that Steggie and I saw him, or more accurately, what was left of him. I was paralysed by fear as I stared at what had caused his body to move.

Four Stalkers were in the process of heaving and pulling Hammerhead, who appeared to be barely conscious, away. They were on the other side of a portal, gripping him by the ankles and lower legs, dragging him across the floor and back through his bedroom mirror. They had already managed to get Hammerhead's lower body, just above his waist, through. Another few seconds and he would have been completely gone. Over-riding our terror, Steggie and I launched into action.

I skidded across the room towards him, grasping him by the wrists and levering myself backwards with all my strength, off the bedroom wall. As he looked up, I saw a glimmer of recognition in Hammerhead's confused eyes. He was badly wounded, and the Stalkers were not loosening their vice-like grip, roughly yanking him further into the mirror. Steggie planted her feet firmly on either side of us, positioning herself barely a foot from the portal, both hands clasped tightly across her chest.

I was uncertain what she was planning to do, as it was very probable her powers were restricted now that we had exited the dream world. As she stood there over us, I desperately tried to think if any of the abilities that I had learnt to master between both worlds could be used. We needed to close the portal, but couldn't begin the process, not with Hammerhead's body stuck in the middle crossing both worlds, for that would most certainly have killed him. It was then that, quite to my surprise, my efforts of straining with brute force seemed to pay off, as I managed to pull Hammerhead's body several inches back through the mirror. Glancing up, my satisfaction soon turned to horror as I realised why.

Two of the Stalkers had released their hold on his legs. One was advancing inch by inch towards the portal, towards me, staring me down menacingly with those lifeless, hollow black eyes. The other had risen to his feet and raised both arms before lowering them in a smooth downwards arc. Like a guillotine in slow motion, he was starting to close the portal. I tugged even more frantically, crying out in desperate exertion, as from the corner of my eye I saw Steggie step forward. She had apparently been waiting for such a moment.

In a flash, she thrust both arms through the mirror. As her palms opened a scorching ball of fire shot out and struck the Stalker who was attempting to close the portal squarely in the chest. The energy she had unleashed knocked him clean off his feet, that oozing, dark and glossy squid-like blood flying from him in all directions as he fell. He did not get back up. In her left hand, she fashioned a barbed and flaming javelin and, with a sweeping movement, hurled it down at the Stalker still crawling towards me, pinning him to the ground.

Steggie drew her hands back through the mirror just in time, as the one she had impaled lashed out furiously at her. The skin on his forearms had peeled back to reveal long, spine covered claws that jabbed and swung towards the opening, reminding me that they were definitely not real children. There rose from those three Stalkers a dreadful howling shriek, and out of the furthest shadowy background on the other side of that portal, more nightmarish shapes emerged.

Dozens more were coming to the Stalkers' aid, and behind them, towering confidently above them, a tall, dark figure approached as well. As the horde reached the portal, a terrifying, screeching chaos ensued. A swirling mass of monstrous claws, some simply tearing, some sinking deep into Hammerhead's legs like fish hooks, while the rest were lashing out viciously through the mirror at us. I felt petrified as I lay there, refusing to release my grip on him while dodging their swiping blows

I heard Steggie pleading inside my head, *"Keep pulling, we can still save him, don't let go!"* as she continued to lunge forwards through the mirror, repeating her attacks. I heard Hammerhead shouting the opposite at me, ordering me to let him go and get Steggie out of there. All the while, those Black-Eyed Children were invading my mind. I felt a cold prickling of fear as I realised what they were trying to do. The increasing pressure of their hypnotically luring voices was becoming unbearable. My head was pounding with their sinister cries. I locked eyes with the nearest Stalker as he strained and tore against the spear that held him down, whispering over and over inside my mind:

"Come with us …be one of us, brother!"

At one point, I had managed to pull Hammerhead so far back into the bedroom that only what was below his knees remained on the other side. Then the tide turned. Despite all of Steggie's valiant efforts, bombarding the Stalkers' reinforcements with all manner of deadly missiles, they had finally swarmed upon the portal. Suddenly a dozen more of them latched onto Hammerhead's lower legs, their combined strength heaving him back through. It was useless: there were just too many of them.

Each time Steggie thrust her arms through to launch another devastating assault, a barrage of those vicious claws and hands swiped at her, trying to grab a hold. To make matters worse, Hammerhead was actively trying to force himself free of my grip. That bellowing, spiteful laughter returned, the very same which we had heard back in the Treetop summit, although it was much closer now, coming from the dark figure standing tall among the Stalkers.

"Simeon!" I heard Steggie hiss through tightly clenched teeth.

Hammerhead looked up at me once more, with desperation in his eyes.

"I was wrong about you, Zoofall. But you know you have to let me go!" he groaned, managing to squirm one wrist free from my grasp. "Protect her! Keep her safe!" Before I saw it coming, he swung that clenched fist with all his remaining strength, striking me straight in the jaw.

"No!" Steggie screamed as I fell back to the floor, and the Stalkers dragged him through. For a moment we could only stare, traumatised, as that swarm of merciless Stalkers descended upon him, savagely tearing him apart.

That ominous figure took one more step forward into the light. It was my first clear view of Simeon Scythe. He looked to be a few years older than me, taller and with muscular arms and shoulders, his skin tanned and weathered, his features pointed, his eyes a deep and glowing shade of green. Now that we were face to face, I felt afraid: intimidated to be in the presence of a more advanced Shifter. His laughter stopped, his lips coming together and then retracting into a shrinking devious sneer until they were tightly pursed in anger. When he spoke, his words rang out with deep, unbridled hatred.

"So, it has finally come to this, Steggie Belle. I warned you all that this day would come. A day of retribution, when I would return and re-balance the scales." His gaze suddenly fell upon me, his voice changing to a sarcastic, mocking tone. "And who might this be? A novice Shifter. I see … very good," he chuckled before turning back to Steggie. "So, you tried to replace me, huh? You always were pathetic. Well, I'm sure I'll find some use for him once all this is done. I guess the biggest question is, are you going to bow down and give up quietly? Now that your ridiculous Inner Circle has gone? You know, it's not too late for you to join me Steggie."

Much to my shock and dismay, with her head hung low in defeat, she shuffled towards the mirror.

"Steggie don't! You can't! Think of the other Freedivers!" I implored her telepathically, but her reply came low, lacking any trace of her usual confidence.

"It's over, Zoofall. I have no choice. I'm doing this for them."

To my alarm, Simeon Scythe's voice broke into what I had thought until then was our private communication. *"That's right. Listen to your fearless leader. You'd be wise to stay out of this and keep*

your thoughts to yourself!"

Miserably I watched as Steggie slowly stepped through the mirror, returning to her physical, visible form as she did so, to stand humbly before him. It was only then that I saw between her hands, clasped submissively behind her back, the jagged shape of a lightning bolt beginning to grow. What happened next was so extremely fast that, had I blinked, I would have missed it.

She threw that godly weapon with such venom that it caught our mutual enemy momentarily off-guard. But his reaction was quick too, turning his head away just enough to avoid it hitting him directly in the face, though not quite fast enough to escape unscathed, the lightning burning its path along his cheek as it sailed past. By the time he had raised one hand to the freshly bleeding wound, Steggie had already dived back through, spinning around to try to close the portal behind her, with me jumping up by her side to help.

Simeon Scythe's shock soon turned to rage as, through gritted teeth and with a wave of his hand, he roared, "So be it!" Every one of those Black-Eyed Children charged at the rapidly closing portal, getting to it fast enough to grip the edges and, through their great numbers, force it back open.

"We've got to get it closed!" Steggie cried out, as the hole gradually began to expand.

"I have a plan," I shouted, turning and running back out of the bedroom. I heard Simeon's bitterly ridiculing voice ringing out through peals of laughter.

"That's a brave one you've got there, Steggie! Ran off and abandoned you like a coward!"

Closely followed by Steggie's desperate voice calling after me, "Hurry, Zoofall! I can't hold it by myself much longer!"

In the darkened hallway, I ripped the large mirror I had seen earlier off of the wall and raced back to the bedroom, awkwardly carrying it with me. Carefully, I slid it across the surface of the other mirror, but not the way that Steggie had expected, so that both mirrored surfaces were facing, pressed tightly against one another.

"That's the wrong way, Zoofall," she yelled. "We won't be able to escape through it like that!"

"Trust me," I replied, secretly hoping that I knew what I was doing, and praying that it would work. Simeon Scythe could still be heard laughing hysterically at what he saw as my sheer incompetence. I tried to ignore him, leaning all my weight against the back of that second mirror and focusing with all my might. It was then that I noticed that the two of them were not exactly the same size. The one I had retrieved from the hallway was a fraction smaller, which would mean disastrous consequences if the Stalkers were able to reopen the portal to its full size. It was too late to do anything about that now, so I just kept going, filling my mind with only one memory, one location: The Wall of Fuse-and-Flux.

As I felt that second Inter-World portal start to form, I strained against the pressure, while the Stalkers on the other side tried to push a gap between the two mirrors. I heard Steggie struggling, breathing hard as, to my horror, I saw the first set of bony fingers protrude past the edges of that first portal, curling themselves around the mirror I was holding.

"I can't keep this up much longer!" Steggie shouted, as more and more hands squeezed their way through the gaps around the edges and began to push. I could feel my feet start to slip, inch by awful inch, backwards across the surface of the carpet. I groaned under the increasing pressure and weight, as the faint sound I had been hoping for reached my ears. Steggie had heard it too and almost smiled as she realised what I was doing.

What started as a slight vibration, rose into a steady rumble and then a heavy pounding, which grew louder with every passing second, becoming a thunderous stampede of the Wokhala. The roar as they closed in on that portal was deafening—just like when they had charged down Steggie and Euryale. The only thing Steggie's earlier story hadn't portrayed was their smell: such a foul and noxious odour, like some awful concoction of stale sweat, rotten eggs and wet dog. Steggie joined me, fixing her palms next to mine for extra support as we tried in those final moments to keep the second mirror in place.

The Stalkers must have caught sight of what we couldn't see: their wild shrieking started up again, and they clawed frantically at the frame as they tried to push the two facing portals apart. We could feel the whole thing shaking violently as those monstrous creatures reached our mirror, working themselves into a frenzy at the chance to break through into the waking world. But by holding the two together however, there was nowhere for the Wokhala to go. They crashed back through the original portal, trampling down the Stalkers with their speed and momentum. We could no longer hear Simeon Scythe's maniacal laughter.

There was no more resistance from the Stalkers, who had either been trampled down or forced back from the two mirrors, so we hurriedly sealed both portals and, totally exhausted, I lowered the second mirror gently to the floor.

Suddenly a new sound echoed through the building: an anxious, human voice, calling out what I guessed must have been Hammerhead's waking world name, and then the sounds of footsteps quickly climbing the stairs. Steggie made a window back to the Treetop summit, and we got out of there as fast as we could.

To escape unnoticed, we were forced to leave behind what would come to be infamously known, by the French police and international media, as the most bizarre crime scene they had ever seen. A mystery which they would later conclude must have been a violent kidnapping of some kind. It is a case which still remains unsolved to this very day.

I can only imagine the agonising wait that Wolfe had been forced to endure all alone up there on that platform, awaiting our safe return. With all that has happened since—looking back—I think it's safe to say that he was never quite the same after that night. Though his relief was obvious, it was fused with sadness too, having watched powerless as that red flame upon the table had finally lost its fight. It was a subdued and far from victorious return, and after some moments our gaze turned with great concern to Steggie, the last surviving member of the Elite.

She told us she needed to be alone for a while, embracing us each in turn for what we were both afraid could be the very last time. She wandered off down that ancient jetty, just as Karmakaze had done, and sat cross-legged at its furthest end, looking out into the darkness, a forlorn and lonely figure. All Wolfe and I could do was wait and watch from a distance, not sure whether she would be next, and disappear like the others into that black and empty sky. For over an hour she stayed there, in silent contemplation, meditating or perhaps planning her next move.

In a low voice, I filled Wolfe in on what had happened in Paris, but despite his shock and dismay at hearing my account, he hardly showed any emotion or managed to ask any further questions. The trauma of the whole evening had left both of us feeling hollow, and physically drained by our ongoing worries over Steggie.

Our hearts were lifted as she finally rose onto her feet, walking determinedly back towards us. She was already speaking as she approached us, her voice infused with a fresh resilience.

"Once we secure the Treetop city, we must summon the remaining Freedivers and return to the training caverns." Simultaneously we both breathed a sigh of relief as—wrapped up in those words—we recognised the defiance in her voice that we had grown to love. Steggie Belle, our leader, was back, and the three of us quickly set to work.

Although the Treetop summit, was well known to be heavily protected, a safe haven for dreamers like us, Steggie insisted we must be prepared for quite literally anything. We set up a thorough series of hidden alarms all over that lofty wooden city, laying invisible tripwires across the entire area, which would alert us should any uninvited guest set foot within that sacred place.

Once we were finished, Steggie told us to brace ourselves— the mental equivalent of covering our ears—as she prepared to issue the summoning. We did so, concentrating on blocking everything out. Still, even so, the volume of her call was excruciating as it rippled forth from our dream world sanctuary, crossing an incredible range. Soon after the summoning was complete Freedivers began appearing, all eager for news but afraid of what they would hear. Perhaps some had been reluctant to return, but it was an assembly which every member was compelled to attend. Under Steggie's instructions, we took a window back to the training caverns, leaving that usually festive and lively home of ours, eerily silent and still.

When all of the Omnivagas had settled there, Wolfe and I weaved our way among them. We lit as many wooden torches and hanging lanterns as we could on the surrounding stone archways, before positioning ourselves at the very back of the crowd, apprehensively waiting for Steggie to speak.

It was a story she had to tell: was forced to face. And yet those wounds were still so very raw and fresh, that I believe I almost heard her heart breaking, her soul weeping with every word she spoke. She gave a full and honest account of all that had happened. The sacrifices and the bravery, and of the person we had learnt was behind it all. It was with great bitterness and sorrow that she explained how the Inner Circle had been so cruelly wiped out.

There were, as one might expect, many reactions among the Freedivers. While Steggie was talking, most of the crowd's responses were restrained and held in check, but once her tale had been concluded and the cold, harshness of reality had sunk in, the general mood began to shift dramatically. From where we stood, Wolfe and I could feel the atmosphere start to turn.

A surge of overwhelming fear had been set loose, and it swept like a disease through those seated rows. Worried whispers ran wild, infecting every ear. I glanced nervously over at Steggie, and amid those rippling waves of discord, as on so many other occasions, her calm expression seemed to say it all— that somehow she had already known or foreseen this outcome. Her gentle words only confirmed that suspicion, as they found their way inside my head. *"It will be alright, Zoofall. This was inevitable."*

For several minutes she remained quiet, allowing ample time for doubt to spread its contagious course among those gathered, before continuing with her announcement.

"In a short while, I will take my seat and give the floor over to anyone who wants to speak. For there are a lot of things that need to be considered, and our time is short. First, allow me to tell you all of a decision that I have made, as the only remaining member of the Elite. From this moment on, there will be no more individual rankings. For this, I have my reasons, but I would ask you all to keep in mind the position and ranking you previously held, as it should weigh heavily on the decision that every one of you soon must make.

"It is, and always has been, a question of free will. From the moment you joined us and became a member of the Freedivers, there has always been a choice. And the choice you now face could not be more crucial or important.

"I will not lie to you. Many dangers lie ahead, and there is a great deal still to do. Our enemies and their plans are still largely a mystery, a threat that we have learnt tonight must not be underestimated. It has been my honour to lead and to walk among you, and you have my word that nobody will be judged for walking away at this point.

"Above all, you will always be my family. But make no mistake, a war is no longer just on the horizon, it's already at our door. Right now, dreamers are not enough, not what we need. I need Dream Warriors."

With those final words, Steggie sat down and closed her eyes, taking in the silence of the cavern, and waited. She didn't have to wait long. Wolfe and I cast a worried look at one another, both sensing where this was likely to be headed. The terror that had crystallised in every Freediver's heart had settled over the room like a dense and heavy cloud. Perhaps all that had been lacking up until then was a mouthpiece. A voice of reason to unite the wavering thoughts that so many there were harbouring.

Miss Avant finally rose to her feet and made her way to the front to address the crowd. She was another highly accomplished Freediver, whom I vaguely recalled sitting next to at my first welcoming banquet; but truth be told, I had had little interaction with her since.

"This won't be good," Wolfe whispered quietly in my ear. "She's got a sharp mind, and an even sharper tongue."

Miss Avant was one of the eldest members present, having worked her way up to #11. Had the Inner Circle been expanded to include twelve members before that night, as had been previously planned, she might well have ended up a target, and not been there to make a speech. She was widely respected, not only for her impressive knowledge but also for her responsible and sensible advice.

"Friends, family, Freedivers. I, like all of you, am both shocked and frightened by this truly devastating news. I share your worries and concerns. I do not doubt that what this situation right now needs is heroes, but I have decided this evening to speak of common sense.

"I, like you all, have nothing but love and profound respect for Steggie Belle, and everything it means to be an Omnivaga. This world that she has shown us and helped us to explore is indeed a magical one, but it is also a very dangerous one. A world full of incredibly powerful tribes, clans and species. Though we as Freedivers are powerful too in our own right, the reality is that we are still only children. And the unavoidable truth is that this is not our fight.

"It would be wise, in my opinion, for us to step back, allow the stronger forces to deal with this dreadful threat. Let the Coven of the North and their associates take up arms and tackle this evil uprising. There are many groups far better suited to take on this challenge. Not us. Remember, when your time comes to decide, who it is exactly that we are."

I was distracted then by a growing number of timid responses, low mutterings which echoed throughout the training cavern. Looking from left to right, I saw many of the Freedivers nodding along wholeheartedly to her words.

"We have lives, families and responsibilities back in the waking world. We must not forget that. I, for one, will never forget the Elite, but that Inner Circle was made up of our bravest, our very strongest. They were the most advanced, and the very best among us. Now they are all gone except for Steggie. Not even they were able to counter this dark army. What hope could we possibly have?

"I'm sorry, Steggie. I truly am, but this is the point where logic tells me it is both safe and sensible to part ways. Goodbye, dear friend, and good luck."

Much to our dismay, we saw Steggie actually nodding along with what was being said. Then, when Miss Avant had finished speaking, Steggie Belle opened her eyes, rose to her feet with a warm smile, and embraced her with a heartfelt farewell. Miss Avant, with a tear in her eye, and a fond wave to the rest of us, then turned away and retreated, heading for the foot of that spiral stone staircase. The same staircase which nearly every

Freediver—at some point in their past—had crept down, filled with such curiosity.

I cannot say for sure whether those heartfelt words of hers were wholly to blame for what happened next. If it hadn't been Miss Avant, perhaps another would have taken her place to speak, and tipped the scales of influence. Regardless, what followed over that next hour can only be described as an exodus, an awful domino effect as, one by one, a mass leaving commenced. In many cases, indecision buckled to doubt, which naturally and in due course led to abandonment. Children walking away from their dreams.

It was in the middle of all this, as the Freedivers numbers were continuously declining, that we heard it: an awful sound, one which meant absolutely nothing to most of those still present but sent a chill right through the three of us. It was the sound of the hidden alarms back in the Treetop summit being tripped.

We put on a brave face and swallowed down our fears. We told the scattered number still remaining that we had to go and check on something and that we would be right back. I remember their blank expressions, their looks of bewilderment and confusion, as we wandered off deeper into the shadows, rustling up whatever courage we could muster. I wondered how many of them would still be waiting in that cavern when, or rather if, we returned.

Once we were out of sight, we paused, looking at one another as though silently saying our own goodbyes should it go terribly wrong. Wolfe attempted to make a joke in the hope of lightening the mood, though Steggie and I found our mouths too dry and our throats too tense to summon even the smallest laugh.

We suited up from head to toe, creating floating sections of thick metallic armour which we attached to our own bodies: the kind that, in the waking world would have been cumbersome, but here weighed no more than a feather. I found my hands shaking with trepidation as we got ready to make a window. Just before we went through, I took a moment to ask Steggie Belle one final question.

"Is there anything else you know? Any other way we could fight the Stalkers?"

"I've only heard a rumour," she said. "But there's no way for us to know how reliable it might be, or if there's any truth to it at all. But someone once claimed that the Stalkers have only two real weaknesses, two things they truly fear: fire, and love."

Wolfe snorted in disgust.

"Fat chance they're going to be getting a hug from me!"

Then the three of us, standing shoulder to shoulder, edged cautiously through the window, back to the Treetop summit. All gripping our weapons tightly and holding them out before us, as we advanced into the shadows. Weapons which, with a nod from Steggie, all ignited into sudden and scorching brilliance. Flames that curled and licked hungrily at the surrounding night, as we closed the portal behind us.

17

The Only Circle

We crept up the spiral staircase towards the Treetop summit, careful to avoid not only our own hidden tripwires but also any creaking floorboards which might give away our position. I was guarding the rear, in case anything should try to sneak up behind us, as we continued up the winding stairs in single file. A part of me was sure that, at any moment, the scars on my arm would start to itch and burn.

Steggie was in the lead and paused as she reached the top, poking her head out carefully to look around the upper platform. There was no noise at all—suspiciously so—and yet the air felt strangely charged, alive with the sensation of impending doom. I imagined that I heard the sound of a distant drum, before realising, it was my own heartbeat. We raised ourselves up onto the platform, wielding our fiery weapons on high. The shadows danced around us, the darkness keeping its distance from the flames and giving the impression of diabolical shapes swaying and lurking in its depths.

"Maybe, whoever it was, has already left?" I suggested quietly.

"For all we know, they could be invisible," came Wolfe's

strained and fearful reply.

Steggie straightened, tilting her head as though she had heard something that we had both missed. She then took a hesitant step backwards, positioning herself beside Wolfe and me, her voice firm but barely audible.

"We're not alone up here!"

Her gaze was fixed on the darkness ahead of us, and I followed it closely, making out the closest corner of the banquet table. I could see nothing, no sign of life: the platform appearing empty. Instinctively I whirled around, back towards the spiral staircase, paranoid of what might be behind me. Still nothing.

Wolfe flinched, grabbing hold of my arm. "Something's moving … over there." He whispered and guided me with his trembling finger, pointing towards what he had seen. The three of us moved guardedly as one, treading lightly on our tiptoes in that direction.

An intruder was squatting on the far end of the banquet table. It had its back to us and its head down, busying itself with something blocked from our view. As we approached cautiously, its small furry ears pricked up, and the creature turned to face us. It was no larger than a kitten, and at first glance closely resembled an average squirrel, except for the flaps of extra skin which dangled loosely from its wrists, down the length of its body towards its ankles. A flying squirrel, I thought to myself.

Yet it had a certain awareness that suggested there was more to it than met the eye. The nut that it had been munching on was still cradled between those tiny paws. The animal froze, guiltily releasing the nut which then rolled off the table and onto the floor. Then the most extraordinary thing happened. It reared up onto its hind legs, appraising the three of us quite intelligently before, with one delicate little arm sweeping out in front very graciously, it lowered its head into a respectful bow.

The three of us stood there stupefied, feeling more than just a little ridiculous with our flaming weapons still held high. Perhaps it was the sum of that night's prior, horrible events, or simply that his nerves got the best of him. Whatever the reason, Wolfe leapt forward towards the table, brandishing his fiery club threateningly, despite us sensing no danger from that harmless, oddly courteous, little creature.

The flying squirrel seemed genuinely shocked by Wolfe's aggressive behaviour, taking a quick step back on those spindly, furry little legs. Then, with the utmost calm, its cute little button of a snout began to swell, elongating speedily until it was well over twenty times the length of the squirrel's entire body. Before Wolfe had time to react or even register what was then directly facing him, the grand, curving elephant's trunk had already sprayed a powerful jet of water, drenching him from head to toe and extinguishing his flaming weapon.

With flailing arms, he stumbled sideways to avoid the continuous torrent of water, knocking into the side of the table, losing his balance, and landing sprawled out on top of it. His morphing *squirr-e-lephant* attacker was far from done. Just as quickly as the large trunk had grown, it shrunk again. Then, in a whirl of fur, the animal mutated once more. In the blink of an eye, I saw a black and white, feline shaped body bounding along the tabletop towards my very confused and disorientated friend. As it drew closer, the skunk turned itself around and with a swift raise of its tail, covered Wolfe with its defensive misty stench before scampering away, dropping off the other side of the table and out of sight.

In shock, Wolfe fell off the table, retching from the horrendous smell that clung to his skin, scrambling blindly along the floor and feeling around for the weapon he had dropped. What grew up from behind the table, rising quickly until it stood over eight feet tall, made my eyes bulge and my mouth drop wide open, as I realised exactly what our mysterious visitor was.

The body was lean and muscular, covered in coarse and dark grey hair. Its eyes were wild and intense, and yet despite the powerful fangs and razor-sharp claws, it had a kind and almost serene expression upon its face. The wolf-man leapt nimbly onto and over the table, approaching Wolfe silently from behind. It was only when his great, dark shadow fell upon our fallen friend that Wolfe turned and froze.

The creature leant towards him, extending one arm down with those fearful claws. Wolfe's terrified mouth began to stretch wide open, a slow-motion prelude to a scream. The piercing sound however never escaped his lips for, in the next instant, that towering animal smoothly transformed into a pleasant and peaceful looking young man, whose outstretched hand gently helped Wolfe up onto his feet. That was how the three of us first became acquainted with one of the phenomenal Loup Garou.

"We're sorry for our friend's misreading of the situation," Steggie began as we stepped forward to greet the young man. "We've been through a terrible ordeal tonight, and are all a bit shaken because of it. We didn't mean to alarm or offend you."

"My dear, it is I who must apologise." the man replied. "Your young friend here was merely trying to defend his home, hardly a crime worthy of being 'skunked' in such an undignified manner." Then, turning to Wolfe, he bowed sincerely. "Please, forgive me, sir."

His words were soft and humble, and his whole presence radiated a sense of pure and natural wisdom. He introduced himself to us with his birth name, Hohnihohkaiyohos, an almost unpronounceable mouthful, but informed us that most of his friends simply called him Kai for short. He then announced that he had been sent there on behalf of his clan. To deliver a response to Steggie's request for an audience with their counsel Elders.

Steggie explained what had befallen the Freedivers, and asked permission, under the circumstances, whether our reduced numbers would be able to travel to the upcoming meeting as a group together.

"Of course, young lady," he replied graciously. "You will all be welcomed into the sanctity of our Hive, and while you talk with our Elders, your other members will be fed and kept safe. On that, you have my word."

Despite Wolfe's slightly awkward initial introduction, by the end of it, Kai seemed deeply fond of the three of us, as though he respected our outlook and positivity, even in the face of such untold dangers. I also heard him joking with Wolfe, saying he admired his bravery, confiding in him that he had rarely met a human with enough spirit and pluck to take on one of the Loup Garou in single combat.

Before he left, he gave us directions to The Wilderness Crossroads, a location that, of the three of us, only Steggie knew. From there, rather cryptically, he instructed us to follow the fireflies until we found the mountain nest, and that our appointment had been scheduled for sundown the following evening. He departed in elegant style, transforming back into the form of that harmless little squirrel and scampering off to perch up on top of the railings. Once there, he lifted those tiny paws up and outwards, stretching out the fine, leathery flaps of skin, before plunging and gliding off into the night with silent grace. We watched until he had disappeared into the darkened canopy below, and then Steggie turned to us.

"We'd better be getting back to the others, they'll be wondering what happened to us."

Upon returning to the training cavern, my hopes were crushed as we stood there, scanning the vast and empty space. We had been gone for less than an hour, but the place was deserted. The torches and lanterns we had lit around where the assembly had been held were all still burning strong. Yet there was not a single Freediver in sight. Wolfe's utter disbelief summed up exactly what was running through my mind:

"I knew things were looking bad, but seriously? Not even one of them decided to stay!"

I noticed Steggie was smiling, but for the life of me could not work out why, until a bashful, disembodied voice responded.

"We, erm, we weren't sure when you'd be coming back, so we thought we'd spend the time practising our camouflage techniques." The voice sounded apologetic and familiar, even though the owner was still nowhere to be seen. Then a leg slowly materialised from one of the nearby stone pillars, then another, and another, and many more.

"So, where did the three of you go anyway?" another voice chipped in over to our right, as figures began emerging all around us.

"And what on Earth happened to you, Wolfe?" enquired someone else. Wolfe could only laugh, shaking his head regretfully to that question as, to be fair, he did look like a soppy sodden mess. As though he had just taken a long shower with all his clothes on. And the smell: the smell was unbelievable. Suffice to say that, as we were happily reunited with that group of loyal Omnivagas he received no warm embraces, everyone giving him a wide berth while covering their noses.

I counted eighteen in total which, including us, made a total of twenty-one brave dreamers who had chosen to stay. I was glad to recognise many of them, Freedivers with whom I had shared many great adventures in the past.

Most of them had been high-ranked Freedivers, experienced and powerful, although there were a few exceptions. In fact, there was only one person within the group who had not been personally ranked within the top one hundred: a rather red-faced, nervous, yet courageous Puddle. Once the brief celebrations had run their course, Steggie informed them where the three of us had gone, and what we had encountered. Meanwhile, Wolfe sat some distance from the rest, furiously scrubbing his body clean in the hope of getting the stink off his skin.

The twenty-one of us talked well into the night, pitching up a honeycomb network of hammocks between the pillars, upon which we reclined, weightlessly swinging in the hopes of getting some well-needed rest. Knowing that the next day would be a fascinating and possibly dangerous one. Feeling gratefully uplifted deep in our hearts that, although our numbers had been significantly reduced and were small, the Only Circle of Freedivers had already been formed.

By late afternoon, as the distant sun was taking its final bow towards the horizon, we arrived at the dusty, windswept crossroads, pausing to examine those desolate surroundings. Steggie was positive that this was the place, and so we waited for the fireflies. There were no obvious signposts where the roads crossed over one another; there were, however, several waist-high towers of loose pebbles stacked precariously, each displaying strange rune-like markings upon their rounded surfaces. They cast lengthy shadows across the dry soil, an ever-growing darkness as twilight crept in. We touched nothing.

In every direction barren plains led away into patches of scrubland, which could very easily have concealed swampy bogs, capable of trapping and sucking down any unlucky traveller. With the receding daylight, we finally saw it: a faint fluorescent flickering, a luminescent dance of yellow-green through the air, in and out from among a nearby clump of brambles. We followed that trail of tiny fireflies with excitement as they set a zigzagging course across the wilderness, putting our faith in the fact that those winged lantern sparks would guide us to safety.

Onwards we went as darkness began to fall, and those natural daylight noises, now unseen, took on unsettling undertones. The wind whistled sharply past our ears, carrying the occasional gaseous, bubbling squelches from those surrounding deadly bogs, reminding us all to watch our step.

It was then that a wholly different sound reached us. From somewhere out there in the dark came a high-pitched distant scream. Then the long, drawn-out wailing of a child calling to anyone that could hear. A despairing plea, asking if anyone was there and could help, that they were lost. The scars on my arm began to tingle. The fireflies started swirling crazily around us, confirming the imminent danger and signalling us to hurry, before shooting off into the night. We raced after them, crashing through the brambles and undergrowth, our path climbing towards a distant hilltop mound silhouetted against the sky.

We were breathless by the time we reached it and immediately set to scrambling hastily up its rugged sides. I became aware of several small creatures poking out their inquisitive heads from the ridge above. Clambering up over the top, I realised they were meerkats, a line of stealthy sentries deliberately positioned to guard that place.

The top platform where we had arrived was circular and sunken, about twenty-five feet wide. Its rounded sides were built up from layer upon layer of twigs and small branches, packed tightly with dried mud and sloping down towards its centre. It took a few seconds, panting and looking from side to side before I realised what it resembled: a giant bird's nest of sorts, except that right down at its centre was a pitch-black hole.

The fireflies were still there with us: they started rapidly circling that opening until it was almost a fluid, hazy glowing ring. It was the meerkats then who approached that centre edge, turning back to face our group and, using uncannily human and earnest gestures, beckoned us over, urgently pointing their little paws downwards. I thought I understood, although, under normal circumstances, no amount of bribery would have convinced me to jump blindly into its dark depths, but right then, we knew we were being hunted. We obeyed. Dropping one by one through the hole, with the meerkats following close behind.

The fall was not too great and the landing soft, like a bedding of straw or grass and feathers. We huddled together, looking up through the hole at the stars and moonlit sky. The fireflies broke their tight formation and raced off out of sight and away from that entrance.

One of the meerkats transformed into a human figure I instantly recognised as Kai. He nodded and smiled warmly at each of us, before raising both arms up towards the night. Shortly there came a gurgling, rushing sound as, much to our amazement, the top of that hole began to fill with water. Defying gravity, it hung right there above our heads, a shimmering lake-like ceiling, as outside, the giant nest quickly filled with water.

"Where are those fireflies headed? Will it be safe for them out there?" Steggie asked Kai, who was standing between the two of us. He looked down at the pair of us, winking reassuringly before whispering his reply.

"Do not worry; they are Loup Garou, too. It was their job to lead you to this place, and now they are the distraction needed to lead those things away. When it is safe, they shall return."

Not more than two minutes went by, in which time the large volume of water suspended above us settled and became still, stirred only by the outside breeze. It reflected flickering spectral hues of deep and rippling blues down upon us as we waited in the shadows. Then we saw movement.

Skulking, swaying in an almost reptilian manner, the Stalkers came into view, creeping their way along the ridgetop. Every one of us held our breath. There were many of them, and they paused menacingly in a line by the water's edge. Although they were only dark, reflected outline shapes to us, we could tell exactly what they were doing. They were searching for our scent. One of them knelt down, studying that stagnant surface, thrusting one arm in, either simply to check that it was real or feeling around to get an idea of how deep it was. That pale arm moved and twisted, grasping in vain to find the bottom. Doing so disturbed the water, creating grotesque and ghastly distortions of an unbalanced world outside, which made me feel queasy and want to grab hold of something solid.

Suddenly the hand was withdrawn, all of them rising together and turning westwards, as though they had heard something or caught a glimpse of movement way off in the distance. Then, as quickly as they had arrived, they were gone, and the dizzying water returned to its glassy state of calm.

When Kai was satisfied that the coast was clear, he walked over to one side of that earthen pit we were in, gesturing for us to follow. He then lifted what appeared to be a muddy wall mingled with tangled roots and other debris, which was, in fact, a marvellously well camouflaged and heavy curtain. Pulling it to one side revealed a dimly lamp-lit mining tunnel that curved away out of sight, winding its way deeper into the hillside. His meerkat companions all scurried through, and it was only from their departing shadows, thrown back towards us against the uneven tunnel walls, that we saw their shapes transform and grow. He looked back at us with an enthusiastic grin before instructing us to follow.

Their home, which they referred to as "The Hive", was— without doubt—one of the most spectacular things I have ever seen, laid out as a steady transformation in its own right the further we ventured in. From the unassuming bird's nest entrance with all its feral and wild ornamentation, our surroundings grew increasingly less primitive as we descended, with evidence emerging of a dwelling constructed with a masterful grand design in mind. Step by step that roughly dug tunnel started to change, the walls becoming smoother, a massive flagstone here and there, and the lighting becoming more regularly spaced and radiant.

Soon we were passing carvings and hanging portraits, with

ancient tapestries and ornate candelabras lining our way. The tiles over which we trod gradually became smaller, depicting swirling patterns of a thousand colours and intricate mosaics that made the very floor a breathtaking work of art. The passage finally ended with an imposing set of double doors adorned with historic scenes depicting the rise and struggle of their species. Unable to imagine what could possibly lie beyond them, we timidly shuffled through, all our jaws dropping as Kai bolted all the heavy locks behind us.

The room we had entered was a sophisticated mixture of elegance and insanity. Even now, I find myself struggling to accurately illustrate the measure of its madness. I suppose it could be best described as an enormous recreational room of sorts, where it seemed the Loup Garou came to relax and unwind. To the casual observer perhaps it resembled a sprawling lounge from an old-fashioned gentlemen's club, the private and exclusive kind so popular a hundred years ago—though even that makes it sound far too normal.

True, it had a huge working fireplace, and several high-backed armchairs, oil paintings and crushed velvet drapes, and the air was tinged with the sweet aromas of flavoured pipe smoke, but that's about where those classy similarities ended. What struck me first was how there was definitely no dress code, or rather, no policy regarding form, be it human or animal.

There was an elderly gentleman with a long white beard and flowing cloak, sitting hunched over a chessboard seriously considering his next move. Every now and then he would look up, dubiously eyeing his opponent, a bald-headed orangutan who seemed to be growing impatient at the length of time the old man was taking. Another man was lounging against the mantelpiece, talking quite earnestly to an eagle, which was perched aloofly on the ledge beside him. A Great Dane was dozing lazily upon the hearth a few feet from them, basking in the warmth of the flames. There was a group of wolf-men—the recently transformed meerkats, we presumed—who had hurried on ahead of us. They were in the process of putting their orders in at the bar, in a respectful manner to a docile, yet nonetheless physically intimidating grizzly bear of a bartender.

We saw an albino python coiled and fast asleep upon another armchair, its forked tongue flickering rhythmically out from between its fangs with every breath. Running along the far wall was an enormous fish tank, whose glass sides shone beautifully, bathing that area of the room in a tranquil turquoise glow. We realised in amazement that this tropical aquarium doubled as an indoor swimming pool as a dazzlingly striped Angelfish jumped clear out of the tank, landing on the carpet and bringing a little puddle of water with it. For a couple of seconds, it lay there flapping around on the floor. But before any of us had time to react and try to save the delicate little thing, it grew at an alarming rate back into its wolf form, standing over seven feet tall on its hind legs. It gave itself a quick and violent shake, the way a wet dog does when it comes in from the rain, before nonchalantly crossing the room as though nothing had happened to take a seat closer to the fire.

I could fill this entire notebook with the remarkable scenes we witnessed down there in the Hive. From the doves nesting up in the roofbeams, to the bats dangling beneath them, upside down and chittering non-stop to one another. The gecko lizard with its little webbed digits, passionately playing a lively tune on the piano in the corner, assisted by a wild hare down below, blindly thumping the foot pedals the gecko could not reach. The plump walrus sipping fine brandy through a straw, and the majestic bespectacled tiger reclining on a couch, intently focused on sharpening its claws. The list would go on and on, and it was from that bizarre and crazy place that Steggie, Wolfe and I were led quietly away by Kai. Perhaps some of the Only Circle would have protested against being left behind, but they barely noticed the four of us departing: such was the enchanting magic of that room.

Following Kai off down one of the many adjoining corridors, we came to what once might have been a cage lift from the original mining shaft. Since then, it had been remodelled into a splendid vintage elevator with spiralling grated sides made of polished brass. Down and down we went until we arrived at the place where the meeting would be held. It was a yawning underground grotto, with impressive rock formations on every side, and one end of the cave ending in a glorious pool, whose light blue reflections danced and played upon the high ceiling.

There wasn't much of a chance to fully take in the place though, as Kai led us directly towards a raised tent, the type one might expect to find in among the rolling sand dunes of some enormous desert. It was there, where the three of us were told that the Elders of the Loup Garou awaited us.

Ducking under those snow-white curtains, we came face to face with seven chieftains all squatting or seated in a semi-circle. Kai took his place beside them, motioning us to step forward. Only he and one of the others were currently in their human form: the rest were wolves, and we soon discovered it was this other human-formed Loup Garou who would be doing all the talking.

"Welcome, dear friends. Welcome. Do please make yourselves comfortable. My name is Quidel, and it is a great pleasure to have you here."

He was an incredibly charming and handsome man, whose age was impossible to guess, but the three of us were certain that he was very old. It was something about his eyes, which seemed to burn with the collected mysteries of many centuries. Before the real discussion began, one by one, we had to introduce ourselves, offering out our hand for him to examine. Steggie went first, and he took her hand very gently in his, a curious expression on his face as he stared intently at her palm.

"Ah, Ms Belle, we have heard so many wonderful things about you already," he began, those eyes lighting up with genuine joy. "Euryale speaks very highly of you, which is no mean feat at all!" Then he paused to peer closer at the lines on her palm, before glancing sideways up at her with one eye. He looked shocked, or perhaps worried would be closer to the mark, before lowering his head once more to scrutinise those folds in her skin more closely. Though we were sitting right beside her and could hear every word spoken, both Wolfe and I were baffled by the conversation that followed.

"Rarely do we see such breaks in one so young. You must have a strong heart indeed to have made it this far." Then he followed with a question so direct that it appeared to take her by surprise. "Does anybody know?"

Steggie seemed almost shy for a moment under his knowing stare, before shaking her head slowly. "No."

"Well, not that it's for me to say, for I have long since learned the dangers of giving advice, but if I might offer a suggestion? Put your faith and your trust in Chance!"

I remember those words of his puzzling me greatly, for they were the complete opposite to the stern lectures from my father, who would often insist to me: "You must never leave anything to chance!" Before I could consider that suggestion further, however, Quidel had moved on and similarly taken Wolfe's hand.

"So you are the one. The boy who was so quick to pick a fight with one of our brothers." He tutted seriously to himself, before regarding Wolfe with a trace of a smile. "While bravery and fearlessness are worthy virtues, ones which cannot be taught, a wise warrior will learn both how to choose his battles, and to know his enemy even better than he knows himself. Reckless bravado can lead one into trouble. And yet, in you I see a future with great potential, should you discover a way to keep yourself safe. Wrapped up in cotton wool, so to speak, and protected from harm."

Next, it was my turn, and I found that I could feel the heat radiating from him as he studied my hand.

"Interesting," he sighed, noting the dark scars upon my forearm. "Shifters are a very useful breed, especially these days. But be warned, it is not only the good who will seek to benefit from your powers, but also the bad. Like a mighty bow, it depends upon the archer, as to which direction he chooses to point the arrow." His expression seemed to sour in the next instant as he peered closer, tracing a particular line carefully with his finger as though somehow he hoped that by doing so, it might be erased or undone. When he looked back up at me, it was with a confusing balance of sorrow, regret and hope.

"I see a lonely road ahead for you. An outcast weighed down by a burden nobody should be forced to bear. I see suffering and heartache and doubt. It is so essential you remain strong, keep your compass steady, and remember that even in the darkest of nights, one can still find a light."

Loneliness, suffering and heartache. Hardly the sort of fortune-telling one hopes to hear, but sadly the sort which once heard is impossible to forget. I was extremely glad when it was over, and the conversation moved on.

"So, Ms Belle, might I ask the reason for you requesting this meeting?"

Steggie cut straight to the point. "We were hoping you would be able to give us information about the Anchor of Perspicax."

"Ah, I see…" he replied, viewing each of us thoughtfully. "Would it surprise you to learn that you are not the first to come to us with that very same question?"

"Simeon Scythe," Steggie whispered, the frustration evident in her voice. Quidel nodded cautiously in response.

"But first, a little test. For not everyone is suitably equipped with the right key to open such a lock." With that, he leant forward, placing both his hands simultaneously upon each of us in turn. One upon our heart, the other upon the forehead. This lasted for nearly a minute until he relaxed and continued. "Where that young boy failed, the three of you have passed. He came to us a few years ago, seeking answers, though we were all able to see straight away that his motives were impure."

Steggie breathed a sigh of relief. "I have to ask though, what did you end up telling him? I can't imagine he would have been much pleased to find out that he had failed."

Quidel grinned a sly grin at this. "Why, we told him he had

passed of course!"

The other Loup Garou who had been silent up until that point, all howled and chuckled mischievously at that.

"You see," he continued, with a casual wink towards Wolfe, "sometimes when faced with the fire of an overgrown ego, the best way to fight it is with compliments and flattery, not force. So we made him feel as special as he already believed he was, before feeding him misinformation, and sending him off on a wild and merry goose chase of our own design!"

We all sighed thankfully at hearing this, while the wolf Elders pounded the floor with their paws, a sound which echoed in waves around that enchanted grotto. Quidel explained, in more detail than we could have ever hoped for, both the history of the Anchor and the purpose for which that mysterious artefact had originally been designed.

"When Pan approached our tribe several thousand years ago and entrusted us with its safekeeping, the Loup Garou brought it down to this very cave, deep within the Hive, to discuss how it should be hidden. It was decided that we should hire a famous dwarf, renowned for his skills in ironmongery and blacksmithing, to dismantle it carefully into two pieces, for we believed that as long as it remained intact, neither world would be truly safe. The larger, most crucial part would stay hidden and guarded within the dream world, while the smaller, less useful piece would cross over and be buried safely in the waking world.

"The Anchor of Perspicax, you understand, had been created by a superior race of angelic beings with a very specific and magnificent purpose in mind. For they believed that one day: when all feuding and fighting would cease, species across both worlds would exist in both harmony and peace and could finally be united. It was never designed to be a weapon at all, but more a machine—not the clunky fuel-driven kind that humans so adore, but a machine nonetheless. One which, upon the perfect future day when such tranquillity had been reached, would be capable of breaking down the dividing walls, cementing the scales in a permanent state of balance, and freeing every being that lived within.

"Sadly, that day has not yet arrived and sometimes, in savagely disheartening ways, still seems so very far off. However, that has not stopped a great many individuals and tribes from desiring to possess the Anchor's vast range of accompanying powers for their own personal gain and selfish ends.

"The Loup Garou, being a clan so in tune with nature that we have developed the ability of crossing between both worlds with ease, came up with a plan. So it was that shortly afterwards, a specially selected group of our brothers took that small piece through and hid it well within the waking world. We had, however, underestimated one thing: humanity's insatiable thirst for power."

Quidel went on to explain how the piece was almost useless: capable only of giving its owner the power to inflict damage and harm upon their own kind. However, much to the Loup Garou's astonishment, humans still ached to wield it. When it was eventually unearthed, it became a legendary weapon, devastating and destroying entire cities and human civilisations. The Loup Garou realised then that something must be done.

"That piece of the Anchor went by many names," Quidel continued. "Though perhaps in the height of its usage it was best known as The Ark of the Covenant. It was about that time that the Loup Garou had crossed back over and successfully intervened. By using our unmatched art of disguise, we were able to infiltrate the palace where the piece of the Anchor was being covetously kept and steal it right out from under those warring nations' noses.

"We took even greater care in hiding it a second time, and through a stroke of pure genius found a place for it, where we are proud to say it has remained safely undisturbed and unrecognised, up until the present day. Its location? Well, that I'm afraid is a secret known only to us Elders."

Steggie tried to prompt more clues about its waking world location but quickly realised that no amount of persuasion would have forced answers from them, even to the three of us.

"Even children do not stay children forever," he had said with a sigh, "and we believe the temptation to misuse such power would be too great for any human being to bear."

We learnt so many things from Quidel that evening, not only of the Anchor but also about the Loup Garou and their strange practices and customs.

"I find it fascinating," I remember him saying at one point, "the way the grown-ups of your world seem so determined to paint us as these ferocious Wolf-men. Telling false tales to children, of how we will hunt down and devour the naughty ones among them. Ha! Well, to set your young minds at ease, never has such a thing happened. We are all about maintaining and protecting the Natural Order. In our experience we have only ever *hunted down* the adults of your kind, whom we have found are not only more willing but far more capable of doing terrible things that disturb and devastate the balance."

He corrected us concerning several misunderstandings that have grown over time to shroud the truth of their clan. How, the more advanced their members become, the wider the variety of animal forms they are able to take, and the faster the speed of transformation. How they can, and still do to this day, cross over freely into the waking world, walking in many forms and go mainly unnoticed among humans. And most curiously, about the myth concerning the One Hundred and One Day Curse.

"Your kind thinks of it that way—as a curse—when of course it is really a blessed opportunity, an ancient custom and secret, privileged test, far closer to a gift than anything else. It is a bond and rite, during which our blood is exchanged, and the recipient is given one hundred and one days to prove his or her worth. If they succeed, their reward is joining and running with our pack. A curse indeed! They should be so lucky. For it is within the long-forgotten wisdom, that the truth resides: that, so many years ago, the Loup Garou were chosen, descended directly from human beings!"

He went on to tell the three of us that, should we ever decide in the future that we were interested, he would gladly nominate us to take that challenge. Although he warned us that passing it was incredibly difficult, and that a being only gets one chance at it in a lifetime.

I have already spoken of the extraordinary wisdom one could physically feel flowing through them while in their company, which I will do my very best here, to sum up. They had an admirable outlook on life, a way about them: a natural ability, to both laugh at the serious things in life, and be serious about the laughable things too. In my humble estimation, a sign of true wisdom.

It was shortly after, when Steggie asked a further question, that the atmosphere in that tent changed quite drastically.

"Where was the piece that remained here in the dream world hidden?"

"In a place that nobody has any desire or business in exploring, don't you worry. We hid it deep in the heart of that impassable wasteland, known to many as the desert of Vumbi Bones."

Steggie shot to her feet, a reaction that alarmed everyone present, while I desperately tried to remember where I had heard that place mentioned before.

"That's where the bounty hunters finally captured Simeon Scythe before!" she cried out. "They said it seemed he was attempting to cross it by foot!"

Quidel stared incredulously back at her, momentarily at a loss for words. "That ... that can't be possible," he stammered. "The seven of us sent him away, searching in the complete opposite direction. How could he have known?"

A heavy silence followed. We noticed all the other Elders solemnly change into their human forms, their faces showing clear signs of worry. They discussed the matter hastily among themselves and then turned back to face us.

"It might be nothing, and yet this could be very serious," Quidel announced, his eyes appearing nervous below a heavily furrowed brow. "We must move quickly. We need to set out to those blistered salt flats where we buried it and check that it's still safe. But first, we must gather reinforcements, as many as we can. We will spend the rest of the night and morning preparing, reaching out to our trusted allies, and making sure we are ready."

"Is there anything we can do?" Steggie asked, eager to help.

Quidel considered that for a few moments before giving his reply.

"Perhaps it'd be best for you all to stay here, make sure your group is fully prepared and ready to move out with us tomorrow at noon. That is, unless any of you are on good terms with any powerful and trustworthy tribes, who you think might be willing to join us?"

Steggie bit her lip in concentration, a wave of curls falling down over her face, as Wolfe and I shrugged, looking blankly at one another. Steggie's sudden exclamation broke the silence:

"I could try to convince the Coven of the North!"

Quidel seemed doubtful at the prospect.

"They can be prickly at the best of times, those witches. They tend to stay out of such matters unless they have a personal interest."

"But surely it's worth a try?" Steggie insisted hopefully.

"Very well," he said reluctantly. "But have you visited them before? Do you know where they are to be found?"

It was with crushing defeat that we shook our heads, admitting we hadn't, but the Elders of the Loup Garou simply turned their heads in unison towards that glistening turquoise pool at the rear of the cave.

"That portal will take you close enough, but be extremely careful. It's a particularly hazardous stretch of coastline there, but if you follow it northwards, you should find them. That Coven is well known for being inhospitable towards uninvited guests, so I hope you know what you are doing. Though I daresay they will find you before you find them, so be on your guard."

As we rose, ready to investigate that tranquil pool of water, I heard Steggie insisting to Wolfe that she needed him to stay and make sure that our Only Circle was prepared for the next day's journey. I dreaded, but half expected, that once she was done with him, she would turn to deliver the same instructions to me.

It was then that I felt a warm hand upon my shoulder, and heard Kai whispering in my ear.

"Stay close to her, and make sure the two of you are back by noon tomorrow." Then, as though reading my surprise: "Yes, she will ask you to go with her, trust me. This piece of the Anchor must not fall into the wrong hands!"

As we continued walking over to the water's edge, I asked him a question that I immediately wished I hadn't.

"What's the worst that could happen if Simeon Scythe managed to get hold of it?"

"Well," Kai replied, shaking his head, "a great many terrible things! You told us he managed to cross over to the waking world with over fifty Stalkers to hunt you … with that piece of the Anchor he could open many Inter-World portals all at once, with no limit whatsoever as to how many or what monstrous creatures he could unleash upon the Earth. And that would be only the beginning of the chaos!"

I swallowed hard, considering the prospect. As we reached the pool, Steggie drew level with me.

"So, you'll come with me, Zoofall?"

I nodded firmly, realising then that Wolfe and the other Elders had already turned away and were hurrying back towards the elevator shaft. Looking down into those pale crystal waters, I found myself wondering how deep it might be.

That was when I suddenly noticed that the pool offered no reflection: no mirrored image of Steggie and I standing side by side. As we looked longer at the water, images began to appear within it. Bit by bit a fascinating coastal landscape came into view, with a long sandy beach, stretching white as snow under the moonlight. The moonlight! In wondrous awe, I counted three moons suspended in an exotic night sky, the largest and brightest of which shone brilliantly with a deep shade of sapphire blue. I heard Steggie mutter something under her breath which I couldn't catch.

"What was that?"

"A premonition from a long time ago," she replied absently, as though she were in a daze, before repeating it once more.

"*Until we meet again, Steggie Belle, blood-drenched under an ink blue moon.*"

I had absolutely no idea of the secrets I was about to discover that night, there on the other side.

We took each other's hand, and jumped.

18

The Blood Mission with Steggie

We hurried along that indigo tinted coastline. The beach led away northwards, as far as the eye could see, a milky blue carpet path of sand and shingle crunching underfoot. I remember thinking that perhaps in the light of day it could have been an idyllic setting, but not then, not that night. Although there were no sounds, no movement, or visible beings, both of us shared the inexplicable certainty that we were not alone. That we were being watched.

To our left, the infinite brooding sea, shimmering and flat: a foreboding and fathomless surface as dark and nerve-racking as an open trapdoor. To our right the beachfront ended in a scattered line of grossly leaning palm trees, whose giant drooping canopies hung like clawed hands, waiting to reach out and grab us. Beyond their blackened rows lay a solid wall of jungle, a thickly shadowed and tangled mass.

We made it about a mile and a half, barely speaking to one another, before our quick footsteps skidded to a halt, sending grains of sand spraying and tumbling in all directions. Steggie had grabbed my arm and was staring out at the dim horizon where sea and sky appeared to melt into one another, giving birth to something else. We strained our eyes, following those faint rises and falls.

"A storm, maybe?" I ventured. My hushed attempt at a whisper seemed far louder than I intended in that deathly silence. Steggie did not answer immediately, still focusing on those dark, wavelike undulations, but from the way she shook her head, she clearly believed it was something else. When her words finally came, I realised with sinking certainty that we were really in trouble.

"We have to go! Run, Zoofall!"

The speed at which we fled was the kind that defines desperation, one that I knew would be impossible to sustain. Both of us stumbled as, with our legs like jelly, we pushed them to move faster than they were ever designed to go.

"Why don't we fly?" I gasped, the air tearing and burning at my throat.

"Not a … good idea," Steggie shouted back, struggling to catch her breath. "If they are … what I think they are … we wouldn't have a hope of outrunning them … not in the open sky!"

The hairs on the back of my neck rose on hearing the real fear in her voice. Out of the corner of my eye, I saw Steggie glancing back towards the sea, but for perhaps that first minute, which pounded out like an eternity, I did not dare to look.

Concentrating on what lay ahead was not much better, with the coastline stretching away forever, a nightmarish never-ending trail offering no sign of safety or salvation. When I did finally look back over my shoulder, I felt a hollow sickness rise within me.

The sea was alive. A swarm of winding threads, far closer

now and rushing towards us, keeping just below that deceptively placid surface. There were dozens, if not hundreds of them, whatever *they* were, and their size was still impossible to determine. My panicked mind tried to fill in the blanks, conjuring endless awful possibilities—yet somehow I knew that the dreadful truth of what lurked beneath those dark waters would soon be revealed as far worse than anything I could imagine. One thing was for sure, with no clear end in sight and no objects behind which to hide, we were running out of time.

"Surely, the jungle?" I panted, unable to draw air and so pointing instead, "... for cover?"

Steggie shook her head vehemently at that suggestion: "Jungle, it's moving ... the shadows ... are alive!"

My whole body shuddered at hearing those words. That barren and desolate place was devoid of hope as, with every passing second, the distance separating those serpentine trails from the shore grew less and less.

"But we're never going to make it!" I cried out, having not even the slightest idea where we were trying to make it to. I heard Steggie gasp and, following her gaze, caught a glimpse of one huge, rolling, scaled hump breaking the surface, ploughing through the water before disappearing once again. The nearest of them were reaching the shallow waters where, within perhaps the next twenty seconds, one way or another, we were going to discover if those devils of the deep were as limber on land.

It was then that Steggie called to me.

"Stop!"

Well, I don't mind admitting that, right then, that seemed to me just about the very worst idea imaginable. But before I had time to protest or even argue, she had tackled me forcefully around the waist and knocked me off balance. There was no going back. In that surreal and slow-motion way, gravity took over, and I realised we were both falling, hurtling down towards the sand. That defeated fall left me without any doubt that it was game over, that our efforts at outrunning our pursuers had failed.

We skidded our way, rolling under our own momentum, to a bruised and battered halt. Panting for breath on my hands and knees, it dawned on me that something had changed. The three moons were still poised exactly where they had been previously, high up in the night sky. To our left, the sound of the waves lapping gently at the beach. To our right, the long and darkened wall of green. And yet something was different.

It was no longer sand beneath us; I was balanced instead upon a strange boulder, and, looking around, it seemed that the entire coastline was made up of them now.

"Hurry! We have to move quickly!" Steggie called insistently, leaving no time for discussion. So we made our way, jumping awkwardly from boulder to boulder until, coming around the next dune-like ridge, I realised what had happened. It was still the same beach, still the same sand, but Steggie had shrunk the pair of us right down to the size of a flea.

Up ahead, lying at a perilous angle on its side, was a gigantic toppled structure. It resembled some mighty shipwrecked vessel, an ancient temple long abandoned and left exposed to the elements.

It was a seashell, conical in shape with a wide and upturned base towering above our heads. Its pointed end was turned slightly upwards into the ink-blue sky, far away in the distance. Quickly we climbed up the ridges, pulling ourselves up onto the lip-edge entrance, to stand side by side in the large, overhanging opening, looking out over that altered landscape.

From the direction of the sea came a deafening roar that vibrated clearly through our feet. In horror, we then watched as those sand-grain boulders all around the shell began to shake and tremble. A loathsome dark torso rose up into the night sky until it blotted out and was silhouetted by the lowest of those three moons. It looked like a mixture between a sea serpent and some mythical dragon, and many others emerged from the sea to rise up on either side of it. We stared dumbstruck for a few moments before Steggie suggested we retreat further inside.

We shimmied and scrambled our way along the shell's sloping inner sides until we found a spot, perhaps three full revolutions from the entrance, where we could comfortably rest. The spiralling passage continued to curl off deeper into the darkness, getting consistently narrower with every bend.

We sat there for some time, hugging our knees tightly to our chests, listening and trying to decipher the series of strange noises reverberating from outside into the depths of our makeshift shelter. There came a continuous rough scratching as those sea monsters slithered paths across the sand, scouring the beach. Combined with the repetitive cataclysmic thuds as massive taloned claws struck the ground, making our whole miniaturised world shudder and jolt, like the aftershocks of an earthquake. This was followed by several short rasping calls from those terrifying creatures: cries of frustration at not finding what they were searching for.

After a long and anxious wait, the two of us began to talk, keeping our voices down to carefully low whispers.

"How long do you think we'll have to stay here?" I asked.

"As long as it takes, I suppose. But with a bit of luck, they'll give up soon enough and head back to wherever it is they came from," Steggie replied rather matter-of-factly, and with an unbelievable level of calm.

"What do you think they are? And why did they come after us like that?" I asked, hoping that answers might help allay my fears.

"I'm not sure. Though the way they moved all together seemed almost territorial, like a pack of guard dogs protecting this coast from intruders."

I could hear her rustling around beside me in the dark, but couldn't make out what she was doing. I found myself more concerned and paranoid about the seemingly unnecessary noise she was making and wincing at every snapping sound. Moments later, there was a spark, and then complete darkness as my eyes tried to readjust to the surrounding gloom. I heard her blowing gently and, with every breath she exhaled, that faint glowing light returned, gradually growing stronger.

Steggie had her hands cupped together, a pile of dry kindling which she had collected held carefully between them, the embers illuminating her face time and time again until there came the crackle of a small flame as a piece of twig ignited. She lowered the smoking pile to the floor, setting it down and patiently tending to it, adding bits of dry brush that were scattered around the inside of the shell, to build it up around the sides.

"Are you sure that's a good idea?" I asked once the little fire had eventually got going, taking in our dimly-lit surroundings. The curving walls were dark and glossy, their surface covered with strange markings: fine grooves that were illuminated by the firelight.

"I think it should be alright," she replied while gathering up more scraps of tiny driftwood splinters to feed the flames, and stoking the fire now and then. "I mean, if the moonlight can't penetrate these walls, any light we make should remain concealed."

"But what about the smoke?" I countered nervously.

"Well, keep in mind the size we are now would be smaller than an ant to them, I mean, this shell is probably not much bigger than our fingernail, so I wouldn't worry too much, Zoofall. Besides, we might as well make ourselves comfortable—it could be a very long night."

That all made sense, but I wasn't anywhere near done with my questions. It was the first time I had Steggie all to myself for an extended period of time, assuming we were not discovered. I can't remember every question I asked her, for there were many, but felt positive this could be the moment for some long-awaited answers. In plenty of instances, my inquisitiveness clearly amused her. Like when I asked her how all of the Freedivers, spread out all over the Earth, could be dreaming at the same time, taking into account the different time zones. Or how we were able to communicate when we spoke different languages back in the waking world. She laughed a great deal when I raised those things before giving me a reply.

"The dream world is not limited by such laws of reasoning and logic, you should know that better than anyone!" she said, shaking her head and continuing in a light-hearted, almost mocking tone. "Really, Zoofall, sometimes you sound more like a grown-up than a Shifter! Searching for answers to things that have no possible benefit, creating problems out of the very air itself!"

It was a criticism which I would not fully understand until much later on in life.

"You see," Steggie went on, "Time isn't really as straightforward or rigid as most people would have you believe. The knowledge simply isn't there yet, not available to those who live only in the waking world. So, for now at least, such ideas and levels of understanding are beyond them." She smiled then, most probably at seeing my baffled expression, before trying to sum up her thoughts as simply as she could.

"Such things are complicated. But for now, let's just say we have been led to believe that Time is real and flows like a river. In one direction, at a steady and ordered rhythm, but that is not the case. Past, Present and Future are only ideas: invented by humanity." She glanced over at me to see if I was still following what she was saying. "In truth, Time is far more flexible: it can be bent, manipulated and even folded right back upon itself. And as for languages, well, try to imagine languages in the waking world as nothing more than music for the ears. Here, in the dream world, we sing the music of our minds. It is a pure and universal sound, which brings people far closer together, despite their different cultures and origins." Steggie sighed with a heavy sadness. "Deep down, on some level, humans still see shadows of such truths, but the waking world distracts them, discourages them from pursuing such trails, insisting to them that such things could not possibly exist."

I nodded along in agreement, committing those words to memory and still trying to wrap my head around their meaning.

When the conversation turned back towards our immediate surroundings, I accidentally stumbled upon another question which was to change, quite by chance, the course of that night's events. I was staring off into the deeper shadows where the sea shell's winding passage curled out of sight towards its innermost point when the random thought occurred to me.

"Steggie," I whispered. "You don't think that this is still some creature's home? That there's something still living in there, further inside, do you?"

Ah, the power of retrospect. The way it can so easily untangle all those knotted and mystifying threads, that make up the unknown of the present moment. I understand now, so many years later, with such clarity that glint of a reaction which shone out her eyes right then. The subtle symbolism of an abandoned shell, a life, and that which is hidden and cannot be seen. It was but a fleeting look, a chink in her armour, and then it was gone. And Steggie Belle turned away, taking some time to examine the walls around us.

"In answer to your question, Zoofall," she briskly replied, after clearing her throat, "I do not think so. If you look at all these written notes around us, you will see they tell quite a fascinating story, like entries in a diary, or journal, you see? Very specific. Notice here ..." she said, pointing to a series of markings, just before where it appeared that peculiar diary ended. "The previous owner explains how he is leaving this home behind, to go and search for a partner whom he lost a very long time ago, during a bad storm, and he is doubtful that he will return. He goes on to welcome any future visitors to make use of his dwelling, should they find it still unoccupied. Rather sad really, but beautiful all the same," she said in admiration.

I looked once more over those old markings that lined the curving inner walls. To me, they did not resemble any form of handwriting I had ever seen, which prompted my next question.

"Steggie, where in either world did you learn how to read and translate these things? Did Euryale teach you?"

She shook her head in a slightly guilty fashion, as though she had already revealed too much. But I refused to let it go and kept on with my persistent string of questions.

"There are just so many things that I don't really understand, things that don't make complete sense. Like how have you come to know and master so many different skills? You haven't been here, in the dream world, that much longer than some of the original Freedivers. And why, when the Inner Circle was being picked off one by one, did you escape the Stalkers' notice? How did they not find you? What secrets are you holding back from me, Steggie?"

I waited, uncertain how she would react, and started to wonder whether I should have kept those thoughts to myself. She shifted her position rather uncomfortably, before looking me straight in the eyes.

"It's complicated," she finally confessed with a heavy sigh. "I have never spoken of these things, not even with the former Inner Circle."

I saw a great sadness then, written in her eyes, and for the first time, I sensed an immense loneliness within her, one usually kept so well hidden. She opened her mouth to explain, to spill out all her unspoken secrets, but at that very moment, we were interrupted.

An awful shrieking wail rose up from those sea dragons outside, what sounded like a defensive cry, alerting the rest of them to some pressing danger. Then, out of the silence that followed, there came a sickening chorus of seemingly innocent children's voices which we recognised only too well.

"Please, would you help us? We are very lost."

Steggie and I crept cautiously back along the curving passage towards the sea shell's entrance, keeping low and peering out over the slanted edge at the shapes moving in the night. A furious hissing filled the air, as the serpents all rose up, making themselves as tall and threatening as possible. Through the darkness of the jungle backdrop, a long line of Stalkers came into view. Too many to count, and advancing in that terrifying way of theirs. Not walking, but vanishing and then reappearing several metres closer. Each time, their pale thin arms transformed grotesquely into devilishly large and elongated claws.

The row of sea-dragons stood firm, defiantly marking their territory, not backing down an inch. Then all hell broke loose. Amid deafening roars and dark, sweeping movements, a ferocious battle erupted. Everything shook violently as those two gigantic, monstrous armies lashed out and fought with one another. From their silhouetted forms, spumes of blood sprayed horribly up into the indifferent dark blue sky.

The next second I felt Steggie tugging at my arm, dragging me backwards away from the edge, urging me to be quiet. It was only when we were back near the fire that she spoke, holding me tightly by the shoulders as we both fought to maintain our balance, the spiral tunnel rocking unsteadily from side to side.

"We can't stay here. We might be crushed underfoot at any moment," Steggie whispered earnestly before dropping to her knees and starting to create a small Inter-World portal. "You wanted answers, and you deserve to have them. But it will be easier to show you."

As the opening widened, blinding light flooded through it. With one arm raised, blinking and shielding my eyes, I quickly crawled through, with Steggie following, closing the portal firmly behind us.

My eyes had grown so accustomed to the dimly flickering firelight that I stumbled around disorientated by the brilliant whiteness until—from somewhere close by—I heard Steggie's voice speaking to me urgently.

"Quickly, Zoofall. As a shadow. We must not be seen here."

Without hesitation, I obeyed, cloaking myself as a fine mist. Perplexed as to where we could be, I forced myself to focus, squinting through one eye. The first blurry image that came into view was a printed wall sign: a red circle with a line crossing through it, and a drawing of a cigarette in the middle. What was written in bold lettering beneath it was not English. I later learnt that it was German. Everything was clean and clinically cold, illuminated by long tube lighting fitted overhead at regular intervals.

I heard Steggie's voice again, tinged this time with a touch of embarrassment and shame, as she gently placed one hand upon my shoulder, turning me around.

"This is where I live."

I found that I was unable to speak, as I stood there trying to take it all in. The room was small and sparsely decorated, consisting mainly of a great many instruments and complicated-looking machines all stacked up and positioned around either side of a bed against the back wall. It was a few moments before I recognised the small figure lying motionless there, beneath the pristine and neatly folded blankets, with her forehead wrapped in layers of cream bandages. With just one rebellious black curl of hair protruding out from under them, falling down across her cheek, lay Steggie Belle.

In shock and disbelief, I took a few steps closer, seeing all the tubes running directly from her, connecting her to all those machines with their flashing dials.

"I ... I ... I don't understand," I stammered fearfully, feeling dizzy as reality set in. "What happened to you?"

She did not raise her head, looking past her feet at the floor as she came up beside me, mumbling her reply.

"You remember that first horse ride I told you about, all those years ago?" I nodded in a daze, the room still spinning. "Well, I guess I didn't clear that fence. I never woke up, Zoofall," she whispered, looking up with tears in her eyes, "and the doctors say that perhaps I never will."

"Oh, Steggie," I replied, taking her trembling hand in mine.

There was nothing I could say. Every mystery and unanswered question suddenly made sense, all those puzzle pieces silently slotting into place. How, when the rest of the Freedivers returned to their earthly lives back in the waking world, only Steggie would remain, forever dreaming. The reason why the Stalkers had been unable to locate her shallow pulse, her fragile heart beating only with the help of those medical machines, while her body lay trapped within a coma.

Something happened then, and even now, I find it difficult to explain.

It was as though I could actually see and feel the terrible burden that rested upon her shoulders, weighing her down. And yet, there in that room I somehow managed to raise it off her, splitting it evenly between us, willingly sharing that awful load.

So it was that, in the dead of night, deep within some German hospital, I learnt the truth. The heartbreaking and tragic secret of Steggie Belle.

We stood there, hand in hand, for what must have been a very long time, before I dared to speak, my heart wishing for nothing more than to rescue her, to save her in some way from her pain. So I broke the silence, attempting to resurrect that wonderful smile of hers.

"If you wanted to, you could show me your home? Your real home?"

There was warm gladness in her eyes and, though it was not quite visible upon her face, when she squeezed my hand, I felt that smile itching to be released, to break free once again.

After taking another window, she led me through an overgrown and wild garden, peaceful in the stillness of the night. We passed through a rustic wooden stable door, making our way quietly across the ground floor of the farmhouse. We stopped in a doorway that led from the kitchen to the sitting room, where a beautiful middle-aged woman was sitting fast asleep within an armchair, the book that she had been reading still resting upon her lap. Steggie was standing glued to the spot in front of me, and I didn't need to see the look on her face to be sure who that sleeping person was. The resemblance was uncanny, and we stood there as shadow forms silently watching, with the pale, serene light of the moon streaming through a nearby window.

It was at that point, the thought suddenly occurred to me and, with great care, I placed both my hands on Steggie's misty shoulders. I closed my eyes, concentrating very hard. In those next few minutes, I managed to pass onto Steggie the most precious of gifts, the one thing she had been deprived of since that freak accident so many years ago. I succeeded in giving her back her temporary physical form.

Though I kept my eyes tightly clenched throughout, I was fully aware of what was happening. I clearly heard Steggie's mother stir. I knew she was awake when the sharp gasp came. Perhaps she thought she must have been dreaming—opening her eyes to see her daughter standing there, large as life within the doorway, encircled by a faint glowing aura behind her. I heard the exclamations of disbelief, followed by the rapid fall of feet quickly crossing the room towards us. Although Steggie and I were two separate forms, we were connected as one by the magic I was channelling through her. I felt everything, I felt the embrace.

I couldn't understand any of the words that passed between them, though perhaps I was never meant to. Within that moment, there radiated the most powerful of bonds. The purest kind of love: that of a mother's for her child.

Time itself appeared to bow to the point of surrender, a compassionate witness stretching itself to the very limits. Steggie's mother relinquished her grasp, planting a final kiss upon her daughter's forehead, before running with tears of joy excitedly from the room. We heard her calling throughout the house, presumably to awaken the father. Wiping fresh tears from her eyes, Steggie turned to face me, her legendary smile spreading from cheek to cheek, and spoke with great reluctance.

"We really must go."

We hurried out from the house, racing down towards a line of thick bushes at the bottom of the garden. Looking back we saw lights being switched on all along the first floor of that secluded farmhouse, twinkling out of the darkness like a Christmas tree. With a broad and satisfied grin, Steggie began constructing a portal to take us back to the spiralled interior of that abandoned shell. I remember noticing at that moment, despite the lack of light, how she appeared to stand taller, reinvigorated and somehow stronger.

Prior to actually crossing back through that small opening I was already feeling nervous. The light inside that curving tunnel had changed dramatically, there was no denying that. Its sloping sides with those strange foreign markings were bathed in a grimly ominous crimson glow.

"Perhaps the fire we left got a bit out of control?" I suggested hopefully, but sharing a quick and doubtful look, we both knew it wasn't so. Seconds later, we were both tentatively crawling through.

The silence which greeted us was a marked contrast from the seismic fury that had been raging when we left. The fire we had built was destroyed, having been thoroughly shaken and scattered, with just a few cherry-red embers remaining: struggling against the shadows.

That unnatural red light was everywhere, seeming sinister in the semi-darkness. It was as though some god-like being had blanketed the whole world with a rose-tinted filter—as if we had slipped on coloured sunglasses. The two of us began sneaking forward along the familiar path that would take us back to the wide seashell entrance. But before we rounded the final bend to reach it, Steggie halted. She pulled me back a step or two, making me suspect she had sensed a threat that I had missed, but that wasn't it.

"Whatever happens out there, I just wanted to say thank you."

Having never been good at accepting praise, I felt a bit uncomfortable but did my best to hold her gaze. That mysterious red glow was reflected in her eyes, and they seemed to sparkle at that moment with the possibility of a thousand heartfelt words, though none were spoken. Instead, out of nowhere, and acting on impulse, Steggie smiled, lunged forward and kissed me.

Before I really realised what was happening, it was over, and yet the feeling lingered. A weightlessness lifted my spirits, empowering me beyond words. The next second we were pushing forwards once more in silence, her hand having slipped so softly that it almost went unnoticed back into mine.

I like to think that I played it cool, but inside my mind was reeling, torn between confusion and disbelief, but somehow caught up in a crazed celebration of endless somersaults and cartwheels. Why had Steggie decided to kiss me, and what could it mean? I knew that then was not the time to try to figure out exactly what it had been about, and that such answers would have to wait. But I made a promise to myself right there that, once things had returned to normal, I would pluck up the courage to bring the matter up with her.

We pulled ourselves up onto the final ledge of the entrance, and what we found there, while explaining the source of the abnormal light, left the pair of us speechless.

What stood between us and the outside world was a gory curtain, a thick dripping wall of dark red blood. Perhaps it was only a single droplet in reality. However, in our miniaturised form it was a dense, viscous barrier, vaguely translucent but keeping the two of us blind to whatever horrors might lie beyond it.

I was about to suggest we could make a window to bypass that sticky and uninviting veil, but Steggie's words were firm and final upon the matter.

"It has to be this way, Zoofall." After which, giving my hand a reassuring squeeze, she led the way straight through.

I closed my eyes, grimacing slightly at the uncomfortable sensation as the blood clung, tacky and warm to our skin, coating every inch of our bodies as we forcefully stepped out into the cool blue moonlight.

Once Steggie had returned us to our regular size, we surveyed the terrible carnage that lay all about us. It was fairly obvious that the Stalkers had succeeded in getting the upper hand: everywhere we looked we saw the sea dragons' torn and charred remains, and although the Stalkers appeared to have suffered losses too, they were nowhere near the same in number. Great swathes of the beach had been scorched with fire, blackened patches from which thin trails of smoke had risen: their pendulous columns awaiting the slightest breeze.

"So, what should we do now?" I asked after we had spent some time wandering through and inspecting that silent and gruesome aftermath of the battlefield.

"I suppose we continue heading north and find the Cov—" Her words fell short, and it was with a sickening dread that I saw she was staring wide-eyed back towards the sea. I spun around to spot what she had seen, fearing the worst. In the distance the sea was moving again, mimicking exactly what had come before.

"Not again!" I cried, my mind whirling through the awful déjà vu. We started backing off, and ridiculously I began scouring the sand in the unrealistic hope of spotting our tiny blood-soaked seashell. Suddenly there came another noise, a low whistling as delicate as the wind moving over leaves.

Then, all around us, tall hooded figures began to rise up

out of the smouldering ashes, a solemn circle of thirteen, with Steggie and I caught in the middle. The Coven of the North had found us.

It was, of course, a great relief to discover that they meant us no harm. Though as far as any initial welcome went, a nod of acknowledgement was all we got at first. Most of them busied themselves with what we had previously been doing: examining the level of destruction there upon the beach. The witches nearest the water's edge turned just in time as those approaching monsters from the deep rose tall and menacingly, taking aggressive steps once more out onto dry land.

Those four witches did not flinch; though dwarfed and vastly outnumbered, they appeared quite unconcerned by the swaying wall of jagged teeth. Steggie's earlier assumption that this legion of sea dragons were guard-dogs of a particular type proved accurate. The Coven of the North proved themselves the dragons' masters, their soothing voices lulling those colossal beasts down onto their bellies in submission.

Only once the sea dragons were settled obediently, like a line of sphinxes in the shallow waters, did the witches turn their attention back to the two of us, reforming a tight circle around our blood-soaked bodies.

One of them stepped forward, raising her slender arms to draw back the hood, and as she did so, the whole Coven followed suit. At that moment we were surrounded by a persuasive gaggle of whispering voices, though not one of their mouths was moving. Then the woman who had stepped forward raised one hand, commanding silence, and immediately those telepathic voices stopped. The conversation that followed was entirely without the use of spoken words.

"So at last you have come to visit us, Steggie Belle. The prophecy has been fulfilled, and..." suddenly she paused, whipping her head to one side, staring inquisitively at me. It appeared she had somehow sensed that I was listening, or rather eavesdropping in on that mental dialogue.

I could feel the blood still dripping from my chin and felt very awkward under the gravity of her stare. Her eyes remained locked on mine, and I felt as if she were actively rooting around inside my head. I did not like that invasive feeling one bit and was grateful when she slowly turned back to Steggie, apparently forgiving my unexpected intrusion.

"So, you have brought a friend with the gift of hearing us too. Well, no matter. In these dark times, such secrets may soon be buried with our dead bodies, to be whispered and shared only with the earthworms. So, what troubles you, Steggie Belle, mentor of the Freedivers, and how might we be of service?"

By the time Steggie had finished explaining all that had happened, the first rays of the rising sun were pushing their light across the expansive sky above, chasing those triple moons away. With the early dawn came a united resolve, although it became clear that not every detail of Steggie's account was to be believed and agreed upon. I remember noticing the way the witches looked at one another with doubt and suspicion when the subjects of Simeon Scythe and the Anchor of Perspicax were brought up. But it was not until Steggie was done with her story that the Coven raised their concerns.

"That boy is trouble! I've said so from the start," the first witch stated assuredly. *"The sacred texts and materials which he stole from us held tremendous and very specific powers. Long since have we tried to understand the 'why'. For what purpose would such things be of*

use to such a waking world dark soul? Now you say it is your belief that he is attempting to locate and take possession of the Anchor. In many ways that would make sense, for it would provide him with immense power, and the key to destabilising both worlds to the point of catastrophe. And yet..."

We waited as she seemed to mull that over, and as all thirteen witches exchanged another silent and knowing look.

"And yet?" Steggie prompted. When the lead witch turned back to face us, there was uncertainty, bordering on genuine fear, flashing in her eyes.

"It is our belief that the Anchor is not the only thing he wants. That it might be just a part of his greater plan and not his only goal. We believe that he is after something else too."

As to what that other motive might be, it appeared they did not know, or would not say, but as the conversation carried on, drawing closer to its conclusion, a desperate tension seemed to grow. Looking back, it was around that point when, whether intentionally or not, through their actions, the Coven managed to briefly separate the two of us.

As I reached up with my right hand to wipe some of the dried and crusted blood from my forehead, my sleeve must have fallen slightly. The witch standing closest to me rushed forward, visibly startled. Very careful not to touch it, as though I was contagious, she proceeded to roll up my sleeve and reveal the dark, handprint scar that was burnt into the skin upon my forearm.

Having done this, several other members of the Coven crowded around me too. I then noticed, from the corner of my eye, the witch whom I supposed to be their leader, the one who had been doing all the telepathic talking, put one arm over Steggie's shoulder, leading her away from the group and towards the water. For the first time that night I clearly saw she was making use of actual words, her mouth moving quickly, as she leant over to whisper in Steggie's ear. I, however, was being distracted, as the remaining Coven tugged at my wrist. Twisting it around at various angles, all trying to get a good look at my arm.

I was bombarded with questions. Where I had got those marks? When had it happened? What had been the precise nature of the event? Whether the scars had grown? If they still hurt? Whether I had any more on my body, and so on. If it was indeed a deliberate ploy to divert my attention, it worked as, during those passing minutes I lost track of Steggie completely. They did, however, seem genuinely concerned about those scars I bore, with the woman who had first noticed them breaking away to have a serious and private talk with another member of the Coven. I strained to hear what they were discussing but was only able to get the tail-end of their conversation.

"But he bears only the one mark! He says that he doesn't have any others," the other witch objected.

"I realise that. But it can't just be a coincidence," the woman insisted.

"It would most likely be a waste of time—time we do not have to spare."

"I sense it to be an omen. That the very winds are changing. I will go right now to ask Proteus. We must know for certain, one way or another."

With that, the witch who had first grabbed me turned and sped off towards the water's edge, whistling sharply through her fingers as she did. When that high-pitched note rang out, one of those patiently waiting sea dragons raised its head, fully alert to the sound of the call. It repositioned itself quickly in the shallow water, flicking out its long and heavy tail, the tip of which slapped down to rest upon the sand. With agile grace that witch leapt up onto it, running swiftly along the creature's bridge-like spine towards the base of its neck, which she straddled in the way one would between a camel's humps, pulling up her hood in preparation.

The next second they were off, ploughing through the waves and leaving the coast behind with incredible haste. Just before I lost sight of them on the horizon, I could have sworn I saw that dark speck rise up from the water with broad scaled wings, glinting in the morning sun for one final, magical moment.

Returning my attention to the beach, I saw Steggie coming back towards us with the Coven leader, nodding her head gravely in agreement. Infuriatingly, I still could not hear what was being said between them. I was only able to catch a small fragment of the witch's last words, which sadly I must have misheard since they made no sense at all.

"It's Sacred Ice! You do know that?"

Steggie nodded once more, showing that, unlike me, she fully understood. When they drew level with the rest of us, the witch gave one final opinion on whatever it was that they had been talking about.

"You don't have to do this, you know!"

Steggie responded by looking up at her with that defiant and mischievous grin of hers.

"But I do, and it's alright. We're all in this together: we will stand or fall, and do so side by side."

The Coven agreed to accompany us on that day's imminent journey into the desert. As they confirmed this, there came an awful racket: shrill cries from the line of sea dragons that had survived the previous night's battle. Though I did not know the meaning of those guttural sounds, I was fairly sure it was a call to be included, the desire for a chance at revenge, should the Stalkers cross our path again. The head witch, whom Steggie had addressed as "E" smiled at hearing their pleas and winked knowingly at the two of us.

"And of course we shall be bringing the dogs along with us."

A wild splashing began in the shallows, as those loyal serpents celebrated the news before racing away into the depths of the sea. The Coven excused themselves, telling us that they too must prepare, bidding us farewell with the assurance they would see us at the Hive by noon. Replacing their hoods in unison and with a miraged sparkle from the morning sun, they transformed into sand statues, which quickly crumbled and disappeared.

I had assumed that we would be heading straight back to the Hive, but Steggie had other plans.

"I need to run a small errand first," she told me while fashioning yet another window. "Would you join me?"

"Of course," I replied, without the slightest hesitation. "Where is it that we need to go?"

"I must speak with Euryale. There is something she needs to know."

Despite my excitement at that prospect, something still niggled at the back of my mind. I couldn't ignore what had passed before and had to ask. Standing there, at the verge of that window, I asked my question.

"What did the Coven leader talk to you about? I need to know, Steggie, and what is the 'Sacred Ice' she spoke about?"

Steggie surprised me by bursting into a fit of giggles at hearing that but abruptly controlled herself, turning to answer me sincerely.

"Sorry, Zoofall. The 'Ice' is nothing to worry about, just another prophecy. Those witches do like their premonitions and riddles!"

I could tell she was avoiding the subject.

"The truth, Steggie. Please!"

Her expression grew solemn.

"She thinks that I could be Simeon Scythe's true target."

19

Leading, and Being Led

I was a bundle of nerves as we hurried along that isolated stretch of coastline, heading towards the solitary cottage set back slightly from the beach. It was just how I had seen it in Steggie's story, but I was awestruck by the sound of the waves. It was a dismal, deafening and constant roar. The kind that is not only a testament to the power of nature but also a reminder of how very small we actually are—an untamed and eternal loop which seemed that morning to signal that a storm was definitely coming.

Steggie advised me to remain at the bottom of that garden while she met with Euryale. A suggestion which raised mixed feelings within me: while a little disappointed at being kept at arm's length, and not properly introduced, a large part of me was relieved to keep some distance from her poisonous living hair and those legendary deadly eyes.

"I won't be long," she promised.

As Steggie made her way up the garden path that she had so lovingly decorated, I realised that my gaze kept returning to the sea. I was scanning it with a degree of mistrust, as though

311

half expecting at any second the water to come alive again with fearsome creatures. I put those worries to the back of my mind, as I heard the hollow sound of Steggie knocking upon the front door.

Though watching the proceedings from afar, what I witnessed impacted me significantly. The figure who emerged from within, stooping low to pass beneath the doorframe, was enormous. With my mouth wide open I realised, intentionally or not, Steggie had greatly downplayed Euryale's full height. She would have been judged a giant among men, and it was with clear ease that she hoisted Steggie up for a fond embrace, as though she weighed nothing more than a rag-doll. Towering at around ten feet tall she held Steggie affectionately close, the wild tangle of snakes seeming overjoyed to see her too, bobbing and swaying in a hypnotic dance. When Euryale finally placed her gently back down upon the veranda, I noticed something quite peculiar happen.

From a distance, I watched transfixed, as Euryale purposefully raised her hands up towards her face. I knew instantly what she was about to do, and yet I was paralysed in that dreadful moment of danger, unable to look away. She was preparing to lift and remove her veil. My mind was urgently screaming commands to my disobedient eyes, to turn away and look any place else, but I could not. Then it happened.

Steggie herself hastily stopped her, appearing to insist that she keep the veil on. That perplexed me, and I tried to recall word for word the exact terms from Steggie's earlier story, relating to Euryale's special sight.

"... Any man or woman with lies and deceit in their minds, or harbouring hatred in their hearts, with just one look into those three

sisters' eyes, would instantly be turned to stone."

Did she stop Euryale simply because I was there, to protect me from harm? Or had Steggie recently fallen from grace, so to speak, in one way or another?

Being well out of earshot, I could only analyse their body language during the conversation that followed, though that gave very little away. They strolled together down the length of the veranda, Euryale's head considerably lowered as she listened to, and perhaps pondered over, Steggie's message. They remained there at the end for some minutes, Euryale staring absently at the horizon, her hair very still, while Steggie continued to talk. The mood seemed sombre, almost mournful. Euryale did not turn, or even alter her gaze, as Steggie gave her a hug with all her strength, wrapping her arms tightly around yet barely reaching Euryale's waist.

Then, in a somehow defeated manner, she let go and stepped away, beginning to walk back to me. Euryale remained absolutely motionless, her eyes fixed on the sea as though she herself had been turned to stone. Before Steggie reached me, that giant, lumbering and lonely figure silently retreated inside, ducking back into that old stone cottage.

"What was all that about?" I asked as we wandered off together down the beach, some distance from the shore. As the words left my mouth, I realised that the truth of what had been spoken between them would never be unveiled. Before she even had time to reply, a faint noise reached us; carried on the wind, it was the definite sound of a door being closed.

We turned back together to witness Euryale, making her way down the garden path, past all those statues of ancient enemies and heading towards the sea. In one hand she held a huge circular shield, the golden disc reflecting brightly in the morning sun. In the other, a long trident spear, nearly double her own height. She never looked our way, but as her feet touched the sand, two ruffled bulges extended outwards from her back. She broke into a swift and silent run, before launching herself forwards into a dive as those majestic wings spread fully wide, and she shot out at a wondrous speed, gliding effortlessly over the waves.

"Where is she going?" I asked, as her impressive outline grew small upon the horizon. There was a hint of sadness and longing in Steggie's voice when she replied.

"She's going to find her sister, Stheno."

The atmosphere down in the heart of the Hive—that deep and spacious cave system—had distinctly changed when we returned. The whole place was bustling with activity: final arrangements and last-minute preparations were already underway. The white-sheeted walls of the tent where we had previously met the Elders had been rolled up and raised, to allow greater numbers to gather underneath and around the edges. We saw Wolfe's face poke out from among the many seated there, clearly delighted that the two of us had returned safely.

The Loup Garou had indeed been busy during our absence, and I took a moment to view the other groups and small tribes who they had succeeded in convincing to join us on the journey.

There was a loose herd of Centaurs meandering through the cavern. Their hooves made a great deal of noise crossing those rocky surfaces, kicking up a fair bit of dust as well, but they navigated the terrain with the nimbleness of mountain goats. They were intimidating creatures, approximately fifty in number, with the lower body of a mighty horse. At the point where the neck and head would typically be on their waking world counterparts, rose the barrel-chested upper torso of a man. They had a cold, wild look in their eyes, a look common in all the ones I encountered that day. I never saw them smile, and though they could speak, they were not lovers of small talk or any sort of conversation for that matter. They were broad and incredibly muscular, preferring not to cover their skin with clothes or armour. They classed themselves as the most talented hunters in existence, each carrying only an intricately carved longbow, and an enormous quiver slung over their backs, packed full of vividly coloured feathered arrows.

Then there were the birdmen, or Garuda, as they liked to be called, a strange tribe who were to be found only on a small secluded island in the South Seas. Back when they existed within the waking world, they had been of invaluable assistance to early man, devouring all types of serpents and snakes. But since relocating to the dream world, they had completely lost their appetite for those legless land lizards and developed an obsessive taste for fish. Their current lifestyle was divided between spearfishing off their tropical shores and eating what they caught. There in the cave, with nothing to fish for, they were busy eating from large, roughly sewn sacks which they had packed in advance. The contents of which, somewhat repulsively, were still bulging and thrashing wildly in the unlikely hope of escaping their fate. It turned out they were mercenaries, of a rather greedy variety. They had only joined us on the promise that the Loup Garou would deliver a considerable haul of freshwater salmon to them as payment, a delicacy that they adored and which was not available anywhere near their remote island.

Last, but certainly not least, were a family of five woolly mammoths. One wouldn't have guessed, as indeed I didn't at first, that these enormous, heavyweight, prehistoric animals each carried a human passenger. They weren't domesticated or owned, mind you, it was more of a mutually beneficial partnership of sorts. Their Inuit riders were a family too, each member buried and concealed beneath the mountains of shaggy fur close to the creature's necks. Due to those animals' distaste for desert climates, their riders dismounted before we left and spent a great deal of time showering them with ice water from head to toe. They were the muscle and brute force of our unusual army.

The Coven of the North had arrived ahead of us, and they were talking earnestly with the seven Elders. All except the one witch who had ridden off into the sea alone, and whose return was anxiously awaited. The sea dragons were there too, playing a quite ridiculous game around the sides of the enchanted pool. They were restlessly flopping back and forth through the blue waters of the portal that led back to their coastal territory. What might have been mistaken for indecision on their part was, in fact, a bloodthirsty, revenge-fueled impatience to get going.

The Loup Garou were all gathered there as well, making up the clear majority of our total forces, numbering just over two hundred. They were well organised and demonstrated a high degree of military experience and professionalism, which was otherwise lacking within that cave. They were arranged in squadrons, tightly formed lines of five, four rows deep, each with their own chosen leader who was circling, inspecting them closely and giving instructions. Steggie and I both noticed that Kai was in charge of one such squad.

It was an awe-inspiring sight to see. For the first time, we viewed them all standing to attention in their wolfmen forms, all uniformly armed in a stylish yet daunting manner. Their weaponry looked brutal and intimidating. Tightly strapped to each of their thighs were long and serrated bone blade daggers, while criss-crossed over their chests were two belts, the kind which soldiers in the waking world would often wear for storing ammunition. Instead of bullets, however, the belts were laden with a row of short curved blades, which, upon closer examination, seemed to resemble something similar to sabre-toothed fangs, or perhaps dinosaur claws. As if that wasn't enough, each of them carried two much larger scimitar swords hanging from their backs, whose carved handles could be seen poking up at outward angles above their broad and muscular shoulders.

Such a magical and formidable tribe, one which I am fairly certain everybody assembled there was thankful to have on our side.

Our Only Circle was positioned alongside one such group, and it was clear that while the two of us had been gone, the remaining Freedivers had become very fond of the Loup Garou, almost to the point of devoted admiration. To the best of their ability, they had attempted to copy our wolfmen friends. Not only by arranging themselves in the same formation but all the way down to the similar style and positioning of straps and holsters.

The hour was approaching, and an enthusiastic buzz was in the air, as the time of our departure loomed. It was then that we saw Quidel beckoning Steggie and me over to the tent where, upon arriving at his side, he began to repeat a vital briefing that we had apparently missed. He barely got started though, and never got the chance to finish telling us the details of that message.

We all heard it before we saw it: the raw, shrill cawing sound of an alarm which echoed throughout the caves. Followed shortly by the crow itself, which made that desperate cry as it swooped down out of the old mine shaft and into the deep cavern. With great skill it threaded its way swiftly through the waiting masses, landing with a wild and frantic beating of its wings by our feet. The second it touched the dirt it transformed into its human form, hurriedly reporting its news to Quidel.

"We are under attack. It's the Stalkers, hundreds of them. They just came pouring over the ridge and down through the Nest entrance. They knew exactly where they were going. I managed to lock the double doors, but that didn't even hold them long. There was no stopping them: they swept through the Hive like a plague. I barely made it down here with my life. We must hurry, they're coming!"

Quidel nodded, stepping forward and laying one hand upon the other man's shoulder, his words kind and consoling.

"Do not blame yourself, brother. Go quickly now, and join your designated squadron."

The Loup Garou messenger bowed and backed away, transforming instantly into its lean wolfman guise and crossed the cave before quickly buckling on its weapons.

All eyes turned to Quidel who, in that awful moment, had to make the toughest of decisions: to make a stand, right then and there, and defend their sacred home, or to flee like cowards, leaving that wondrous place to ruin at the hands of those evil intruders. At that moment, we all heard a click, and then the mechanical whirring strain as the elevator pulleys stirred into action, slowly taking the empty lift upwards.

"We go now!" Quidel cried out in a booming voice. The

squadron leaders immediately set to work, opening a line of wide doorway portals to lead us out of the caves.

Three of the witches leapt forward. With their arms outstretched and faces seriously set, they focused their combined efforts on a six-foot rounded boulder which, before our very eyes, began to fade and disappear. In one sweeping, united movement their palms all swung towards the mine shaft where, to our amazement, through the grated metalwork of the ascending lift, we saw that massive rock reappearing within the cage. Its weight proved to be beyond the lift's maximum capacity. The whole thing coming to a noisy, grinding halt, buying us all some crucial seconds.

From far above came those chilling, inhuman voices of the Black-Eyed Children. Calling down without a trace of emotion, their repeated hollow pleadings for help. As soon as those ten portals opened up, our divided numbers hastily followed the Loup Garou squadrons through, leaving those caves silent and empty behind us.

We had been forced to evacuate the Hive, and from that necessity came the decision to obliterate those doorways once we were safely on the other side. By doing so, the Stalkers would not be able to follow and attack us from behind, but it also meant that our safe exits of escape were destroyed. It was a decision that would eventually be our undoing.

The new terrain we faced was staggering. The Desert of Vumbi Bones stretched out infinitely before us in all directions: an even and unbroken plain of incalculable size. Ahead, the salt flats shimmered a dazzling white, the ground's surface flaky, parched and crystalline. It wasn't long before the woolly mammoths were irritably making their displeasure known, their thick coats becoming suffocating under the sweltering midday sun.

A deceptive heat haze hung low to the ground, meaning that despite the uninterrupted view for miles towards the horizon, close to the floor it was a blurred mirage, an obscure steaming film that danced in a thin layer, creating potential blind spots. Added to which, fine salt particles were constantly being stirred up, floating invisibly through the choking air, stinging our eyes and impairing our sight further. That, however, as we were soon to learn, was far from the sum of our problems.

Our newly formed army was spread out along that desert basin. Within that line, we—myself, Steggie, Wolfe and the remaining Only Circle—were centrally located, sandwiched somewhat reassuringly between two squadrons of the Loup Garou. From further to our right, we saw Quidel signalling to Kai who, once the message had been received, quickly approached Steggie and I. He went on to explain a summarised version of the briefing we had missed.

It turned out that the salt flats had been chosen for the Anchor's hiding place, partially due to a peculiar characteristic of that surrounding area. There was something about the air itself in that place, that interfered with the use of windows. Whether it was the density, the heat, or some chemical reaction from the salt itself was not known for sure. The result, however, was an unbreachable barrier of limited travel, which meant the rest of the journey had to be made on foot. He continued to point out that, where we currently stood, although unable to be seen by the naked eye, was the boundary line, encircling the entire plain that lay ahead of us. Behind us—he gestured towards the empty space where the ten doorways had stood only moments ago— was the last point where windows or any other type of travel portal could successfully be created. He ended by letting us know that he, together with his squadron, had been given strict orders to stay close, and keep a watchful eye on us Freedivers, and in particular Steggie Belle. Two things then happened before we started to march across that salt-encrusted landscape.

Steggie retraced her steps about a dozen or so paces and, with the help of a few other Freedivers, began building a large window, reinforced with thick beams and supporting bars, which led directly back to the safety of the Treetop summit. While that was happening, I took several steps forward and dropped to my knees, unaware that Wolfe, Puddle, and others within our tight-knit group had followed and were silently watching me.

I'm not sure why I tried, perhaps a curiosity to understand, or some misguided belief that maybe, just maybe, I was special. With all my energy and effort, I focused and tried to create a window, building it carefully from the ground upwards. I heard astonished gasps behind me as, inch by inch, the foundations of the portal began to form. I raised it with great difficulty until it was almost six inches off the floor, and then I seemed to hit a solid barrier, an invisible and unyielding wall. After a further minute of futile struggling, my optimism was gone and, with sweat trickling down my cheeks, I was forced to admit defeat. It could not be done. The portal could not rise tall enough, and a window was indeed impossible.

We journeyed towards our destination mostly in silence, apprehensive and fearful of what we might find. Steggie had insisted to me that I not mention to the others what she had shown me back in Germany, within the waking world, and I respected her wishes.

"Wolfe," I asked privately at one point along the way, "have you ever heard anything about Sacred Ice?" He looked blankly back at me, then up towards the blazing sun. He was clearly suffering from the intense heat, panting heavily with his clothes caked in a mixture of salt dust and sweat.

"I haven't got a clue," he finally replied. "But whatever it is, it sounds lovely. I wish we had some with us right now!"

Soon we spied signs that the ground had been disturbed up ahead, with the faint shape of something dark and unmoving in the distance, and so we fanned out into a semicircle, approaching the site warily. It wasn't until we had gotten quite close that everyone halted, uncertain exactly what to make of what was lying there in front of us. It clearly had the Coven and the Elders of the Loup Garou very worried, turning suspiciously in every direction, searching for some sign of danger which they were unable to find.

Kai had crept quietly alongside us, his eyes totally focused on the object ahead.

"Is it," Steggie whispered, barely breathing, "the dream world part? The Anchor of Perspicax?"

He only nodded gravely in response, his gaze never faltering from it.

"Something's very wrong!" he finally replied, leaning forward and inquisitively sniffing the air. The tension was spreading and quite unbearable. The Anchor was just positioned there, out in the open, in the middle of a strange and circular platform. It was box-shaped, large and antique looking, and gave the sure impression, without even needing to touch it, that it was extremely heavy. My lips were dry and cracked, and it hurt to open them as I prepared to ask a question. Before I got the chance, Kai started talking again, whimsically, as if he was speaking purely to himself:

"Someone's been here before us. Recently too, that's for certain. We buried the Anchor deep beneath the surface here, in an unmarked grave. It makes no sense how they managed to find it. Even less why, once dug up, it would have been left here unattended."

"Perhaps it was heavier than they expected?" Wolfe suggested. "Maybe they didn't have the right equipment to take it away with them straight away?"

Kai did not seem convinced, and I noticed then that some of the Coven had gathered around the perimeter of that raised platform. Several of the Loup Garou had also advanced, getting down on all fours, and smelling for a scent along its rounded edge.

"Seems more like some kind of trap to me," Kai concluded ominously. It was Steggie who was the next to speak up.

"Well, be that as it may, trap or not, we must do something. This could be the one chance we have to get it someplace safe."

Although that line of reasoning seemed sound, it became obvious that nobody was overly keen to step forward first. It was one of the witches who finally took that leap of faith, moving closer and raising one leg up to step onto the platform. As soon as she made contact, there was an almighty bang and a flash of light, as some electrical charge threw her backwards several feet, skidding across the salty plain. We were relieved to see, after a few seconds, that she had not been too badly hurt, dusting herself off and gingerly rising back onto her feet.

Kai was the next to try, leaping forward, curling himself into a ball in mid-air, in what would have been the beginning of a high aerial somersault. In doing so, he vaulted clear over the edge of the platform, but before he even came close to a landing, that same force field struck him, sending him reeling backwards with great violence and tumbling painfully over the loose ground.

Moments later, a seed of worry darted through my mind, a premonition of sorts. The kind of sinking gut feeling that turns the stomach. It soon became a reality, as Steggie moved closer beside me, offering her hand for me to take.

"Zoofall, will you try with me?"

Feeling sure this was an awful gamble that we would regret very soon, I steadied my nerves, and we stepped forward together. I closed my eyes, wincing in anticipation of the same high voltage current shooting through the two of us and propelling us back across the desert floor. But it never came. Still half-expecting the sudden delayed shock to strike, I hesitantly opened one eye, to find the two of us standing there unharmed on top of the flat raised platform.

Perhaps we should have known right then that something was wrong, but there was so little time, as we found ourselves caught up in a wave of excited celebrations. A plan was quickly formed and implemented. One squadron of the Loup Garou was chosen, and they lined themselves in two long columns facing away from where we stood. They then promptly transformed into a team of great packhorses, which their squadron leader hastily reined and tethered together.

While that was going on, the Coven took charge, issuing instructions to everyone assembled: orders that were immediately carried out. The birdmen, with their long spear hooks angled downwards, were joined by the fleet of sea dragons, creating a great circling ring flapping through the air high above our heads, keeping a lookout from way up in that milk-blue sky. The mammoths positioned themselves on either side of the packhorses as protection, with the Loup Garou and Freedivers assisting. Every one of us remained vigilant and on high alert.

The giant leather straps attached and trailing behind that team of horses were thrown up to Steggie and me, and we set to work, looping and securing the ends around the Anchor of Perspicax. It was amid that panicked fumbling and tying of knots that events began to spiral rapidly out of control. Even now, looking back, it's hard to be sure of the precise order in which those things unfolded. It all happened so quickly, but I will do my best.

It was the Centaurs that got wind of something first. Their hooves aggressively stomped at the ground, and I remember looking up to see them circling that platform at high speed, drawing their bows and keeping them raised and at the ready before anyone else noticed anything. I had just finished tightening my last strap, as the call rang down from above. Our lookouts up above had spotted something, far away, in the direction from which we had come.

All eyes followed the angle in which the birdmen's spears were pointing. Out of the cloudless, light blue sky, a single dark speck appeared, growing larger as it flew towards us. Steggie and I rose to our feet. Before we could make out what was headed our way, a terrible sound rose up, reverberating over the salt flats and sounding as if it was coming at us from all sides. It was the deafening war cry of thousands of roaring creatures. Still, we could see nothing.

The two of us spun around up there on the raised platform.

We looked wildly in all directions in a desperate attempt to find the source of that fearsome noise—but the horizon appeared clear and empty. That layer of heat haze revealing nothing, just a blurry film of brilliant white, reflecting the salt that surrounded us for miles, and nothing more. The next voice to reach us over the escalating din was a reassuring one. The leader of the Coven's calm and steady voice rang clearly inside both our heads.

"The shape approaching in the sky. It is our sister returning from her meeting with Proteus. She's calling to us with news, but she's still too far away. Out of range, and we cannot hear her clearly."

It was then, as I continued to stare at the horizon that I saw it. The semicircle of the salt flats further past the platform changed. To my utter horror, like a blotch of ink spreading upon an unmarked page, the white heat haze beyond us turned black. Through the frantic flapping in the sky above, I heard the birdmen raise the alarm, shouting to all of us down below:

"They're coming up out of the ground! They've been lying in wait beneath the salt!"

From the corner of my eye, I saw a flash of fur as the squadron leader sprung up to stand on the backs of the lead two packhorses, straddling them and urging them to move. As all twenty strained and began gathering momentum, the straps became taut, and the Anchor started to slide away towards the edge of the platform. That was when Steggie and I both felt it: the platform began to move.

Stumbling to maintain our balance, we saw the Anchor drop off the side, heard the weighty crunch as it hit the salt plain, and then watched it being successfully dragged away. Any joy was short-lived as, looking at one another, we knew we had a serious problem. The platform was rotating, turning on the spot like a merry-go-round in the park, but with no handlebars to hold onto and it was rapidly picking up speed.

The world was fast becoming a spinning cloud of blurred colours as we clung firmly to each other for stability. Our friends— so close, and yet beyond our reach—became an indistinguishable patch of black, flashing by at regular intervals, unable to help us, as round and round we spun. The whole thing was already moving so fast that even the smallest step was enough to make us lose our balance and fall. Right then, the piercing cry reached us. The returning witch's telepathic message projected as though she was screaming at the top of her lungs, over and over again:

"It's not Steggie they're after! They want the boy! The Shifter… the one with the scar!"

That shocking sentence wailed like a siren through my head as, in that very moment, I lost my grip on Steggie Belle. As I flailed dizzily, trying to reconnect with her, I saw both her hands, palms facing out, hurtling towards me at a brutal speed. I felt her incredible strength as, with all the power that she possessed, she pushed me clear off of that platform.

Falling backwards, in that weightless and timeless spell, I realised that Steggie had just saved my life. Unknown to me, as I crashed ungracefully like a sack of potatoes through the salt flakes, it was not to be the last time she would do so that day.

20

How We Lost Her

Perhaps I was knocked unconscious in the fall, but if so, it must have only been for a few seconds. When I opened my eyes, Wolfe was kneeling over me, shaking me roughly by the shoulders. Puddle and the rest of the Only Circle were crowded close by and looking down at me with great concern.

"Come on, Zoofall, you have to get up!"

Though I was dazed, I could hear the fear in his voice. Staggering to my feet, I looked around. There was no sign of the platform—or Steggie.

"What happened?" I asked, totally bewildered. Wolfe pointed one finger into the distance and following it, I saw a wide trailing furrow carved deep through the surface of the plain, starting from where the platform had previously stood.

"Just after she pushed you, the whole thing sped off that way, with her still stuck on top of it. It was a trap, Zoofall! That whole platform … with the Anchor as bait, it was all one massive trap!"

I strained my eyes down the line of that endless trench. Just before the dark backdrop of the heat haze horizon, I thought I saw a glimmer of movement. I focused, placing both hands up to my temples, concentrating and trying to channel the vision of the Owl Totem's power. My eyes widened as the strength of my sight was magnified. About two miles from where we stood was a lone figure running desperately towards us. It was Steggie Belle. I could see her raising a small thin instrument to her mouth, and heard the faint note of a whistle rise bleakly on the wind. All the while that black wall, still cloaked within the shimmering haze, rose up all around her, closing in.

"We have to help her!" I cried out. Wolfe grabbed my shoulder, pulling me back and pointing once again, off at a slightly different angle.

"The Centaurs are already headed her way. They'll reach her long before we ever could. Besides, the Coven has said we have to get you and the Anchor out of here, right now!"

In the distance I could just make out two forking trails, the Centaurs, racing along either side of the trench towards her, hidden by the billowing clouds of salt their hooves were kicking up. Meanwhile, Wolfe continued insistently to drag me away. The team of packhorses, towing the Anchor in their wake, was already far ahead, with the woolly mammoths in pursuit, doing their best to keep up.

As we fled, retreating towards the window Steggie had previously made, I realised that the Freedivers and I were being closely guarded by both the Loup Garou and the members of the Coven. That was when, over their heads on either side of our army, I saw two dark and swirling clouds rise up into the sky. Soon we could hear it too, the familiar droning buzz as those enormous clouds swept towards us. What was even more terrifying was how, as they got closer, we could clearly make out their size and features: their giant wings and barbed, spear-like stinging tails.

"There must be thousands of them!" I yelled at Wolfe, just as daylight appeared to fade, with their endless numbers actually blotting out the sun. Looking up, we watched as our winged cavalry, those agile birdmen, divided themselves into two groups and flew to protect us from those plague-like swarms of giant hornets.

"Geez!" Wolfe cried out as we continued running, and those two opposing sides clashed overhead, not too far away from our fleeing column. "They must really love that salmon!"

The birdmen's limited numbers disappeared and were entirely swallowed by those dark, seething clouds. Although we could not see the battle that was raging within, soon we heard the screeching cries of the mutant hornets. Then they began to fall lifelessly from the sky, their four-foot bloated bodies slamming down into the salt all around us.

Nor, we realised, was the fighting restricted to the air. Beyond the rows of our Loup Garou guardians, we saw several hugely bulbed and pointed scorpion tails rising up over twelve feet into the air, before striking down in our direction with horrendous force. Each attack was closely followed by the scraping sounds of the Loup Garou's blades fending them off, keeping them at bay and deflecting those deadly stabbing tails.

Up ahead we were just able to make out the top frame of Steggie's window and, it seemed the runaway train of packhorses had nearly reached it with the Anchor. Despite all our friends' valiant efforts as they escorted us onwards, through that final stretch of desert, they could not protect us from everything. By the sheer size of those monstrous hordes, we were overwhelmed.

One of those giant hornets dive-bombed, breaking through

our defensive ranks and only narrowly dodged one of the sea dragons lashing claws. It swooped down through the middle of us, its body contorting so that its lance-like tail was sticking out in front, seeking a victim. I heard the sickening scream and turned to see the tail pass clean through Rosethorn's thigh, impaling her and for one awful second lifting her off her feet and into the air. We all swerved as one, desperate to help, with Wolfe and I reaching her first, our minds creating deadly weapons held aloft within our tightly clenched fists. The hornet was scratching at Rosethorn with its spindly hairy legs, trying to get a better grip on her thrashing body, while madly beating its wings in the hopes of taking off once more into the sky. Wolfe's club came down splittingly hard on the back of its hideous head, while I thrust the sword I had fashioned repeatedly into the creature's chest.

We were so close to reaching that window, but with Rosethorn so badly injured our retreat had been slowed considerably, giving time for our attackers to unite and form an even more devastating assault. As she hobbled and limped her way onwards with our support, I noticed the other Freedivers glancing expectantly at me. In Steggie's absence, they were looking to me to lead. Over the chaotic sounds of battle and tremendous blows raining down close by, I tried to stay calm and collect my thoughts.

"First, we must get Rosethorn safely back through the window. Then we have to make a stand and fight. We have to keep the portal open for as long as we can—until Steggie reaches us! We need to buy her more time!"

It had sounded far easier in my head, but over that short remaining distance, our casualties began mounting up. Toejammer was injured by another diving hornet, and ScaleFist suffered a grazing blow down his right arm from a scorpion's sting, which soon became puffy, red and swollen. The packhorses had already dragged the Anchor through onto the Treetop jetty where, right then, two of the Loup Garou Elders were busily preparing to spirit it away to another secret location. Once the horses had transformed again into their wolf forms, they helped us get our wounded safely across before charging back out onto the battlefield.

"If anyone wants to stay behind, now's the time," I told our small group as we stood on the verge of the window. But not one of those Freedivers chose the easy way out, shaking their heads defiantly in unison. "Keep your distance from the Stalkers if you see them," I warned the sixteen of them as, for the first time the running was over and, we turned to face the carnage. "If you have to fight them, do it with fire!"

Looking out, with our backs to the safety of the Treetop summit, the scale of the fighting was shocking. Not far away, the Coven were spread out in a curved row, like a crescent shield and last line of defence. With their arms raised high, I watched the savage level of destruction they were unleashing upon the enemy. They were harnessing the phenomenal power of nature, using the elements to crush and slow down the advancing dark army. From gale-force blasts of wind that buffeted and pushed back those abominable creatures, to blinding salt storms and wildly tilting tornadoes that tore winding paths across the salt flats, side-swiping through the enemy lines. Every now and then, white-hot and well-aimed fireballs would shoot forth from their open palms. Right then I saw one such blast strike down the first Stalker who had managed to claw his way through the Loup Garou, sending him flying back across the ground and combusting into a ball of flames.

The towering mammoths, though slow, were effectively holding the centre of our front line, trampling anything that dared to come that way. By doing so, they had divided the enemy on the ground, forcing them to attack from either the left or the right and creating a clear channel down the middle, which reminded me in an abstract way of that biblical tale in which Moses parted the Red Sea.

It was clear from where I stood that Simeon Scythe's strategy had been to lead with that expendable army of hornets and armoured scorpions who, in their infinite numbers, had distracted us and kept us busy. Now we could see his army of Black-Eyed Children pushing through. Over the tops of their diabolical heads, I caught glimpses of him pacing to and fro in the distance, a maniacal look of delight upon his face. He resembled some evil chess Grandmaster examining the board, looking for a weak spot, some way forward, to break through and destroy us.

Our group of Freedivers advanced, veering towards the fierce fighting on the right side of the window, spreading out and heading into the fray. As we passed by the Coven, their leader stopped what she was doing, speaking to me in her wordless way.

"Don't go far, Zoofall. He'll be coming for you, and we can't afford you to be taken!"

Glancing back at her as I pressed on, I saw she'd clearly had second thoughts about allowing me such a loose rein, and was signalling two of the Coven to follow us and remain by my side. Reaching the front line, where the fighting was thickest, I watched as Wolfe leapt straight in with his barbaric club engulfed in flames and swinging wildly, taking on one of those massive scorpions all on his own.

It lashed out at him with one of its enormous pincer claws, which he avoided by the skin of his teeth, rolling through the salt as its tail came hammering down, missing him by inches. He was quick though, managing to scramble up onto its back—it drove the scorpion crazy, lurching and bucking like some Rodeo beast, trying to throw him off. I managed to slice through one of its legs which, despite toppling it momentarily as it shrieked in pain, unfortunately, seemed to make it all the more berserk.

Our efforts had been enough of a distraction to allow one of the Loup Garou to sneak in close, silently drawing one of the long daggers from the sheath on his thigh. He somehow anticipated the wounded creature's next move, launching himself through the air towards it. The scorpion reared up fiercely, just as our friend reached it and plunged the blade up through the soft underside of its neck, killing it instantly. Before the scorpion's body had even struck the ground, that Loup Garou soldier had already spun away, moving on to a new target.

There was something mesmerising about the way they moved, the Loup Garou. A fluid beauty of lethal simplicity and accelerated reflexes, flowing to complete their brutal and graceful dance. While everyone else groaned and grunted, fought and struggled, the Loup Garou simply glided. They saved each of our lives repeatedly throughout that battle, often intervening and rescuing us from dangers we hadn't even noticed. On several occasions those short claw-like blades were pulled, lightning-quick from their criss-crossed belts and hurled with incredible accuracy. Sometimes they sailed past us so close that we could feel their whistling draught pass over our skin, before striking down an enemy who had crept up right behind us unseen.

Out from among such dazzling displays, I became aware

that, like my personal witch bodyguards, Kai was never far away, always circling and staying close.

His strength, agility and speed were beyond compare, and he had a mystifying way of fusing full transformations into his battle-dance. I saw him kill one of those diving hornets neatly in mid-air while simultaneously tossing his weapon straps—swords and all—far ahead of him into the middle of the approaching mob, before curling into a ball, landing and rolling after them. What rose up from that mass of fur, gaining momentum as it charged towards the nearest line of Stalkers, was a stampeding rhino which ploughed straight through without hesitation, sending them scattering. From there he changed again, from the head downwards, springing ferociously at the startled enemy in a way a rhino never could. By the time he struck, he was a fully formed Bengal tiger, sinking claws into flesh, tearing and slashing indiscriminately. For a split-second, I was worried, as one of the scorpions lunged towards him from behind. I almost called out to warn him, but before I could, I saw one of his tiger paws reaching down towards the ground, reverting to its wolf form and picking something up. Twisting at an unbelievable speed, Kai spun, swinging the retrieved scimitar sword upwards, as that bulbous tail came crashing down, lopping it cleanly off with just one blow.

As the battle raged on, what I had hoped at first was nothing more than an unpleasant coincidence gradually became an undeniable pattern. Wherever I was, a growing number of Stalkers would gather, pushing forward relentlessly in waves and trying to cut me off from the others. It appeared that not even the threat of fire would discourage them or hold them back. Indeed, on one occasion they almost succeeded, stopped only by a joint effort from Kai, my Coven chaperones, and a team of sea dragons swooping down from above to wreak havoc and divide them. Were it not for them, perhaps I would not be writing these lines tonight.

At times it felt that we were not only holding our own but even gaining the upper hand. Glancing backwards, however, only proved the grim reality of our situation. Without us realising it, our forces had been steadily pushed and driven so that, quite literally, our backs were up against that window. What only made matters worse was that there was still no sign of Steggie Belle.

Over the course of the fighting, many more of the Freedivers had also been injured. And while only a few needed to be carried back through the portal, most of us were then nearing exhaustion. Even the courageous Loup Garou had suffered casualties and losses and, like our shrinking numbers, hope was also fading fast. The battle lines had been pressed tightly on both sides to within fifty feet of the window, leaving the Coven with no alternative but to fight at close quarters. We were being surrounded, squeezed in and funnelled backwards, and we were running out of room to retreat.

The great woolly mammoths were the only thing keeping that ever-tightening channel open, a hopeful runway through which Steggie might return. I remember an awful tremor as the ground beneath our feet shook, and looking up, we realised that the smallest of the mammoth family had fallen, and only four remained. Shortly after that, I felt a warm hand upon my shoulder and the Coven leader's firm voice inside my head.

"Zoofall, it's time we get you and your group safely through the window. Our situation here is circling the drain!"

"We can't! Not without Steggie!" I retaliated, baring my teeth at the horde of Stalkers who were lunging towards us on all sides, staring with their dark, hollow eyes. In a defiant move I had learnt from Steggie herself, I raised both palms, unleashing a lightning bolt which tore through that advancing line, taking at least two of them down. Within seconds, though, the smoking gap where they had been was refilled. Their places were taken by even more, and though I didn't want to admit it, inside, I knew our struggle was hopeless.

"It's no good," she insisted, summoning the rest of the Coven to her side. *"We will not be able to hold them back much longer. I made a promise to Steggie Belle that I would keep you all safe."*

So it was that amid the dying minutes of that desperate battle—against our will and with some among us kicking and screaming in protest—the last of the Only Circle were physically restrained and forced back through the window. From behind the large frame of that opening, all we could do was watch helplessly as the seemingly futile last stand was made.

Suddenly there came a deafening crash, like an almighty thunderclap, which rolled menacingly over the desert sky. All our eyes instinctively peered upwards, leaning as close to the window frame as we could get, to see what had happened. Seconds later, two flashing missiles shot into view, travelling at such high speed that at first, they were nothing more than arrow-like blurs. They climbed steeply into the blue sky before separating and then slowed to hover briefly and take in the breadth of the battlefield far below.

I recognised Euryale at once. Her partner was even larger

than she, and I assumed it must have been her sister, Stheno. The two of them descended in unison like terrifying angels, carving out ferocious paths of destruction through the encroaching army of Stalkers. Watching them swoop down, I shuddered at seeing their lower legs which transformed into monstrous weapons as their claws came out. We watched in awe, daring to believe that just maybe the two of them alone might tip the scales back in our favour. We were not the only ones.

Their arrival seemed to have spurred on both the Coven and the remaining Loup Garou, who began launching a series of re-energised attacks. I spotted Kai racing off, leading a team of his brothers, cutting a narrow channel towards those overwhelmed and isolated great mammoths who were in such desperate need of support. What happened next caught us quite unawares, our eyes following the movement for several seconds, uncertain of what exactly we were witnessing. From out of the distance, a thick dark cloud had risen, floating in a patterned stream, like fine rain rising upwards from the ground. It was headed our way, and it was only when it began to curve and dip back down that we realised what it was. We were watching an immense volley of arrows.

That moment filled our hearts with the promise of hope. The Centaurs were returning, which in turn led us to one possibility: that Steggie Belle was with them. I will never forget the moment when, through that tunnel of carnage and chaos, for one fleeting second, the two sides were prised apart, and I saw her, fighting her way back towards us.

Before those arrows even hit their targets, a fresh wave was already shooting silently through the air. These were quickly followed by another, then another. The victims never even saw it coming, as those hundreds of shafts whistled and struck. The Centaurs' aim was breathtakingly accurate, as all around those Black-Eyed Children began dropping like flies. One, no more than twenty feet from that window ledge where we were crowded, fell onto its back staring up at the desert sky, an arrow protruding from each of its sightless, darkened sockets.

If there had ever been a time for cautious celebration, it was then but, as we were soon to discover, Fate had other cruel plans in store for us.

We didn't notice it at first: our attention being glued to what was going on outside. But suddenly one of the supporting beams above our heads splintered and broke, and we knew something dreadful was happening.

The window was slowly starting to close. We clambered over one another, shouting and bracing ourselves against its shrinking sides. Some fashioned new brackets made of iron and steel, wedging them into the corners, but even those soon began to bend and crumple. The various wounded were crawling across the jetty's ancient planks towards the window, desperate to try to help. I glanced at Wolfe, who was straining with all his might, not even allowing himself to breathe, his cheeks and face turning from red to a deeper purple. We were failing to slow it down at all.

In that moment of despair, I looked out over the bloodied salt flats searching for the culprit, the one who was crushing that window despite all our efforts. My eyes travelled quickly, scanning the rows of nearest Stalkers, though they did not seem to be the guilty party, at that time clearly having their work cut out for them. They were being picked off by the steady, hollow thudding of deadly arrows, while simultaneously doing everything they could to avoid being incinerated by the Coven and their vengeful pet dragons. Then the thought struck me.

"Simeon Scythe!" I hissed through clenched teeth, as my right knee began to buckle. It took some time to locate him in amongst the madness, but there he was, standing tall and actually living up to his name. He was wildly swinging an enormous scythe, already dripping with blood, out in front of him. With great frustration, I realised it wasn't him who was doing it either, as he too had his hands full, locked in a fierce and deadly duel with two of the Loup Garou.

By that point, several of the Freedivers had no alternative but to jump back down onto the jetty, as the window continued to shrink. Only Wolfe and I remained up there, with our feet and hands pressed stubbornly against the frame, refusing to let it close.

That was when I saw it. That singular sight that made my heart and spirits sink and shatter at one and the same time. It was Steggie. She was no longer running back to us: her feet were rooted firmly into the salt, both her arms stretched purposefully in our direction, shaking her head at me in anguish. It was Steggie who was sealing the window shut.

"No! Steggie, no!" I cried out, not even considering to do so telepathically. My mind could not accept what I was seeing, and with each pounding heartbeat, I could feel my desperation rising. She was far too strong, and we couldn't fight it. Without thinking, my next move was instinctive and reckless. It was perhaps the only way I could think of, to make her stop what she was doing.

With one last heave, I rolled out and dropped back down onto the salty desert floor. Steggie must have alerted the Coven, for they all whipped around, forming an intimidating line to stop me. With tears welling in my eyes, I charged at them, and somehow scrambled through. Plotting a course straight for Steggie, I broke into a crazed and foolhardy run, aiming for the clear and narrow channel between us, vaguely aware of the sea of Stalkers pushing forwards and closing in from both sides.

I tried to take off into the air to escape their burning clutches. In that nightmarish moment, I found, perhaps due to my unbalanced emotions, that I was unable to fly more than a few feet off the ground. I didn't care. There was no time to come up with a better plan, so I settled for focusing on speed instead.

Looking back at it now, it was an impossible route. The Stalkers were far too many, striving with every ounce of strength to grab me, no matter what the cost. It was a gauntlet I could not win.

My adrenaline was such that, at first, I did not even feel the touch of their sickening rows of pale hands. I crashed my way through, oblivious to their grasping fingertips. Then the pain finally caught up with me. Searing burns tore across my body as that deathly crowd closed in. Their combined clawing was starting to slow me down, until one of their hands clamped down firmly on my ankle, gripping it tightly, before swinging me violently through the air in a completely different direction.

I was expecting to be mauled right then and there, so it was a strange relief not to feel any more of those terrible hands taking hold of me. Disorientated, I managed to roll over and make it to my knees, wincing from the pain of freshly burnt scars all over my body. It was then, looking around, that I realised how extremely bad my situation was. I was surrounded by a leering wall of Black-Eyed Children, some of whom had allowed their arms to grow into those diabolical, sharp claws. That was not the worst of it for, while they were keeping their distance, for the time being, there was another tall figure standing not far from me within that enclosed ring.

The look of pure evil and hatred upon Simeon Scythe's face was terrifying as he towered threateningly over me.

"One click of my fingers and my servants here will tear you limb from limb!" he shouted, before cackling with glee, and then calmly lowered his voice, which somehow sounded even worse. "That is … unless you would be willing to come quietly?"

He pulled a colossal length of jangling metal shackles out from behind his back and threw them in disgust onto the ground in front of me.

At that moment I heard frenzied howling cries rise up from beyond that crowd: it appeared that some of the Loup Garou were trying to force their way through and attempt a rescue.

"Time is ticking …" he taunted venomously, kicking at the salt with his boot.

From not far away, I heard my name called, and I recognised the voice. It was Kai. My eyes followed the sound, and I saw one of his curved scimitar swords being hurled over the heads of that horde. It was spinning as it flew, and landed with a clatter only a few feet from where I knelt. Simeon eyed the blade suspiciously. Pivoting slightly onto his back foot, he raised his scythe in preparation before glaring at me expectantly.

I didn't hesitate, scrambling through the salt and grabbing it by the hilt, retrieving it just before the scythe came down. I rolled away, struggling to get back onto my feet as he swung at me again. His next blow came down hard, in a wild curving arc, and I was barely able to block it, our blades locking just above my head. With my free hand, I released a ball of white energy that struck him in the chest, knocking him backwards and off-balance. He laughed contemptuously at the attack before coming back for more.

What followed was a brief and nail-biting game of cat and mouse, as he chased me around that ring, and it was all I could do to stay out of his reach. He was just too strong, too powerful, and the proximity of our Black-Eyed audience was causing all the scars upon my body to burn with excruciating pain. He cornered me at last, our blades locking again and, even with both my hands resisting against his weight, he forced me down onto one knee. Grimacing, I remember feeling certain it would soon be over, that neither Steggie, the Coven, nor the Loup Garou would be able to get to me in time.

Simeon Scythe bore down with all his might, the tip of his curved blade only inches from my face. Suddenly the ground opened up beneath me, and I felt hands take hold of my legs, pulling me sharply down. I collapsed there, safely back on the planks of the Treetop jetty, gasping and staring incredulously at Puddle, who was lying breathless beside me. Where everyone had failed, he had found a way. As though to illustrate how close a call it had been, despite having quickly closed his puddle portal behind us, half of Simeon Scythe's scythe was embedded there, sticking up vertically through the wooden planks.

I ran back to the window, which had already begun to close again and was then only a little bigger than a picture frame. As I did so, the other Freedivers all rushed around, desperately holding me back.

I caught sight of Steggie, just as the desert floor between her feet began to rise and open up. Straight out of the salt it grew, first the head whinnying and shaking itself free, then the long flowing mane, followed by the torso and legs. Its nostrils flared and snorted out salt dust as the animal stamped its way determinedly out from the ground, with Steggie seated on top of it. From the way she patted and lovingly caressed its forehead, I instantly knew it must be Tiger, the horse from her past, her first friend and guide within the dream world.

"Puddle," I cried, turning around and shaking him roughly by the shoulders. "Make another of your portals and get me back out there. I'm begging you. There's still enough time ... we can still reach her." That was when her voice reached out to me, calmly projecting her words inside my head.

"Chance has been a fine and wondrous thing to me, something that I have unexpectedly grown to love and treasure. You must let me go. It was always meant to be this way. You have to promise me that you will not come back."

Looking back through the window, which was by then no larger than an envelope, I saw that her horse had sprouted great white feathered wings, and risen up like the fabled Pegasus into the sky. As they rose, I swallowed hard, knowing then that, even if Puddle had wanted to, it was too late to get to her and pull her back through.

"You must promise me, Zoofall!" she repeated insistently. My whole body was shaking, even my fingertips were trembling as they gripped that diminishing window frame. My mouth betrayed me, and I unwillingly gave her my word.

"I will not come back ..." I mumbled as all around me I heard the other Freedivers sobbing, and even Wolfe desperately choking back his tears.

She reared up further into the blue upon that flying stallion, pausing to turn back and whisper her final words to me.

"No matter what, Zoofall, dreams are worth living."

I watched as she veered off, joining up with Euryale and Stheno, both of them flanking her on either side. The very last thing I saw before that window closed, was the three of them swooping down together, with Steggie Belle leading the charge, heading straight for the heart of that dark army, with Simeon Scythe screaming at its centre.

After that, the window was gone, with only the stillness of the jungle canopy stretching out down below. Moments later, there came a tremendous explosion, out there on the distant horizon, somewhere to the west.

Then nothing. Not even a single birdsong to sweeten the air.

I sank to my knees and buried my head in my hands. For I understood right then that I had misheard Steggie's previous conversation with the Coven leader, out there upon that beach.

There had never been any such thing, or mention, of 'Sacred Ice'.

I couldn't control myself. The tears flowed freely.

The word had been 'Sacrifice'.

21

Thirty Years and a Phone Call

Even though you and I have not met, you must believe me when I say that I did not give up on Steggie Belle easily. Far from it. We all waited up there in the Treetop summit for her to return. Around nightfall, we spotted the twinkling glow from many fiery torches, moving through the forest far below. No noise accompanied them, but the line was advancing steadily towards us, and so the decision was made to retreat to the training cavern, where we were certain she would find us.

It was to be the longest wait I had ever known. Looking back, I do not blame the other Freedivers for returning to the waking world. Wolfe was the last to leave and did so reluctantly, but he knew that, with the weekend coming to an end, his mother would soon be returning and his absence would not go unnoticed long. I, however, refused to leave or give up hope. I made a pact with myself that, no matter how long it might take, I would stay to make sure Steggie was safe.

My vigil was to last well over three months. Even to this day, I still regret the suffering and worry I must have caused. With no trace, or sign of me back in the waking world, I was declared missing: search parties were launched, and in time it was presumed that I had probably been kidnapped, or worse. Wolfe was the only one who knew exactly where I was but, for obvious reasons, was sworn to secrecy and unable to utter a word.

Loneliness became my shadow, my silent cellmate down there, and time passed so very slowly. I wasn't completely alone all of the time, mind you. Each evening it became a regular source of relief to hear the footsteps of the Only Circle tiptoeing down those spiral stairs. One by one, their visits became less frequent as, I suppose, they gradually began to face the reality that I could not. I lost track of days altogether, but Wolfe assures me it would have been just after Christmas Day that I finally received a visit from the dream world.

My heart leapt as I watched the outline of that portal appear and start to form, but sadly it was not Steggie who stepped through. It was Kai, and from the way he approached with lowered head and a reluctance to look me in the eye, I knew he was not the bearer of good news.

"She's not coming back, Zoofall," he sighed, sitting down cross-legged on the floor beside me. "The Coven wanted to be the ones to tell you, but I insisted it should be me."

I found myself unable to speak or lift my gaze from that smooth stone floor as Kai continued to deliver his solemn report. I remember there was a tiny green shoot, a weed no longer than my fingertip, growing up in between two heavy flagstones. I focused on it while he spoke, as though it symbolised some last strand of hope, a final chance of salvation, with the power to somehow change the way things were. Everything else melted into insignificance: it was a lifeline, and I was the drowning man.

He, together with the surviving nine members of the Coven,

347

had spent the last several weeks since the day of that terrible battle attempting to understand the whys, the real motives behind what had transpired. As to the exact fate of Steggie, Euryale and Stheno, nobody could be sure as, from the final moments of that fight, none of them had been seen or heard from again. Kai himself had witnessed the three of them leading that heroic charge, and then the next moment the entire salt flats had been lit by a blinding flash—an explosion that rocked the whole desert and stretched to the limits of the horizon. They had been at its centre, and he assured me with great sadness that nothing within either world could have survived such a blast.

Even so, those among our allies who had managed to pick themselves up off the scorched surface had held out hope, wanting so desperately to believe. Yet, despite long and extensive efforts, not a single trace of the three of them was found. Wide-scale searches had been repeatedly launched but, discovering nothing, had finally been called off.

What of Simeon Scythe, and his dark army? Kai admitted that concrete knowledge was scarce, but that rumours had been running wild throughout the dream world ever since. That somehow, by using many of his evil Stalkers as a kind of human shield, he had succeeded in escaping. Several unconfirmed sightings had been reported, placing him within the dead and barren lands where some believe he is taking refuge, licking his wounds, deep within the bowels of the former Temptors' Lair.

Kai went on to explain the other mystery they had unravelled, and the revelations which had been revealed. To a large extent, he continued, that was the reason for him coming to see me. They had finally figured out the reason why Simeon Scythe had gone to such extraordinary lengths to try to capture me.

He lay in front of me an exquisite old book, similar in some ways to the golden one we had recovered from the cellar of the ruined mansion years before. Opening it to a specific page, he pointed and waited for my reaction. There was a faded drawing, with a brief description underneath in a language I did not recognise. At first, I did not put two and two together. The picture was of a dark figure, whose identity was quite unrecognisable, with features obscured by deliberate thick and heavy shading.

Then I noticed the patterns, subtly blended within the portrait. There were slightly lighter markings across that mysterious figure's body, marks I knew only too well. They were, without doubt, the scars I bore, many of which were still in the early stages of healing, from that painful attempt of flying to reach Steggie Belle. By the figure's feet within that drawing was the equally dark shape of a large rectangular box. My curiosity had been awakened.

"You see? It was the text beneath that gave us the most difficulty," Kai remarked, encouraging me to focus on those archaic looping symbols. "Because it is written in an ancient angelic dialect, which has not been seen or spoken for over twenty thousand years. But, at last, the Coven has succeeded in deciphering the text:

'The worlds will give birth to a being of coincidence. Only by such an individual's hand can the Broken be carried to the Temple of Restoration. Blessed and cursed will that person be, for every covetous eye, will try to guide the hand that can raise the Anchor.'"

A full minute of silence passed before Kai reluctantly continued.

"Steggie believed. She had an inkling of who you might be

the whole time. She was willing to lay down her life to protect it. That's why she made you promise, made you give your word, no matter how hard it might be. It's just too dangerous, Zoofall. Who knows what Simeon would have you do if he was able to get his hands on you. That is why you must not, under any circumstances, come back. Even these training chambers are not completely safe."

I looked around the cavern which held so very many special memories, feeling a great sadness welling up inside of me.

"What if he should come for me again, within the waking world as he did for the Inner Circle?"

"We cannot guarantee that he won't. But do not fear: though you may not recognise us, the Loup Garou pack and I have sworn to keep a close eye on you, for as long as needs be. My advice to you is simple. Keep your guard up, be forever watchful, and if possible, try not to stay in one place too long or draw suspicion upon yourself."

I was devastated. Faced right then with such an unfair future and all its implications. It would take a long time for me to learn how to live with so harsh a sentence. Before Kai got up to leave, I tried returning his scimitar sword that I had been holding onto since that day in the desert, when he saved my life from that cursed ring of Stalkers. He refused to take it back, offering it to me instead as a parting gift.

"You keep it safe. You never know when you might have need of it in the future," Kai said, shaking my hand meaningfully, as true friends do. "Take care of yourself, and keep your chin up. Perhaps one day, we shall meet again. And remember, the Loup Garou will be watching you."

With those words, he was gone, and I waited there, a

miserable wretch upon the floor. Hoping that soon, as regular as clockwork, Wolfe would be arriving down those stairs to check up on me. Meanwhile, as a symbolic gesture, so she would never be forgotten, I decided to fashion a humble gravestone made of marble, right there in the middle of that cavern, under the central arches. The inscription I carved upon it was a simple memorial: In Memory of Steggie Belle—Leader of The Dream Warriors.

Standing back to regard my work, it struck me that something about it was totally wrong. It didn't need any embellishing, grand wreaths, or flowers, but it just seemed too terrible and lonely an end. So I stepped forward once more and carved a smaller headstone beside it, which read: Zoofall—Her Friend, and fellow dreamer.

When Wolfe arrived and saw them, without any words he understood; he put one arm comfortingly around my shoulder, and we stood there in silence for a while. Before I agreed to return to the waking world, I asked one final favour from him. He said he would do it, on the firm condition that I did not follow.

He opened a window straight out onto the Treetop jetty, looking very cautiously around first, then stepped softly through. In our last act as the survivors of a dying group, he dashed across those planks, right to the very edge, understandably nervous about what might be lurking out there in the stillness of the night. He planted a five-foot pole, wedging it in the middle of the wooden boards, from which he hung and lit a brightly burning lantern, then scampered quickly back through.

That was our closing gesture, a hope against all the odds, that someday Steggie might see that flame burning through the darkness and find her way home.

351

Well, the rest—as adults are so fond of saying—is history. What none of us could have possibly foreseen, the impossible, the unimaginable, finally happened. We grew up, and we grew old.

I fear I have become a mere shadow of the fourteen-year-old boy whom the police found wandering alone along a country road in the middle of the night, all those years ago. Yet another misunderstood miracle, this time of a supposedly kidnapped boy having escaped or been released from his captors. Of course, they had many questions for me, almost two days' worth in fact, but I played dumb, remaining vague on any details. They photographed my many scars and concluded with misguided sympathy that I must have been the victim of some cruel and truly horrific ordeal, tortured and psychologically traumatised, and still in a state of shock. I refused to talk and was eventually returned to my hugely relieved parents.

Growing up is seldom easy, partly because life passes by in such a bright and furious collage of scattered images and moments, almost like a dream. Even by denying the inner child and taking on the guise of a grown-up, life still finds a way of throwing up surprises and taking one on a journey which could never have been planned or prepared for.

With barely any candle wax remaining at all, how would I be able to best sum up the last thirty years? A period of time that has ended just recently with an astoundingly bizarre event. An incident, so unexpected, so unpredictable, that it has forced me to confess these secrets, on such a cold and stormy night.

So, what became of the Dream Warriors? That Only Circle? It may please you to hear that we have tried over the years to keep in touch, no matter how determined the world has sometimes seemed to divide us. For the most part these days, we send and receive strange holiday and birthday cards to, and from, one another, which I'm sure to an outsider must appear quite peculiar. "Seasons Greetings!" with a savage and sinister-looking werewolf with blood dripping from its jaws. Or a Coven of ugly witches gathered around a cauldron. Or a photograph of the Amazon rainforest canopy, taken from a dizzying height, with an arrow and a question mark drawn in pen upon it, aiming towards a distant lofty outcrop.

Last year I received a birthday card from Marble Tap, a print of a classical painting depicting those three dreaded and monstrous Gorgon sisters, Euryale, as I remember her, unrecognisable among them. All that was written inside was: "Heroes take on many shapes and sizes!"

These little things keep us somehow connected, help us to smile through the hard times, and remind us of those wild and early dreaming days.

For me personally, there are two members of the group whom I have kept in regular close contact with and still consider my dearest friends. They are Puddle and, perhaps not surprisingly, Wolfe. Two individuals who, as fate would have it, could not have possibly walked more differing paths.

Puddle has grown into a quite remarkable man. He moved to live in England by the time he was in his early twenties, in a small town just outside of London. He became a jeweller by trade, but outside of this regular work he succeeded in bringing back a skill from the dream world which he had always had a natural knack for—Healing. Having learnt how to balance such powerful energies, he now offers this rare ability for free to anyone

353

in need. A wonderful man who, even if you were to pass him in the street, you would recognise and believe you knew somehow, so strong are those natural forces of peace that it creates an aura which radiates from his being.

He has since got married and raised three beautiful children. And in the most tender mark of love and respect, he even managed to squeeze in a middle name for his first-born daughter: Fiona Belle. I have visited him many times, and it has been one of the greatest pleasures to watch his family grow. It has happened on occasions when he has invited me along to a dinner party, that some other adult present has raised the subject of dreams. "Oh, I had the strangest dream the other night. I wonder what on earth it could have meant?" or some such innocent anecdote. It doesn't seem to matter how old we get, but in those instances, the two of us feel as brave as the children we once were, stealing glances towards one another. A large part wishes we could tell them all we know, explain the truth and set them free. But sadly, some secrets must remain hidden, which, in a roundabout sort of way, brings me to Wolfe.

Ah, Wolfe, my closest ally and childhood partner in crime. Long have I agonised and worried over you, my friend, and yet now, as the hour of our destiny approaches, I see everything so clearly. I understand there was never any need to doubt you.

When he first told me of his plan, barely a week after his eighteenth birthday, I was horrified and told him it was utter madness. Yet despite my strong disapproval and constant pleadings, he followed through with it anyway. He started telling the world, and anyone who would listen. Not all of it, mind you, but certainly enough of our secrets to stand out in the modern world like a sore thumb.

Naturally, the rational minds of this world concluded that something must be done to safeguard society from such an unstable man. So it is that Wolfe has spent the last three decades securely locked inside a psychiatric hospital. He never appeared bothered by that outcome—quite the opposite actually, almost content or satisfied.

Over the time that has passed, I have visited him as often as I could, or that his doctors would allow. And it is only here in these pages that I will admit with shameful regret that there have been a few times when I have wondered whether my dearest friend had indeed lost his mind. He has always been delighted to see me and would talk incessantly and with great enthusiasm about so many things. I found myself often asking him the same single question:

"Wolfe, don't you want to get out of here?" while looking around his small and solitary white cell. But until very recently, I never understood the answer he would always give:

"Don't worry, Zoofall, it's just part of my retirement plan."

Well, I guess that brings my story full circle back to me. What, you may ask, would a young Shifter be expected to do with his life, when the one thing he longs for the most, to dream, has been forbidden and denied? Perhaps, with the skills I have already carried over and mastered, I should have become a modern-day superhero or vigilante fighting cruelty and injustice. It is true, that on a few occasions, I have interfered with the ongoing violence of men, but only when there was no other alternative, through fear of drawing too much attention to myself.

For the most part, rather wisely, I have taken Kai's advice, remaining ever watchful and alert. As soon as I was old enough, I left home, with one clear intention of keeping on the move.

I have spent many years wandering and travelling the world. Memorising every foreign and exotic location I possibly could, preparing escape routes all over the globe, to which I could open portals and run, should Simeon Scythe and his Black-Eyed monstrosities ever succeed in tracking me down.

It may also come as little surprise to know that I made my way back to a particular small hospital in Germany and, though I located the exact same room, I did not find what I was looking for. The bed was empty, the machines all gone, and despite all my efforts, I found no trace of Steggie Belle.

It has been extremely tiring, living in fear, and continually looking over my shoulder. And it has been a long and lonely road, as Quidel once predicted through reading my palm. But through my travels, I have met many remarkable people, have hunted down lost wisdom, and have devoted myself to searching for forgotten knowledge. Those solitary labours have not been in vain. For I have, after thirty years of looking, succeeded in discovering the location and secret hiding place of the second half of the Anchor of Perspicax. I believe that shall be a secret for me to take quietly to my grave, no matter what the future holds in store. Though, to put your mind at ease, I can confirm that for the time being within the waking world, it remains safe, unnoticed and protected.

Like many adults, I have become a creature of habit. At night I often sit alone, wondering what could have been and sometimes, when I feel burdened by that indescribable weight, I even begin to doubt myself. It is in such moments that I stand up and draw the curtains and lock the door, close my eyes, and lift myself weightlessly from the floor. Sometimes it is enough to simply hover or to fly in smooth circles around the room, but it is always a chance to smile and confirm what I already know.

I walk a great deal, at peace with my thoughts. And every day I am thankful that the odd, dark handprint scars that still remain at various points all over my body have been dormant all these years and no longer burn.

Occasionally, when I mingle with the crowds, I have heard children giggling, or have noticed them staring incredulously at those fingerprint marks I have been branded with. Having travelled to many shores, it is quite possible that perhaps our paths have crossed, though as a figure I am easily forgotten, and for the most part my strange practices and I go largely unnoticed. An obsolete and quiet individual, that peculiar person you might have only glanced at, who was feeding breadcrumbs to the ducks and pigeons and squirrels in the park. Perhaps your curiosity would have caused you to look a little longer, a little closer. Then you might have noticed that the crazy, lonely man before you was actually whispering and talking insistently to those animals. Perhaps? But by now I am sure you know, through the secrets I have shared, that for such things I have my reasons. I remain forever hopeful that maybe one day the Loup Garou might reach out, from one of those everyday disguises of theirs and contact me.

That was, and has been, my existence, my life, up until one week ago. It was quite suddenly, early on a very typical Sunday evening, that this extraordinary event occurred.

My telephone rang.

Now, maybe that would seem like a very normal thing to you. But it startled the living daylights out of me as, despite owning such a device, I knew that nobody had my number and that the phone had never rung before. I approached it suspiciously, and carefully picked up the receiver, putting my ear right up close. I could hear shallow breathing on the other end, but at first, the mystery caller did not say a word.

"Hello?" I inquired hesitantly. Whoever it was cleared their throat, though nothing could have prepared me for the words about to come.

"Mr Zoofall?"

I froze. Even among the Only Circle who still kept in touch, we would rarely ever address each other in the waking world by our dream names. After a few seconds, I regained my composure and found my voice.

"Who is this?" I stammered, and then rather secretively whispered, "Puddle, is that you?"

I don't know why I asked that as, even before the reply came, I knew it wasn't him.

"No," was the eventual and quite abrupt response. My brain was an absolute melting pot of confusion. I waited in silence, trying desperately to gather my thoughts. I analysed what I could from our minimal conversation thus far. It was a young child's voice, there was no doubt about that, but most definitely not one that I knew. Although the English appeared reasonably good, there was a noticeably strong accent, which cast my mind back to my travels through India. But how on earth could this random child have gotten hold of my number, let alone have known my dream name? The young voice came crackling through the phone again.

"She needs you!"

Instantly my blood ran cold. My mouth dried up, and I shivered uncontrollably at hearing those words.

"We all do!" the voice gently persisted.

"Who is this?" I demanded, more defensively than I had intended to sound. I noticed a slight hint of pride in the caller's next response, which seemed vaguely familiar.

"This is WakingCrow, rank number five of the Wild-Divers."

I gasped and actually dropped the phone at that point, finding that I could not put a single word together, as I fumbled to pick up the receiver from the floor.

"She needs you!" the message came again.

"Who does? Who needs me? What is all this about?" I finally managed to splutter.

"Steggie Belle."

Those two words echoed in my ear.

"That's not possible! Are you saying that you've seen her?"

There followed an infuriatingly long pause.

"No."

"But you're telling me that Steggie's alive?"

There was no answer, only silence.

"Tell me, is she alive?" I repeated, my voice quivering. Still no answer. Then, in a rushed and nervous tone, the caller spoke once more.

"You must hurry, Mr Zoofall. Come quickly!"

Then the line went dead.

The last seven days have flown by. They have consisted of me pacing relentlessly around the house. Resulting in noticeably worn trails across the carpets, through every room, showing the routes that I have taken. Every single day I have gone to the asylum to visit Wolfe, a pattern which I fear has aroused the suspicion of his doctors, and probably has them preparing for me the cell next door to his.

If I still have enough time remaining, I will quickly tell you what happened on my first visit to see him, the morning after that phone call. Perhaps it was my excitement as I burst into his room that gave me away, but as soon as we were left alone, he leant forward looking at me earnestly, and whispered,

"So, they contacted you too! Well, it's taken long enough! I was beginning to think that I would never be able to move forward with my retirement plan."

That was the moment I realised the truth of his situation: Wolfe's own cunning little secret. He too had quite deliberately chosen his own unique path. I remembered Quidel's assessment of him, all those years ago, deep within that cave of their Hive.

"...Reckless bravado can lead one into trouble, and yet, in you, I see a future with great potential, should you discover a way to keep yourself safe, wrapped up in cotton wool, so to speak, and protected from harm..."

Wolfe, my dear friend, with the patience of a saint, had taken those words to heart and, instead of cotton wool, had found that a padded room, under lock and key, would suit his purpose just fine! And, as I have since discovered over the last several days, he has not been idle either. Lying in wait these last three decades, he passed unseen below every radar, so convincingly that even his oldest friend began to question his sanity, and all the while focusing, training and preparing for this very night. The retirement plan he would so often refer to was never designed or destined for the waking world, but for returning without fear, back into the dream world.

During our plotting through the week, I have been forced

to make a tough decision in regards to Puddle, a decision for which I hope he will forgive me. I have wanted to reach out and include him so badly. I even stood on his doorstep two nights ago for a full half-hour, one hand poised and ready to knock. It was the sounds echoing from within that stopped me: the sound of children's laughter.

For I have absolutely no doubt that, were we to ask, he would join us in a heartbeat. But he has a family of his own now, just as we were once a part of his. And sometimes, life has taught me, the best bonds are both the hardest yet the most necessary of which to let go.

Besides, Wolfe and I are under no illusions as to where this journey may very well lead us. This call of new children from out of the blue could be nothing more than a cunningly prepared trap, one from which neither of us will likely return. Now I realise perhaps it was always destined to end this way. I must break my word, the promise I made so many years ago—for the simple reason that I miss my friend. And that a life without Steggie Belle, is a dream not worth living. If she is still alive, we will find her.

Before this final candle burns itself out, and I sign off this confession of mine, I will leave you with these last thoughts.

I am speaking right now to the person that fate has decided should hold this book. Even if you are unable to believe the truth of my account, please humour a lonely old man, and keep what is written here safe, keep it moving, keep it alive. Place it in the hands of dreamers, for though their hands may be young, their minds and imaginations are mighty. Be careful not to whisper the name of Steggie Belle too loudly, should the wrong person overhear you. And if you should ever come upon that spiral staircase leading down, or find your way to the training caverns, or even the Treetop summit—keep an eye out for us! And if, by some wild chance, you should ever come across Steggie Belle herself, and I am not there, by her side, please tell her that Zoofall did his best and that he tried.

Beneath this book, which I shall leave upon this writing desk, you should find an envelope containing a list of nine names, together with various newspaper clippings that I have worked tirelessly to collect. Those nine are the ones we lost, thirty years ago: the Inner Circle. The articles relate to their disappearances, all on the very same night, across countries and continents throughout the world.

On the next page, I have also done my best to put together a glossary of terms mentioned already. It is unfinished, a work in progress, and I must apologise for that. But I hope it will shed some light on the research I have made in recent years.

Last night I found my way back to the woods directly behind Wolfe's childhood home, where I dug up Kai's sword, that Wolfe had buried there for safekeeping so many years ago. Right now it lies hidden beneath the pillow on the bed behind me, but very soon, after I put down my pen, that blade will once again be firmly in my hand.

Our plan is set. What plan?

Well, I see no danger now in revealing to you the details of the plan Wolfe and I have made as, within minutes, it will be set in motion.

This morning I smuggled into the asylum an oval mirror, tightly wrapped and strapped under my clothes across my back. When nobody was looking, we swapped it over, and Wolfe now has it hidden under his mattress. By now, the last of the doctors will have finished their rounds, and in a few moments, I will create a portal straight to that mirror within his padded room.

In this way, I plan to break him out of his cell, and together we shall crawl our way back through, here into the barricaded safety of my attic. From this room, once fully prepared, we shall uncover this mirror that stands right before me now, and cross over, Plunging and travelling blind back to the world where we both belong. Two old dreamers, reunited once again and side by side. Just like in those days gone by, to recklessly face whatever may await us.

A Secret Unfinished Glossary:

Ah, information, such a wondrous and peculiar gift: the more one unwraps, the less one seems to know.

-(The) Anchor of Perspicax: The angelic instrument, designed to one day unite both the waking and dream worlds in harmony. Long ago divided into two pieces, which were hidden respectively within each world. Perspicax derives from the Latin for sharp-sighted or penetrating.

-Centaurs: A half-human, half-horse breed of hunter, last mentioned in Greek Mythology within the waking world, before they migrated long ago as a tribe to the dream world where they roam wild in search of a challenging hunt.

-Chupacabras: A small reptilian creature, not often sighted in the waking world. Vicious and bloodthirsty by nature, there have been reports of them attacking livestock through the Americas, and beyond. Their name comes from Spanish, meaning "goat-sucker", as animals are often found drained of blood. They originate from Volcanaton, a fiery area of the dream world where some say these rabid dragons are hatched directly out of the lava pools.

-Drifters: Also known as "Movers", and incorrectly labelled as Ghosts within the waking world, they are separated selves, possessing energy, and are launched out into the eternal realm of dreams to wander. Though they have vastly differing powers, they are rarely harmful and not something to be feared.

-E: The voice of the Coven of the North. I never discovered if the "E" stood for anything. Although some members of our Only Circle are fairly certain that all of the Coven addressed one another by only single letters, for simplicity's sake, finding no use in full names.

-Euryale: One of the three Gorgon sisters, completely misrepresented through history, and the wildly embellished legends that have since arisen. A firm and loyal friend of the Freedivers and Steggie Belle. Her fate, like her sister Stheno, still up to this date, remains unknown.

-(The) Forests of Crepusculum: The enchanted area of woodland, infested by mountain trolls, along the border of which our group of the Freedivers found the Golden Book within the ruined mansion, where I was also first touched by a Stalker, narrowly escaping with my life.

-Garuda: The race of Birdmen, who accompanied us as mercenaries on the day of that terrible battle. They are referred to within Hindu and Buddhist mythology, known within the waking world for their insatiable appetite for snakes. They have since adopted a seafood diet, with a particular obsessive fondness for salmon.

-(The) Hive: The sacred and magical home of the Loup Garou. I still remember so vividly the incredible room where they would go to rest and relax. It was invaded by the Stalkers, and I often wonder whether our friends were able to reclaim that wonderful place. I hope so, and also that it was not too badly ransacked and destroyed.

-Hohnihohkaiyohos: The full name of our good friend Kai, one of the most graceful and deadly of the Loup Garou. I have since discovered that his full name derives from the Native American word, meaning "High backed wolf".

-Indiacs: The formal name for the most common type of dreamer, more commonly known amongst the Freedivers as "Floaters". I have as yet been unable to trace the roots of the word, but suspect it might have been formed similarly to the term "Insomniac" (someone who is unable to sleep), and think perhaps Indiacs might refer to those who are, essentially, unable to dream?

-Krumlov: The fairy-tale place to which I followed that shadow column of Stalkers through the mirror. I have since discovered that the town really does exist. And I have travelled there many a time, to admire its astounding beauty. It is located in the south of the Czech Republic: the town's full name is Český Krumlov.

-Loup Garou: A tribe of stunning creatures, descended from early humans, who reached such a level of natural balance that they can change at will into a great variety of animals. While transformed, they remain completely in control, while making use of the chosen species' heightened senses and strengths. Often mistakenly connected to Werewolves and other Lycanthropic beings, they have become in the eyes of humanity nothing more than a fairytale monster with which to frighten naughty children.

-Lucid Dreaming: Amongst grown-ups, this state is supposedly the most advanced form of dreaming, an awareness allowing one to both control and change the subject and direction of the dream itself. Though as you now know, there is a whole other world existing beyond this.

-Omnivagas: The most advanced category of human dreamers, a far step beyond the limits of Lucid Dreaming. Our group of Freedivers were all of this category, perhaps too this unknown group calling themselves "Wild-Divers", though Wolfe and I will soon discover if this is true or not. Research has shown me that the word derives from the Latin, meaning "to wander or roam everywhere", which I believe is quite a fine definition of what and who we are.

-Ostery: The region of the dream world where our two safe-havens: the Treetop city and the sacred cave are located and protected by the Coven of the North's magic. Should you ever find yourself navigating this realm, try to find these special places, and do make sure the lantern at the Treetop summit is still burning brightly.

-Pan: The ancient Forest God, associated with the countryside and wilderness, who was the unlikely first guardian of the Anchor of Perspicax. He was last referred to within Greek Mythology, where much about him has been written.

-(The) Pit of Obliviscor: The terrible dungeon in which Simeon Scythe was once imprisoned, although it still remains unclear exactly how he managed to escape its depths. From the various accounts I heard, I believe it to be similar, though perhaps on a far grander and terrifying scale, to the French Oubliette, a punishment reserved for the most fiendish villains within the dream world. The word Obliviscor is derived from the Latin word meaning "to lose the remembrance of something, or to forget".

-Plunging: A dangerous technique of travelling through the dream world, also known as "travelling blind". One does not know exactly where one is headed, and therefore runs a high risk of walking straight into danger or an ambush.

-Proteus: A Sea God from Greek Mythology, to whom one of the Coven travelled to learn the truth about the dark scar upon my arm. Within the waking world, he is also known as the 'Old Man of the Sea'. He is supposedly able to foretell the future, but always unwilling to do so.

-Quidel: One of the leading Elders of the Loup Garou. Looking back, I can say with some certainty that he was able to predict the three of our futures, although of course Steggie

Belle's fate still remains unclear.

-(The) Rising Four: The stages which reflect how an individual sees the dream world. Four differing states (all Astral): the Inferno; the Tower; the Sea; and the Cloud. A more detailed description sadly would require far more time than my situation allows.

-Shadow People: A hugely important element of both our worlds. One that, after careful reflection, I have decided not to discuss in detail within these pages, and have only mentioned them in passing. They are a mystery, I feel, too dangerous to divulge here.

-Shifters: A rare breed of dreamer, even among the Omnivagas: some would say the rarest. I myself am one, although so too is Simeon Scythe, which highlights how dangerous a Shifter's abilities can be. We possess the ability not only to cross back and forth physically between both worlds but also to carry objects and skills through as well.

-Skimmers: Also known as the "Ostrasighted", they are the middle major category of dreamer, falling between the Indiacs and the Omnivagas. Through their more advanced awareness, they are at times able to descend further into the world of dreams, often bringing fragments of what they have seen back to the waking world.

-Sophists: The favoured name the unfortunate race of Temptors liked to go by. They possess the uncanny ability to squeeze themselves into the waking world where they would influence sleeping men and women, by whispering awful suggestions in their ears. Some say they are mostly responsible for the evils which human beings have committed. The word Sophist, I have since learned, is derived from Ancient Greek, referring to "a teacher of philosophy and rhetoric", or an individual who "reasons with clever but false arguments".

-Stalkers: Our dreaded nemeses within the dream world, first known as "The Lost Ones" and then in the waking world as "Black-Eyed Children". They possess some degree of telepathy and mind control, and their appearance of pale, lost children is but a mask for the evil that lurks beneath. Take it from me, their touch burns, and perhaps could even kill. Together with Simeon Scythe they brutally massacred our Inner Circle, also attacking and wiping out the Temptors.

-Thistle-Wisps: The mysterious organ stolen from the Temptors, perhaps allowing the Stalkers to cross back over into the waking world. Possibly connected to "Kundabuffers" which was mentioned by a spiritualist leader of the twentieth century, by the name of Gurdjieff.

-Vumbi Bones: The desert where our final battle took place, where the Loup Garou had hidden half of the Anchor of Perspicax. An immense barren landscape of salt flats. The word Vumbi, I have since learned is Swahili, and means "Dust".

-(The) Wall of Fuse-and-Flux: An immense cliff-face within the dream world, which held thousands of tiny portals upon its surface, through which the Temptors were somehow able to pass through into the waking world. Charged by some form of electrical current, it still stands to this day, I believe, as a thankfully limited passageway between our worlds.

-(**The**) **Wokhala:** The vast horde of monstrous creatures that lie in wait for Inter-World portals to open. You may have noticed that their description in this book is rather vague: that is mainly because their frenzied stampedes do not often allow one the time for a more detailed examination! I have since learnt that the word possibly comes from the African language of Chichewa, meaning either "resident", or "opportunist".

-**Zoofall:** The name Steggie Belle once gave me, which I had always presumed was a reference to the day I met Wolfe—and the accident in the zoo. In recent years I discovered it is actually a German word, spelt Zufall, which means "coincidence" or "chance". I realise now that all the times when she spoke of "chance", Steggie may have been actually referring to me.

Epilogue: An Unlikely Witness

Detective Fred Charmers finished reading and placed the notebook on the desk. He picked up the large envelope which had been lying underneath it and sifted through the loose pages that were inside: newspaper clippings of various sizes, all frail, brown and faded, as though they had been soaked in tea. Most were written in foreign languages, and sadly he was no linguist. Children's faces stared innocently up at him from those old articles. Something caught his eye. He hurriedly flicked back through the ones he had already passed to double-check his eyes were not deceiving him. All of those collected cuttings referred to incidents which had occurred on the same day some thirty years ago.

"What on Earth have you gotten yourself into?" Fred wondered out loud, carefully replacing the flimsy, wafer-thin pages, before standing up and walking confidently over to the one small window up there in that dusty attic.

The view was grey and bleak, broken by dark silhouetted

trees with bare and lifeless branches. A late frost had recently settled and, though it was almost April, there was no sign of spring pushing through anytime soon. The days were still miserably short, and one look outside at that dismal sky and the sombre shadows reminded him that very soon it would be dark. He tried pulling himself back to the matter at hand, but a surge of disappointment broke back into the forefront of his mind.

This was his first assignment since being promoted to the rank of detective and, no matter how unrealistic it might have been, he had been hoping for something juicier, something to really sink his teeth into. Okay, so investigating the first murder of a future prolific serial killer might have been a bit of a far-fetched pipe dream, but an armed bank robbery would have been good, or even a bog-standard kidnapping, but not this.

A possible missing person's case just seemed so mundane, and a far cry from what he had wished to begin his promising career with. So the man hadn't been seen for a few months, so what? According to the few neighbours he had interviewed, the missing guy had been a bit of a loner, keeping mostly to himself. And yet, Charmers had been up in that attic for a good few hours now, far longer than he had anticipated, and he was still no closer to reaching any conclusions. It was becoming apparent that even the less compelling cases were not always a piece of cake.

"Think, damn it, think!" he scolded himself, knowing that there was no way he was going back to the station and facing his captain after all these hours with nothing to show for it.

He turned on his flashlight, since the afternoon was quickly fading into twilight, and turned his attention back to the window frame. Nothing. No marks of disturbance or fingerprints in the dust. And besides, the lock looked like it had been rusted over for

many years. He tried using brute force for good measure but no, the window would definitely not open.

"Well, the guy didn't just vanish into thin air," he tutted, crossing back through the room which he had no desire, until it was absolutely necessary, of labelling as a crime scene. He paused. "Great! Your first day, and you're already talking to yourself."

Charmers shone his torch into every corner, into every nook and cranny, hoping perhaps he had missed something. He was glad that he had taken all the necessary photographs first—before he had stumbled upon that book. Though it was obviously written by a person more than just a few sandwiches short of a picnic, he had found it oddly engaging and had ended up reading the whole thing from beginning to end.

He very much doubted that those photos would shed any light on the puzzle anyway. He retraced his steps methodically, determined to re-examine everything. He even checked under the pillow, which the writer of that journal had referred to. As he had expected—and feeling a little bit silly for even entertaining the possibility—of course, there was no sword. That was when the thought occurred to him: just because the missing man may well have been mad, it did not necessarily mean that he didn't honestly believe the things he had written. Most importantly: perhaps there was some fragment of truth hidden within his warped fantasy.

The detective walked over to the open trapdoor and called out loudly to his colleague on the floor below. A few moments later, the young constable's face appeared near the bottom of the stepladder.

"Yes, sir?"

The new detective inwardly relished the ring of authority and respect on hearing that title.

"Jenkins, find out if the owner has any prior history of being reported missing, would you?"

"Of course, sir. I'll radio in right away and find out."

"Thank you."

The detective took a step back and glanced at the trapdoor and the pieces of furniture and debris scattered behind it. In the distance down below, he heard the faint sound of radio static. It had taken both of them over ten minutes to force open that hatch from below. There must have been well over one hundred kilos of junk piled up on top of the trapdoor entrance. Had the man really built that barricade to keep something out?

He steered himself clear of such dead-end musings. He re-examined the candlestick, with the wax melted right down to the blackened wick; the free-standing mirror, whose reflection in the torchlight nearly blinded him. Then he knelt alongside it, studying the crumpled bed sheet cloth, which he presumed had been previously draped over the mirror and was now lying in a pile on the floor. Then his attention turned to the next conundrum, the shoes. Yes—the shoes. Not one pair, mind you, but two. Both positioned neatly side by side, a short distance from the mirror. On the left, a well-worn pair of walking boots, and next to them a battered old pair of cheap and simple slippers.

"So the guy enjoyed walking a lot but preferred to wear his slippers up here to write," Charmers reasoned under his breath, mulling the whole thing over. "But why not take the boots off at the front door? Why all the way up here?"

Then it hit him, like a bolt of lightning. The two pairs were different sizes, how could he not have noticed that before?

"There were two people up here!"

At that moment his train of thought was interrupted by his colleague's head poking up through the trapdoor. It startled him a little, but he managed not to let it show.

"Uh, sir?"

"Yes, constable?"

"They said there was a report of the owner going missing a long time ago, for a few months, when he was just a boy, only—"

"... Fourteen years old," the detective interrupted. The constable looked astonished.

"Yes, sir. How did you ... what even made you think to ask about that in the first place?"

"Just being thorough, Jenkins," Detective Charmers replied somewhat smugly, feeling like he was getting the hang of this. He turned his attention back to the shoes but, moments later, noticed out of the corner of his eye that the constable was not leaving.

"What is it, Jenkins?"

"Sorry, sir, it's the captain. He was asking when you're going to wrap this up? Says you should have reported back by now."

"Just finishing up, I'll be down in a few minutes."

Fred Charmers waited until the constable's footsteps had faded away before picking up one of the slippers, turning it over in his hand. He read what was neatly printed on the sole out loud, then scribbled it down in his pocket notebook: "Property of Brimstone Asylum".

Instinctively, he cast a quick glance back at the book, still lying on the writing desk, before carefully placing the slippers into an evidence bag.

"What happened up here four months ago? And where did you run off to, Mr Zoofall, if that's the name you insist on being called?"

The attic was growing darker by the minute. By now, Detective Charmers had stopped even caring that he was talking to himself. He ran one hand inquisitively over the multiple lines of deep markings scratched with great force across the floorboards. Several long and ragged furrows. He leant forward at that point, to line his eye up and follow their directional trails.

"All leading back towards you," he whispered, looking up at the mirror, where the scratches all ended abruptly. In the wavering torchlight, he imagined that there would be plenty of people willing to lap this all up—but not him. For despite feeling he might be onto something, above all else, he prided himself on being a rational and logical man. He was a detective now after all, and something about all this struck him as fishy. An elaborate hoax of some kind, inventive and well-planned, but surely a hoax nonetheless.

A sealed room with no exits. A mysterious confession from the missing man. A pair of slippers from a local psychiatric hospital. And those monstrous claw marks, which had ripped through and torn up that hardwood attic floor.

His mind began to race with possibilities. Some attempt at financial fraud? A tall tale calling out for attention in a desperate bid to get into the newspapers? Or a false claim on a life insurance policy? That sounded like it might hold water. It was at that very second he stopped dead in his tracks: could this all be a work-related test, an initiation of sorts?

A peculiar case that his captain and co-workers had deliberately given to him to test his mettle. To gauge whether the newly promoted detective would keep a level head, or jump to absurd conclusions. Of course, that had to be it. Charmers

scratched his stubble pensively. Jenkins was probably in on it too. Well, it wasn't going to work: he had no intention of embarrassing himself by taking such nonsense seriously. His report would be professional and firmly grounded by logic, and he would not be wasting another minute up there.

He put all the evidence he had collected into his shoulder-bag and went back to the desk once more, to take the book with him. He folded the envelope with the loose clippings and wedged it inside the book's cover. Heading towards the trapdoor he had to laugh, partly because of how nearly he had fallen for the whole thing, partly impressed by the sheer amount of effort that must have been spent creating this entire charade.

With one foot Fred began lowering himself onto the stepladder.

He stopped, sure in that instant that he had heard a noise. There it was again. A loud thud, which sounded as though it was coming from somewhere at the other end of the room. The detective shone his torch wildly from corner to corner but saw nothing. The sounds were definitely getting louder, starting to resemble the rumble of an approaching train, but he knew that they were miles from the nearest tracks.

He took another step down, feeling increasingly less sure of himself.

He retreated quickly down a few more rungs, still shining his torch back and forth across the darkened attic. For a moment, his courage returned, and he found himself taking one cautious step back up the ladder. Suddenly there came a sound that made him freeze. All the hairs on the back of his neck rose up at once. The voice rang out crystal clear—a child's voice—coming from the place where that long, tall mirror stood.

"Excuse me, can you help me? I'm lost."

Detective Charmers reached up and gripped the handle of the trapdoor, lowering it gently without a sound, until it was barely a few inches from being totally closed. Through that gap, he angled the torch directly at the mirror, wide-eyed and watching in disbelief what happened next.

The smooth reflective surface appeared to tremor and vibrate. Then he saw it. Right at the mirror's centre were fleeting and repetitive imprints of a human hand, fist clenched, pounding and thumping upon it as though from the other side, leaving a slight indentation each time for a mere millisecond. As unimaginable as it was for him to accept, it looked like someone was desperately trying to get out.

Then it stopped, the attic becoming eerily silent in the semi-darkness. Just when he was summoning the will to go back up, the whole surface of the mirror changed, rippling like water under the torch beam, then turning dark.

"What in the name of—" the detective began to exclaim in amazement before, out of the mirror's darkness, a pale face appeared, a child's face, with two black and hollow eyes.

He slammed the trapdoor shut, fumbling to lock it, and half stumbled, half fell down the rungs of the ladder, landing ungracefully in a heap on the hallway floor below. Before the constable found him, he did something quite inexplicable and out of character. Charmers knew the rules and procedures for gathering evidence by heart, and yet he broke them: he slipped the envelope and book quickly into the inner pocket of his jacket.

"What was all that racket? What happened up there? Sir, you look like you've seen a ghost!" the constable demanded, clearly alarmed. From the genuinely shocked expression on his face,

Detective Charmers knew that none of this was a test or a hoax.

"Rats! Biggest ones I've ever seen!" he replied, pushing his way past and heading towards the front door.

Opening it, he saw that a faint drizzling rain had begun to fall.

"So, we're all finished up here then?" the constable inquired hopefully, standing on the threshold of that creepy, empty house.

"No! Keep the building sealed. Nobody goes up there, you understand?"

"Yes, sir," the constable replied automatically, though his expression remained confused. "But, what do I tell the captain?" he called out, as the detective raised his collar against the elements and made a dash towards his car.

"You tell him it's a crime scene now," he shouted back, opening the car door.

"But where are you going, sir?"

"I'm going to track down a Wolfe."

"Beg your pardon, sir?"

"I'm headed to Brimstone Asylum. To find out if they've had an escaped patient that they failed to report."

The constable watched bewildered as the car door was slammed violently shut.

Detective Charmers was still shaking slightly as he pulled the book carefully from his pocket and laid it on the seat beside him. He rested one hand upon it for a moment, as though it were a bible, and he was swearing an oath.

"Keep it safe, keep it moving, keep it alive." he repeated, whispering those quoted words beneath his breath, before turning the engine on, gripping the wheel tightly to stop his hands from trembling, and speeding away into the night.

"Then we'll come from the shadows."
-Leonard Cohen (from The Partisan).

SPECIAL THANKS TO
MY PATRONS

Alan Lee
Ozan Fahri
Anne Matthews
Lucía Nieto

For any generous readers and fans of my work, please check out my Patreon Page and consider supporting my journey further. Any help, no matter how small, will never be forgotten.

www.patreon.com/eliaspell

ABOUT THE AUTHOR

Elias Pell is a London-born, previously published poet and dream-inspired writer of both short stories and novels, for adults and children. He left England in 2016, putting all his savings towards the lifelong dream of writing full-time.

In March 2020, Elias published a collection of short stories for adults, entitled *Scapegoats & Crowbars*. He is currently working on the sequel to *Steggie Belle & the Dream Warriors*, alongside other exciting new writing projects.

If you have enjoyed this novel, please consider reviewing it (either on Amazon or Goodreads) and recommending it to friends and family. Word of mouth can really make an enormous difference to an unknown author. As Zoofall implores: "Keep it safe, keep it moving, keep it alive."

If you have any further queries or wish to get in touch, Elias can be contacted directly at:

elias.pell75@gmail.com

Printed in Great Britain
by Amazon